DEATH DIVE!

"Torpedo still on our tail!" exclaimed the voice of Joe Carter that was now being broadcast over the *Cheyenne*'s P.A. system. "Range 1,000 yards and closing!"

They were spiraling downward now into the black, frigid depths at a speed of thirty-three knots and Aldridge momentarily visualized the hard rocky floor of the fjord waiting to greet them in an embrace of instant death.

"Mr. Murphy," he ordered. "Pull us up, now!"

The helmsman yanked back at the steering yoke and the *Cheyenne* slid to a depth of 450 feet before beginning its climb upward.

Aldridge knew this was the moment of truth. He'd been gambling the torpedo wouldn't be able to pull out of its dive as quickly as the *Cheyenne,* and that he hadn't underestimated the depth of the fjord. His fate and that of his crew were in another's hands now.

Seconds later he heard the sound of a deep, thundering explosion and the deck beneath his feet began to tremble and shake. . . .

RICHARD P. HENRICK

THE GOLDEN U-BOAT

ZEBRA BOOKS
KENSINGTON PUBLISHING CORP.

ZEBRA BOOKS

are published by

Kensington Publishing Corp.
850 Third Avenue
New York, NY 10022

First printing: May, 1991

Printed in the United States of America

10 9 8 7 6 5 4 3 2

The author wishes to thank Karl Ivar Bjornsen and the rest of the members of NUEX. Without your sharing of the "Norwegian experience," this book wouldn't have been possible.

"When one considers that right up to the end of the war there was virtually no increase in heavy-water stocks in Germany . . . it will be seen that it was the elimination of German heavy-water production in Norway that was the main factor in our failure to achieve an atomic bomb before the war ended."
— German scientist Dr. Kurt Diebner

"The political stability of the Bonn government is slowly being undermined by millions of old fighters . . . who are deeply committed to a Nazi comeback. They dream of a military establishment with supermodern weapons . . . in order to regain for Germany the status of a great world power."
— T.H. Tetens

"We must hand down the brave, self-sacrificing U-boat spirit to our children and grandchildren."
— Admiral Karl Donitz

Chapter One

August 8, 1941

The footpath was little more than a narrow, earthen track that led from the rail yard into a thick birch forest. Mikhail Kuznetsov first spotted it late the previous afternoon. They were still busy moving into their temporary barracks at that time, and he was forced to postpone any exploration of this promising trail until some free time presented itself. The opportunity came the very next morning.

The twenty-one-year old, newly commissioned junior lieutenant awoke long before reveille. There was a slight chill to the air as he slipped off his hard, straw mattress and headed for the latrine. The hut they had just moved into was normally reserved for railroad workers. Far from being luxurious, it was simply constructed out of native timber, but at least had indoor plumbing.

The dark blue sky was tinged with the first hint of dawn as he stepped outside. A gust of crisp air, fresh with the scent of the surrounding wood greeted him as he surveyed the compound. Several gray freight cars could be seen parked beside the main rail line. Directly adjoining this central track was the fuel depot. A massive heap of black coal was stored here, beside which was a soot-covered loading ramp. A large repair shed stood nearby, its grimy structure graced with several broken

7

windows and a five-pointed, red star painted beneath its gabled roof. All in all, the view was far from inspiring, and Mikhail gratefully turned to his left and began his way toward the encircling birch wood.

The footpath that had called him from his warm bed led him into the forest of slender white trees. Soon the world of man was replaced by the lonely cries of a raven, and a muted creaking as the wind gusted through the tree limbs, causing them to sway like a single entity.

Mikhail felt instantly at ease in this peaceful environment. Having grown up near a birch forest much like this one, he was no stranger to such a place. Yet for the past year and a half he had lived exclusively in the bustling city of Leningrad. Here, along with his twin brother Alexander, he attended the Frunze Naval Academy. Their pace of study was intense, and innocent forest jaunts had all but become a pleasant memory. Thus to be out on his own this morning on a real hike was like a trip homeward, even though his birthplace was actually a thousand kilometers east of this spot, outside the city of Kirov.

As he followed the path into a dense thicket of underbrush, a fat, brown ground squirrel darted out in front of him. Seconds later, a covey of quail exploded from the nearby brush with blinding swiftness. Mikhail's pulse quickened with the unexpected commotion. Regretting that he didn't have a shotgun to bring with him, he began his way down into an oak-filled hollow. Many of the trees were gnarled with age, and an almost reverent atmosphere prevailed.

The sound of rushing water sounded in the distance and Mikhail soon set his eyes on the swift current responsible for this pleasantly distinctive racket. It proved to be a good-sized stream. Many of the crystal clear pools appeared quite deep and no doubt provided a comfortable habitat for the local variety of trout. Halting beside a portion of the brook where the bubbling waters swirled against a series of partially submerged

8

boulders, Mikhail's thoughts went back in time, for it was at a spot much like this one that his father had taught him and Alexander their first lessons in the art of fly fishing.

Their father had been an avid fisherman, and devoted much of his free time designing and tying his own lures. As a veteran naval officer, whose specialty was submarines, Dmitri Kuznetsov had spent much of his adult life at sea. His leaves were therefore precious to him, and he utilized them to their fullest extent.

Family outings drew the Kuznetsovs to such diverse places as beautiful Lake Baikal, the desolate Siberian taiga, and the tropical shores of the Black Sea. On each of these trips, Dmitri made certain to take along a variety of fishing and hunting gear, so that he could further instruct his twin sons in the intricacies of wilderness survival.

Trout and salmon fishing were his father's greatest passions. He would spend hours working a stream, applying the same intense concentration that he used to stalk a naval target on the high seas. More often than not, his efforts paid off in the form of a trophy-sized fish, whose flesh could feed the entire family and then some.

Mikhail was proud of his father's skill with a rod and reel, and had tried hard to emulate him. Patience was a virtue that every good fisherman had plenty of, and Mikhail did his best to control the natural impatience of youth and focus solely on the prey at hand. He thus did his best to imitate his father's every move, often working a single pool for an entire afternoon.

His twin brother, Alexander had found it impossible to summon such self control. Easily bored, Alexander would give the fish an hour or so to take his bait before giving up and taking off to explore the surrounding countryside. In this aspect he was more like their mother, who was content to limit her participation in fishing to preparing the catch for dinner.

Mikhail peered out to a promising pool of deep water

9

and sighed as he recalled the last family outing that had taken place two years ago. They had camped deep in the Ural mountains. It was early summer, and both Mikhail and Alexander were celebrating their recent acceptance to the Frunze Academy. Though proud that his boys were following in his footsteps, their father had seemed preoccupied during the entire stay. The fishing was poor, and several times they had to resort to shooting game to fill their empty plates.

It was three weeks after their return home from that trip that they received notice of their father's death at sea. The submarine he had been commanding failed to ascend from a test dive. Though a faulty valve was suspected, the true cause of the tragedy that took the lives of sixty-three Soviet sailors lay hidden in the frigid depths of the Barents Sea.

Sobered by the news, Mikhail and Alexander applied themselves to their studies with renewed intensity. Their efforts had recently been rewarded as both graduated in the top tenth of their Academy class. When queried as to the nature of their future naval service with the Motherland's fleet, both chose submarines without a second's hesitation. Though their mother had wept when told of their choice, all eventually agreed that this was the way Dmitri Kuznetsov would have wanted it.

Mikhail turned from the stream and began his way back through the stand of oak. It was only when he crossed the clearing that he realized the sun had long since risen in the intensely blue sky. It appeared as if it would be another hot, sultry day, for the newly commissioned naval officer's brow was already shining with sweat. Mikhail was reaching for his handkerchief when the deep-pitched whistle of a distant train broke the silence. Suddenly reminded of his duties, he looked at his watch and saw that over an hour had passed since he left the barracks. He had only planned to be gone half that time, and he immediately sought out the trail that would take him back to the rail yard. He had just reentered the birch wood when a familiar voice rang out nearby.

"Misha! Misha, are you out there?"

"I'm here, Alex. On the trail!"

No sooner were these words spoken, when his brother broke through the underbrush. Since both wore matching khaki uniforms, a stranger would have had to look very closely to tell the two apart. Both sported muscular, six-foot, three inch frames, identical mops of wavy blond hair, and the same handsome features down to the round dimple that split their chins. Only the most conscientious observer would note the difference in the twins' eye coloring. Mikhail had inherited his father's vivid blue eyes, while Alexander's were a deep sea-green like his mother's.

"Ah, there you are, Misha," said Alexander. "For a moment I feared that you had gone AWOL."

"Now why in the world would I do that, my dear brother? It's only been seventeen days since the Nazi hordes crossed over our borders, and now it looks as if our sworn duty to the Rodina will finally prove interesting."

"If only you knew the truth of those words," Alexander said. "Rumor has it that the Germans have already reached the outskirts of Pskov. From there it's only 250 kilometers to the gates of Leningrad, with us smack in between."

"Surely we won't be here much longer," replied Mikhail. "What good can a naval squad do this far inland? I'll bet the orders directing us to the navy base at Tallinin are on the way even as we speak."

Alexander answered with a gloomy shake of his head. "I'm afraid not, Misha. Less than a quarter of an hour ago, a packet arrived by courier from Lieutenant General M. Popov himself. We've been instructed to make our way with all due haste to the monastery of Tsarkoe Selo, outside of Luga."

"There must be some mistake! Such duty falls under the auspices of the People's Army. We belong out at sea

11

with the Fleet."

"Tell that to Lieutenant General Popov. Right now, we have no choice in the matter. Orders are orders. If we don't hurry back to the station, there's a good possibility both of us will be shot by the NKVD as deserters!"

Without waiting for further argument, Alexander turned back toward the rail yard. His brother followed close on his heels, and they both broke into a run as the shrill whistle of a train sounded once again.

"Most likely that train is our means of transport to Luga," Alexander said without breaking his long, fluid stride. "If we miss it, there's no telling what could happen to us."

The birch forest passed in a blur as the two junior lieutenants sprinted down the footpath. They broke through the tree line in time to see a massive black locomotive enter the yard followed by a trio of box cars and a caboose. On the roof of this last car was a sandbagged machine gun emplacement manned by a pair of soldiers.

It was Alexander who pointed toward the group of khaki-clad men gathered on the track-side loading ramp. "There's the squad now, Misha. Father must be watching out for us, because it looks like we'll just be able to join them in time."

As the locomotive screeched to a halt beside the loading ramp, Alexander and Mikhail hurried across the tracks and climbed up the ramp where they were met by Senior Lieutenant Viktor Ryutin. Their grizzled superior officer wasted no time venting his wrath.

"So the Kuznetsov twins have decided to grace us with their company after all," spat the red-cheeked veteran. "I was going to send the NKVD out looking for you. But I really wasn't worried, because if our men couldn't find you, the Nazis would. So come on, comrades. Onto the train with you. We've got ourselves a real live war to fight."

Though Mikhail would have liked to get a clarification of their orders and find out why they weren't being sent to the nearest navy base, he didn't dare incur more of the senior lieutenant's anger. Meekly saluting to the veteran's orders, he followed his brother into the boxcar.

Inside they found the rest of the squad huddled around a seated figure, who was propped up against the wooden slat wall. The twins wasted no time joining their comrades and listened as the bandage-wrapped stranger described his experiences on the front.

". . . I tell you, those Nazis came upon us like crazed demons!" exclaimed the infantryman, scanning the faces of his rapt audience. "I was assigned to guard a hospital unit that was supposed to be well within our lines. I had heard gunfire for most of the day, but most of it was a good distance away and nothing to worry about. It was getting toward sunset, and I was just thinking about breaking for chow, when all hell broke loose. First came the Stukas, diving out of the sky screaming like banshees from the underworld. The bastards didn't bother dropping bombs. They were content to strafe with their infernal machine-guns. I can still hear those exploding rounds as they ripped through our tents. Our wounded boys never stood a chance!"

The boxcar shifted as the locomotive jerked forward and began picking up steam. The infantryman took a deep breath and continued.

"I'm not afraid to admit my hands were shaking like an old woman as I shoved a live round into my Dekyarov and tried to draw a bead on one of those Lufwaffe bastards. Yet just as I was about to let a round fly, a new racket caught my attention. It sounded like a hundred locomotives and when I dared to look to the south, my worst fears were realized. Headed our way was a line of more than a hundred Panzers! It was then that my rifle jammed, and I had no choice but to run for cover and find a new weapon!"

"Sounds like a German blitzkrieg to me," said one of the young sailors. "With such a lightning attack, the Nazis were able to conquer Poland and France all in a matter of days."

"Nonsense!" said another ensign. "Such tactics might have worked in Poland and France, but never in the Motherland. Everyone knows that we have the Stalin Line to protect us."

"That's a good one!" the infantryman said with an ironic grin. "If we had saved the millions of rubles it cost to build that ridiculous line of ineffective tank traps and bought rifles instead, we'd be much better off. I was right there, comrades, and saw with these very eyes how those Panzers broke through our lines and mowed down our troops without quarter."

Alexander Kuznetsov nodded. "There are said to be many in our General Staff who have doubted the effectiveness of the Stalin Line all along. No fortress can ever provide one hundred percent protection. One only has to look back at France's so-called impenetrable Maginot Line to demonstrate this point."

"Well said, comrade," spoke the infantryman. "It's too bad we turned a blind eye to history, because even as we speak, the Germans continue their penetration of the Motherland. Soon they'll be unstoppable. First they'll rape and pillage our beloved Leningrad. Then it will be onto the gates of holy Moscow itself!"

The train was travelling at full speed and the deafening clatter of the wheels made conversation difficult.

"I wouldn't give up hope just yet, comrades," Mikhail said. "Even if the Stalin Line has indeed been circumvented, there are still many battles to be fought before the walls of Moscow and Leningrad are breached. No country on this planet can summon as many brave men and women to arms as the Soviet Union. Our Air Force is equipped with thousands of modern planes, and we're living testament to the awesome power of our Navy. Yet one thing still puzzles me. Why are we being taken further inland to Luga, instead of joining our comrades in the fleet? Surely as trained sailors we can best strike back at the enemy from the sea, as we were taught to do in the Academy."

"That is not ours to question, comrade Kuznetsov," answered the gruff voice of the senior lieutenant. "Our orders come direct from the High Command. We can only trust that General Popov and his staff know how we can best serve the Rodina. And no matter where they might send us, we will go into battle without flinching. To die in the defense of the Motherland is to die the death of a hero!"

The infantryman was suddenly possessed by a violent fit of coughing, that brought bloody spittle to his cracked lips. As the medical corpsman bent down to attend to him, Mikhail and Alexander retreated to the boxcar's opposite corner and sat down on the straw-covered floor.

"I still think Command has made a major screw-up," said Mikhail in a forceful whisper. "For the sake of Lenin, we belong at sea!"

"Easy, Misha," cautioned his brother. "Like the senior lieutenant says, we're just going to have to trust in General Popov's judgement. And who knows just what's waiting for us outside of Luga?"

"One thing we can be certain of," Mikhail said. "It won't be a submarine!"

Alexander sighed. "My greatest fear is that the Motherland doesn't have enough time to properly mobilize. The Germans caught us completely off guard, and unless we can reorganize, they'll continue to slice our forces to pieces."

"Come now, brother," Mikhail said with a grin. "You're beginning to sound like that scared old infantryman. Have you so little faith in the power of our people? We'll drive this foe from our borders, just as our ancestors sent Napoleon's legions home in defeat. The German supply lines are probably stretched so thin that a single spirited counterattack will turn the—"

A loud explosion from the outside suddenly sent the

boxcar swaying from side to side and the distinctive stac- cato blast of the caboose-borne machine gun could be heard from the rear of the train. This was accompanied by the rousing voice of Senior Lieutenant Ryutin.

"Stuka attack! To your rifles, men!"

Another deep explosion sounded outside and the brothers rose to arm themselves with their newly issued carbines. Well acquainted with the workings of a rifle, they loaded their weapons, ran to the rear of the boxcar and climbed a ladder that led to a hinged door that had been cut into the ceiling. Scrambling through the open- ing, they crouched on the roof of the swaying boxcar. The machine gun chattered behind them. Mikhail was first to spot the lone, silver-skinned, single-engine fighter in the process of sweeping down out of the cloud- less blue sky.

"On the eastern horizon! It's headed straight for us!"

"Surely they don't expect us to shoot it out of the sky with rifles," Alexander shouted.

"We don't have much choice in the matter, do we, brother? Besides, all it takes is one well placed bullet to take the Stuka down. And perhaps one of us will be the lucky one to do it."

Alexander raised the barrel of his rifle as the Stuka screamed toward them, strafing the train with a salvo of bullets. Several of the rounds crashed into the machine gun emplacement on the caboose, killing the two sol- diers who had been manning it.

"Our only chance is that machine gun," Mikhail yelled as the Stuka turned to begin another pass.

With the train steaming northward at top speed, they managed to jump onto the roof of the caboose. The sandbagged emplacement was covered with blood, as they pushed the dead gunners aside and took up posi- tions behind the machine gun.

"It still looks operational," Mikhail said as he fed in a fresh belt of ammunition. He was in the process of clear- ing the breech, when his brother called out excitedly.

"Here it comes! Out of the east!"

Mikhail gripped the trigger with both hands and swung the barrel up to meet the diving war plane. It was coming in head on, and Mikhail waited until he had its swirling propeller in view before pressing the trigger. The machine gun bucked wildly, but with his brother's help, he was able to stabilize the barrel. The sound of exploding shells rose with deafening intensity as the Stuka loomed like a giant winged beast, sweeping low over the surrounding forest of pines, on a collision course with the speeding train. With his machine gun still roaring, Mikhail raised his aim, centering the vibrating barrel on the aircraft's cockpit. He could actually see the German pilot hunched over his controls, when the Stuka suddenly blew apart and disintegrated before his startled eyes. The heat of this mid-air blast singed Mikhail's hair but that was of little consequence. The brothers had stood up to the best that the Luftwaffe could throw at them, and had come out victorious.

The twins looked up as Senior Lieutenant Ryutin climbed down onto the caboose and offered his hand in congratulations.

"Thank the heavens I didn't leave you two back at the rail yard," said the grinning veteran. "It takes a real man to face almost certain death like the two of you did. I'm proud to have you under my command. What do you say about scaring up some vodka? I don't know about you two, but this old-timer needs a drink."

A series of shrill blasts of the train whistle accompanied them as they climbed down into the boxcar. A bottle of clear, potent potato-distilled liquor materialized, and as the spirits were passed around, the senior lieutenant delivered a blow-by-blow description of their encounter with the Stuka. Mikhail humbly accepted the handshakes and hugs of his comrades. Yet after only a single sip of vodka, he seated himself on the straw-covered floor and fell soundly asleep and allowed his brother to take all the laurels of their victory.

Mikhail awoke several hours later. As his eyes opened, he realized the train had stopped moving. The boxcar was empty, and he stood up stiffly and went to the open doorway. Outside, he spotted his detachment gathered on a broad, clover-filled clearing. Behind them was a walled compound. A golden-domed cupola capped by a Russian Orthodox cross graced one of the structures that lay inside, and Mikhail knew they had reached their destination, the monastery of Tsarkoe Selo. The sun was high in the sky as he climbed down out of the boxcar and joined his comrades.

"The hero has awoken," greeted Senior Lieutenant Ryutin. "You're just in time to hear the rest of our orders. Make yourself comfortable, comrade Kuznetsov. I'm certain that you'll find this briefing most fascinating."

As Mikhail sat down beside his brother, Ryutin cleared his throat and continued. "As I was saying, because of the continued rapid approach of the German Sixth Army, Command has ordered us to this location to initiate an evacuation of certain state treasures that must be kept out of Nazi hands at all costs. Stored in the basement vault of the monastery behind us is a virtual fortune in jewelry, icons, and other ancient art masterpieces. Of even greater importance are the five hundred gold bars that have also been held in safekeeping here. Originally minted during the reign of Czar Nicholas II, the gold has been kept here as an emergency reserve, to aid the Motherland in times of crisis.

"Because of your spotless service records, you have been entrusted with the vital job of loading this collection onto the train we have just disembarked. Once this task has been completed, you will be responsible for providing security during the trip back to Leningrad. To be chosen for such a mission is a great honor. The Rodina is putting it's trust in you to properly carry out this assignment in these trying times. You mustn't let your Motherland down! So if there are no questions, we'd better get started. Time is of the essence. The Germans continue their advance, and have been reported as close as the neighboring village of Verduga."

As the senior lieutenant turned for the monastery, Mikhail saw his brother beckoning to him.

"So Command hasn't forgotten about us after all," Alexander said. "This might not be as glamorous as duty aboard a submarine or battleship, but our assignment sounds just as vital to our countries future survival."

"So it does," said Mikhail, as he gazed over the monastery grounds. "I must admit that it was an ingenious idea to hide a treasure in such an unassuming spot. Who would have ever expected it?"

"During the time of the Mongol invasions, monasteries such as this one were utilized for similar purposes," Alexander replied. "Supposedly the barbarians feared our chapels were filled with black magic, and whenever possible they kept their distance. Too bad the Germans can't be so easily deceived."

A bearded priest escorted the group through an icon-lined chapel. The air was thick with the scent of incense, and by the light of dozens of white candles they were led to the back of the central altar where a descending stairway led to the basement.

They were not prepared for the glittering treasure trove that awaited them in the cramped subterranean vault. Glistening in the candlelight were gilded chests filled with gem-studded jewelry. Stacked among the chests were exquisite icons, golden cups loaded with precious stones, and an assortment of expertly rendered paintings. Yet it was the rear of the vault that drew their eyes. Stacked on a thick wooden pallet were the gold bars stamped with the double eagle seal of the Romanoffs.

"An incredible sight," Ryutin reflected as he joined his men in the vault. "I had no idea of the treasure's true

19

extent. This could take days to properly catalogue and remove."

"I think that we should get started with the gold," said Mikhail. "Then if time allows, we can see about transferring the rest of the collection."

The senior lieutenant attempted to pick up one of the gold bricks and grunted. "That sounds good to me, Comrade. Moving this gold isn't going to be such an easy task by itself. Each bar must weight well over 20 kilograms."

"Just knowing the Nazis are out there will be enough to motivate us," said Mikhail.

"Why don't we form a human chain, and transfer the bars upstairs in that manner?" Alexander suggested.

"Good idea," agreed the senior lieutenant. "But while the actual transfer is in progress, I want both of you down here at all times with loaded weapons. If any of the men even touch any of the other objects you have my full blessings to stop them . . . permanently."

It was late in the afternoon by the time all of the bars were removed from the vault to the courtyard. Here they were loaded onto a cart and trundled to the train. They were in the midst of this process when the compound was buzzed by a dual-engine German surveillance plane. A tarp was hastily thrown over their glittering treasure, but it was not in place until the aircraft had made two complete passes.

"Get those bars loaded into the train with all haste, lads," Ryutin shouted. "If the Nazi's have spotted us, they'll be upon us like vultures."

The men were a good two-thirds done with their task when the sound of muffled gunfire could be heard in the distance, accompanied by several booming explosions. A column of thick, black smoke could be seen rising to the west. As the gunfire intensified in volume that Ryutin decided it was time to make a run for it.

"Unload that last cartload and board the train, lads. Comrade engineer, I want you to break all speed records from here to Leningrad."

"But the rest of the treasure," said one of the ensigns. "We can't leave it for the Germans!"

"The hell we can't," Ryutin said. "By the sound of that gunfire, the Germans are just a few kilometers away. If we don't get going now, we'll lose the gold as well."

A rumbling detonation caused another plume of black smoke to swirl up on the western horizon. Within minutes the last of the gold bars was loaded inside the boxcar located directly behind the locomotive. The squad was instructed to board the car behind, while the Kuznetsov twins were ordered to stay with the gold.

Mikhail and Alexander watched from the open doorway of the freight car as the priest refused Viktor Ryutin's invitation to come to safety with them. As the locomotive built up steam and began chugging out of the clearing, the bearded man of God could be seen chanting and tossing Holy water in their direction as a blessing to insure the trip's safe conclusion.

"I wonder what the Nazi's will do to the occupants of that monastery when they overrun the place?" Alexander said.

Mikhail shook his head. "Funny that he should be leaving us with a blessing, because those poor souls are going to need a miracle to remain alive. One look at the treasure we left behind and those Germans are going to become a bunch of crazed sharks in a feeding frenzy. They'll suspect that additional loot is buried nearby and will utilize every torture in the book to find out where it's located."

"Maybe we shouldn't have left them, Misha. At least we could have gone down fighting."

"Those are noble sentiments, dear brother," Mikhail replied. "But you're forgetting the purpose of this mission. The gold bars are worth a fortune. Think of how much medicine, food, rifles and ammunition it will buy. To sacrifice this treasure merely to show how brave we are would be an injustice to the rest of the citizens of the

21

Motherland."

Mikhail turned toward the doorway, his attention riveted on the countryside they were leaving behind. He could still see the golden, onion-shaped dome of the monastery. It was just visible beyond the thick branches of the forest. As the track snaked in the opposite direction, the last vestiges of the holy enclave disappeared altogether. Mikhail could still see the setting sun as it dipped beneath the tree line. All too soon it would drop below the horizon, and the night would swallow the forest in a veil of blackness. Mikhail guessed it would be under the shroud of night that the Nazis would close in on the monastery and transform the sacred site into a pure hell.

He gritted his teeth in anger. The encounter with the attacking Stuka had unlocked a primal instinct from deep within his subconscious. He had never gotten joy from taking another life before. Yet this was war. The Nazis had willfully violated their border; now it was either kill or be killed.

What power he had felt as he sat on the roof of the caboose perched behind that machine gun! Like a god, with the power of life and death in his hands, he accepted the challenge of the Luftwaffe pilot, and without fearing the consequences, put his very life on the line to defend his homeland. With the adrenalin pumping through his body he felt invincible, even though the greater firepower and maneuverability lay with his adversary. Yet the fates had sided with Mikhail, and as the diving aircraft exploded in the air before him, his enemy's fiery death was almost anticlimactic. At that moment he remembered thinking how very thin was the line between the living and the dead. And it was then he realized that he had transcended the normal bounds of mortal fear.

The freight car shifted hard to one side as the track began winding its way around a broad bend. Reaching out to the edge of the doorway to steady himself,

Mikhail listened as the locomotive's powerful whistle cried out in the gathering twilight like a howling demon.

It was only after the curve was behind them that he noted what seemed to be a decrease in the train's forward speed. The loss of velocity was gradual at first, and Mikhail was wondering if it all wasn't a trick of his imagination, when the ear-piercing squeal of the brakes told him otherwise. Thrown violently off balance by this unexpected loss of speed, he started to tumble forward. Only the firm grasp of his brother kept him from being tossed out of the partially open doorway to the track below.

"What the hell was that all about?" cursed Mikhail.

Alexander leaned outside and surveyed that portion of the track that lay before them.

"Sweet father Lenin! It's a tank, and it's just sitting there, smack in the middle of the damn track!"

Quick to have a look himself, Mikhail peered out the doorway. Dusk had fallen, yet barely illuminated by the last glow of twilight, less than two dozen meters away, was a massive armored vehicle, its gun turret pointed right at them.

"It's a German Panzer," revealed Mikhail. "And from the look of it, they're not in any hurry to let us pass."

"Perhaps if we put up a full head of steam we could ram it and push it out of the way," Alexander said.

"I seriously doubt they'd just sit there without firing and let us get away with such a thing, dear brother. Our only alternative is to reverse our course while the track is still clear behind us, and find another route to safety."

Mikhail was prepared to jump from the car and inform the engineer of this tactic, when Senior Lieutenant Ryutin climbed down onto the track from the boxcar behind them.

"Comrade Senior Lieutenant, perhaps we should try reversing our course!" cried Mikhail. "We could transfer to an alternative route at the switching station at Luga."

"That's just what I had in mind, Kuznetsov," answered

the veteran. "But no matter what happens, you're to stay with that gold above all else. Now hang on, lads. I'm afraid the ride is going to be a bit rough."

Mikhail watched as Ryutin ran down the track and disappeared inside the locomotive. Seconds later, the brakes released with a loud hiss. There was a sudden lurch as the engineer reversed gears, followed by a steady movement backward. Mikhail watched as the tank that had been blocking the track grew smaller.

"I wonder why they didn't shoot at us while they had the chance?" Alexander asked with a relieved sigh. "Surely it would have only taken a single well-placed round to blow our locomotive to pieces."

Mikhail had been contemplating the same thought as he leaned out the doorway in an attempt to view the conditions of the track in the direction that they were now moving. As they prepared to round the curve they had transitted only minutes before, he spotted another Panzer blocking their escape route. And in that instant, he knew the answer to his brother's question.

"It's an ambush!" warned Mikhail. "The bastards had us set up the whole damn time."

The engineer also spotted the new obstacle, and as he slammed on the brakes, the train once more lurched to a sudden, squealing stop.

"Now what?" asked Alexander.

"You'd better make sure you have a fresh magazine in your rifle, brother. The way it looks to me, the only way we're going to be able to get out of this train is to fight our way out."

Alexander fumbled for his carbine. "Perhaps we should make a run for it on foot while we still have a chance, Misha."

Mikhail firmly shook his head. "This is as good a place to die as any other. Besides, I think I'd rather be dead, than live the rest of my life as a coward."

Alexander's moment of indecision was cut short by the gruff voice of their senior lieutenant. "Alexander

Kuznetsov, I want you to take up a defensive position inside the caboose. Your brother's to stay with the gold until I say otherwise."

"This is it, Misha," Alexander said. "Do take care."

There could be no doubting the fear and confusion that clouded his brother's sea-green eyes, and Mikhail stepped forward and hugged him tightly.

"Have faith, dearest Alexander. We've gotten out of worse scrapes before. This will be no different. You'll see."

Alexander stood back and stared into his brother's intense blue eyes. Finding himself unable to find the words to express his deep emotions, he could only shake his head and then turn for the open doorway. The last Mikhail saw of his twin was as he sprinted off to his new position at the rear of the train.

Moments later Mikhail spotted his first German infantryman slowly moving out of the nearby tree line. Because of the limited light, he couldn't determine if there were more. But it became apparent there were when his comrades in the boxcar behind him opened fire. Quick to respond to this meagre volley, a multitude of muzzle flashes erupted from the black depths of the wood and Mikhail knew that they were vastly outnumbered.

Determined to send as many of the enemy to their early graves as possible, Mikhail raised his Dekyarov and began firing. He picked his targets carefully, diligently waiting until an exploding Nazi shell gave him something tangible to shoot at. He expended over a dozen cartridges before the first German mortar rounds arrived. One of the shells landed on the edge of the track directly in front of him, and Mikhail ducked for cover just as a shower of shrapnel and debris flew in through the open doorway.

Seconds later, another mortar round crashed into the freight car behind him with a deafening explosion. The floor rattled beneath Mikhail, and he could hear the

25

horrified cries of his wounded comrades as they screamed out in anguish. Fighting the impulse to leave his position and see what he could do to assist them, Mikhail began choking on the thick, black smoke that was another by-product of the blast. His eyes stung with pain, and it took a supreme effort just to breathe. Yet not to be denied his chance to revenge this attack, he lifted his rifle and blindly sprayed bullets into the tree line.

It was while he was inserting another magazine that the first German soldier reached the side of his boxcar. Mikhail intuitively sensed this man's presence moments before he could actually see him. With trembling hands he did his best to get a fresh round into the chamber, but a jam kept the breech from clearing. When the Nazi soldier could be heard climbing into the entrance of the boxcar, Mikhail had no choice but to put down his rifle and pull out his combat knife. He used the roiling smoke as an effective veil and waited until the German was almost upon him before springing up and thrusting the knife deep into the enemy's soft gut.

The German howled in pain. Bathed in spurting blood, Mikhail backed away as the Nazi collapsed onto the floor. It seemed to take an eternity for him to stop his pained whimpering. Barely aware of the scattered gunshots that still emanated from outside, Mikhail listened to the labored breathing of the man whom he had just stabbed. Remorse replaced his previous anger, and he only wished to flee from this cursed place. Yet his legs were heavy, and feeling suddenly drained of all energy, he dropped to the floor himself, not noticing the wounded German's last desperate gasp before he surrendered to the arms of death. He was equally unaware of the fact that outside, the shooting had finally come to a conclusion.

It proved to be the sound of nearby voices that eventually broke him from his shocked reverie. Still finding himself without the energy to stand, Mikhail listened as a German officer barked out a flurry of orders. The blindingly bright shaft of a battery-powered torch split the blackness and a group of soldiers noisily climbed up into the boxcar.

Mikhail winced in pain as the powerful shaft of light hit him full in the eyes.

"Well, what do we have here?" asked an icy voice in broken Russian.

As Mikhail's eyes adjusted to the sudden illumination, he viewed the face of the man responsible for this question. There was a cruelty to this stranger's expression that belied his relatively young age. Peering down at Mikhail like he was a poisonous contagion, his steel-gray eyes displayed pure hatred. His sharp features were dominated by highly etched cheekbones, a narrow forehead, and a head of closely cropped white hair. A nervous tick caused the right side of his mouth to lift in a sneer, as he addressed Mikhail in German-flavored Russian.

"You and your comrades fought admirably. Unfortunately, you were no match for the Waffen SS. May I ask what it was that you were willing to give your lives up to defend this evening? Surely it wasn't for this empty train."

"Go to hell, you Nazi pig!" spat Mikhail viciously.

The German merely snickered. "My, you are certainly an emotional people. You're crude and mannerless as well."

Turning away from Mikhail, he spoke in rapid German. Two black-uniformed infantrymen appeared out of the darkness, and took up positions on each side of Mikhail. Each of the muscular soldiers took a hold of one of his arms and pinned them back until he was a helpless captive. Doing his best to hide the pain, Mikhail watched as his white-haired interrogator bent over and picked up his blood-stained combat knife.

"So this is evidently the weapon that you used to kill my corporal with. I understand that a knife wound is a

27

most painful way to die."

Briefly examining the finely honed blade, he accidentally nicked his finger. Blood oozed from the tiny wound, and he quickly brought it to his lips.

"This is certainly a most lethal weapon, comrade," observed the Nazi, who regripped the knife and waved it menacingly before Mikhail. "It would be a shame to ruin such a handsome face." Then he stepped forward and pressed the tip of the blade up against Mikhail's left temple. "I'll give you one last chance, comrade. Where was this train bound and what is your cargo?"

Mikhail could only think of a single fitting response. Even though his mouth was dry, he managed to summon forth a wad of thick, white phlegm, which he proceeded to deposit squarely onto his interrogator's forehead.

"Insolent Red heathen!" cried the Nazi, who without bothering to wipe off the spittle, pressed down onto the knife until its tip just penetrated Mikhail's skin. Then with a single slashing motion he traced a bloody line from the tip of Mikhail's left eyebrow all the way down to his jaw.

Any further retaliation on the Nazi's part was cut short by the excited shouts of one of his subordinates. "Over here, Herr Koch! You'll never believe what I've found hidden beneath a tarp just waiting for us!"

Oblivious to the seering pain that filled the left side of his face, Mikhail watched as the white-haired Nazi turned in the freight car's smoke-filled interior. He couldn't help but catch the glint of gold as the Germans excitedly scanned their find. A pain just as intense as that which racked his torn face filled his being with pure anguish.

With the realization that he had failed his assignment, Mikhail collapsed into his captors' vice-like grasp. As the blood from his wound splattered down onto the floor, he listened as the Germans sang out in celebration. Their incredible find brought pure joy to their lips. As a way of expressing his satisfaction, the white-haired officer known as Koch decided to spare Mikhail's life. Instead of a bullet to the back of his head, he would be shipped off to experience a living death in a hellhole known as the Bergen-Belsen concentration camp.

While Mikhail Kuznetsov was granted yet another temporary reprieve from his pain by slipping off into blessed unconsciousness, his twin brother Alexander had just experienced his own near brush with death. He had been positioned inside the caboose when the first Nazis were spotted. Standing beside him, Senior Lieutenant Viktor Ryutin gave the order to open fire.

The light was poor, and Alexander waited for an enemy muzzle-flash to show itself before taking aim and squeezing off a shot, and then another and another. His confidence was reinforced when several of his bullets hit their mark. But when the mortar shells began falling, he knew they were fighting a losing cause.

When one of these rounds detonated right outside the caboose, Alexander looked to his left and saw that Senior Lieutenant Ryutin had been hit. There was no need for him to apply first aid, for the entire top portion of the veteran's skull had been blown off by a piece of razor sharp shrapnel. Finding himself on his own, Alexander decided that in this instance, discretion was the best policy, and off he went through the shattered window on the opposite side of the railroad car.

He didn't stop running until he was a good fifty meters away from the train tracks. Here he took advantage of a dense thicket and dove for cover. With his pulse pounding madly in his chest, he dared to look back and cringed when he saw the column of black smoke rising from the boxcar located immediately beside the caboose. It was here that the majority of his comrades had been stationed, and the smoke surely meant that they had taken a direct hit.

An even greater concern crossed his mind as he

peered at the adjoining freight car, for it was here that not only had the gold been hidden, but his own brother as well.

The conspicuous absence of gunfire certainly meant that the battle was over. The Nazis had succeeded in overwhelming them and Alexander watched as a squad of German troops assembled at the trackside. The deep, rumbling roar of an advancing tank broke the temporary quiet. He looked on in disbelief as the armored vehicle broke out of the woods and smashed into the caboose and the still smoking boxcar that was attached to it. As the cars tumbled off the track, the Germans loaded themselves into the remaining freight car, where both the gold and his brother had been situated.

The locomotive built up a head of steam, and to a heartrendering blast of its whistle, the now shortened train roared off in reverse, without ceremony to the presumed safety of the German lines.

The tank disappeared back into the trees, and Alexander waited until the sound of the locomotive had completely faded in the distance before leaving his hiding place. Ever fearful of what awaited him alongside the tracks, he carefully returned to the site of the ambush. The smashed boxcar was still smoking, and by the flickering light of the burning wreckage, he searched for any survivors. As he expected, there were none. Only the smashed, lifeless corpses of his comrades met his eyes.

Yet one observation was a bit more heartening. Nowhere within the twisted wreckage were the remains of his brother. Was his corpse still inside the boxcar alongside the gold? Or had he perhaps been wounded and taken prisoner? With this hope in mind, Alexander reluctantly left this site of carnage and death, to get on with the huge task of ridding his homeland of the bloodthirsty scourge that was responsible for this slaughter.

Chapter Two

The Present

The Bell 212 helicopter lifted off its dockside pad with a grinding roar. From the copilot's seat, David Lawton peered out the plexiglass windshield, and watched the city limits of Haugesund, Norway take form down below. Unlike his hometown of Houston, Texas, there was a noticeable absence of steel and glass high-rise buildings in evidence. Instead there was a preponderance of quaint, wooden structures of approximately three stories, painted in soft pastel shades. Most were situated near a wide channel of water that allowed direct access to the open sea. A variety of boats ranging from compact sloops to cabin cruisers, fishing trawlers, and ocean-going freighters were docked along the shoreline.

As the chopper gained altitude, Lawton caught a glimpse of the breathtaking scenery visible inland. Huge, sharply-etched mountains formed the eastern horizon, while magnificent sparkling green fjords filled the deep valleys. The Texan would have loved to explore this fascinating terrain more closely, but unfortunately his destination lay in the opposite direction. Already the pilot had pointed the rounded nose of the helicopter to the west. They would remain on this course until they were well out over the surging grey waters of the North Sea.

"Excuse me for not getting the chance to properly introduce myself back at the heliport," offered the pilot as she turned toward her passenger, pushing back her chin-mounted microphone. "I'm Kari Skollevoll. Welcome aboard Noroil One. I hope you're enjoying Norway, Mr. Lawton."

To be heard over the whining rotors, the Texan responded firmly. "Actually, I haven't seen much more than the Stavanger and Haugesund airports. I flew in from Edinburgh a little less than two hours ago."

"Have you visited our country before, Mr. Lawton?" asked the pilot, as she reached forward to make a minor adjustment to the fuel mixture.

"This is my first time, and I must admit what little I've seen so far is impressive. That countryside behind us looks magnificent. And Haugesund appears to be quite the charming fishing village."

"It's much more than that," answered the young pilot, whose blond curly hair could just be seen beneath the confines of her helmet. "In my grandfather's day herring fishing was indeed the city's primary industry. Today Haugesund is much more diversified. We have a huge shipyard, where vessels up to 150,000 tons can be repaired. The city is also a primary supply and research base for the offshore oil business."

"So I understand," replied Lawton, infected by her enthusiasm. "How long have you been with Noroil?"

"I'm approaching my third anniversary. I learned how to fly helicopters in the Air Force, though I've been flying fixed-wing aircraft since I was a teenager."

"I gather you're from around these parts," said the Texan.

"I was born and raised in Haugesund. In fact, most of my family still lives there. One good thing about my job is that I get a chance to visit them quite frequently."

David Lawton nodded and peered out the window to the sea below. Though the sky was slightly overcast, the visibility was good, and he was afforded an excellent view of a series of small islands that barely managed to poke their rocky surfaces above the white-capped waters. The forty-seven year old Texan scratched his thickly bearded chin.

"I have to admit," he said, "that I was expecting to be greeted by waist high snowdrifts the moment I stepped foot on Norwegian soil. So far, considering it's late autumn, the temperatures seem incredibly mild. And the only snow I've seen has been on the summits of those coastal mountains behind us."

"You can thank the warming influence of the Gulf Stream for that, Mr. Lawton. An offshoot of the current flows just off our coast, and because of it, we have some of the mildest winters in all of Scandinavia. But just you hang around a little longer, and you'll see plenty of snow around here. That I can guarantee you."

As Lawton continued his inspection of the waters below, he spotted what appeared to be a large ship looming in the distance. It was only as they got closer to the monstrous object that he identified it as a huge oil platform. Supported on thick concrete legs, the platform was in the process of being towed out to sea, clearly dwarfing the trio of powerful ocean-going tugs that had been chosen for the task.

As a veteran oil-service worker, the Texan had seen many similar rigs, yet none could compare to this one for sheer size. Dominating its equipment-packed surface was a towering derrick. A complex maze of snaking pipes and a vast assortment of pumps, cranes, and other heavy machinery was tucked beneath the latticed steel framework. Its living module rose over ten stories high, and was capped by a circular helipad and a number of white satellite dishes. All in all, it was an awesome structure, that proved impressive even to a jaded Texan.

Noting his interest, the pilot identified the rig for him. "That's the new Ice Field's production platform, sir. It was just completed in Haugesund, and is designed to be placed in 200 meters of water off the Arctic island of Svalbard. I've been told that its total weight is over one million tons. From the base of its legs to the tip of the derrick, it's over 350 meters high. The legs alone required 240,000 cubic meters of concrete, and the total quantity of steel utilized is the equivalent to the weight of ten Eiffel towers."

"That's mighty impressive, even by Texas standards," reflected Lawton, as the platform passed beneath them. "How much longer until we get to the Falcon?"

"We should be touching down on the ship's helipad in another ten minutes," answered the pilot. "Why don't you just sit back, relax, and enjoy the flight. I've got a thermos full of hot coffee in the supply cabinet. If you'd like a cup, just let me know."

Lawton shook his head. "No thanks, Kari. I've already had my caffeine fix for the day."

"Then would you mind some music?" she asked. "I just got a new Oslo Philharmonic recording of Edvard Grieg's *Peer Gynt*. During the chopper's last refit, the ground crew installed a cassette player and some pretty decent speakers up here. It sure beats listening to the constant chop of those rotors."

"Sounds good to me, Kari."

While the pilot reached up to activate the cassette player, Lawton attempted to stretch his tall, lanky frame. The equipment-packed cockpit was far from spacious, and the bulky, bright orange survival suit that he wore over his normal clothing only made the cramped cabin that much tighter.

As the spirited first chords of the Grieg symphony broke from the elevated speakers, he took his attractive pilot's advice and did his best to sit back and relax. The stereo system was indeed first class, and the resulting music did much to filter out the harsh, grinding roar of the Bell's engines.

Though he wasn't much of a classical music buff, the opening movement had plenty of old-fashioned fiddle playing in it. The spirited folk rhythms were easy to lis-

34

ten to, and had an almost country flavor to them.

The island of Utsira passed below. This compact, rock-strewn landmass was the western-most extension of the Norwegian mainland, and as they zoomed over it, nothing but the lonely gray sea stretched to the horizon.

Lawton stared out at the seemingly endless expanse of water and contemplated the man whose invitation had brought him so far from home. He had first met Magne Rystaad a year ago, at a symposium in Washington, D.C. The two were introduced immediately after a seminar on the latest hyperbaric welding techniques. The fair-haired Norwegian was tight-lipped at first. Yet Lawton liked him right off, and invited the Chuck-Norris look-alike for a drink. Since they were practically the same age, and had both been employed as oil industry divers for over a decade, they were soon chatting away like old friends.

It was during their second beer that Magne accepted Lawton's offer to visit an oil platform that the Texan was helping put in off the Louisiana coast. They left for the site immediately after the conclusion of the seminar. This was the Norwegian's first visit to the American south, and he thoroughly enjoyed his exposure to both the balmy weather and the variety of unique southern customs.

Magne seemed genuinely impressed by Lawton's project. His main interest was the crew of two dozen divers that Lawton was responsible for and he was surprised to learn that a good majority of the men were ex-U.S. Navy. In Norway, a military diver was seldom allowed to transfer to the civilian sector and apply the craft that the government had spent so much time and money teaching him.

When Lawton admitted that he was an ex-Navy diver himself, who had seen action in Viet Nam, Magne's eyes opened wide, and for the rest of the day the Norwegian pestered his host to share some of his wartime experiences. Lawton reluctantly did so

35

later that evening, while sipping longnecks on the platform's deserted helipad.

The war had been a traumatic time in Lawton's life that he would have preferred to forget about. During his two-year tour in the jungled hell of Southeast Asia, he had witnessed atrocities that had broken stronger men than he. Only by the greatest of miracles did he come out of the conflict with some degree of sanity. Yet the nightmares still returned from time to time, and just sitting there on that platform, with the humid Gulf winds hitting him in the face, brought back many a poignant memory of his exploits as a U.S. Navy SEAL.

It was well after midnight when the two veteran divers finally parted company, with their new friendship all but sealed. To reciprocate Lawton's hospitality, Magne invited the Texan to visit him in Norway. Lawton accepted, though it was to take him a full year to find the time in his hectic schedule to fit the trip in.

With the spirited strains of *Peer Gynt* still filling the cockpit, Lawton sat forward expectantly when the bare outline of a ship became visible on the distant horizon. The vessel's unique silhouette became more discernable as the helicopter continued its approach. Though he had previously only seen pictures of the *Falcon*, there was no doubt in his mind this was the Norwegian dive ship he had travelled thousands of miles to visit. There could be no mistaking the bulbous helideck that was positioned on the ship's bow, or the massive bridge and dual engine stacks situated amidships. The rest of the bright yellow vessel was dominated by an immense crane. This was the operational portion of the *Falcon*, where its moonpools were located. Through these openings to the sea, the ship's remotely operated vehicles, or ROV's for short, and manned diving bells would be lowered.

"Looks like we made it," said the pilot matter of factly. "I'll have you safely on deck before you know it."

The good weather allowed their approach to be a routine one, and with a minimum of difficulty the Bell 212 landed on its shipborne helipad with a bare jolt.

"Thanks for the smooth ride, Kari," said Lawton as he unbuckled his safety harness. "Will you be staying on board for awhile?"

"Afraid not, sir. I'll only remain long enough for them to unload that mess of supplies back in the main cabin. Then I'm off for Stavanger to pick up a new load of computer hardware for the main office."

"Well, take care, young lady. And thanks again for the lift."

The helicopter's rotors were whirling to a halt as Lawton exited the vehicle through its main hatchway. Outside, he was met by a gust of cool, salt-filled air and a weather beaten crew member dressed in orange coveralls and matching hard hat.

"Welcome aboard the *Falcon*, Mr. Lawton. I'm Olav Anderson, the ship's quartermaster. Magne is sorry that he wasn't able to greet you personally, but he's in the midst of an operation in the ship's diving control room. If you'll just follow me, I'll take you down there."

The Texan nodded and followed his guide down a latticed steel ladder to the main deck. Here they passed a silver suited figure, who stood with a fire hose in hand, his gaze riveted on the nearby helicopter. Nearby, a fully enclosed, orange life boat was stored, and Lawton was impressed by the Norwegian's exacting safety standards.

A hatch led them below deck. While transitting a spotlessly clean passageway, the quartermaster offered an impromptu briefing.

"The *Falcon* is the newest multi-purpose vessel in Noroil's ever expanding fleet. Its main functions are to act as a diving support ship and provide fire fighting services. The *Falcon* is 101 meters long, with two fully equipped engine rooms, three tunnel thrusters in the foreship, and two Azimuth thrusters in the aft. All of these systems are automatically controlled through a dynamic positioning system with dual redundancy."

"To what depth is your diving system rated?" asked

37

Lawton, as they passed by the ship's mess room.

"350 meters," answered the quartermaster. "If needed, this rating can be easily modified for 500 meters."

Yet another ladder led them to a spacious compartment filled with various machine tools. While crossing its cluttered length, the quartermaster continued his briefing.

"The *Falcon* has two moonpools, and is outfitted with a pair of diving bells, each capable of holding up to seven individuals. For decompression purposes there are three separate transfer chambers, and a central four-man chamber for extended stay, saturation purposes."

Lawton caught a brief glimpse of one of these large, cylinder-shaped, white chambers as they stepped through a hatchway and began their way over a narrow catwalk that bordered one of the open moonpools. A thick cable linked to an overhead winch extended into the water here. Several crew members could be seen gathered around a nearby console, and the Texan couldn't help but vent his curiosity.

"Is there currently a bell down below?" he asked.

"Actually, it's a ROV," answered his guide, without breaking his brisk stride. "We call it Solo. Inside that umbilical is the latest in fiber optics, allowing high quality video and data feedback at depths up to fifteen hundred meters. Solo has also got the latest in side scanning sonar, that allows for high speed pipeline sonar surveys at velocities up to four knots."

Well aware that such a vehicle would certainly make life easier for the *Falcon*'s divers, Lawton followed the Norwegian into a narrow passageway lined with snaking electrical cables. The corridor led directly into a large compartment dominated by a central cluster of consoles. Seated in front of this assemblage of high-tech equipment were a trio of technicians. Each wore yellow overalls, and had their attentions focused on the complicated assortment of video monitor screens mounted before them.

38

The middle figure sported a familiar mop of wavy blond hair, and David Lawton spotted the name *Rystaad* printed across the broad back. Magne seemed unaware of his guest's presence behind him, his right hand glued to an airplane-like joystick, his eyes riveted to a video monitor. The Texan gingerly stepped forward until he was immediately behind his host and could just make out the flickering images visible on the video screen.

The monitor was filled by an object that appeared to be a large boulder. A digital depth gauge showed that it was laying on the seabed 283 meters beneath the sea's surface. Yet it was a single sharp spike that emerged from the top portion of the object that indicated it wasn't a boulder at all, but a manmade object.

"My God, is that a mine?" blurted the Texan.

Without taking his eyes off the monitor screen, Magne Rystaad coolly answered. "As a matter of fact, it is. Welcome aboard the *Falcon,* David. Sorry I can't offer you a proper handshake, but I'm currently utilizing our ROV to place six kilos of dynamite at the base of that baby, that we believe to be a relic of World War I."

"No apologies necessary, Magne," replied Lawton who watched intently as his host gripped yet another joy-stick with his left hand.

Almost instantaneously, an articulated manipulator arm came into view on the screen. At the tip of the artificial appendage was a sausage-shaped cannister that was being deposited beside the base of the mine. Only when this process was completed did Magne push back from the console, turn to face his guest, and exhale a full breath of relief.

"It's really good to see you, David," the Norwegian said as he stood and offered his hand in greeting.

Lawton found Magne's firm grip a bit clammy as he replied, "Likewise, my friend. It seems I got here at an opportune moment."

"Your timing's impeccable, David. You'll get to see the fireworks firsthand."

Magne issued a flurry of instructions in rapid Norwegian to his co-workers, before returning his attention to his guest.

"We just found this mine yesterday, while in the middle of a routine examination of the seabed for the laying of Ice Field's new oil pipeline."

"With all of your other pipelines in this area, I would have thought that the seabed here had long been cleared of any obstacles," said Lawton.

"So did I," Magne answered. "But as you very well know, the open seas are full of surprises. We only learned from the Norwegian naval authorities this morning that the mine appears to have been originally laid in 1918. At that time some 70,000 mines were deposited in a minefield between Norway and Great Britain to prevent German submarines from gaining access to the Atlantic."

"Couldn't you just reroute your pipeline to go around the mine?" asked Lawton.

"We tossed the idea around, but decided it just wasn't worth the risks involved. As you well know, during pipelaying the laying barge hauls itself along on anchors. Some of these anchors extend several kilometers from the barge, and it's therefore imperative that a cleared corridor over five hundred meters wide exists. Because of the presence of massive, house-sized boulders on the seabed beneath us, the route can't be significantly altered; thus we've been saddled with the job of ridding the seas of this potential hazard along with all the others once and for all."

One of the technicians interrupted with a brief comment and Magne provided the translation. "The blast will be triggered by our ROV. Solo has just attained its firing position. Though I'm afraid that there won't be much to see, keep your eyes on the central monitor screen."

Lawton did just this as Magne returned to the console. Illuminated by the ROV's powerful mercury-vapor spotlights, the fiber optic video camera showed nothing but an expanse of grey water. It was just after Magne depressed a circular red button that the screen filled with a swirling vortex of roiling air bubbles. It took several minutes before the agitation settled.

"I'll move Solo in now," said Magne as he activated the joystick. "But I doubt if there will be much left of that mine but an empty crater in the seabed several meters deep."

Soon the video screen filled with just such a feature and David Lawton said thoughtfully, "That sure beats the hell out of deactivating mines like we did in Nam. Back then we were still doing it the old-fashioned way — with divers."

"Two hundred and fifty kilos of TNT can pack a wallop," said Magne. "I certainly wouldn't want to have to go down there and personally deal with such a monster."

"Tell that to the C.O.," said Lawton with a wink.

Magne smiled and stood to rejoin his guest. Only then did Lawton notice that Magne was wearing the alligator-skin cowboy boots that the Norwegian had bought in Houston the year before.

"I see you still have your boots," observed the Texan.

"Most comfortable pair of 'shoes' I ever owned, David. I almost gave you a call before you left to ask you to bring me another pair."

"That can be arranged," said Lawton. "Do you still have your Stetson?"

The blue-eyed Norwegian shook his head. "As a matter of fact, I don't. My oldest boy Karl took a liking to it from the day he met me at the airport. That was the first real cowboy hat he'd ever seen. When he asked me if he could wear it to school the next day, I couldn't refuse. Needless to say, that was the last I ever saw of it." The Norwegian's warm eyes sparkled. "Why don't I give you an update on the family over something to eat."

41

Oil field support ships were widely known for the excellent quality of their food, and the *Falcon*'s galley was no exception. The buffet table displayed a wide variety of both hot and cold delicacies. At Magne's suggestion, Lawton chose a plate of fresh herring, served with sour cream and chopped onions. For his main course he selected broiled chicken, steamed potatoes, beets, and an apple tart for dessert.

The mess was designed to hold up to one-half of the *Falcon*'s one hundred person complement at a time. Yet less than a dozen crew members were present as the two sat down at a vacant table near the room's rear bulkhead.

"I hope you find the food satisfactory, David. The *Falcon*'s head chef was trained in Paris, although he still can't duplicate the wonderful chili that was served on your rig. I don't suppose you would happen to know the recipe."

"That, my friend, is an official Texas state secret," laughed Lawton as he piled a piece of herring onto a slice of black bread. "But I'll tell you what—though I'm not much of a cook myself—when I return to Houston, I'll see what I can do about getting a copy of Cooky's famous Rio Grande chili recipe and send it off to you. Maybe I could even manage to smuggle out a couple of packages of real Texan chili powder."

As Lawton took a bite of herring, he appreciatively added, "This concoction's damn tasty itself. When I eat fish back home it's usually prepared deep fried or blackened with cajun pepper. But I think that I could learn to enjoy this herring. Yes, I think I certainly could."

"Well, you'll be having your fill of it during your stay with us," said Magne as he dug into the Ceaser salad he had selected. "Herring is a staple part of our diet, and hardly a day goes by without it being served. My wife Anna likes it raw for breakfast. I myself prefer the pickled variety, like the type that you're eating."

"Is Anna still teaching?" questioned the Texan between bites of his appetizer.

"She certainly is, David. This is the start of her third year, and she's just as enthused about those fifth graders of hers as she was on the day she first began."

"What ever happened to your oldest boy, Magne? Did he enlist in the Army like he was threatening to do?"

Magne put down his fork. "Fortunately, Karl listened to the voice of reason and decided on college. A full scholarship to the University of Missouri is not something to pass over on a mere whim. He'll have plenty of time to serve his country once he graduates and returns home in four years."

"You must be very proud of him, Magne. What's the little one been up to?"

The Norwegian grinned. "Thor is as full of the devil as ever. It's hard to believe he'll be graduating secondary school in another year. Where in the hell does time fly?"

"Tell me about it," said Lawton as he cut into a chicken breast. "I still find it hard to believe that a whole year has passed since your visit. It seems like it was just the other day that we were out there on the Gulf of Mexico sipping Lone Star longnecks and swapping the stories of our lives."

Magne nodded. "What ever happened to your daughter? Did you hear from her like you were hoping last year?"

There was a hint of bitterness in Lawton's tone as he answered. "To tell you the truth Magne, I haven't. Though I did hear from one of her close girlfriends that Susan's doing real well. She's got her own place in Santa Monica, California, and is studying to get her real estate license. I still think it's her mother's fault for her never answering my calls or letters. My ex has filled her with so much poison that she probably thinks I'm a demon of some kind. I should have fought harder for custody from the very beginning."

Magne sensed he was treading on sensitive ground, and was all set to change the direction of their conversation, when he was paged over the public address system. He left his guest to his dinner, and stood up to cross the mess hall and pick up a wall-mounted telephone. He was back to their table in less than a minute, his eyes wide with wonder.

"Solo's made yet another surprise discovery," he said without bothering to seat himself. "Would you care to join me back in the diving control room to have a look?"

Without a second's hesitation, Lawton put down his knife and fork and stood. "You'd better believe that I'd like to have a look, partner. Is it another mine?"

"Why don't you wait and see for yourself, David. From what my assistant says, neither one of us should be too disappointed."

There was a deliberate vagueness to this answer that immediately aroused Lawton's curiosity, and he followed his host out of the galley area and aft toward the *Falcon*'s stern.

This time when they entered the compartment where the *Falcon*'s diving operations were monitored they found the room buzzing with excitement. Several jump-suited technicians stood blocking the central console, as they watched the scene unfolding on the video monitor. Magne impatiently pushed his way through this crowd, with David Lawton close on his heels.

Once the Texan was past this gawking mass, his eyes went at once to the video monitor. The screen was filled with an immense, elongated black, tubular structure, that he assumed to be a shipwreck of some sort. Slowly the ROV's camera continued its sweep of the mysterious object, and several distinguishing features showed themselves, causing Lawton's pulse to quicken.

Illuminated beneath Solo's floodlights was a rust-streaked hull, whose length was perforated by a number of regularly spaced free-flood holes. Yet only when the Texan viewed the streamlined conning tower that had two dual cannons set into each end, was he certain enough to express himself.

"It's a German Type XXI U-boat!" he exclaimed. "During my UDT training, we dove on a similar wreck, that had sunk off the coast of Georgia. No other submarine has a fin with two cannons set into each end like the Type XXI. I'm absolutely positive that's what we've got here, Magne."

Seemingly oblivious to this spirited revelation, Magne Rystaad calmly questioned the technician seated to his right. "Tell me, Knut, how did Solo make this discovery? Was it by sonar?"

"It was," replied his associate. "We were just completing a visual inspection of the debris field generated by that exploding mine, when the side scanning sonar unit made the first contact. At first I thought it was one of the large boulders we've previously seen on the seabed here. But since our bathymetric chart had no mention of such an object positioned in this quadrant, I decided to eyeball it to get a definite I.D."

"You did well to do so," said Magne. "Yet I wonder why a wreck of this size wasn't previously uncovered by past survey teams?"

"Perhaps it was hidden beneath the same sediment that veiled that mine you found earlier," offered the Texan.

"He could be on to something, Magne," added the technician. "The seabed in this region is mostly comprised of sand and muddy silt that could have shifted during last week's gale."

As the pointed bow of the wreck came into view on the video screen, Lawton said, "If that's the case, now what? Can you lay the pipeline around it?"

"No chance," replied Magne. "Because of the irregular shape of the neighboring seabed, the new pipeline must pass through this corridor. That means we'll have to thoroughly salvage this wreck to make absolutely certain it doesn't contain unexploded ordinance."

"When will you start?" asked Lawton. "I'd love to have a look inside her myself."

45

Magne grinned. "Perhaps in exchange for that chili recipe and a new Stetson, I could arrange such a thing. But before we rush into such a dangerous venture, I feel it's best if we call in some experts. We've got a group of young divers who are specialists in this type of thing. They call themselves NUEX, for Norwegian Underwater Explorers. Their specialty is military salvage, and no matter the degree of danger or difficulty, if a job can be done, they can do it.

"The last I heard, they were working inland beneath the waters of Lake Tinnsjo. Thor, I want you to get a hold of them. And if they balk at our invitation, don't forget to remind that group of hard-headed misfits who signs their paychecks. We've got a multi-billion dollar job on the line here, and as far as I'm concerned, this project takes precedence over all others, no matter what they may think."

Approximately 175 miles due west of the *Falcon*, another group of Norwegians were gathered around a shipborne video monitor, intently watching a picture being conveyed by an ROV. Though not as sophisticated as the system deployed on the full-sized North Sea diving vessel, the fiber optic cables of this smaller, portable unit conveyed a sharp, finely tuned portrayal of the black depths of Norway's Lake Tinnsjo.

"Are you certain that both mercury-vapor lights are working, Knut? It's so damn dark down there at 350 meters that I can't make out a thing."

These comments came from Jon Huslid, NUEX's chief underwater photographer. Only in his mid-twenties, the red-headed Bergen native already had a reputation as one of the tops in his field. One of the original co-founders of the group calling themselves the Norwegian Underwater Explorers, Jon was the team's self-proclaimed spokesman, and was not afraid to step into the role of leader if called upon to do so.

"Both lamps are on, all right," replied Knut Haugen, who was seated before the ROV's compact control board with one hand on the joystick. "I sure wish we had that portable sonar unit. Then we'd know just where the hell we were."

Knut Haugen was in charge of engineering. A soft spoken native of the Telemark region, he was a mechanical genius who was responsible for the operation and upkeep of their gear. His broad-shouldered, six-foot, four-inch frame was currently squeezed into the small trawler's forwardmost cabin, the only vacant interior space large enough to hold the assortment of gear needed to run their current operation.

Seated beside Knut was diver Arne Lundstrom. Arne was also from Telemark. He was slightly built, and had a full, bushy beard and dark eyes that lit up with enthusiasm when he talked.

"Try taking her deeper, Knut," suggested Arne. "Why, I bet we're still not even on the bottom as yet."

Quick to heed this advice, Knut pushed forward on the joystick and watched the digital depth gauge begin to drop further.

"Easy now," warned Jon Huslid. "Our last scan showed some pretty sharp rock formations down there, and if we were to smash into one of them, that could be the end of everything."

To ease the photographer's anxieties, Knut gently eased back on the joystick and lessened the ROV's forward velocity to a bare crawl. All eyes were glued to the video monitor, that continued showing nothing but a black, watery void.

"I still say that the wreck of the *Hydro* doesn't want to be found," broke a deep voice from the hatchway. "No matter how hard we look for the ferry, all of our effort is destined to be in vain."

The speaker of these pessimistic words was another of NUEX's young divers. Jakob Helgesen was from the far-off northern city of Tromso, the so-called gateway to the Arctic. Lapp blood flowed in his veins, and it was said that Jakob had inherited the gift of foresight from his maternal grandfather, who was a spirit chief of this nomadic people.

"Don't start up with that spooky crap again, Jakob," countered Jon Huslid. "The *Hydro* is just another wreck, like the dozens of others we have searched out and salvaged from all over Norway."

The black-haired Lapp shook his head to the contrary. "I beg to differ with you, Jon. Don't tell me that you've already forgotten the twenty-six poor souls who went down with the doomed ferry when the saboteur's charges blew its bow off. The spirits of this lake have veiled the wreck to protect their final resting place. That's why no one else has ever succeeded in locating the *Hydro*."

"And NUEX is going to change all that," said the photographer confidently. "Besides, we're not interested in disturbing the wreck itself. All we want to do is find the *Hydro*'s main cargo."

"It's all part of the same," said Jakob with a sigh.

Jon Huslid turned away from the monitor screen to argue otherwise, when Knut's excited voice redirected his attention.

"We've got something! Right there, on the upper right hand portion of the screen. It looks like it's part of a boat's superstructure."

As he moved the ROV in to have a closer look, the monitor filled with a jumbled mass of twisted, rust-covered steel. Careful to keep the ROV and its umbilical free from this obstacle, Knut expertly guided it forward. Soon pieces of rotted plank could be seen, along with an elongated tubular structure that Arne Lundstrom eagerly identified.

"It's one of the *Hydro*'s dual smokestacks, just like we saw in the old photographs!"

"I believe you're right, Arne," said Jon Huslid. "That means that we've done it, lads. After forty-seven years, we're the first to actually find the wreckage of the *Hydro!* Now if we can only extract a suitable piece of salvage to document our find."

Knut nodded. "You don't have to say any more, Jon. When the ferry originally went down, eyewitness reports indicated that before she disappeared from sight, the railroad flatcars that *Hydro* was carrying broke loose, rolled off the deck, and then sunk straight down. That would put them somewhere closeby."

As Knut utilized the joystick to initiate an organized sweep of the surrounding seabed, Jon looked up at his dark-haired associate.

"So much for the spirits of the lake, Jakob."

The Lapp's scowl magically turned into a broad grin as he stepped forward to offer the group's photographer his handshake.

"Congratulations, Jon. Some events are just destined to happen, and this discovery is one of them. So once again, NUEX has made the history books."

"That we have, my friend," replied the smiling photographer. "No other human has laid eyes on the *Hydro* since that February morning back in 1944, when her cracked hull slid beneath these very waters. Now if the fates are still with us, perhaps we can locate that all-important portion of the *Hydro*'s cargo that precipitated this disaster."

"I think I saw something, Knut," interrupted the voice of Arne Lundstrom. "In the foreground, in the center of the screen."

All eyes immediately returned to the video monitor as the ROV was sent in to investigate this sighting. Its dual mercury vapor lights cut into the blackness. And when a faint distant glint momentarily flashed onto the screen, Knut needed no prompting to open the throttle wide and cause the ROV to surge forward in a sudden burst of speed.

Seconds later, the screen filled with a image that caused gasps of wonder from the four men. Illuminated by the spotlights was a large steel canister, like the sort industrial chemicals were stored in. It sat upright on a relatively flat subterranean ledge. Cautiously, the ROV closed in, and soon the four awestruck observers spotted a label that had long ago been stenciled on the cannister's rust-streaked side.

"It's in English," said Jon. "And it reads, 'potash lye.' "

"Then it's not the heavy water after all," said Arne, a hint of disappointment flavoring his tone.

"Like hell it isn't," retorted the excited photographer. "Forty-seven years ago, when the last of the heavy water was removed from the Norsk Hydro plant for the trip to Germany, it was stored in cannisters marked, 'potash lye'. We've done it, friends! NUEX has found the greatest treasure to be hidden in Norwegian waters since the days of the Vikings!"

A round of shouts and applause was followed by the ever practical voice of Knut Haugen. "Shall we get on with the actual salvage attempt, gentlemen?"

Though Jon Huslid was more in the mood to break open one of the bottles of aquavit that sat in the adjoining galley, he resisted temptation. "You may proceed, Knut. Just make certain that the collar is snuggly fitted around the cannister's base before we inflate it."

"Come off it, Jon," replied the straight-faced engineer. "Do you think I'm an amateur? Don't forget who it was that perfected this salvage technique."

The photographer apologetically shook his head and smiled. "I'm sorry, Knut. It's just that now that we're so close to realizing our dream, I don't want anything to happen to spoil it."

Knut merely grunted, and went to work utilizing the ROV's articulated manipulator arm to place a deflated plastic collar around the cannister's base. Once this device was properly positioned, a pump would be activated topside. Air would be sent rushing down the umbilical, inflating the collar and causing the cannister to attain a state of positive buoyancy, which would send

50

it floating to the surface like a cork.

Confident that Knut could do the job, Jon turned toward Jakob Helgeson. "How about joining me on deck with your wet suit? You'll have to go over the side to attach the winch cable."

"Some fresh air sounds like a good idea," said the Lapp, who turned and led the way up a narrow wooden ladder.

Both divers arrived topside, where a bright blue, cloudless sky greeted them. The air was brisk and hinted at the long, cold winter that would soon be upon them. There was a light wind blowing in from the southwest, and the boat that they had rented for the week bobbed up and down in a gentle swell.

With a photographer's practiced eye, Jon Huslid surveyed the encircling countryside. Lake Tinnsjo was an elongated, sausage-shaped body of fresh water that was over thirty kilometers long and barely three kilometers wide. Situated on the southeastern corner of central Norway's Hardanger plateau, the lake was set in a deep valley. From its boulder-strewn shores, the surrounding hills rose dramatically upward, to a ridge some thousand meters above sea level. Sturdy pines hugged rocky soil that would never see a farmer's plow.

They were currently positioned over some of the lake's deepest waters, approximately one kilometer from the shoreline. Jon knew very well that the saboteurs had planned all along for the ferry to sink in this portion of the lake, for in this manner, the *Hydro*'s precious cargo would sink to depths that were, at that time, totally unsalvageable.

He briefly looked to the northwest, where a small spur of the lake extended to the town of Mael. This had been the spot where the railcars holding the heavy water had been loaded onto the ferry for the short trip to Tinnoset. Nearby was the village of Rjukan, where the cargo originated at the infamous Norsk Hydro plant. This facility still existed, though its days of manufacturing heavy

51

water were long over. Today it merely generated enough hydroelectric power to feed a plant whose main product was fertilizer.

When first told about NUEX's intended expedition to Lake Tinnsjo, the townspeople of the region rose in angry protest. Though the war had been over for well over forty years, there were many still alive in the area who had lived through the Nazi occupation. They were very content to forget all about those nightmarish times, and looked at any attempt to salvage the sunken ferry as an intrusion on their privacy.

The members of NUEX had argued that it was their historical duty to find the wreck once and for all. Of course, to convince the state-run organization that sponsored them to support their efforts, another line of reasoning was used. Beyond the historical significance of their expedition was the fact that the *Hydro*'s cargo was worth a virtual fortune in today's marketplace. They argued successfully that if the thirty-three drums of heavy water were still intact, that they could subsequently be sold for over five million dollars. The executives at Noroil couldn't ignore such a figure, and deciding that it was worth the risks involved, gave the project their blessing.

It was in high school when Jon first read about the attack on the *Hydro*. The incident inflamed his imagination, inspiring him to read other narratives regarding his people's daring exploits during World War II. Yet because of the significance of the *Hydro*'s cargo, this mission stood out in importance above all the others. To him it was the crowning point of the Norwegian underground's undeclared war against the Germans, and could have very possibly saved the entire world from Nazi domination as well.

The key ingredient to manufacturing an atomic bomb was heavy water. A totally harmless compound on its own, heavy water gained importance when it was learned that it was an exceptionally efficient moderator for slowing down neutrons in a uranium pile. This enabled the neutrons to collide with and split up uranium-235 atoms, until the reaction would sustain itself and thus make possible an atomic explosion.

What few people realized was that most of the early research into nuclear physics was done in Germany during the 1930's and early 40's. In fact, the Germans were only months away from producing a working prototype of a bomb, and had only one major ingredient lacking — heavy water. Since the Norsk Hydro plant was the only facility in the world making that substance at the time, the Nazis decided to occupy Norway with all due haste. They did so without much difficulty, and every effort was made to produce the great amounts of heavy water needed by German scientists to initiate that first self-sustaining atomic reaction.

By this time the Allies had their own atomic research projects going. Intelligence operatives closely monitored the Nazi effort, and when it looked like they were about to win this critical race, commando teams were sent into Norway to destroy the heavy water stocks before they reached Germany. After several failed attempts ended in tragedy, a group finally succeeded in penetrating the plant and blowing up much of these existing stocks. But the Nazis ordered them replenished, and in early 1944 the final load was packed up in drums, loaded onto a freight car, to be sent off to Germany. Thanks to a daring operation in which a Norwegian commando team hid a time bomb in the *Hydro*'s hull, the shipment only made it as far as the bottom of Lake Tinnsjo. The rest was history.

Proud to play a part in the final chapter of this incredible story, Jon Huslid prepared his Nikon for the moment when the first cannister popped to the surface. Hopefully, it and the others that would follow would still be sealed. His country would then have a liquid treasure on its hands, to do with as it pleased.

Barely aware of the distant chopping sound of

a far-off helicopter, Jon's attention was caught by a deep, familar voice behind him.

"Knut's got the collar in place, and Arne's started up the compressor. The drum should be surfacing off our port side, any moment now."

Jakob Helgesend joined his associate beside the boat's stern railing. The Lapp was dressed in a full black rubber wetsuit, that had *NUEX* stenciled on its back with bold white letters.

"I'll go over the side as soon as it shows itself," he added. "That way I can make certain the collar is firmly in place when you throw me the winch cable."

The characteristic clatter of the helicopter seemed to intensify, and Jon briefly scanned the blue sky in an effort to locate it. His examination was cut short by a booming voice that emanated from below deck.

"It's on its way up!"

The photographer's pulse quickened as he returned his glance to the waters off their port side. No sooner did he pull off his camera's lense cap than the surface of the lake erupted in a frothing circle of agitated white bubbles. Just as he snapped off the first picture, the drum responsible for this wake shot out of the depths in which it had been buried and smacked back into the blue waters with a resounding slap.

Without hesitation, Jakob plunged into the icy water to stabilize the cannister. Jon was able to continue his picture taking when Arne arrived topside to handle the winch cable. He was so engrossed in this process that he didn't even notice the helicopter that was now circling the boat, only a few hundred meters above them.

"What do you make of that chopper, Jon?" asked Arne, who now had to practically scream to be heard.

Only then was Jon aware that they no longer shared this historical moment among themselves. "Don't pay attention to it, Arne!" he yelled. "It's most likely just a bunch of journalists who are trying to scoop the competition. We'd better concentrate on getting that line out to

Jakob before we lose our treasure before we even have it."

With a mighty heave, Arne hurled the steel cable out into the nearby waters. Jakob had to swim over to reach it. Then began the tedious job of securely wrapping it around the bobbing cannister so that they could finally haul it aboard.

Jakob was well into this task, when the loud amplified voice of a woman boomed out from above.

"Hello NUEX, this is Kari Skollevoll! I've got a top-priority dispatch for you from the Chief. Sorry to crash your party, but I'm dropping it down to you now."

Clearly audible even from the water, this unexpected message caused Jakob to temporarily abandon his efforts and look up into the sky. He watched with astonishment as a familiar orange and white Bell 212 helicopter swept down from the sky and hovered only a few meters above their boat. It was from the main hatch of this vehicle that a small container was lowered on a thin guide wire. Arne was the one who retrieved it, and as he waved the container overhead, the helicopter dipped its nose and, following orders, shot off to land on the nearest shoreline.

Jakob turned back to the drum, and had just completed securing it with the winch cable, when Jon could be seen on the boat's stern madly waving for him to return. Jakob wasted no time fulfilling this request, climbing back on board to be met by a thick terry cloth towel and the typed dispatch that had just been delivered them. He quickly read it.

"Most urgent that you return at once to the *Falcon*. This is a top-priority request. Magne Rystaad."

After hurriedly rereading this message, Jakob handed it back to NUEX's disappointed chief photographer.

"Do you believe Magne's rotten timing?" stated Jon disgustedly.

"Maybe if he knows our progress, he'd let us finish up here before returning to the *Falcon*," suggested Jakob. "If

55

the rest of the drums are as easy to locate as this one was, we could have the whole job done in a day at most."

Jon shook his head. "Nice thought, but you know the Chief better than that. He wouldn't send Kari out here for us in the chopper unless he was damn serious."

By this time Knut had joined them on the stern. A good five inches taller than his co-workers, the team's engineer read the dispatch and then looked out to the secured drum that now floated off their port beam.

"So this is going to be the end of it, huh?" said Knut. "And it's a rotten shame, because while you guys were up here securing that drum, I did a little searching with the ROV. Not ten meters away from where we spotted the first cannister, I found the remains of the flat bed railroad car. And strapped securely on its back is the rest of the shipment, all thirty-two drums! All I have to do is put together a big enough lifting collar, and I can raise the whole damn thing in a single stroke."

Jon only needed to deliberate a second before responding. "Then do it, Knut. Can you manage it alone?"

"It won't be easy, but I can do it," replied the giant with confidence. "I've got plenty of trusted family and friends in these hills, and I can always count on them to give me a hand."

"Then it's settled," said the photographer. "Magne is going to have to be content with only three of us, because this is an opportunity that we just can't let slip by. Now are you certain that you can complete the salvage on your own, Knut?"

"I can do it, Jon. And I'll make certain that those drums are under lock and key the moment I get them on dry land."

"Excellent," returned the photographer, while his associates readied the Zodiac raft for the trip to shore. "God be with you, big fellow. All of our dreams are on your capable shoulders, Knut. We're counting on you to make NUEX a part of living history."

The two shook hands, and Jon turned for the Zodiac, his palm still smarting from Knut Haugen's powerful grip.

From the opposite shoreline, hidden in a dense thicket of Norwegian pine, a white-haired old man watched the Zodiac set sail. The veteran's powerful Zeiss binoculars allowed him a clear view of the three young men who sat inside their grey, rubber raft. The bearded member of this trio positioned himself at the stern and started the Zodiac's outboard engine. Even though they were over a kilometer distant, the elder could hear the whining growl of the engine as the raft sped off to the nearby shore to rendezvous with the awaiting helicopter.

Returning his line of sight back to the wooden trawler where the Zodiac had originated, he looked on as a single, muscular figure stood beside the boat's transom. This blond-haired giant was a bear of a man, who was busy starting up a motorized winch. A taut steel cable extended out into the water from this piece of machinery. The old-timer had watched breathlessly as the rust-streaked drum shot up from the depths earlier. It floated innocently on the surface now, and was slowly being pulled toward the awaiting ship.

A familiar throbbing pain suddenly coursed down the entire left side of his face, causing the man to flinch and momentarily put down his binoculars. With trembling hands he reached up to gently massage the jagged scar that extended from his temple to his jaw.

For fifty long years, Mikhail Kuznetsov had been forced to live with this ugly reminder of a war that he would never forget. And though plastic surgery had somewhat masked the scarred facial skin, the deep knife wound had caused permanent nerve damage that no physician on earth could ever repair.

Certainly no stranger to physical pain, Mikhail

forced himself to take a series of deep, calming breaths and gradually the discomfort dissipated. Only when his hands stopped trembling altogether did he regrip his binoculars. By the time he returned his glance back to the boat, the modern day Viking was in the process of lowering the steel drum onto the deck itself. As he proceeded to unwrap the cable that was still coiled around it, Mikhail noted that the cannister appeared to be intact. He feared just such a thing, and knew very well that if this drum was still sealed, the others would be as well.

Inwardly cursing, Mikhail's gut tightened as he considered the grim possibilities. When the trail had originally led to the nearby village of Rjukan one week ago, he got his first hint that his sworn enemy was after the *Hydro*'s treasured heavy water. They had apparently been drawn to Lake Tinnsjo when it was announced that the group known as the Norwegian Underwater Explorers were about to initiate the first salvage of the sunken ferry.

Mikhail had first heard about heavy water while a prisoner at the Bergen-Belsen concentration camp. He had been stricken with typhus at the time, and was laid up in the camp's filthy, overcrowded infirmary, when his emaciated bunkmate introduced himself. As it turned out he was a Jewish physicist from Hamburg, who had been actively involved in Germany's earliest efforts to split the atom. Though he was to die in less than a week's time, he was able to share with Mikhail his greatest fear — the Nazis' perfection of an atomic weapon.

Mikhail had never heard of such a device before, and could only listen in complete horror as the Jew gave him his first elementary lesson in nuclear physics. Time after time, he emphasized the utter importance of heavy water to moderate the fission process. Only when the war was finally over, and Mikhail literally crawled from the camp as one of its few survivors, did he learn how a group of brave Norwegian commandoes had destroyed the *Hydro*'s cargo of heavy water, which would have made Hitler's nightmarish dreams of world conquest a reality.

With the war's conclusion, Mikhail had returned to his homeland a sick, broken man. By the grace of fate, his twin brother Alexander had also survived, and had emerged as a hero in the People's Navy. Their reunion was a tearful one. As Mikhail's weakened body gradually regained its strength, he swore to devote the rest of his life to a single cause. So that the Fascist beast would never raise its ugly head again, he would roam the world in search of fledgling Neo-Nazi movements. Only by destroying their ambitions in their infancy could their dreams of a resurrected Third Reich be thwarted.

Mikhail operated under the auspices of the KGB, and even had a small staff at his disposal. Much of his early work took him to South America, where thousands of Hitler's henchmen fled after the Axis went down in defeat. It was in the jungles of Paraguay that he first learned of the fascist organization that went by the code name, "Werewolf". This group was only one of many that Mikhail was attempting to infiltrate. When a photograph arrived on his desk showing Werewolf's supposed leader, Mikhail was shocked to find an unforgettable face staring back at him from a vine-encrusted veranda. Not even forty years could mask this individual's cruel gray eyes, highly etched cheekbones, and narrow forehead. The only feature that was drastically different, was that in place of closely cropped white hair, he now was completely bald.

Like a nightmare come true, here was the very man responsible for not only the scar that still lined Mikhail's face, but for the emotional scars generated by his incarceration into the living hell of a concentration camp. After a half decade of tortured dreams and sleepless nights, at long last he was on the trail of former SS Gauleiter Otto Koch!

Like a man possessed, Mikhail dropped all other investigations to concentrate solely on bringing this demon to justice. With the assistance of a top-secret team of specially trained Soviet commandoes, Koch's plantation was located and penetrated. Unfortunately their man had moved out only hours before and it took another two years of intense, frustrating work to once again come across the trail of this elusive quarry. This time the tracks led to the Telemark region of central Norway, where representatives from Werewolf made contact with a local right-wing group known as the Nordic Reich's Party, or NRP for short. Mikhail's intelligence network was a bit stronger in this part of the world, and it was through a tip from a local KGB informant that he was drawn to the shores of Lake Tinnsjo.

Only two days ago, four members of the NRP were seen in the nearby village of Hakanes. They were accompanied by a pair of tall, blond-haired middle-aged strangers, who were introduced as business associates from abroad. Knowing full well that they were representatives of Werewolf, Mikhail was able to follow them to a mountain hut that lay hidden in the trees of the opposite shoreline, not far from where the orange and white helicopter had just landed. From this vantage point they would have an uncluttered view of the lake, much like his own. This led Mikhail to one shocking conclusion. Werewolf was also after the heavy water, which they hoped to utilize to construct a weapon of such destructive force that even the world's superpowers would have to stand up and take notice.

Mikhail returned his gaze to the lake. The fair-haired giant could still be seen on the trawler's stern, securely strapping the drum that he had just extracted from the water to the boat's deck, while on the opposite shore, the Bell 212 helicopter lifted off into the sky with a grinding roar, its cabin now filled with the three young Norwegians who had arrived here by means of the Zodiac raft.

Wondering where they had been called to, Mikhail Kuznetsov angled his binoculars up into the thicket of trees that overlooked the clearing where the helicopter had just taken off. Even though the pines effectively veiled the wooden structure that he knew to be hidden here, the seventy-one year old Russian visualized the gloating representatives of his arch nemesis as they also peered down to the lake's surface, patiently waiting for the rest of the liquid treasure to be brought up from Tinnsjo's icy depths.

Chapter Three

The snowmobile zoomed over the freshly fallen powder, and Alexander Kuznetsov dared to open the throttle wide. As he did so the engine instantly reacted with an ear-shattering whine, and the vehicle shot forward like a sprinting thoroughbred. The speed was intoxicating, and the seventy-one-year-old naval officer felt totally invigorated. The fresh, bitterly cold Siberian air was like a youth-giving tonic to him, and in the blink of an eye he was a lad once again, his spirit renewed by the thrill of adventure. It was only when he left the flat valley that he had been following and began climbing a steep hillside that he cut back on the throttle. The snow was encrusted with ice and dotted with dozens of jagged boulders. Taking care to steer well around these obstacles, Alexander reached the summit of the ridge and briefly halted.

In the distance he could just make out the outskirts of the city of Vorkuta. It was a drab outpost, as were most Siberian settlements, dominated by older, corrugated steel huts, and newer, four story concrete buildings. Dwarfing these uninspiring habitations were several massive oil platforms. The derricks of these huge structures rose high against the horizon, while their equipment-packed bases were like miniature cities unto themselves. Two of these platforms had only just gone operational, with the rest soon to follow. It was projected that they would be in service for decades to come, pulling up the black gold that had been found beneath the permafrost in an incredible abundance.

This was Alexander's first visit to this region and his heart filled with pride as he thought about the thousands of brave, resourceful men and women who chose to make their homes here. Cut off from the rest of the U.S.S.R. as they were, they braved both isolation and the raw elements to do the all-important job at hand. They were true heroes who deserved the Republic's heartfelt thanks.

Alexander couldn't help but wonder why he had been picked to attend this conference. He was but a Vice Admiral assigned to Northern Fleet headquarters in Murmansk, and had no business mixing with the likes of such notables as Defense Minister Vladimir Kamenev, Energy Minister Pyotr Glebov, and Deputy General Secretary Viktor Rykov. All the same, he had been summoned to attend, and now he only had to wait for Viktor Rykov to arrive to learn the reason for his presence here. Anxious to get to the bottom of this mystery, he decided to take a brief excursion to clear his mind and help pass the time before Rykov's plane landed.

The local militia commander had sketched out a route which would allow him to safely enjoy the area's scenic splendors and not take him too far away from the city. This was a once in a lifetime chance to see a portion of the Rodina that was far from the nearest Intourist office, and he returned to his snowmobile eager to get on with his adventure.

His route led him down the opposite ridge. He was travelling straight into the piercing wind, and he pulled up his woolen scarf to cover as much of his exposed face as possible. As he reached the bottom of the hill, he began following a narrow ravine. The snow was deep, and he had to make certain to keep moving along at a good clip to keep from sinking.

Soon this ravine opened up to yet another broad valley. This one was coated completely in a veil of white, and contained not a hint of human habitation. Alexander readily crossed its virgin length, all the while pondering a thought that the local militia commander had shared with him. In several weeks time the sun would set beneath the western horizon, not to be seen again for three months. This would signal the time of darkness, when the frigid Arctic night prevailed twenty-four hours a day. The commander had mentioned that at this time the crime rate usually shot up in Vorkuta as the locals vainly struggled to adjust to this occurrence. With their biological clocks abruptly knocked off kilter, insomnia was shared by all, while a handful of unlucky individuals were driven to even greater extremes of hallucinations, schizophrenia, and even suicide. Having participated in submarine patrols, submerged for up to two months at a time, Alexander was no stranger to a perpetual world of darkness. But he had to admit that undergoing such a phenomena while on solid ground would be very disorienting.

The snowmobile skimmed over a frozen lake. Beyond a distant ridge, Alexander spotted a lofty mountain range that he knew to be the northernmost extension of the Urals. This chain stretched for over twelve hundred kilometers, efficiently cutting the U.S.S.R. in half, and acting as the natural dividing line between Europe and Asia.

Wishing that he had the time to continue right up into these foothills, Alexander caught sight of a group of dark alien forms in the snow beyond and instinctively cut back on the throttle and guided his snowmobile up onto a small hillock that lay beside the frozen lake bed. With the assistance of a pair of binoculars, he identified the previously alien forms as being a herd of musk-ox. This was only the second time that he had seen such creatures in the wild before. They were covered completely with long, shaggy brown hair, with yoke-shaped horns that tapered down to stiletto-sharp points. They were feeding on dwarf shrubs that lay exposed beside a large boulder, totally unaware that they were being observed from afar.

Alexander was in the process of deciding whether or not he should try getting closer to the herd when a distinctive, low-pitched growl redirected his attention to the area right behind him. At first he could see nothing but pure white snow. But when the growl once more sounded, he scanned the ravine again.

Then he spotted the snow bear. It was an awesome looking beast of incredible proportions completely covered in a thick coat of white fur. Only its jet black eyes and nose gave it away. Since it was only twenty meters or so distant and appeared to be headed straight for him, Alexander knew he had to act at once. Having ignored the militia commander's suggestion to take along a weapon, he found himself with two alternatives: he could make a break for the snowmobile and pray that he could get it started in time to escape, or make his stand right where he stood.

Again the beast angrily growled, and Alexander decided at that moment that making a dash for it was much too risky. Even though it was against all his instincts, he slowly dropped to the snow-covered ground. His heart was pounding wildly in his chest as he pulled himself into a tight fetal ball. As long as he kept himself absolutely still, he knew he had several things going for him. First off, was the fact that the bear was still upwind. Notorious for its poor eyesight, the bear would have an equally difficult time spotting him because of Alexander's white snowsuit.

The crunch of broken snow and the sound of heavy

panting signalled the bear's arrival. It was passing only a few short meters away, and Alexander could actually smell its musty odor. Any second he expected to feel its razor-sharp claws rip into his back, and he braced himself for the inevitable. Yet with each passing second, his chances of survival increased, to the point where he finally summoned the nerve to peek out and see what had happened to the beast. To his utter amazement, the bear was nowhere to be seen!

Alexander guardedly raised himself up. His arthritic limbs were stiff with the frigid cold, and he found it difficult to catch his breath as he scanned the hill for the bear's tracks. He found them only a half meter away from the spot where he had been crouching. By a miracle, the beast had passed right by him.

As Alexander turned in the direction the bear was now headed, he soon saw that it hadn't been the divine hand of providence that had saved him—it had been the herd of musk-oxen! Gathered in a tight circle, the shaggy herd faced the stalking bear head on. Their pointed horns appeared to offer an impenetrable barrier, but that didn't stop the snow bear from savagely charging the pack. As the lead bull lowered its head to thwart this attack, the bear knocked the fully grown musk-ox aside with a single swipe of its paw. Then with a cat-like agility it sprang into the herd, finally emerging with a calf between its jaws.

Bright red blood stained the white snow as Alexander sprinted over to his snowmobile. Having seen his fill of nature in action, he turned the ignition and listened to the sweet sound of the engine roaring alive. Without fear of life or limb, he opened the throttle full, and the snowmobile leaped off the hillock. Seconds later he was shooting over the frozen lake bed, the wind at his back, his course set straight for Vorkuta.

Suddenly a dark green, prop-driven Antonov cargo

plane roared overhead. The aircraft had its wheels and flaps down, and appeared to be on its final approach. With the expectation that it carried Deputy General Secretary Viktor Rykov in its cabin, Alexander guided the snowmobile down the ridge and ducked his head down for the final sprint into town.

Waiting for him in front of the bust of Lenin that stood outside the government house was the corpulent figure of Vladimir Kamenev. The Defense Minister was dressed in a full-length fur coat, and looked like a nervous brown bear as he paced to and fro beneath the watchful eye of the founder of the modern Soviet state.

"At long last, there you are, Admiral Kuznetsov," greeted Kamenev as Alexander's snowmobile skidded to a halt on the snow-packed roadway. "Deputy Rykov has already arrived. He's waiting for us in the conference room."

Alexander took his time turning off the ignition and climbing off the snowmobile's padded leather seat. "Because of a hungry snow bear, I almost didn't make this meeting at all," he answered grimly. The bureaucrat stared in mute surprise, then began leading the way toward the entrance to Vorkuta's newest and most modern building.

"A snow bear, you say," mumbled the distracted politician. "What on earth would such a creature want with the likes of an old salt like you, Admiral? Surely he'd find your hide much too tough."

Alexander's joints were still stiff with the cold, and he didn't even try to keep up with Kamenev.

"You're most likely correct, comrade," returned Alexander. "But as you very well know, extreme hunger can even make a tough old bird like me look appetizing."

Barely acknowledging this remark, Vladimir Kamenev reached the main doorway and hurriedly yanked it open. He impatiently held it for Alexander, who hobbled past him with a slow, pained gait.

Inside, the sudden heat was stifling. Before continuing, Alexander stopped to remove his parka, gloves and hat. Seeing this, a pained expression crossed the bureaucrat's pudgy face.

"Come, Admiral," he prompted. "One does not keep the likes of Viktor Rykov waiting."

"I'm coming as fast as these old bones will allow me," returned the veteran naval officer.

His own brow now soaked in sweat, Vladimir Kamenev stubbornly waited until they reached the closed doors of the conference room before taking off his fur. A uniformed attendant took their coats, and informed them to proceed inside.

The interior of the conference room was lined in rich, polished wood. A single round table and four chairs were the extent of the furnishings. The room's dominant feature was a large stone hearth that had a picture of Lenin hung above it. In the process of putting a match to the assortment of logs and kindling that were stacked inside this fireplace was an immaculately dressed, middle-aged gentleman, with wavy dark hair and sparkling brown eyes.

"Ah, now that should take the chill out of this room," he said, backing away from the hearth and watching the flames begin to grow.

Standing beside him was a thin, balding, bespectacled figure dressed in an ill-fitting brown suit. Completely engrossed in the crackling fire, both individuals were completely unaware that they had company.

An awkward moment of silence followed as the newly arrived Defense Minister shrugged his shoulders and loudly cleared his throat. Thusly introduced, both Alexander Kuznetsov and Vladimir Kamenev solemnly walked up to the blazing hearth.

"So look what the Arctic winds have blown in," said Deputy Secretary General Viktor Rykov, the debonair figure who had started the fire. "I was wondering if you two were going to stand me up for a plump Inuit woman."

"I'm indeed sorry that we were delayed, Comrade Rykov," replied the sweating Defense Minister.

"I do hope everything's all right at the Ministry," probed Rykov.

To this, Alexander Kuznetsov responded. "It's nothing like that, comrade. Actually it's all my fault. I was out on a snowmobile, and I allowed the time to get away from me."

"Good for you, Admiral," shot back Rykov with a grin. "If my plane hadn't been held up by weather in Kirov, I would have been right out there beside you. I do hope that you managed to get a good distance out of the city. To me, there's nothing as beautiful as a gleaming Siberian snowfield. So, tell me Admiral, did you see any wildlife?"

Alexander liked this young man at once and answered him directly. "I was lucky enough to see a herd of musk-oxen, and then a snow bear that just missed having this worn-out old veteran for its supper."

"A snow bear?" repeated Rykov. "Why, that's incredible. No wonder you were late. Tell me, was it very far from here? Perhaps we'll have time to track it down later this afternoon after our meeting's concluded."

"I doubt that would be possible," replied Alexander. "The last I saw of the bear was as it was running off into the tundra with a musk-ox calf in its jaws. Surely it has eaten its fill and is contentedly snoring away, dreaming of the next juicy meal."

"I'm sorry to hear that," said Rykov, who seemed genuinely disappointed. "I've always wanted to see a snow bear in the wild, but I never seem to get the opportunity."

"There's plenty of them out there, Comrade. You'll get your chance yet," offered Alexander.

Redirecting his thoughts, the Deputy Secretary General got on with the formalities of their meeting. "All of you know our esteemed Energy Minister here. During a recent conference with Premier Korsakov, Comrade Glebov presented some excellent points as to the future direction of the Motherland's energy policy. The Premier gave these points much thought, and subsequently requested that this meeting of minds be called. Though Premier Korsakov would have loved to be here in person, he's currently preparing for next week's trip to New York City, where he'll be addressing the United Nations Security Council. You can rest assured, though, that your suggestions will reach his ear the moment I return to the Kremlin. So with this said, I'd like you to join me at the conference table, and we can get on with the matters of state that have brought us together today."

Placecards indicated their positions at the table. Viktor Rykov sat with his back to the fire. On his left sat the close-lipped Energy Minister, Pyotr Glebov, while Vladimir Kamenev placed his sweating bulk to the Deputy Secretary General's right. This left Alexander Kuznetsov seated directly across from the dapper Rykov.

No sooner did they get settled when Rykov began speaking. "This meeting has been called today to discuss one extremely important factor of the Rodina's future energy policy. It is because of outposts like Vorkuta that our homeland now finds itself in the enviable position of having vast amounts of oil available for export.

"In this era of *perestroika,* the very foundation of socialism is being reformed. As our nation prepares to enter the twenty-first century, this readjustment is taking place on many levels. Comrade Kamenev's De-

70

fense Ministry was one of the first areas to feel the tide of reform. Rather than emerging as a weaker organization, I'm certain that Minister Kamenev would agree that today's Soviet defense forces are stronger than ever. The fat has been cut out. Wasteful, obsolete, and redundant weapon systems have been scrapped, and hundreds of thousands of troops redeployed to the civilian sector, to create a lean, efficient fighting force second to none.

"Times have drastically changed since our founding fathers first raised the red banner of Communism. Now, to compete in the new world marketplace, the U.S.S.R. has had to make fundamental changes in the way it does business. Our people cry out for more basic foodstuffs and consumer goods, but before we can satisfy these demands, our industries must totally reorganize. The radical shift from making tanks and other military hardware to automobiles and household appliances can't be completed overnight. It will take time and most importantly, a great deal of money. Like never before, hard currency will be needed in enormous amounts to pay for the high-technology production systems, many of which will have to be imported from abroad. Where will this hard currency come from? It is this difficult question that we've been called together today to discuss."

Halting at this point, Viktor Rykov took a second to carefully scan the faces of his rapt audience before continuing. "What we currently lack in consumer goods, we more than make up for in basic raw materials. The Rodina is particularly blessed with abundant reserves of oil. Beneath our very feet lies a virtually untapped supply of rich black crude. Only recently have our rigs begun pumping up this treasure. While flying into Vorkuta this morning, I personally saw these platforms at work. Many more will soon be online. The potential here is enormous. Yet how do we best make use of this valuable commodity?

"Ten days ago, Pyotr Glebov came to the Kremlin to discuss this very subject with our Premier. Our Energy Minister's thoughts on this matter were most clear, and I'm certain that all of you would be enlightened to hear them. So if you don't mind, Comrade Glebov, would you please share a portion of your plan with us today?"

All eyes went to the bespectacled Energy Minister, who seemed totally surprised by this request. As he pulled the heavily starched collar of his white shirt away from his scrawny neck, he nervously cleared his throat.

"I had no idea that I was going to be called upon to make a presentation, Comrade Rykov. At the very least I would have brought along my charts and maps to make things clearer."

"Relax, comrade, you are among friends today," said Viktor Rykov. "It was my express desire to make this meeting as informal as possible. So merely do your best to share with us the high points of your visionary plan to distribute the by-products of the Vorkuta oil field. Would a map of Europe help you?"

"By all means," replied Glebov.

Viktor Rykov reached into his briefcase and pulled out a map, unfolded it and spread it flat on the table, revealing a chart that showed the European continent extending west to the Ural Mountains.

Satisfied with this visual aid, Pyotr Glebov again cleared his throat and continued. "The main purpose of my recent trip to Moscow was to present to the Premier the final route of the soon-to-be started Vorkuta-to-Moscow oil pipeline. Stretching over eighteen hundred kilometers, this project will be responsible for conveying millions of barrels of oil to where it's most needed, the industrial heartland of our country.

"Our enlightened Premier was most concerned

about the ecological impact of such a project. My ministry has done an extensive study of this aspect, and I was able to allay the Premier's fears by sharing with him the unique design of the pipeline itself and our emergency contingency plans, which deal with almost any type of disaster." He looked intently into each face.

"After he was completely satisfied with our efforts in this field, I approached the Premier with an idea that's been on my mind for some time now. Since the Vorkuta field is capable of producing much more oil than is presently needed by our own industry, why not sell the excess petroleum on the open market? And what better way to distribute this product than to build a pipeline to the West that will carry our oil straight into the heart of energy-starved Europe!"

Newfound confidence guided the Energy Minister's actions as he reached forward and traced an imaginary line from Moscow to Hamburg, Germany. "By doubling the length of the Vorkuta-to-Moscow pipeline, we could have an outlet that will guarantee the Rodina an enormous amount of hard currency for decades to come."

"That's quite an idea," interrupted Defense Minister Kamenev. "But wouldn't such a project be incredibly expensive to implement?"

Pyotr Glebov shook his head. "Not really, comrade. By ordering the extra pipe now, we could save millions of rubles as the Vorkuta-to-Moscow order is fulfilled, and our market trends show that even at the going rate for energy, the line will pay for itself in less than five years. Oil will only increase in value as the years go by."

"But what of the route itself?" countered Vladimir Kamenev. "Once it leaves our borders, it would be a political nightmare."

"I beg to differ with you," returned Glebov. "Over

half of the route lies on Russian soil. The majority of the rest goes through the territory of our Warsaw Pact allies, Poland and East Germany. They too have great energy needs, and I'm certain that a compromise could be reached without too much difficulty."

The Defense Minister nodded and Alexander Kuznetsov alertly broke in. "Such an ambitious project indeed looks attractive, comrades. But aren't we forgetting that Europe already has energy suppliers? What about Great Britain, the Netherlands, and the Arab states?"

"Your observations are most astute, Admiral," replied the Energy Minister. "But we have already factored in these external sources, and the results are the same. As their resources dwindle, ours will increase. It's as simple as that."

"But what about Norway?" quizzed the Deputy General Secretary. "Don't the Norwegians already have such a pipeline in operation?"

His ardor abruptly cooled by this remark, Pyotr Glebov answered softly. "As a matter of fact, they do. The Norwegians have one such pipeline feeding North Sea oil directly into Emden, in the Netherlands. Another line will terminate in Zeebrugge, Belgium."

"What about Norway's available reserves?" asked the Defense Minister.

"Unlike our other competitors, Norway can continue its oil production at today's rate for more than a hundred years," answered Glebov gloomily.

Viktor Rykov sat forward. "Then it appears that the bottom line is this, comrades. Can the U.S.S.R. successfully compete against such an experienced producer as Norway, to get Europe's business?"

"We can always undercut the Norwegians when it comes to price," offered the Energy Minister. "In the long run, we'll more than make up this deficit with our sales volume."

"I can tell you right now that the Premier is not about to approve such a massive project if its success hinges on a price war," retorted Viktor Rykov. "That philosophy crippled OPEC, and we don't want any part of such a thing."

Disappointed with the firmness of this reply, Pyotr Glebov sat back sheepishly in his chair, eyes downcast. Across from him, his contemporary in the Defense Ministry offered his own thoughts on the matter.

"If a price war can't be relied upon to stop the flow of Norwegian oil, why not try a more . . . dramatic . . . approach? In fact, I know the ideal plan, one designed to be implemented in the event that military hostilities break out between us and NATO. Since the continued flow of Norwegian oil to the West would be essential during such a conflict, an operational plan exists in which elements of our special forces would strategically place a nuclear device in Norway's North Sea oil fields. This device then only needs to be detonated to shut down Norwegian production for centuries to come."

This novel suggestion was met by an ominous silence, and to further support his idea Kamenev quickly added. "For our purposes all this could be achieved without anyone having to know that the U.S.S.R. was responsible for the blast. The area is a notorious hotbed for submarine operations. NATO is continually active there, and who's to say that one of their nuclear warships wasn't responsible for such a tragedy?"

Most pleased with the direction the meeting was now going, Viktor Rykov slyly turned to meet the gaze of the white-haired veteran seated directly opposite him. "Perhaps Admiral Kuznetsov would care to share his ideas with us. If I'm not mistaken, weren't you just involved with a white paper that concerned just such a matter?"

Surprised that the bureaucrat had knowledge of this recently concluded, top-secret study, Alexander nodded. "Yes I was, Comrade. The report was undertaken as a result of a war game that involved the Northern Fleet. During this simulated battle, that had yet to escalate to nuclear weapons, it became essential for the Soviet Union to immediately halt the flow of Norwegian oil. The scenario that the Defense Minister mentioned was proposed, but because it involved a nuclear detonation it was deemed too risky. I was charged with the job of finding an alternative, less conspicuous way to take the oil fields."

"And just what did you propose?" quizzed Rykov.

Conscious now of the reason he was invited here, Alexander answered. "Since eliminating the oil fields themselves was out of the question, I recommended doing the next best thing."

Reaching out for the map of Europe that lay on the table before him, Alexander pointed to the southwestern coast of Norway between the cities of Bergen and Stavanger. "All of Norway's North Sea oil is piped directly to a single refinery and pumping station, here at Karsto. Therefore, I suggested a simple act of sabotage, aimed at knocking out this facility. This operation could be carried out with conventional explosives by as few as three commandoes, who could be landed by submarine. They could be in and out of there before anyone was the wiser."

"Do you mean to say that only three men and a load of conventional explosives could stop the entire flow of Norwegian oil into Europe?" questioned the Deputy General Secretary.

"I don't see why not," replied Alexander. "It wouldn't take much to destroy the pumping facilities, and the Norwegians are notoriously lax when it comes to security matters."

"Why that's amazing!" reflected Rykov. "What do

you think of the operation's chances of success, Comrade Kamenev?"

Irritated that he had never been given a copy of Kuznetsov's white paper to read, and not liking the idea of being showed up by a mere vice-admiral, Vladimir Kamenev sighed. "I feel that it would be a great mistake to be deceived into thinking that such an operation would be as easy to pull off as Vice Admiral Kuznetsov makes it sound. The landing of special forces on foreign soil can never be taken for granted. This is especially true when it comes to Norway. Its irregular shores are riddled with tiny islands and twisting fjords. Since much of these waters remain uncharted by us, merely navigating a submarine there would be a challenge."

"What do you say to this, Admiral Kuznetsov?" asked Rykov. All eyes turned to the Navy veteran.

Not wanting to provoke the Defense Minister, Alexander deliberately softened his response. "Comrade Kamenev has made an excellent point. Of course, my entire scenario was based on pure supposition. If such an operation were to become a reality, a thorough reconnaissance of the Karsto region would have to be initiated."

"Then by all means get us this information, Admiral," Viktor Rykov replied without hesitation. "It sounds to me like the entire idea of a trans-Siberian pipeline transferring gas products directly into Europe hinges on our ability to disrupt our competitor's flow of oil, if needed. Thus, if I hear no objections, I will officially adjourn this meeting with the stipulation that we reconvene as soon as Admiral Kuznetsov has completed his task."

Thrilled that the idea of an extended pipeline was still being considered, Energy Minister Pyotr Glebov eagerly nodded in agreement with Rykov. Having no real objections of his own, Vladimir Kamenev also concurred. This left Alexander Kuznetsov with the sole responsibility for organizing a clandestine reconnaissance mission deep into enemy territory, through some of the most hazardous waters on the entire planet.

Chapter Four

It was a typical cold, overcast fall morning in Dunoon, Scotland, as Captain Steven Aldridge, his wife Susan, and six-year-old daughter Sarah strolled through the town's central shopping district. The narrow sidewalks were filled with dozens of other pedestrians, most of whom were bundled up in thick woolen sweaters and carried several parcels each. Unlike America, travelling by foot was still practical in a small town such as Dunoon, and the Aldridge family fit in as if they were locals.

"Oh look, Daddy. There's a pastry shop. Can we go in and get some cookies?"

Sarah Aldridge followed up this request by catching her father's glance and flashing him her warmest smile. This tactic never failed to do the trick, yet just as her dad was about to agree, her mother intervened.

"There will be no more cookies for you, Sarah Aldridge, until you've had your lunch. Why, you've already eaten two pastries this morning, and you put away a breakfast earlier that could have fed a horse."

"Oh Mom, you're no fun," said Sarah with a pout.

"You're the one who will be no fun when I put you to bed with a bellyache," returned her mother.

"Look Sarah, there's the fishmonger's shop," observed her father in an effort to change the subject. "Shall we go in and see what the day's catch is?"

Sarah's eyes opened wide. "I'll say, father. Maybe Mr. Angus has still got that octopussy in there."

They entered the shop and found its portly proprietor perched over the concrete counter cleaning a load of flat, hand-sized fish. He only needed to take one look at the newcomers who had just entered for a wide grin to turn the corners of his wrinkled face.

"Well, if it isn't my very favorite Yank family," greeted the old-timer, who had fluffy white hair and long gray sideburns.

"Good morning, Mr. McPherson," replied Steven Aldridge. "We just stopped in to say hello and check out the day's catch."

"Mr. Angus, do you still have that octopussy?" questioned Sarah. She watched the fishmonger split open the flat belly of the fish he was cleaning.

Stifling a chuckle, Angus shook his head. "So the wee lass wants to see an octopus. I'm sorry, my dearest. I'm afraid you'll have to make do with these lovely Dover sole that came right out of the sea only a few hours ago."

The fishmonger picked up one of these fish by its tail and bent over to show it to his fair-haired guest. "Why, I bet you never saw a fish with both of its eyes on the same side of its head before," he added.

"Look at that, Father!" exclaimed Sarah in amazement. "It really does have two eyes on one side. Why's that?"

Steven Aldridge accepted a playful wink from the fishmonger as he attempted answering his daughter's question. "The sole's a bottom fish, Sarah. That means it spends most of its life laying flat on the surface of the seafloor. Instead of having one eye constantly buried in the sand, mother nature moved both of them together like this, so that it wouldn't be wasted."

Not really certain what her father was talking about, Sarah was already bored with the sole. She gasped in wonder when she viewed a tank of live lobsters on the shop's opposite wall. She quickly ran over to have a closer look, leaving the adults to their conversation.

"So tell me," asked Angus eagerly. "How did you like Iona?"

This time it was Susan Aldridge who answered. "It was gorgeous, Angus. In fact, the whole trip worked out just perfectly."

"Even the weather cooperated," added Steven. "We only had one full day of rain."

The fishmonger seemed genuinely impressed with this. "Now that is something. The gods of the Highlands must have been smiling on you."

Pleasantries were interrupted by the sight of a police car with its emergency lights flashing passing down the street. Angus was quick to explain its significance.

"Looks like they're clearing the streets for the parade. At least it looks like the rains will hold off until it's finished."

Suddenly realizing the late hour, Steven Aldridge called out to his daughter.

"Come on, Pumpkin. It's almost time for the parade."

This served to pull Sarah away from the tank. As her mother took her hand and led her to the door, the youngster looked up to the old fishmonger and waved.

"Goodbye, Mr. Angus."

"Goodbye to you, lass," returned the old man.

"Save three of those sole for us, Angus," added Su-

81

san Aldridge. "I'll pick them up later on our way home."

"Will do, Mrs. A. Enjoy the parade."

As they stepped outside, Steven said his own goodbyes before turning to follow his family. "See you later, Angus."

"I'll be here, Captain. By the way, why no uniform?"

Aldridge shook his head. "As far as the U.S. Navy is concerned, I'm still officially on leave, my friend. Uncle Sam will have me back in the flock soon enough."

"I hear you, Captain. Enjoy it while you can."

Steven returned the Scot's salute and hurriedly left the shop. The foot traffic was headed one way now, down toward the wharfside war memorial where the ceremony would be taking place. Securely linking hands, the Aldridge family followed the crowd past the collection of quaint one-story shops that made up this section of Dunoon. They passed the new YMCA building, and entered an open square, that was bordered by a park on one side and the blue waters of the Firth of Clyde on the other. It was beside the parkside walkway that a large group of townspeople had gathered. Steven recognized several denim-clad American sailors in this crowd. Even in their civvies, these young men had the good old U.S.A. written all over them.

The war memorial itself was nothing but a large stone cairn with several bronze plaques set into it. Inscribed on these tablets were the names of the brave local servicemen and women who died as a direct result of World Wars I and II. Immediately in front of the cairn, facing the empty street and the waters of the firth beyond, a compact wooden reviewing stand had been set up. No sooner did the

Aldridge family fall in alongside the mass of onlookers, when the shrill sound of massed bagpipes broke in the distance. Hearing this caused the crowd to buzz with excitement, and even Sarah found herself thrilled.

"Listen, Father, the pipers are coming!"

Steven anxiously looked to his left, and soon spotted the marching column of kilted musicians responsible for this distinctive clamor. They were dressed in green, yellow and black tartans. Together with a line of drummers, they were playing a spirited rendition of *Scotland the Brave*. The music was an excellent arrangement, and Steven couldn't help but be inspired when he spotted the squad of U.S. Marines who followed the band. Dressed in traditional olive green parade uniforms, the leathernecks marched with exacting precision. Each of the soldiers was well over six feet tall, and in superb physical shape. Steven knew that this crack complement came from the nearby navy base at Holy Loch, where they provided security.

Behind the Marines followed a unit of junior cadets, a group of local dignitaries, and a dozen or so disabled veterans, several of whom were in wheelchairs. Two white-haired veterans carried the Union Jack and the Stars and Stripes, and as the band turned toward the crowd, the two flag carriers broke from the ranks and approached the reviewing stand. Here they were greeted by a tall, erect figure, dressed in kilts, a brown tunic, and the regimental bonnet of a senior army officer. This individual waited for the marching column to come to a complete halt before signalling the sergeant major to order, "Parade rest!"

The senior officer then approached the marchers and reviewed their ranks. He paid particular atten-

83

tion to the veterans, each of whom he engaged in a brief conversation. He also questioned several of the cadets, and appeared to convey a job well done to the leader of the Marines. Then after a cursory inspection of the band, he returned to the reviewing stand, saluted, and initiated a short speech.

"We are gathered today on the fiftieth anniversary of the United States of America's official entrance into World War II. This is a solemn occasion, yet it is a joyful one all the same, because without America's invaluable help, the United Kingdom would have been forced to continue the struggle against Nazi tyranny on its own.

"Hundreds of thousands of our sons and daughters died for this cause. Even a small village like Dunoon paid its share of the ultimate price of freedom, with the brave lads and lasses whose names are etched in bronze behind me. We shall never forget them. Nor shall we ever forget the individuals who serve our country's armed forces today. It is because of their selfless vigil that world conflict no longer stains our shores in blood.

"I remember a time not so long ago, when the waters of the firth before me were filled with hundreds of vessels drawn from ports throughout the free world. These convoys risked death on the cold seas to provide England with urgently needed supplies to fuel its continued war effort. As a young ensign, I was assigned to a frigate whose responsibility was to provide convoy escort, and I personally shared the horror of a German U-boat raid.

"Today the mighty warships that patrol the waters of the firth fear no such attack. In these times of fragile peace, their job is to deter any aggressor from ever again attempting to force their way of life upon ours. Because of this, we enjoy a life of freedom and democracy that is the envy of every other nation on earth. We shall always remember the names of those whose lives were taken so that this greatest of all gifts could be ours. God bless you all, and may peace by with you always."

Issuing yet another salute, the senior officer nodded to the sergeant major, who ordered the column to resume its march. They did so to the strains of such traditional pipe favorites as *Captain Orr-Ewing, Culty's Wedding,* and *Farewell to the Creeks.*

A blustery wind began gusting in from the northwest, and the crowd wasted little time dispersing. As Susan bent over to zip up the collar of Sarah's parka, Steven noticed that a familiar duo of blue-uniformed naval officers had gathered beside the war memorial. They were in the process of speaking to the officer who had just given the address, and Steven couldn't resist going over to pay his respects himself.

"Susan, why don't you take Sarah and get started with lunch. I see Admiral Hoyt and Bob Stoddard over there, and I just want to say a quick hello before joining you."

As a veteran Navy wife, Susan was accustomed to doing things on her own. "Go ahead, Steve, but don't be too long. I know that you're dying to find out how things are going on the *Cheyenne.* But don't forget that you're still on leave. And besides, you should have worn a heavier coat if you're going to be out in this wind much longer."

Thankful for her wifely concern, Steven glanced down at his daughter. "Now be a good girl and eat all of your lunch, Pumpkin. And then we can stop off for those cookies that you wanted."

"Can I have chips 'n fish, Father?" asked the six year old.

85

"Chips 'n fish it is," laughed Steven, who caught his wife's eye and playfully winked. "I'll meet you at the Old Mermaid. Go ahead and order me a pint of Export. I'll be there to drink it by the time the head settles."

Though Susan would have liked to lay odds against this, she smiled, took her daughter's mittened hand, and began walking back toward town. Steven watched until they were safely across the street before walking back toward the war memorial.

The taller of the two U.S. naval officers was the first to spot him. There could be no missing Lieutenant Commander Robert Stoddard's gangly six-foot frame, wholesome Nebraska-bred good looks, and the unlit corn-cob pipe that perpetually hung from his mouth. As Executive Officer of the 688-class attack submarine, *USS Cheyenne*, Stoddard was Steven's right-hand man. They had been together for over a year now, and had long ago established that tight bond that every succeful command team needs to be an effective one.

Beside his XO, in the process of addressing the kilted master of ceremonies, was Admiral David Hoyt, Jr., commander of the U.S. submarine base at Holy Loch. A former history instructor at Annapolis, Hoyt was a competent administrator, who earned his dolphins in the days before Nautilus and the advent of Rickover's nuclear navy. A bit given to long-winded discourses when his favorite subject, maritime history, was being discussed, the admiral was also well known for his love of golf. He thus accepted the orders sending him to Scotland with open arms, for he was finally stationed in the legendary birthplace of his favorite sport, and had his choice of its many fine courses. Steven Aldridge wasn't a bit surprised as he approached the trio of officers and heard the nature of Hoyt's animated remarks.

". . . and there I was, all set up for my first real crack at a birdie on Glen Eagle's infamous eighteenth hole, when what sprints out onto the green and steals my ball but a fox! That damn red varmint must have thought that my Titleist was a grouse egg, the way he snagged it in his jaws and took off for a nearby creek bed. You know, I never did find that frigging ball again."

"My Lord, Admiral," chuckled his kilted colleague. "How on earth did you ever score that one?"

Deadly serious, the admiral answered. "As far as I was concerned, I was already out a damn good ball, so to hell with taking a penalty stroke. But wouldn't you know that I proceeded to three putt a ten foot shot. And out of all that, I ended up with a bogey."

To the roar of laughter, Steven Aldridge closed in on the trio. It proved to be his XO who greeted him.

"Good afternoon, Skipper. I didn't expect you back until tomorrow."

Aldridge accepted his second-in-command's firm handshake and that of his base commander.

"It's good to see you again, Captain," added Admiral Hoyt, who realized additional introductions were in order.

"Brigadier General Hartwell, I'd like you to meet Captain Steven Aldridge, commanding officer of the *USS Cheyenne*."

While the two men shook hands Admiral Hoyt continued. "Brigadier Hartwell is with the Scot Guard, and as ranking senior officer in this district, was responsible for today's ceremony."

"I enjoyed your speech very much, sir," said Aldridge.

The Scot looked directly into the newcomer's eyes

and curtly replied, "Why thank you, Captain. It was an honor to have been chosen to give it."

"Now what's this about you being back from your leave a day early," interrupted Admiral Hoyt. "I hope everyone is all right in that wonderful family of yours."

"They're doing fine, Admiral. In fact, Susan and Sarah are waiting for me to join them for lunch at the Old Mermaid. We had a great time in the Highlands. But since they'll be flying back to the States tomorrow afternoon, Susan decided to get back early."

"Captain Aldridge has a wonderfully precocious six-year-old daughter by the name of Sarah, who loves a proper fish 'n chips," said Admiral Hoyt to Brigadier General Hartwell.

"Or chips 'n fish, as she calls them," added Steven.

The Scot's expression warmed. "I've got a six-year-old granddaughter myself, Captain Aldridge, who's a devout aficionado of your MacDonald's hamburgers. Why, whenever we pass one, no matter what time of day it is, she's after me to stop and purchase her a sandwich."

The sudden arrival of Dunoon's mayor gave Aldridge and his XO time to step aside and have some words in private.

"It really is good to see you again, Skipper. I can see in your face that your leave was a relaxing one."

"I wouldn't go that far, XO. Susan and Sarah had me on the go every free moment of the day and night."

"Did you have any difficulty driving on the wrong side of the road, Skipper?"

Aldridge grinned. "It was a bit tricky at first. Of course, I figured that if I could pilot a seven-thousand-ton submarine down a foggy channel in the dead of night, driving a Rover on the left hand side of the road couldn't be that difficult."

The two laughed, and Aldridge's tone turned serious. "How is the refit going, Bob?"

The XO shifted his pipe from one side of his mouth to the other before answering. "As far as I can see, right on schedule, Skipper. We'll be taking on the first of our SUBROC's tonight, with the final modifications to the Mk117 fire control system due to be completed twenty-four hours later."

"So you managed it without me, huh, XO? I knew you would, especially with the able assistance of our esteemed weapons' officer. So tell me, did Lieutenant Hartman get much sleep while I was away?"

"You know better than that, Skipper. From the very beginning, the good lieutenant took on this project like it was his responsibility alone. He's on it day and night, and nothing gets done without Hartman's personal okay."

"We're very fortunate to have a guy like Ed Hartman aboard the *Cheyenne*, Bob. I know that he can be a real pain in the ass sometimes, but his attention to detail can really make the difference if we're ever called on to launch those fish of his."

"I hear you, Skipper. But I still think that the guy has to lighten up some. You know what they say about all work and no play."

Suddenly aware of the time, Steven Aldridge grimaced. "Speaking of the devil, I've got a date over at the Old Mermaid to keep. Would you care to join us?"

"It sounds like it would be fun, Skipper, but we're due at a formal reception at city hall."

"Well, make me proud, XO," said Aldridge as he prepared to convey his goodbyes to Admiral Hoyt and their Scot host. "And I'll see you back on the ranch sometime tomorrow afternoon."

By the time Steven arrived at the pub they had picked for lunch, the creamy head on the pint of beer his wife had ordered had long since disappeared. Yet the lukewarm lager was tasty all the same, and the thirsty fifteen-year navy veteran managed to empty the pint in three lengthy swigs. Their fish and chips were as delicious as ever, and only after stops at both the bakery shop and the fishmonger's did they return to their cottage overlooking Hunter's Quay.

Later that evening, long after Sarah was tucked warmly in her bed and while Susan was still busy packing, Aldridge slipped on his overcoat and went outside. The wind that had been with them all afternoon had turned icy. Pulling up his woolen collar to counter these frigid gusts, he glanced up into the sky and found a myriad of twinkling stars shining forth from the crystal clear heavens. Pleasantly surprised by this breathtaking sight, he looked around him. From his current vantage point, he could see the entire length and breadth of that inlet of water known as Holy Loch. Having supposedly gotten this auspicious name several centuries ago when a sailing ship bound to Glasgow sunk here with a load of soil from the Holy land in its hold, the loch was currently home to a U.S. Navy submarine base. A major component of the base itself could be seen floating on the choppy waters of the loch. This ship was the sub tender, *USS Hunley*. Inside the *Hunley* was stored almost everything that a submarine would need to continue extended operations. This included food, spare parts, fuel, and even weapon reloads.

It took a trained eye to spot the minuscule red light that lay amidships, near the waterline of the

Hunley. Also bobbing with the swells, this light was the only visible evidence of Aldridge's present command. It belonged to the sail, or conning tower, of the *USS Cheyenne.* During its current refit, the *Cheyenne* was berthed beside the *Hunley,* their hulls separated by a line of hard rubber fenders.

If there was more light present, Aldridge knew that he would also see the upper portion of his boat's black hull. Three hundred and sixty feet long from the tip of its conical bow to its tapered stern, the *Cheyenne* was almost as long as the massive tender, though the majority of his command's mass lay perpetually hidden beneath the inky waters.

127 men made this vessel their home. Designed primarily to hunt other submarines, the *Cheyenne* was powered by a single pressurized, water-cooled nuclear reactor that drove geared steam turbines. A single shaft could propel the ship at speeds well over thirty knots, while its specially welded, high-yield steel hull allowed it to attain a maximum diving depth of some fifteen hundred feet. The sub was also fitted with the latest in digital electronic sonar and fire-control systems.

In addition to carrying a full complement of MK 48 torpedoes, the *Cheyenne* was also equipped with Harpoon anti-ship missiles, the Tomahawk cruise missile, and with the completion of their current refit, the SUBROC antisubmarine rocket. All of these advanced weapons were designed to be launched from one of the vessel's four twenty-one inch midship's torpedo tubes, thus giving Aldridge an incredibly diversified arsenal of firepower.

Altogether, the *Cheyenne* was one of the most awesome warships ever built. Proud to have been picked to lead her into harm's way, Steven Aldridge could visualize his men at work inside its cylindrical hull.

Only a spartan crew would currently be manning the control room. This space would be completely lit in red to protect their night vision. The majority of action would be taking place in the forward torpedo room, where the modification to their fire-control system would go on throughout the entire night. Ever vigilant in this portion of the ship, Lieutenant Edward Hartman would be doing his best to insure that the work was being done correctly. Most likely the bleary-eyed weapons' officer would be sipping on one of the innumerable mugs of hot black coffee that he had already downed today, counting the minutes remaining until the refit was scheduled to be completed. Hartman was a consummate worrier and a stickler for detail, two traits that made him one of the finest young officers in the entire submarine force.

Back in the *Cheyenne*'s engineering spaces, a full detail would be on duty monitoring the ship's reactor. This was Lieutenant Rich Lonnon's exclusive realm. The brawny New Yorker was a graduate of MIT. Highly intelligent, Lonnon was never afraid to get his hands dirty along with the rest of the enlisted men. He also put in his fair share of work hours, and was most likely on the job at this very moment, insuring that all was well with *Cheyenne* Power and Light.

The ship's galley would also be open at this late hour. By its very nature submarine duty could be boring, tedious work, and Petty Officer Howard Mallott and his devoted crew made meal times something to look forward to. Right now the *Cheyenne*'s brightly painted mess would be rich with the scent of perking coffee. A variety of fresh sandwiches would be available, along with an assortment of other suitable late night snacks. Only recently, Mallott had managed to bring a corn popper on board, and was proud of the fact that he could serve the crew piping hot popcorn at fifty fathoms. This snack was also greatly appreciated when the *Cheyenne*'s very own movie theatre was operational.

One of the few compartments that would most likely be empty at this hour would be the sonar room, or as it was affectionately called, the sound shack. Recently the *Cheyenne* had been lucky enough to get the services of one of the best sonar men in the business. Petty Officer First Class Joe Carter had previously been an instructor in his arcane art at the San Diego Naval Facility. Blessed with ultra-sensitive hearing and an uncanny degree of intuition, Carter was versed in every aspect of their BQQ-5 sonar suite. Such a system was incredibly complex, and the twenty-six-year-old, black St. Louisan made the most out of its large active/passive spherical bow sonar, conformal passive hydrophone array, and PUFFS fire-control system. He was also responsible for the boat's BQR-23 towed sonar array. Designed to allow pinpoint spotting of the enemy, without having to be distracted by the inherent sounds of the *Cheyenne*'s own signature, the array was housed in a prominent fairing that ran almost the length of the hull. The winch that deployed it was located between the bow itself and the forward end of the pressure hull. Thus the *Cheyenne* was equipped with the state-of-the-art when it came to the critical sonar functions, that were, after all, the eyes and ears of the boat whenever they were submerged.

Twenty-four hours from now, Steven Aldridge would be dressed in dark blue coveralls and be an integral component of this team. But right now he had other responsibilities. A familiar voice broke the silence around him.

"Penny for your thoughts, sailor."

Thus brought back to dry land, Aldridge turned and set his eyes on his beloved wife. Susan was wrapped in her ski parka and carried two steaming mugs of herb tea in her gloved hands.

"My guess is that you were thinking about another woman," added Susan as she reached her husband's side and handed him a mug. "And I bet her name is *Cheyenne.*"

"I confess. You're right. Do I still get to keep my tea?"

Susan flashed a warm smile and cuddled up to him. "You know I'm not the jealous type."

"No, come to think of it, you never were," reflected Steven fondly.

As they stood there silently sipping their tea, Steven's thoughts returned in time to the day they first met. Twenty years ago, both of them had been aspiring sophomores at the University of Virginia. As a participant in the school's excellent Naval ROTC program, Steven knew from the beginning that his goal was a career in the Navy. He therefore made certain to take a full curriculum of mathematics and science courses, in which he excelled. It was basic English that proved to be his downfall. A tutor was therefore suggested, and into his life walked Susan Spencer, a bright-eyed, vivacious, English major from Norfolk. Steven got that peculiar feeling in his stomach from the first time he laid eyes on her. She was petite, with dark eyes, curly brown hair, and a figure kept trim with daily aerobics. She seemed cool to his ardor at first, though when Steven learned that she was a Navy brat like himself, the two found a common bond.

In an incredibly short period of time, Steven's English grades improved to the point where the tutorial sessions were no longer needed. They had never gone out on a real date, and as their professional relationship came to its end, Steven summoned the nerve to ask her for dinner and a movie. Miraculously enough, she accepted readily.

They saw each other regularly after that, and by the time summer vacation rolled around, Susan felt comfortable enough to invite him to meet her folks. The Spencers lived in Virginia Beach. Her father worked nearby, at the Oceana Naval Air Station. He was a Viet Nam veteran who held the rank of commander and had over 400 carrier landings under his belt. When Steven learned that he was currently involved with the P-3 Orion program, his nervousness quickly faded into a barrage of questions relating to the science of anti-submarine warfare. The two talked for hours, and Susan and her mother actually had to pry them apart just to get them to the dinner table.

One month later, Steven asked Susan to marry him, and she immediately accepted. One thing that they both agreed upon from the outset was that they would wait until Steven's career was well on-line before having children. It was on the day that he was promoted to the rank of Lieutenant Commander that Sarah was conceived. And they were currently working on a brother for her.

"Finish with the packing yet?" asked Steven dreamily.

"The last trunk is nearly full," said Susan with a sigh.

"Then how about going in and giving little Andrew one more try," offered Steven.

Susan squeezed his hand and purred. "I'd like that very much, sailor. I truly would."

The dawn was all too soon in coming. With the

95

bare light of the new day filtering into their bedroom, they once more made love, this time with an urgency that hinted at their inevitable parting. With the warm aftereffects of their shared passion still fresh on his mind, Steven reluctantly rose from their bed. As he stepped from the steaming hot shower, the aroma of strong coffee greeted him, he dressed himself in the freshly pressed set of khakis that he found hanging on the bathroom door.

Breakfast was a sad affair, with Sarah rattling on about her desire to go hiking with a flock of sheep once again, and the forlorn lovers silently staring at each other from across the kitchen table. Time seemed to fly by, and all too soon the suitcases were securely stowed inside the Rover's boot. And the last thing Susan saw, as she left her home of the past two months, was the barely discernable, black upper hull of the *USS Cheyenne*, as it floated on the calm surface of the nearby loch.

"Be good to my man," she whispered to the wind, as she ducked into the Rover, feeling almost as if she *were* handing Steven over to another woman.

The ferry that would take them to Gourock, the first leg of their long trip to America, was faithfully waiting at Dunoon's main dock. Sarah was an avid sailor and couldn't wait to board the sturdy vessel. As she ran ahead to begin her exploration of the ship, Steven loaded their suitcases onto a trolley, which he handed over to a grizzled deckhand. He included a five pound note and strict instructions that once the ferry reached Gourock, the deckhand would make certain that both his family and their baggage found its way onto the train to Prestwick airport.

Steven Aldridge took his wife in his arms, and as sailors and their women have done from the first time that man went away to sea, they kissed, and cried, and parted, each to go their separate way until the fates willed them together again.

Steven waited on the docks until the ferry was well across the waters of the firth. He could still see images of Susan and Sarah gathered at the stern railing waving their goodbyes as he heavily turned to get on with his duty. His own sea bag lay in the Rover's boot, and he sped through Dunoon, proceeding directly to Hunter's Quay.

Two serious-faced Marine sentries, who most likely were participants in yesterday's parade, thoroughly checked his I.D. before allowing him entry into the base itself. Aldridge returned their salute, and drove to the parking lot reserved for officers. He was fortunate to get down to the dock just as a launch was getting set to leave for the tender.

With thoughts of his family already slipping from his consciousness, Aldridge seated himself in the whaleboat's bow and peered out at the massive tender that they were rapidly approaching. The USS Hunley's distinctive squared hull was packed with equipment and dominated by a large crane. Sailors scurried over its deck, their efforts focused solely on caring for the needs of the partially submerged, black-hulled vessel that lay floating close beside it. Several individuals could be seen gathered in the top of the Cheyenne's relatively small sail, and Steven Aldridge felt as if he had been gone from his command for months, instead of a mere seven days.

Security concerns forced him to be dropped off on the Hunley, instead of right onto the Cheyenne's deck. As he climbed onto the tender, he had to pass the inspection of yet another duo of no-nonsense Marine sentries. One of these leathernecks held a German shepherd on a short steel leash. Stationed here to detect illegal drugs, the canine nonchalantly sniffed Steven's seabag then backed away, signalling that he was free to continue on.

To get to the gangway leading to the *Cheyenne*, he traversed a passageway that led him past a cavernous storeroom packed with spare parts, and a compartment holding one of the *Hunley*'s many fine machine shops. To the hiss of a welder's torch, he climbed down a ladder, traded salutes with a trio of enlisted men, and began his way down an exterior corridor, whose ceiling was lined with snaking electrical cables. One of the sailors who was busy working on a portion of this cable network was a young woman. Interestingly enough, there were several hundred women on board the tender, making it one of the most integrated ships in the entire fleet.

A section of the *Hunley*'s railing had been removed and replaced with a covered gangway that led down toward the waterline. Alertly perched at the top of this gangway was a denim-clad sailor with a Browning combat shotgun at his side. The slightly built enlisted man had a bristly brown moustache, and Aldridge readily identified him.

"Good morning, Seaman Avila."

"Good morning to you, Captain. Welcome home," returned Petty Officer Second Class Adrian Avila.

The bright-eyed Hispanic enlistee from Plano, Texas had been with the *Cheyenne* for six months, and was showing himself to be a bright, inquisitive young man, well on his way to qualifying for his silver dolphins.

"Who's the current OOD?" questioned Aldridge as he began his way down the gangway.

"Lieutenant Laird, Sir," answered Avila efficiently. "Shall I let him know that you're on the way down?"

"You needn't bother," said Aldridge with a shake

98

of his head. "The good lieutenant will know soon enough."

Aldridge entered the submarine through a deck hatchway positioned just abaft of the sail. As he climbed down the ladder's iron wrungs, the familiar scent of machine oil met his nostrils. All too soon, the direct light from above was blotted out as he continued climbing further downward into the *Cheyenne*'s artificially lit interior.

He continued on, straight to the officer's wardroom. Seated at his customary spot near the head of the table was his XO. Bob Stoddard was totally engrossed in the examination of a detailed bathymetric chart, and Aldridge stood there silently for a moment before announcing his arrival.

The wardroom directly adjoined the portion of the boat that contained the officers' living quarters. It occupied a rather spacious compartment lined with woodgrain paneling. A single rectangular table was situated in the center of the room. Here the officers ate their meals, talked shop, and held court with other elements of the crew when necessary.

The chair at the head of the table was reserved for the captain. Hung on the bulkhead beside it was a large photograph showing a gently rolling plain, covered with brightly colored wild flowers and clumps of golden scrub. This picture had been taken outside the city of Cheyenne, Wyoming, their warship's namesake.

Aldridge recognized the piece of music softly emanating from the wardroom's stereo as being from the soundtrack to the movie, *Lawrence of Arabia*. Two months ago, while on leave in London, Bob Stoddard got the chance to see a newly edited, 70mm version of this classic movie. Infatuated by its exotic score, he purchased a tape of the recording, which

99

he brought back to the ship and had since listened to religiously. Though Aldridge himself preferred jazz, he had to admit that he had grown quite fond of Maurice Jarre's Academy Award winning score. Most of the other officers also enjoyed it, prompting one of them to go out and buy a video tape of the movie for the *Cheyenne*'s film library.

The sudden entrance of Petty Officer Howard Mallott alerted the others to Aldridge's presence. The portly, bespectacled chief of the *Cheyenne*'s mess burst into the wardroom carrying a tray of food.

"Why hello, Captain," said the personable master chef as he placed the tray beside the XO. "Can I get you some lunch?"

With this, the XO looked up from the chart he was studying and cast a surprised glance on the boat's commanding officer.

"Greetings, Skipper. I didn't realize that you were aboard."

"I just got here, XO," replied Aldridge as he walked up to the table. "What are your serving, Chief?"

"Turkey burgers, Captain," answered Mallott proudly. "It's something new that I just got the recipe for. Half the cholesterol of beef, and just as tasty."

Aldridge inspected the plateful of food that included mashed potatoes, steamed broccoli, and a gravy smothered turkey patty that looked much like a chopped beef steak. A slice of apple pie and a mug of black coffee completed this meal.

"Looks awfully good, Chief," reflected Aldridge. "Why don't you go ahead and bring me a tray. But forget the pie. I'm carrying along a couple of extra pounds that I didn't have when I left here last week, and the only dessert that I'm going to be having on nis next patrol is an extra twenty-five sit-ups."

"I'll be back in a few minutes, Captain," said Mallott, smiling. Aldridge was well known for his insistence on physical fitness.

Aldridge helped himself to a mug of coffee and sat down at the head of the table. "Go ahead and eat while it's hot, Bob. I'll just have a look at this chart."

While the XO cut into his meal, Aldridge commented, "Looks like someone's planning to take the *Cheyenne* out to sea shortly."

"I didn't get a chance to tell you, Skipper," managed the XO between bites. "Our sailing orders came in about a half hour ago. We're due out on this afternoon's tide."

"Then it looks like I got back here just in the nick of time," added the Captain. "Any hint as to why the rushed departure?"

The XO spooned down a bite of mashed potatoes before replying. "The entire packet's on your desk along with your other mail. It seems that Command needs us to shake up a NATO ASW exercise that's currently taking place out in the North Sea."

"That's all fine and dandy, Bob. But is the *Cheyenne* ready to go on patrol right now? We were supposed to have until midnight tonight to finish up that Mk117 modification and get the boat ready for SUBROC."

"Everything's been taken care of, Skipper. As we expected, Lieutenant Hartman has been right on top of those engineers. It looks like they'll be done a couple of hours early, which means we can get those civilians off of here and still catch the late afternoon tide. I made certain that all personnel on leave were called in. In fact, I was just about to have the quartermaster track you down when you showed up here."

"At least you weren't going to set sail without me," returned Aldridge with a wink. "How's that turkey?"

"Marvelous, Skipper. I would have never known it wasn't beef unless Chief Mallott told me otherwise."

"Did I hear someone mention my name?" interjected the chef as he arrived with another tray of food. "Bon appetit, Captain."

"I understand from the XO that you've got a winner with this turkey," commented Aldridge. "Nobody loves a thick, medium rare chopped beefsteak smothered with onions more than me, Mr. Mallott. So let's see what this new recipe of yours is all about."

Howard Mallott looked on as the captain picked up his fork and cut into the patty. The *Cheyenne*'s commanding officer smelled the piece he had cut off before putting it into his mouth and thoughtfully chewed.

"Well, what do you think, Captain?" expectantly asked the chief.

Without allowing his expression to reveal his verdict, Aldridge nodded. "I'm impressed, Mr. Mallott. Would you mind writing down the recipe for me? My wife is going to love this dish."

"With pleasure, Sir," replied the beaming chef, who marched out of the wardroom thrilled by the captain's compliment.

"Did Susan and Sarah get off on time?" quizzed the XO. He cleaned off his plate and went to work on his pie.

"They should be well on their way to Prestwick by now. Susan's so well organized that they made the 10:15 ferry with time to spare. That should put them at the airport about ninety minutes before their flight to the States is scheduled to depart. Susan's folks will be picking them up in Norfolk. But they've got a lot of territory to cover until then."

102

Steven Aldridge chewed in reflective silence, his thoughts unexpectedly returning to the joy-filled week that he had just completed. The XO was content to polish off his pie and quietly sip his coffee. While in the background, the graceful strains of *Lawrence of Arabia* filled the wardroom with the magic of the desert.

The spell was broken by the arrival of a short, stocky officer, who held a clipboard in his hand. Lieutenant Andrew Laird was a relative newcomer to the crew. He was the boat's navigator, and currently its OOD. It was in regard to this latter responsibility that he was presently functioning.

"Lieutenant Commander Stoddard, I have that personnel update that you requested," offered the young officer stiffly.

The XO took the clipboard and hastily skimmed it. "Well, you can scratch the Captain's name off of the list of those we're still waiting for, Lieutenant. That leaves us only three crew members short."

"Seamen Thomas and Crawford are on their way from Hunter's Quay even as we speak, Sir," replied the OOD. "That just leaves us without Petty Officer Carter."

"We certainly don't want to leave for sea without our best man in sonar," interrupted the captain.

"He should be here within the hour, Sir," returned the OOD. "I called the Glasgow telephone number he left us. A woman answered and said that Mr. Carter left for Gourock on the eleven o'clock train. That should put him in Dunoon at approximately one, Sir."

"That's still cutting it awfully close, Lieutenant," said Aldridge. "I want someone down at the ferry terminal with a car, right now. And if Carter's not on that one p.m. boat, the driver's to call in immediately."

"Yes, Sir," snapped the OOD.

Yet before Laird could leave to carry out this order, he had to field one more inquiry from the XO.

"I see that those four civilian engineers are still with us, Lieutenant. Will they be able to finish up in time, or will we have to take them out to sea with us?"

The OOD answered a bit hesitantly. "I'm waiting for an update from Lieutenant Hartman, Sir. He promised to give me a definite time, but as of five minutes ago, I still haven't heard from him."

"Well then, get on it," urged the XO. "Otherwise you're going to have to be the one to tell those civilians that they've been picked to be the exclusive guests of the USS *Cheyenne* for the next eight weeks."

"I'll do so at once, Sir," said the OOD.

Only then did the XO return his clipboard, indicating that his audience here was over. As Lieutenant Laird disappeared through the forward hatch, the XO grunted.

"We'll make a proper officer out of that kid yet."

Steven Aldridge offered his own opinion of Laird's competency while sipping his coffee. "I don't know, Bob. I think he's coming along just fine. He's only been with us less than two months, and don't forget what it was like when you pulled your first patrol on a 688."

The XO rolled his eyes back in their sockets. "Guess I'm just turning into the same type of hardnosed, insensitive taskmaster that I always despised when I first got into nukes ten years ago."

"That, my friend, comes with the territory," quipped Aldridge stoically. "Now I'd better get back to my cabin and unpack, then I'll get to work trying to put a dent in that paperwork that's been piling up on my desk all week. See you topside when the tide turns, Bob."

"I'll be there, Skipper," returned the *Cheyenne*'s second-in-command as he watched Steven Aldridge push away from the table to get on with his duty.

Two and a half hours later, both senior officers were gathered in the sub's exposed bridge as promised. The sun was peeking through the clouds as the USS *Cheyenne* engaged its engines and headed for the open sea.

With a patrol boat leading the way, the 360-foot attack sub remained on the surface as it exited Holy Loch. The town of Dunoon soon passed on the starboard, and Steven Aldridge spotted the ferry that had conveyed his family across the firth earlier in the day just leaving its berth at Gourock on the opposite shore. Ever alert for any nearby surface traffic, the sub hugged the deepwater channel that would take it almost due south.

The large cement stack and trio of huge fuel storage tanks belonging to the Inverkip power station soon passed to their port, while the flashing beacon known as the Gantocks signalled the starboard extent of the channel. Beyond this beacon on the firth's western shore rose a sloping, tree-filled hillside that culminated at the summit called Bishop's Seat, 1,651 feet above sea level.

"Believe it or not, you can just make out Ailsa Craig with the glasses, Skipper," observed the XO.

Putting his own binoculars up to his eyes, Aldridge soon enough spotted this distinctive volcanic-like formation splitting the channel up ahead. "Well, I'll be," he muttered. "That's a good forty-seven miles away."

"That's certainly a first for me," revealed the XO. "Usually from here we'd be lucky enough to spot the

Cumbrae isles, or even Arran."

Notorious for thick fogs, blinding rains squalls, and heavy winds, the Firth of Clyde was more often than not a navigator's nightmare. But Steven Aldridge had already learned never to anticipate the weather in Scotland, as he found out during the glorious week just passed.

"I guess we should count our blessings, XO," reflected the Captain. "This transit looks to be one of the easiest yet. And it's a tribute to the crew that we're right on schedule."

"They sure worked some miracles, Skipper. Although for a moment there, I didn't think we'd ever get away on time. Lieutenant Hartman kept those engineers on board to the very last second. Those white shirts were sweating bullets, afraid that they'd have to go along with us. And as they were climbing up the gangplank to the *Hunley,* who passes them going the other way but Petty Officer Carter."

"We can be thankful for that," said Aldridge. "Did anyone find out what held him up?"

The XO flashed a wide grin. "Scuttlebutt says that our romeo in the sound shack met a comely little Gourock lass on the train down from Glasgow. Luckily she didn't keep him in her apartment longer than an hour, or we'd be without his services."

"I thought he already had a girlfriend back in Glasgow," countered the Captain.

Again the XO snickered. "From what I hear, Mr. Carter attracts women like my wife collects bills."

"He does have that certain air about him," added the Captain, who looked up as a Boeing 747 airliner could be seen climbing into the blue heavens above the eastern shores of the firth.

Steven Aldridge knew that this plane originated in nearby Prestwick airport, and could very well be the one carrying his family homeward. And as the plane turned to the west and disappeared into a thick cloud bank, Aldridge found himself forming a silent prayer: that both of their long journeys would be safe ones.

Chapter Five

To the rousing strains of Greig's *Peer Gynt*, the Bell 212 landed on the *Falcon*'s helipad. Jon Huslid had been seated in the co-pilot's position, and made certain to compliment the helicopter's attractive pilot before joining his teammates in the main cabin.

"That was a wonderful landing, Kari. Are you going to stick around the Falcon for awhile?"

The pilot answered while skimming the cockpit's instrument panel. "It doesn't look that way, Jon. Since the Chief hasn't said any differently, it looks like I'll be returning to Stavanger to get on with the job I was on my way to when they diverted me to Lake Tinnsjo."

"Well, I hope that we didn't inconvenience you too much. God knows what Magne's got in store for us here. Now don't forget, I still owe you that photo session. Just name the time and place, and I'll try my best to be there."

"You're on, Jon Huslid. I'd like to give my folks a decent portrait of me for the holidays."

"With a face like yours, it won't be hard to do," remarked the grinning photographer. He unbuckled his harness and turned for the main cabin.

Kari Skollevoll was blushing as she watched him

exit. "Good luck, Jon. Don't let the Chief talk you into doing anything that he wouldn't do himself."

NUEX's co-founder flashed her a thumbs-up as he disappeared into the helicopter's fuselage. Waiting for him in the main cabin were Jakob Helgesen and Arne Lundstrom. The black-haired Lapp was in the process of reaching for his dive bag, stored in an overhead bin, while his bearded co-worker was stretched out on the cabin floor, sound asleep.

"Come on, Arne. Rise and shine," prompted Jon.

Oblivious to this request, the bearded Telemark native continued his snoring unabated.

"Damn, Jakob. I hope that you didn't have to put up with this racket all the way from Lake Tinnsjo," remarked Jon.

The Lapp shook his head and pointed to his ears like he couldn't hear the photographer's words. Only then did he reach up and pull out his earplugs.

"You industrious northerners never fail to amaze me," said Jon, who bent over to shake his sleeping colleague's shoulder. "Come on, sleeping beauty. Snap out of it. We've got a job to do."

This served to do the trick, and Arne groggily stirred and opened his eyes. "Where the hell are we?" he questioned with a wide yawn.

Jon answered this query by grabbing hold of the cabin door and sliding it backward. A gust of cool, salty air surged inside, while the distant crashing of the North Sea swells against the *Falcon*'s hull provided an appropriate backdrop.

Jon and Jakob climbed outside onto the helipad, with their groggy co-worker slowly bringing up the rear. The rotors of the Bell 212 were still spinning above them, and they instinctively ducked until they were well clear.

No sooner did they step off the helipad when the roar of the chopper's engines intensified. A deckhand in a silver fire-fighting suit stood alertly beside the foam gun, and Jon Huslid turned to watch the orange and white vehicle take off into the overcast sky.

"Welcome home, NUEX," broke a deep voice from behind.

Jon pivoted and set his eyes on the rugged face and figure of their diving supervisor, Magne Rystaad.

"Hello, Chief," replied the photographer. "It's good to be back, although if you would have just given us another day or so, we could have brought back one of the greatest treasures to have ever been pulled from Norwegian waters."

Not paying this remark much attention, Magne surveyed the deck area and inquired, "Where's Knut?"

Jon inhaled a deep breath and answered. "He's back at Lake Tinnsjo, along with the first piece of salvage ever brought up from the ferry, *Hydro*." His voice betrayed his excitement. "We've got one of the sealed drums, Chief! And if all goes well, Knut will have the other thirty-two up by this time tomorrow."

This revelation commanded Magne's full attention. "You mean to say that you managed to actually locate and begin salvaging the heavy water? Why, that's fantastic news, lad! But unfortunately, a matter of even greater importance has come up that requires your immediate attention."

Stepping to the side, Magne briefly turned his head and beckoned forward a tall, lanky, bearded stranger, who was dressed in orange coveralls. He

110

appeared to be about Magne's age, and had his same no-nonsense expression.

"Jon, I'd like you to meet David Lawton. David's a friend of mine from Houston, Texas, who has his own group of oil-service divers to supervise."

As the two shook hands, Magne continued. "David was with me in the *Falcon*'s control room when Solo discovered a hazardous object on the seafloor, one that could very well jeopardize the entire Ice Field's gas pipeline project."

"What in the world could possibly block the route of the pipeline?" asked Jon. "Especially in these waters. Why, with all the other pipelines that we've already placed here, the seafloor west of Utsira has to be one of the most carefully charted areas on the planet."

"I thought the very same thing," replied Magne. "But as all of you know, just when you take the sea for granted, it has a way of surprising you. I learned this lesson once again two days ago, when we chanced upon a World War I mine that was supposed to have been long ago cleared from these waters. David arrived on the Falcon just as we were in the process of detonating the mine.

"It was while *Solo* was inspecting the aftereffects of this explosion, that we discovered another military relic. This one is from World War II, and is a bit more complicated to get rid of than that mine. 283 meters below the hull of the *Falcon,* smack in the middle of the new pipeline's proposed route, is a sunken German U-boat."

"It's a Type XXI to be exact," added David Lawton. "Such vessels only became part of the German fleet in the latter years of the war, and were the most advanced underwater vessels to have ever

111

sailed beneath the seas in those days."

Magne nodded. "David's our current resident expert in the matter, since as a U.S. Navy SEAL, he actually explored the wreck of a Type XXI that had been sunk off the coast of Georgia."

Not really too concerned with the nature of this obstacle, Jon Huslid questioned, "Can't Noroil merely route the pipeline around this U-boat?"

"That's impossible, lad," responded Magne. "Our safety margin on the pipeline's corridor is only five hundred meters wide. To reach the main pumping facility at Karsto, it has to circumvent the boulder-strewn seafloor on this side of Utsira island, so this route has to be followed exactly. And since the laying barges are forced to haul themselves along on anchors, we have to make absolutely certain that there is no unexploded ordinance inside that sub's hull."

"Then I guess that's why we're here," remarked Jon matter-of-factly. "When do we get started?"

Magne looked at his watch. "The bell will be ready to go in another ten minutes. Since you left Knute behind, I hope you won't mind taking along David in his place."

The photographer didn't like the idea at all. "With no offense meant toward Mr. Lawton, we're a team, and NUEX works best by itself. The three of us can manage very well on our own."

Magne briefly caught the Texan's glance before replying to this. "I understand, Jon. But I'd feel much better with four divers down there. This will be a bounce dive, so one of you is going to have to remain behind in the bell. The rest of you will only have an hour to get into that sub and give it a complete once over. I seriously doubt that two of

112

you can do it. Since David's already familiar with this class of U-boat, and has almost more hours at that depth than all three of you combined, I'd appreciate it if you'd make an exception in this instance."

Knowing very well that this was as close as Magne would ever come to actually coming out and ordering them to take along the stranger, Jon looked to his teammates for support. Arne didn't appear to be too concerned one way or the other. And when Jakob merely shrugged his shoulders, Jon reluctantly gave in.

"Very well, you can come along, Mr. Lawton. But please, no showboating."

The Texan looked to his host, and stifling a grin, responded to this request. "You don't have to worry about any such behavior from me, young man. And by the way, I want all of you to just call me David. I've been in this game for more years than I'd like to remember, and I've got nothing to prove but my desire to stay alive."

Jon looked to Magne. "Then let's do it, Chief. We're going to need an assortment of tools to pry open those hatches, and some of those new mercury vapor torches to light our way once we get inside."

Magne explained just what equipment had already been reserved for them as he led the team of divers below deck. Taking up the rear of this group, David Lawton anxiously awaited his first bell dive in the North Sea. His host had previously briefed him on his diving companions' backgrounds. As an outsider, David was anticipating some resistance, and true to form, the red-headed photographer expressed it. Yet this was a natural reaction. NUEX had been together as a team for over five years now,

113

and it would have been totally out of character for them to welcome a stranger into their ranks with open arms.

Formed originally as a social club, the Norwegian Underwater Explorers grew from a bunch of teenagers with a shared love of diving, to a money-making organization with a long list of projects to choose from. Magne had explained how the missing member of the group, Knut Haugen, had inherited his father's dive shop in Oslo. His friend from the Telemark region, Arne Lundstrom, was called in to give him a hand running the business. Their future teammates, Jon Huslid and Jakob Helgesen, were customers, and it was in this way that they met and planned their first dives together.

Jon's love of photography inspired Knut to design several watertight housings for his camera equipment. The first underwater photos he took were just for fun, but all this changed when a picture he snapped of a sunken German fighter plane won first place in a nationwide photo competition. Fiber optics and ROV's were not yet readily available in those days, and Jon was asked to initiate a photographic inspection of a newly installed North Sea oil platform. He brought along his teammates for help, and together they successfully completed their first professional dive job.

The Norwegian oil-service business was a tight-knit group, and when it was learned that NUEX provided excellent, dependable work for a reasonable cost, other jobs followed. Many of these assignments took them to a depth of three hundred meters, the maximum their current technology safely allowed. They accepted these jobs without hesitation, and were not afraid to go through the

114

long hours of decompression that such depths necessitated.

Magne hired them to do a hull inspection of one of Noroil's many diving ships. He was satisfied with their work, saw their potential, and offered them a full-time job. They only agreed to sign on when they were told that their first assignment would be to document in pictures the wreck of the German heavy cruiser *Bleche,* that sunk in Oslo fjord in the opening days of World War II. The *Bleche* still held the corpses of over fifteen hundred men, and its rusted fuel tanks were beginning to leak oil into the pristine waters of the fjord. Noroil was called in to see what could be done about stopping this flow of pollutants.

The resulting dive made international headlines. The pictures were excellent and made many a front page newspaper and magazine cover worldwide. Because of this notoriety, and the excellent publicity it generated for Noroil, it was agreed that NUEX would be called in whenever a difficult salvage job presented itself.

Magne had also explained to David the nature of NUEX's current project in Lake Tinnsjo. The exploration of the *Hydro* sounded like an exciting adventure that took on additional dimensions when the heavy water was taken into consideration. Though Magne hated to call them away from this historic task, he had no choice in the matter. Hopefully, after a quick inspection of the submarine, the route could be cleared and the pipeline survey continued. Then NUEX would have plenty of time to return to Lake Tinnsjo and complete their work there.

Curious himself as to the condition of the ferry's

special cargo after all these years, Lawton followed the team into that portion of the *Falcon* where the diving bells were stored. There were few words spoken as several attendants helped them into their heavy, black latex diving suits. Because these suits would not keep them absolutely dry, and since the water temperature at 283 meters was near freezing, hot water would be pumped into a network of tubes that lined the suit's interior, conveyed by a rubber hose that made up part of their individual umbilicals. Also included in this lifeline to the ship above was the tube that carried their breathing gases, and that which allowed their communication topside.

The diving bell that would convey them to the seafloor was an oblong, cylindrically shaped object that was painted bright yellow. It had an assortment of ballast tanks and air capsules welded onto its outside skin. And as Lawton was soon to learn, it was just spacious enough inside to allow the four of them room to stand upright, shoulder to shoulder.

"You'll be breathing a 96% helium to 4% oxygen mixture," instructed Magne. "Of course, as during any bounce dive, the bell will be lowered and only then pressurized to your working depth. Once the lower hatch falls open signalling that the proper pressure has been attained, you'll have sixty minutes to get into that submarine and see what it's carrying. I suggest heading right for the sub's forward torpedo room to determine its weapon's load."

"What about its aft tubes?" quizzed Jakob.

"It doesn't have any," answered Lawton. "The Type XXI is equipped with six bow tubes only. Thus all of its ordinance, whether it be torpedoes or mines, should be found in the forward portion of the boat."

116

Satisfied that their suits were properly fitted, Magne pointed toward the awaiting bell. "I'll be in constant contact with you at the diving console. At all times keep me updated on your positions, and don't take any unnecessary chances. If the vessel doesn't look right to you, get the hell back up here and we'll figure out another way to attack the problem."

As the members of NUEX solemly climbed into the bell, Magne took his special guest aside. "And that warning goes especially to you, David. I want you around so that I can collect on that chili recipe and Stetson that you're going to owe me after this dive."

"Don't worry, partner. As long as the gear holds up, it should be a piece of cake."

"Be gentle with my boys," added the veteran diver as he guided the Texan into the bell.

Lawton squeezed himself inside and listened as the hatch was tightly sealed behind him. He was able to lean back on a narrow ledge, and listened as the winch mechanism activated. The bell was then swung over the open moonpool, and unceremoniously dumped into the gray waters below.

As they initiated their descent, Jakob Helgesen pulled out a Sony Walkman cassette player. The Lapp then clipped on a set of headphones, adjusted the Walkman's volume control, punched its "on" button, and proceeded to close his eyes.

"Odds are that Jakob's listening to Pink Floyd's, *A Momentary Lapse of Reason*," offered Jon. "Lately, he never goes to depth without it."

"When I'm in the chamber, I like plenty of old-fashioned jazz," revealed Lawton. "Have any of you ever heard Aker Bilk blow the licorice stick?"

117

Neither Jon nor Arne had any idea what the Texan was talking about, and shook their heads to express this fact. David Lawton smiled.

"Too bad. Old Aker and his Strangers on the Shore has gotten me through many a nasty decompression. And there's the Professor of Brass himself, Dizzy Gillespie. That man can hit notes that even the angels in heaven can't reach."

A bit doubtful as to the sanity of this lanky American, both Norwegians seemed relieved when Magne's steady voice broke from the bell's p.a. speakers.

"Hello, gentlemen. You're presently breaking the fifty meter threshold. How do you read me?"

"Loud and clear, Chief," answered Jon.

"And how are you doing, David?" added the voice of Magne.

"It's a walk in the park," replied Lawton. "You know, I forgot to ask you, Magne, but what do you have planned to keep me occupied during decompression?"

The supervisor of Noroil's diving operations hesitated a moment before responding. "You'll have to give me some time to work on that, David. I'll spread the word and see what the crew is holding in the way of English books and magazines."

"I appreciate that, partner. And if any of the crew has any jazz tapes, send them along, too. It's time my fellow divers down here got a dose of some real music."

"I copy that, David. I'll do my best. You're presently breaking one hundred meters."

Lawton yawned wide to clear his blocked eardrums. Other than the alien pressure in his ears, there were no other physical symptoms of the great

118

depth that they had already attained.

"What kind of depths were you working with during the job that you left for this one?" asked Lawton in an attempt to break the ice.

"Our initial sonar contact with the sunken ferry was at 415 meters," answered Jon. "So needless to say, we were able to keep our feet dry for most of the project, and let our ROV do all the work for us."

"How did we ever do it without those ever-loving ROV's?" reflected the Texan.

"Our teammate, Knut, who's the technical genius of NUEX, says that in a few years, with all the electronic advances in robotics we're seeing, that human divers won't even be needed anymore," offered Arne.

"I seriously doubt that," said Lawton. "But I must admit that we've got ROV's doing things that we never dreamed possible just a couple of years ago."

"You're breaking 150 meters," observed the calm voice of Magne from above. "Continuing pressurization."

After clamping shut his nostrils and blowing out hard to clear his ears, Lawton added, "Of course, when I started in this business, just a dive to our current depth would have been unthinkable. So who knows, maybe ROV's will progress to such a stage that the really deep, dangerous work can be handled solely by the machines. Though as far as I'm concerned, nothing will ever beat having a real live diver on the job."

"I'm with you, David," broke the voice of Magne. "You're all starting to sound like a bunch of ducks. Approaching two hundred meters."

Magne was referring to one of the aftereffects of

119

breathing almost pure helium, the phenomenon known in the diving industry as "Donald Duck" voice. Inside the bell, the four divers weren't aware that they sounded any different than normal, and instead found their main concern being to keep the pressure on their eardrums equalized.

At 250 meters, Lawton found it a bit more difficult to catch his breath. But like someone who lives in a mountainous region, his lungs soon became adjusted to the new gas mixture, one quite different than that found at sea level.

"You're at target depth," said Magne as the bell gently jerked to a halt. "Initiating final pressurization."

For one last time the divers were forced to equalize the pressure on their eardrums. By the time this task was completed, the bottom hatch popped open, signalling that the pressure inside the bell was the same as that outside.

At this point, Jakob neatly stashed away his Walkman and began gathering his diving equipment. Both David Lawton and Jon Huslid also reached for the tools of their dangerous trade. Their bell man helped each one make the final adjustments to their masks, which entirely covered their faces. Arne would remain inside, with his own gear closeby, ready to leave the bell should one of the others need his assistance.

"Getting ready to leave the bell," said Jon, his mouth now covered by his mask.

Magne's tinny voice broke from the mask's small recessed speakers. "I read you. You now have sixty minutes and counting to complete your work and get back to the bell."

With his umbilical held carefully in his right

120

hand, Jon climbed down through the hatchway. Before leaving the bell altogether, he put on his fins, switched on his mercury-vapor torch, and grabbed the canvas sack full of tools that Arne handed him. As Jon swam free, Jakob followed, with David Lawton once again bringing up the rear.

The Texan was genuinely excited to be back at work again. The hot water that circulated throughout his suit effectively countered the frigid cold of this depth, and since hypothermia could kill a man just as quickly as a poor breathing mixture could, he was especially careful with his umbilical. Only when he was absolutely certain that it was playing out smoothly did he begin swimming away from the bell with speed.

As it turned out, he didn't have to go far. His teammates' torches lit the black waters like a flare, and as he swam up to join them, he spotted the immense gray hull of the vessel that they had been sent down to investigate. Lurking in the blackness, like a monstrous behemoth, the U-boat almost appeared imbued with life itself. Only when they swam in closer did he spot the vessel's rust-streaked hull and saw for certain that this object was man-made after all.

"We have the target in sight, Chief," reported Jon. "It appears to have settled upright on its hull, and looks to be listing a few degrees to its port side."

"Excellent," replied the distant voice of Magne. "See about finding those hatches set into the base of its sail."

"Will do, Chief," said Jon, who swam forward almost immediately.

The two Norwegians were strong swimmers, and it took Lawton's total effort to keep up with them.

He slowed down as he reached the sub's hull. It appeared to be intact, and he could still make out the dozens of free-flood holes that allowed such vessels to go from the surface to periscope depth in an unprecedented ten seconds.

It was as he reached the aft end of the sail, that a bright strobe lit the blackness forward. When this blindingly bright light repeated itself, Lawton closed in to see what it was all about. What he found in the waters ahead of him caused goosebumps to form under the black wetsuit.

Positioned beside the forward portion of the conning tower, Jon Huslid had a small waterproof camera aimed toward the sail itself. As Lawton reached the photographer's side, he turned toward the sub to see what the Norwegian found so interesting. What the Texan saw caused him to momentarily gasp, for still visible in white paint on the rust-covered steel plates was the sub's identification number—U-3312.

"We know the old wolf's name now," observed the photographer. "It's U-3312."

"Got it," replied Magne. "While you see about getting inside, I'll get the fellows at the Naval Ministry started on pulling up its history. You've got fifty-one minutes to go, gentlemen."

Immediately below the I.D. number, Jakob could be seen struggling to open the hatch that was set into the sail's base. While his teammate went to his aid with a crowbar, Lawton decided to give the hatch on the after end of the sail a try. The last time he had explored such a vessel was off the coast of Georgia, this same hatch had provided him an entryway, so he wasn't really shocked when he gripped its circular iron handle and found it give with the slightest of efforts. The doorway opened inward, and only after Lawton peeked into the flooded sail's interior and spotted a clear ladder leading downward, did he go to retrieve his fellow divers.

The Norwegians were still gathered around the forward hatchway, stubbornly straining on its jammed handle with a pair of crowbars, when he arrived.

"Put down those crowbars and follow me," instructed the Texan.

"Excuse me, Sir," countered Jon Huslid. "But we're just starting to make some progress here."

"Do what you like," shot back Lawton. "But if you want me, I'll most likely be found in the sub's control room, that I'll be accessing through the open hatchway positioned ten meters behind you."

Not waiting to give them a chance to respond to this revelation, Lawton swam off to do just as he said. No sooner did he reach the open hatch, than a pair of lights could be seen rapidly approaching from the sub's forward end.

"We'll I'll be damned, Jon," observed Jakob as he spotted this entrance.

The photographer swam by David Lawton and skeptically peeked inside. "It looks clear, alright," he said. "Let's give it a shot. Watch those umbilicals, Jakob. I'm going in."

The Texan reported their movements to the surface. "We're proceeding to enter U-3312 through its sail-mounted aft, starboard hatchway."

"I read you," replied Magne. "Good hunting. You've got forty-seven and a half minutes and counting."

Lawton signalled Jakob to go on and enter the sail. The Norwegian did so readily. Lawton made certain that their umbilicals were clear before

123

entering the hatchway himself.

It was eerie as he carefully swam down the length of the well and emerged into the vessel's control room. The curious Norwegians had already begun their inspection of this space, and Lawton did his best to carefully scan the compartment with the limited light available to him.

The cold water had kept most of the fittings in a fairly decent state of preservation. He swam by the diving station, and was able to identify the assortment of large brass wheels that would be turned to adjust the U-boat's trim. Nearby he found the remnants of a cracked gyro-compass, and a compact, barnacle-laden table that he supposed was reserved for the navigator's charts. A closed bin lay beneath this table, and curious as to what lay inside, Lawton bent over to have a look.

He laid his torch on the deck and grabbed the bin's handles. When they didn't give at first, he put his foot up against the adjoining bulkhead, and using his back for leverage, yanked backward with all his might. The doors parted, and out shot a black creature with a slimy narrow body, bright yellow eyes, and massive, snapping jaws. His pulse pounding in terror, Lawton blindly dove to his left, causing the giant eel's slithering body to smack up against his side and then dart off into the blackness.

He was still trying hard to regain his composure, when he heard one of the Norwegians cry out in disgust. "Oh, for the love of God, just look at what's left of that poor fellow!"

His curiosity now fully satisfied, Lawton backed away from the open bin and swam toward the flickering lights at the center of the compartment. Both of the Norwegians were gathered there, their torches illuminating the skeletoned figure of a man, who was still dressed in a ragged black uniform complete with a white hat, draped over what appeared to be the partially deployed periscope.

"Looks like he died right at his station," observed one of the Norwegians somberly.

Lawton felt a heavy lump gathering at the back of his throat as he pulled his glance away from this macabre scene. "Come on, lads. We'd better be moving now," he managed.

This time he led the way to the forward hatchway. He found it jammed shut. While Jakob utilized a crow-bar to free it, the central portion of the control room flashed with a photographer's strobe. Soon after this strobe faded, Jon joined them at the stuck hatch, and with their combined strength, they finally succeeded in wrenching it open.

A long, narrow passageway led to the boat's forward spaces. With no time left to explore the various spaces that bordered this corridor, they continued on toward the sub's bow, stopping only when they came to another closed hatch.

"This should be the entrance to the torpedo room," remarked Lawton. "Make certain that those umbilicals have plenty of slack in them while I give the hatch a try."

Using a crowbar, the Texan managed to turn the circular locking mechanism, which opened with a loud, rusty squeal. His pulse quickened as he pulled the hatch toward him and swam into the spacious compartment that lay beyond.

While he circled this cavernous space with his light held up before him, Lawton listened as one of the Norwegians sent a report topside.

"We've entered what appears to be the forward

torpedo room, Chief. But strange as it may seem, there doesn't appear to be anything in it. The whole room looks like it's been stripped bare."

"Why that's impossible," returned Magne. "Are you certain you're in the right space?"

"It's the torpedo room alright," said Lawton. "I just passed its six bow caps. But the compartment does appear to be completely empty."

"Get a load of this, Jon!" interrupted Jakob. "What in the hell?"

"You're down to less than a half hour, gentlemen. It's time to clear out of there and return to the bell," warned their conscience from above.

Totally ignoring this advice, the three divers gathered on the port side of the compartment, where the Lapp had just made a puzzling discovery. Cut into the side bulkhead was a neatly cut rectangular hole that extended all the way through both hulls and led directly into the open sea.

"Good Lord!" exclaimed Jakob. "It looks like this cut is recent, and it appears just wide enough to fit a single diver."

"Did you hear me, gentlemen?" repeated the sharp voice of Magne. "I said that it's time to return to the bell! Do you copy that?"

"Magne, this is David. We hear you all right, and we'll return to the bell in a minute. But in the meantime, just hold onto your horses a second. We'll be getting back to you right shortly."

Without waiting for Magne to respond, the Texan made certain that he had plenty of slack in his umbilical before fitting his head and shoulders up against the mysterious opening. Seeing that he could just clear it with a couple of inches to spare, he kicked himself forward and entered

126

the void that lay between the sub's inner pressure hull and its outer skin.

"David, I want you out of there right now!" screamed Magne urgently. "Jon, Jakob, what the hell is going on down there? Either get back to the bell, or I'm going to have to send Arne in to carry you back by force!"

Oblivious to this threat, the two Norwegians followed the American's lead, with Jakob going into the hole first. Instead of heading right for the outer skin of the vessel, the Lapp plunged down into the black space that separated the two hulls. It was easily wide enough to fit two divers, and Jakob knew that somewhere down here was stored the sub's ballast tanks. With his mercury-vapor torch held out in front of him, he continued downward toward the keel, as the infuriated voice of his boss rattled forth from his mask mounted speakers.

"Arne, I want you to suit up right now. Then get out there and pull those guys up out of there if you have to."

It was obvious that Magne was furious, and before Arne was forced to needlessly leave the shelter of the bell, David Lawton responded.

"Hold on, partner. I've seen what I had to see, and now we're headed on back to the ranch. Keep dry, Arne. We're comin' home."

Both David Lawton and Jon Huslid returned through the hole that they had swum through and re-entered the empty torpedo room. Yet one umbilical still remained on the other side of the opening, and the photographer was quick to speak out.

"Come on, Jakob! What the hell's keeping you?"

Mysteriously drawn to the black void that continued beckoning him onward, the Lapp ignored the call of his colleague. Only one thing mattered now, and that was reaching the bottom of this manmade pit, where no diver before him had ever penetrated. It was just as his torch illuminated the flat keel of the boat, and he prepared to turn upward, a glittering reflection shot up from out of the blackness. It appeared to have emanated from a portion of the keel only a few meters distant, and Jakob reached out into the void with his torch.

Then he saw it. About the size of a large brick, it looked to be comprised of a golden, metallic substance, and had a pair of familiar eagle-like creatures engraved on its surface. He reached for it and found it to be incredibly heavy. Swiftly he turned to join his companions for the long decompression that would soon follow.

It took Knut Haugen an entire day to locate an inflatable collar large enough to lift the entire railcar from the lake bed. He did so at a deep-sea salvage firm that was based out of nearby Konigberg. While the collar was being expressed out to him, he got on with the task of finding some trustworthy assistants. He recruited a cousin that was working part-time on the construction of a new hydroelectric plant outside of Eidsborg, and an old friend, who lived in the village of Heddal.

A major concern was where the heavy water would be stored once it had been extracted. The thirty-three drums promised to take up a lot of space, and Knut finally settled on a partially empty warehouse that was owned by a Hakanes-based lumber company. Though he would have preferred to find a more secure location, the building was close to the salvage site, and since the heavy water wouldn't be there long, he supposed that it would do.

Ever practical, Knut made certain that the logistical problem of transferring the containers to the warehouse was solved long before the drums reached the lake's surface, by renting a flatbed truck, a dozen wooden pallets, and a small forklift. All of this equipment arrived on the same morning that the salvage collar reached him. This unique piece of gear weighed several hundred kilos, and took the combined efforts of both his muscular assistants to get it loaded onto the trawler.

By the time he returned to the site of the wreck, the excellent weather that had prevailed began turning for the worse. A stiff northerly wind was beginning to blow, and the once cloudless sky was gray and overcast. Fearful that the weather would only continue to deteriorate, Knut decided to go on with the attempt regardless.

A previously placed sonar transponder guided the ROV down to the sunken railcar. The heavy collar was rolled overboard, and as it sank it was guided down to its proper resting place by the ROV, until it was securely tucked beneath the wreckage. Knut started up the air compressor, and a steady stream of air was pumped via an umbilical down into the icy depths. As the collar began to fill, slowly the railcar began to lift.

To insure that it rose on an even keel, he expertly utilized the ROV to insure that the partially inflated collar was evenly distributed. It took several long, frustrating hours to accomplish this task, and as he was nearly finished, a cold rain had begun to fall topside. Trying his best to ignore the worsening weather, he restarted the compressor and anxiously waited for this novel salvage technique to show the desired results.

It seemed to take forever for the collar to fully inflate, but when it finally did, the results were quick in coming. Rushing from the ROV's control board in the trawler's cramped, forward cabin, Knut reached the boat's stern just as an agitated circle of white bubbles in the water beyond signalled the treasure's imminent arrival. He looked on in wonder as the railcar shot onto the surface at a slight angle, its bent, rust-streaked frame completely surrounded by the fully inflated collar. Knut barely had time to count the thirty-two sealed drums that lay securely strapped to the car's interior as he slipped into a wet suit and dove overboard to secure the collar with a winch-borne tow line.

The darkening sky didn't really open up until the trawler was well on its way back to shore, but by this time, Knut really didn't care. Ignoring the icy gale, he pulled up to the small wooden dock and screamed out in triumph. Yet his celebration was brief, for he still had to get the heavy water unloaded onto solid land.

Though he had planned to immediately transfer the drums to the warehouse, the rotten weather and advancing dusk kept him from accomplishing this goal. It was all they could do to get the containers out of their bobbing raft and onto the dock before darkness was upon them.

Knut and his exhausted assistants decided to spend the night on the trawler. His original intention was that they would sleep in shifts, so that one of them would always remain awake to watch their treasure. Yet this was not to be, for Knut fell

130

soundly asleep on the very first watch.

He awoke with a start several hours later, shocked to find the shiny barrel of a pistol pointed at his head.

"Don't try anything brave, Viking," warned a strangely accented voice from the darkness.

"What in the hell is going on here?" quizzed Knut as he started to sit up.

The cold, hard side of the pistol smacked into his jaw, sending him crashing onto his cot.

"Now, not another move out of you, Viking!" shouted his mysterious attacker. "Or I'll use this weapon like it was intended."

Certain that he meant it, Knut dared not flinch. As a stream of blood poured from a broken blood vessel in his nose, Knut summoned the nerve to question.

"Where are my crew mates?"

With his face and figure still hidden in the cabin's dark shadows, the intruder answered. "The lads are merely giving us a hand completing the job that you did not finish earlier today."

Only then did Knut hear the characteristic whine of a forklift truck in the background, beyond the pattering sound off the constantly falling rain.

"You've got to be kidding!" blurted Knut. "You don't really think that you can get away with stealing that heavy water, do you?"

"Who said anything about stealing it?" returned the icy voice. "We're only taking back what was rightfully ours in the first place."

Out of sheer desperation, Knut violently kicked up his foot in an effort to dislodge the pistol, but the stranger had been expecting just such a move and parried this blow with his forearm. Again Knut

131

tried to sit up, and this time the solid butt of the pistol smacked into his temple. As the diver tumbled backward, unconscious, his attacker cursed in perfect German.

"You stupid swine! May your dreams last an eternity, Viking!"

From the thick wood of Norwegian pine that bordered the dock area, Mikhail Kuznetsov watched the tall blond stranger leave the trawler. Even through the sheets of pouring rain, the scarred veteran could see the chrome Luger that this figure carried in his right hand.

"The other one is taken care of," said the stranger in German to his co-workers. "But hurry all the same. I want to be on our way long before dawn."

His colleagues were hard at work loading the recently salvaged drums onto a flatbed truck. There were five of them, together with the two unnerved Norwegians, who had been pulled from the trawler and forced at gunpoint to do the majority of the heavy labor.

Mikhail recognized four of the thieves as being from the local chapter of the Nordic Reichs Party. They readily took orders from the two blond-haired figures that accompanied them. These were the ones in which Mikhail had the greatest interest, for they would unknowingly lead him to the lair of his archnemesis. Only then would Mikhail move in, to wipe from the face of the earth the Neo-Nazi organization known as Werewolf.

A gust of rain and wind hit him full in the face, and as Mikhail wiped his eyes dry, he briefly massaged his throbbing scar. One step closer to finally bringing to justice the demon responsible for this wound, Mikhail anxiously readied himself for the next stage of his lifelong quest. For the place these thirty-three drums of heavy water were ultimately destined would be the place where he'd find Otto Koch, and destroy forever his twisted dreams of a reborn Reich.

Chapter Six

The *Falcon*'s main single lock living chamber was located on the ship's upper 'tween deck. It was here that David Lawton, Jon Huslid, Jakob Helgesen and Arne Lundstrom patiently waited for their decompression to be completed. This critical process actually began inside their diving bell, as they were slowly pulled up from the depths after their exploration of the German U-boat. It would continue for another seventy-two hours, inside the comfortable, but cramped, cylindrical structure that provided their current home.

The transfer from the bell took place without incident, and for the first couple of hours, the exhausted divers did nothing but sleep in their bunks. As they began to awaken, they moved around a bit, and were even able to sit down and have a meal, especially prepared for them in the *Falcon*'s galley.

David Lawton had sampled this excellent chow before, and wasn't the least bit disappointed as he wolfed down a tasty bowl of fish chowder and a delicious Caesar salad. Afterward, he went back to his cot to begin an Ian Flemming book that one of the crew had surrendered. Though the well-written exploits of James Bond were thoroughly engrossing, the Texan couldn't help but be distracted by the conversation of his diving companions.

". . . then say that seal carved into the gold brick indeed turns out to be Russian in origin. What in the world would it be doing on a German U-boat?" quizzed Arne. He sat at the table, sipping a mug of hot chocolate.

"I'd like to know why that torpedo room was completely emptied out like it was," added Jakob, who sat beside his bearded teammate.

Jon Huslid was propped up in his bunk reading a technical manual, which he put down to join this discussion. "It's only too obvious, Jakob. That compartment was cleared out so that it could hold something other than torpedoes."

"Then you really think that there was more gold than that single brick?" asked Arne.

"You better believe it, my friend. Lots more," offered Jon with confidence.

"That hole in the boat's hull convinced me," said Jakob. "It was cut there only recently, and intended for a single purpose, namely to remove whatever was being stored inside that compartment. That brick was probably left behind by accident, when the rest of the cargo was carried out into the open seas."

With this, Jon sat up and reflectively commented, "Then that leaves us with one question. Who in the hell was responsible for the heist?"

Before any of them could offer an answer, the chamber's centrally mounted video monitor popped on. Magne could be seen seated at his console in the nearby diving control room.

"Good morning, gentlemen," greeted the diving supervisor. "I hope everyone slept soundly and ate well. Your decompression is continuing smoothly. Right now, you have only seventy-one hours and

135

fifty-two minutes to go. I just got back some photos from the ship's lab that I thought you'd like to see."

Magne reached into an envelope and pulled out a stack of large prints. All eyes were on the video monitor as he continued.

"It looks to me like NUEX's master photographer has outdone himself once again. See for yourself."

The first photo that he displayed showed the bare outline of the U-boat's sail. The next one was a closeup of this same streamlined structure, and clearly showed the sub's I.D. numbers.

"I've already faxed a copy of this shot off to the Naval Ministry in Oslo," revealed Magne. "We'll hopefully soon know more about the history of U-3312, and then perhaps we can figure out what it's doing sunk in our waters. Now this next photo is a bit macabre, but I think that it could be a real prize winner. What do you think, gentlemen?"

The screen filled with the skeletoned remains of a lone seaman, draped over a corroded periscope. This ghostly shot had been one of those that Jon took in the vessel's control room, and was lit in such a way that it had an almost ethereal quality to it.

"Now that's something!" observed Arne, who had been waiting in the bell when this gruesome discovery had been made. "I wonder who that poor Kraut was?"

Magne was quick to reply. "Most likely, he was U-3312's captain. We can make this assumption because of the remnants of the white cap that he's wearing."

Several more ghostly photos of the sub's control room were followed by a single, well-lit shot that had been taken inside their diving bell. Practically

136

filling this print was the gold bar that Jakob had retrieved from the space between the U-boat's hulls. Clearly outlined, etched on the bar's surface, was a crest showing two ornate eagles back to back. Beneath this seal was a barely discernable series of numbers.

As a wondrous gasp filled the chamber, the monitor returned to Magne, who had just been handed a dispatch of some sort. He quickly read this report, then looked up to the camera to explain its contents.

"Good news, gentlemen. We just heard from the Naval Ministry. It seems like we've helped the authorities clear up one of the great remaining mysteries of World War II. They indeed have a record of the vessel known as U-3312. It was one of the German's newly introduced Type XXI class attack submarines. It had been stationed in Bergen, and the last that was ever heard of the sub was when it set sail on the last day of the war, along with its sister ship, U-3313. Both vessels were believed to have sunk in the mid-Atlantic while on their way to South America with a full complement of highly placed Nazi officials."

"I bet those Nazis were the ones who took that gold along," offered Arne.

"Any new ideas as to where the gold originated?" asked Jakob.

Magne was quick to reply. "It appears to be Russian. Though the bar itself is locked away in the *Falcon*'s safe, we sent along that photo of it to Oslo. Our friends in naval intelligence will know soon enough exactly where that gold originated."

"If it does turn out to be Russian, I wonder if we'll have to return it to them?" reflected Arne.

The phone inside the chamber began ringing, and it was Magne who explained the nature of this call. "I believe your associate's on the line for you from Rjukan, gentlemen."

"Damn, it's Knut!" exclaimed Jon as he sprang for the receiver.

Both Jakob and Arne anxiously gathered around the phone as Jon initiated an intense conversation.

"What do you mean, they're both dead?" questioned the astounded photographer. ". . . Why that's simply horrible, Knut. Are you going to be okay? . . . No, you shouldn't leave until the doctors allow you. A concussion can be serious business . . . I understand, Knut. But your life is much more important than that damn heavy water. As soon as we're out of this decompression chamber, we'll be there, big fellow. That you can rely on. Just listen to those doctors and be cool. The police will find the bastards responsible, and then they'll rot in jail for the rest of their lives . . . I will, Knut. You know where to find us. Take care, my friend."

Jon thoughtfully hung up the receiver and looked up to meet the concerned stares of his teammates.

"My God, Knut's in the hospital at Rjukan with a concussion, and both his cousin Lars and friend Thor have been found shot to death!"

This surprise revelation drew David Lawton from his bunk, as the shocked photographer continued. "They had just finished bringing up the rest of the heavy water; and were waiting for morning to transfer the drums to the warehouse when a group of armed men broke into the trawler. Both Lars and Thor were apparently forced at gunpoint to load the heavy water onto a truck, while Knut was pistol-whipped inside the trawler's auxiliary cabin. When he eventually snapped back to consciousness, not only did he find the thirty-three drums of heavy water gone, but the bodies of Lars and Thor as well. Both had been shot a single time in the back of the head, and were long dead by the time the first ambulance got there."

"Oh, that's horrible!" managed Jakob.

"Will Knut be okay?" quizzed Arne.

Jon shook his head. "I hope to God he will, Arne. Fortunately, the big guy's tough, though he's really taking the news of the shootings badly. He feels personally responsible, and was carrying on about sneaking out of the hospital and tracking down the murderers himself."

"That would be a big mistake," interjected David Lawton. "The police are the ones that are best prepared to handle such a dangerous investigation. Your friend will only be interfering, and also very possibly putting his life needlessly on the line."

"Try to tell that to Knut," retorted Jon. "He's already made some calls to his local network of friends and family in the Telemark region. If those cold-blooded bastards are still anywhere in the area, Knut will soon know about it."

A moment of thoughtful silence was broken by the return of Magne's solemn image to the video monitor.

"I just heard what happened to Knut, gentlemen. I want you to know that I'm deeply sorry, and that Noroil won't rest until the ones responsible for this heinous crime are brought to justice. We'll be sending in a specialist from Oslo shortly to have a personal look at Knut's injuries. Since this is a company matter now, our internal security division will be getting involved. You can rest assured that

139

once your decompression is completed, one of our choppers will be available to convey you to Rjukan if you so desire. Meanwhile, I'd better let you in on some other important news that just arrived. The *Falcon* has been ordered to proceed north with all due haste. It seems that the new Ice Field's production rig, that was being towed to the waters off Svalbard, has hit some heavy seas. It's in danger of capsizing, and the *Falcon* has been called in to stabilize it. So just hang in there, Gentlemen, while we pull anchor and get some steam up. We'll be relaying to you position updates as they're available."

With this the monitor went blank, and for several seconds the group of divers continued staring at the empty screen, their shocked thoughts still focused on their wounded colleague, the senseless deaths of his friends, the stolen heavy water, and the type of sick individual that could be responsible for such a heinous thing.

Charles Kromer looked up expectantly from the book he had been reading when the Braathens Safe Boeing 737's 'fasten seat belt' sign activated with a distinctive chime. The forty-six year old former West German naval officer was a veteran traveller, who long ago learned to always keep his seat belt fastened during a flight. Thus he only had to pull it a bit tighter around his lower waist as the plane began its descent into Svalbard's Longyearben airport.

Kromer wasn't surprised to learn that it had been the Norsemen who made the first mention of this isolated archipelago back in 1194 A.D. Four centuries later, while looking for the fabled shortcut to

China, two boats under the command of Willem Barents sighted a land of snowcapped mountain peaks which they called Spitsbergen. Today this collection of frozen islands was known as Svalbard, with Spitsbergen being the name of its largest island. Situated in the Artic Ocean, Svalbard was only 10 degrees and four hundred nautical miles from the North Pole. With a total landmass of 23,958 square miles, it was one-fifth the size of Norway, its mother country.

Because of its strategic location, it had been a jumping off place for many hopeful Arctic explorers. This long list included Salomon Andree, a Swede who in 1897 tried to get to the North Pole by means of a balloon, and died on one of Svalbard's frozen fjords. Twelve years later, the American Walter Wellman attempted to fly to the Pole from Svalbard. He too crashed on the way to his elusive goal, but was rescued by a group of Norwegians from Tromso.

Svalbard was covered by immense glaciers and towering mountain peaks. It had no indigenous population, and was instead permanently settled by a handful of hearty Norwegians and Russians, who worked its many coal mines. Other Europeans also had a small stake in the hunt for this valuable fuel, as did the German consortium with whom Charles Kromer was currently affiliated. Still undiscovered by tourists, Svalbard was a relatively pristine wilderness, much of which was still uncharted.

Anxious to see such a place with his own eyes, Kromer closed his book and peeked out the window as the plane lowered its landing gear and began its final approach. Only a few years ago, this landing would have been on the frozen tundra itself. The asphalt runway was a recent addition, as was the terminal building that they were next bound for.

There were only a handful of passengers on the plane, and Kromer exited quickly via the rear stairway. As he climbed down onto the tarmac, briefly halting at the bottom of the ramp, he looked out to survey the surrounding landscape. A range of black, snow-capped mountains met his eyes. They had a stark, foreboding quality to them, and Kromer knew without a doubt that this was the most unique place that he had ever visited. Feeling as if he had just arrived on an alien planet, he made his way to the nearby terminal.

A stern-faced Norwegian policeman stood immediately outside the modern terminal structure, carefully scrutinizing each of the new arrivals. There were no formal customs' personnel on the island, and it was up to this individual to spot any potential troublemakers. Kromer looked him right in the eye and passed inside without incident.

Next to the baggage claim area the former German naval officer spotted a young, blond-haired man dressed in blue coveralls, holding a sign that read, *Rio de la Plata Coal Co*. Kromer went up to him and spoke casually.

"There'll be one going to North Cape."

"Very good, sir," returned the young man politely. "If you'll give me your claim check, I'll take care of the bags. The van is just outside, in the holding area."

Kromer handed over his claim check and gratefully left the assemblage of noisy passengers who had gathered here. He zipped up the collar of his parka, put on his mittens and woolen cap, and headed out the exitway. The quiet was immediate as

142

he stepped outdoors, the air brisk and fresh.

He stretched deeply, and turned around when he heard voices behind him. The other passengers were leaving the terminal, the majority of whom got into a large, yellow bus that took up much of the holding area. Behind this crowd followed his driver. He pushed a large push cart in front of him that was packed with an assortment of cardboard cases and wooden crates. On the very top of this heap was Kromer's battered seabag. By the time the veteran climbed into the van's front passenger seat, his driver had neatly stacked this baggage inside, and soon they were on their way.

A narrow asphalt roadway led from the airport. To the right were the mournful mountains, to the left the gray waters of Advent Bay. Several piers jutted out into this broad expanse of water. Massive piles of coal were heaped up beside these piers, along with the equipment needed to load it into a ship's hold. Assorted clapboard buildings and steel warehouses did little to distract from the area's remoteness.

"Do you get into Longyearben often, young man?" questioned Kromer in an effort to get a conversation going.

"Approximately once a week, sir," replied his driver. "And that's usually just to pick up our mail and basic foodstuffs."

"Well, it sure doesn't look like much of a settlement," observed Kromer.

"Don't let this portion of town fool you, sir. Up in Longyear valley there are some very nice accommodations. Over a thousand people live there all year round, and they have a really nice community center with a cinema, a restaurant, school, church, and several large meeting rooms for community functions."

"Will we be passing this facility?" asked Kromer.

"I'm afraid not. We're headed straight for the central wharf."

Established originally as a coal town, Longyearben was founded in 1905 by John Longyear of Boston. In 1916 Norway bought the mines from him, and had since produced over 14 million tons of coal.

"I understand that you were formerly the commanding officer of the Emden," remarked the driver a bit shyly. "You wouldn't happen to know my brother, Hans Schmidt, would you, sir?"

"Ensign Schmidt was my weapons officer for over a half dozen patrols," revealed Kromer, who half grinned. "You wouldn't happen to be that kid brother of his who went off and joined the merchant marine at the age of seventeen?"

"That's me all right," the driver admitted proudly. "But I've settled down since then. I've been with Rio de la Plata for over a year now."

"Your brother always spoke very highly of you, lad."

"That's nice to hear, sir," said the driver as he turned off the roadway and guided the van into a complex filled with various warehouses. "It's because of Hans that I ran off to sea. How's he doing, anyway?"

"The last I heard was that he'll be a duly qualified submariner by the years end, lad. He's a hard worker, and if he continues to do as well, he'll have a full career just like I had."

"Was it tough leaving the fleet, sir?" dared the driver.

Kromer shook his head. "I put in my twenty years and then some, lad. It was time for a change of scenery."

"Well, you'll have plenty of that, sir. Wait till you see these mountains in the daylight. It's like nothing you've ever dreamed of before."

A narrow alleyway led to a spacious wharf area. Several large ships were docked there, including a good-sized modern warship.

"Is that a frigate?" asked the naval veteran from the passenger seat.

"That's the Norwegian Coast Guard cutter *Nordkapp*, sir. It just pulled in this afternoon. From what I hear, the ship is here on a routine patrol."

Kromer knew such cutters to be extremely well equipped. Along with the various fishery, law enforcement, and rescue functions, the Norwegian Coast Guard also provided coastal defense in times of war. Much like a frigate, such cutters could also be used to track down submarines, and were armed with a full assortment of depth charges and torpedoes to finish off the job.

"There's our ship, sir," observed the driver, as he pulled to a stop beside the dock's edge. Floating in the water was a sturdy, forty-ton vessel, about fifty-seven feet long, with the clean lines of a motor sailor.

"We call her the *Weser*, sir, after the river. She was originally a Norwegian rescue boat. Now she's completely equipped with automatic pilot, echo-sounder, direction finder, and radio telephone. Her 150-horsepower diesel puts out a smooth ten knots, and she even has 1,178 square feet of sail should a good breeze present itself."

The mere fact that this vessel once belonged to

145

the Norwegian rescue service spoke well for it. This exclusive outfit was an all-volunteer force that sailed the coast of Norway in search of boats in trouble. Since they sailed in even the worst of gales, their equipment was some of the best ever made. Thus Kromer wasn't really worried about the hundred mile journey through ice-infested waters that still lay before them.

Kromer wasted no time boarding the ship, where he was intercepted by a short, wire-haired old salt with a game leg.

"Welcome aboard the *Weser*," he greeted in Norwegian-flavored German. "I am Captain Hansen. Herr Kromer?"

The newcomer nodded and Hansen led him to a small cabin. It was immaculate, and the former submarine commander knew that he was in the hands of expert mariners.

"When do we get started?" he questioned.

"As soon as the baggage is stowed away," returned Captain Hansen.

Kromer stifled a yawn, and the *Weser*'s observant Captain was quick to add, "I'm certain that you've journeyed far today. I've taken the liberty of preparing a stateroom for you in the forward cabin. I'm certain that you'll find it cramped but comfortable."

"That's very thoughtful of you, Captain," said Kromer, who once again tried not to yawn.

"Would you like something to eat first?" asked the Norwegian.

"Thank you, but that won't be necessary, Captain. Right now, that bunk sounds awfully inviting."

"Well in that case, follow me and I'll show you the way. Soon we will be on our way to North Cape."

The stateroom that Charles Kromer soon found himself in was more than sufficient. It was over twice the size of his cramped cabin on the *Emden,* and had a bunk bed, a desk, chair, and a small wash basin.

To the chugging sound of the boat's diesel engine, Kromer removed his shirt and went over to the basin to wash up. It felt good to bathe his face in hot water, and as he reached up to dry himself, he caught his reflection in the round mirror that was mounted beside the towel rack. His dark eyes were bloodshot, and had noticeable fatigue lines beneath them. His once jet-black hair seemed to have more gray in it than ever before. Thankful that he kept it regularly trimmed in a short crew cut, he scratched his square jaw, decided to wait until later to shave, and turned for his bunk.

By the time he was stripped down to his skivvies, they were out to sea. As he lay on his back, with the fjord's gentle swells rocking him to and fro, the veteran mentally visualized the route they would now be following. The *Weser* would leave Advent Bay and head due west down Ice Fjord. Soon the Russian coal town of Barentsberg would pass to their port and the boat would turn to the north, following the irregular coast of Spitsbergen to its northernmost extremity. Here they'd turn to the east for the final leg of their journey.

All too soon these same waters would be choked in impenetrable ice. Such a trip would be impossible then, and would have to be accomplished by long-range helicopter. Glad to be travelling by way of his old friend the sea, Charles Kromer closed his eyes and drifted off into a deep, dreamless sleep that lasted nearly eight hours.

He was jarred awake when a series of massive swells smashed into the boat's hull. Nearly thrown out of his bunk by the force of these waves, Kromer did his best to stand and dress himself. With the deck rolling wildly beneath him, he decided to forget about trying to shave. Merely walking was difficult enough as he left his stateroom and entered the main cabin. A bald seaman was seated at the table here, calmly chewing away on a piece of raw herring and onion, while loose gear rattled away on the deck beneath him.

"Hello, sir," greeted the weather-beaten seaman with a gravelly voice. "Would you like some breakfast?"

Kromer was beginning to feel a bit seasick and graciously declined this offer. "Where can I find Captain Hansen?" he asked.

"The skipper's up in the wheelhouse with the ice pilot," answered the seaman, who was also the *Weser*'s cook. "Perhaps I can whip you up some bacon and eggs."

Kromer shook his head. "Maybe in a little while, my friend. Right now, I'd just like to have a few words with the Captain."

The cook shrugged his skinny shoulders and went back to his meal, as Kromer crossed the constantly pitching deck like a drunken sailor on shore leave. He reached the shut hatch, and made certain that his oilskin was zipped up securely before ducking outside.

The morning sun hung low in the blue sky and did little to counter the freezing gusts of wind that whipped over the ice-coated deck. Extra careful to keep a secure handhold, he began his way up the semi-enclosed stairwell that led directly to the wheel-

...use. He gratefully ducked inside this compact, ...ell-heated compartment that was dominated by a ...rap-around windshield and a modern control console. Seated before this console was the ship's captain and an alert, broad-shouldered young man who currently had the *Weser*'s helm. A taut steel cable crossed the width of the cabin behind them, and it was on this object that Kromer steadied himself.

"I see that we have a bit of a swell this morning, Captain," observed Kromer as he tightly gripped the shoulder-high cable with both hands.

Captain Hansen replied without diverting his glance from the windshield. "This is nothing, Herr Kromer. You should see these waters when a real gale is blowing. Why, just to remain seated in our chairs, we are forced to utilize our harness mechanisms. I hope that your quarters were sufficient. I'd like you to meet the *Weser*'s ice pilot, Sigurd Bjornsen."

The hefty young Norwegian nodded curtly, all the while keeping his line of sight focused on the waters before them. Charles Kromer peered out the windshield himself and immediately spotted the huge floes of fractured ice that were a deadly hazard.

"I'm surprised that these waters are even passable at this time of the year," remarked Kromer.

"They won't be much longer," returned the ice pilot with a grunt.

"This will most probably be the last trip of the season," added Captain Hansen. "The lead that we're currently following is a result of our closeness to the coastline. Further out to sea, the ice pack is solid, and only specially designed vessels can transit it."

A monstrous berg of ice, many times larger than

149

the *Weser*, passed by them to the starboard, a~~n~~
Kromer shuddered to think that nine-tenths of th~~e~~
giant was still hidden beneath the water. Still more
bergs followed, yet the ice pilot didn't actually pull
back on the boat's dual throttle until they spotted a
nearly solid field of ice up ahead. A constant moan-
ing, creaking groan accompanied this floe and they
inched forward. A splintering crunch announced
their first contact with it.

Sigurd Bjornsen seemed unaffected by the steady
grinding noise of the ice that sounded above that of
the *Weser*'s engines. With an expertise developed
after many years of experience, the Norwegian
steered them through the thinnest portion of the
floe with a minimum of backtracking.

"At least we don't have any fog to contend with,"
offered the boat's captain. He watched the ice pilot
expertly steer them into an open lead of gray water.
"Then Sigurd would really have to earn his paycheck."

The ice pilot grunted again and reached forward
to reopen the throttles. Soon the solid flow was behind them, and Kromer noted that even the seas
themselves were calmer here, especially when the
Captain took the wheel and rerouted their previously north-easterly course to the south.

A series of jagged black peaks formed the shoreline of the fjord that they soon entered. The wind
had long since dissipated, and the sparkling, mirror-
like waters were calm as a lake.

"You can see our destination just up ahead of us,
Herr Kromer," said the Captain. "On the western
shore of the fjord, beyond that flashing beacon."

Charles Kromer looked in the direction that the
captain was now pointing and easily spotted the

150

beacon Hansen had mentioned. It took a bit more searching on his part to pick out the actual settlement. Set at the foot of a mountainous ridge was a barely visible collection of man-made structures that made the remote outpost of Longyearben look like a bustling metropolis by comparison.

As they continued their approach, Kromer identified the settlement's dock area, that wasn't much more than a wooden wharf with several mounds of coal heaped beside it. A single road led from this pier, passing half a dozen white-washed, two-story structures that appeared to be dormitories. Other than several corrugated steel warehouses, this seemed to be the extent of the town.

As they passed by the beacon, the *Weser's* captain pointed almost reverently to a single cottage that stood on the summit of a steep ridge of solid rock, that dropped straight down to the waters of the fjord below.

"That's the Director's cottage," he proudly revealed. "They say that its interior is furnished just like a Bavarian hunting lodge. Unfortunately, I've never been invited there to see for myself if this is true. Perhaps you will be luckier."

"Perhaps I will," mumbled Kromer as he peered up at the sturdy A-frame structure that overlooked the majestic fjord and the settlement of North Cape down below.

Kromer left the confines of the wheelhouse and headed toward the foredeck as they prepared to dock. The air was cold and invigorating, and because the winds were gone, easily bearable. Several dockhands could be seen on the wharf. A large flag, fluttering from a tall metal pole, showed the earth with a golden star crowning the North Pole. The

151

submariner had seen this pennant before, and knew very well that it represented the German-Argentinian consortium that had bought this coal settlement from a Dutch concern over half a century ago.

He couldn't help but grin as he scanned the dock and spotted a tall, fair-haired, middle-aged man in a long navy peacoat. Quick to also spot Kromer, this figure waved and called out in greeting.

"Welcome to North Cape, Captain!"

Charles Kromer waited to respond until the boat reached the dock. The deckhands officially secured the *Weser,* and as he climbed onto solid land, Kromer accepted his welcomer's firm handshake.

"It's good to see you again, Senior Lieutenant Kurtz," said Kromer warmly. "It's been much too long."

"It will be one year exactly this January," replied the former West German naval officer with a smile.

"Well, is civilian life all that it's cracked up to be?" asked Kromer with a wink.

"I guess you'll soon enough find out for yourself, eh, Captain?" returned Hans Kurtz who added. "Do you have much luggage?"

"Only my seabag," answered Kromer.

"Then let me get it for you, and we can get going. The Director wants to see you at once."

In a matter of minutes Kromer's seabag was stowed away inside the boot of their black Rover, and they were on their way down the settlement's only road.

"That's some sea voyage from Longyearben, isn't it Captain?" quizzed Kurtz as he guided the vehicle past the collection of dormitories.

"That it is, my friend. Though I must admit that I slept through much of it. Those Norwegian rescue boats are solidly built, and my accommodations were surely more luxurious than aboard the Emden."

A grin turned the corners of Kurtz's mouth at the mention of this sub. "She may have been a bit cramped, but the old lady was really something special. Are any of the old crew still aboard, Captain?"

"The gang is long gone, Hans. Since you mustered out, the others followed in quick succession. Even Chief Dortmund left me. Though your replacements may have been young and bright, there seemed to be something lacking in their characters. Why, the majority of this new generation of submariners doesn't even know what it means to be a real German anymore."

"I'm sorry to hear that," replied Kurtz as he guided the Rover up into the surrounding hills.

Charles Kromer took advantage of the moment of reflective silence that followed to absorb the passing landscape. The road on which they drove had obviously been laid out originally for the coal mines that were dug into this ridge. He counted over a half dozen of them, all of which were currently boarded up. The very nature of this work caused a perpetual sifting of black dust to settle on the rock and snow here. But, in a way, this shroud seemed to fit well with the stark, treeless ridge that they continued to climb.

A switchback finally led to the summit of this ridge, and Kromer set his eyes on the A-frame cottage that he had seen from the boat. This structure looked much larger from this vantage point, and as the Rover pulled up in front of it, he saw that it had been built out of whole tree trunks. A trace of smoke curled from its stone chimney, while a massive rack of antlers was mounted above the door mantle.

Hans Kurtz put the vehicle into neutral, and without turning off the ignition, turned to address his passenger. "Well, good luck, Captain. I'm certain that you'll find the Director as full of life and feisty as ever. He's really something for a man in his seventies."

"You're not coming in with me, Hans?"

"This audience is all yours, Captain. We'll be together again soon enough — and then we can really talk about the old days."

A bit confused by the arrangements, Kromer questioned, "But where are our facilities, Hans? I thought that the meeting was to take place there."

A devilish gleam flashed in Kurtz's eyes, and his answer was evasive. "You'll be seeing what this whole operation is about in good time, Captain. Now, you don't want to keep the Director waiting for you, do you?"

Kromer realized that he wasn't going to be getting any answers from this end. Anxious to learn exactly what was going on here, he left the Rover and walked up to the entrance of the cottage. The door was fashioned from a huge slab of highly polished wood, and had an iron knocker in the shape of a wolf's head. Kromer rapped three times, and didn't have to wait long until it swung open, revealing a shapely blond woman in a white servant's uniform.

"Good morning, Herr Kromer," she said in perfect German. "We've been expecting you." Smiling, she beckoned him to enter.

From the moment he stepped inside the foyer, it

154

seemed as if he were magically transported back to the Bavarian foothills of his birth. Panelled completely in polished oak, the hallway was crowded with familiar bric-a-brac that included an authentic German cuckoo clock, a rack of stag horns, and an assortment of beautifully framed photographs of various alpine scenes. Several exquisite Dresden plates were also hung there, along with a collection of hand-carved walking sticks. The stirring strains of a Prussian calvary march could be heard in the background. Kromer readily followed the young woman further into the cottage's interior.

The room that he next entered was breathtaking. A solid wall of glass allowed a magnificent view of the sparkling waters of the fjord. Glacier capped mountains could be seen in the distance, glistening beneath the rays of the rising sun. Two high-backed leather chairs sat in the middle of the carpeted room, turned so that they could take full advantage of the spectacular vista. Beside these chairs was a bronze telescope on a tripod. A stone fireplace with a blazing fire dominated one end of the room, and a well-stocked library stood on the opposite side.

The Prussian calvary music that he had heard came from four elevated speakers, strategically mounted in each of the room's corners. Kromer recognized the piece as the Fehrbellin calvary march. Certainly never expecting to hear such inspiring music in this isolated location, he handed the young servant his jacket and gloves. As she left the room, he took a position beside the fireplace. With his gaze still riveted on the extraordinary view, he wondered when his host would join him. Thus, he was taken completely by surprise when one of the high-

155

backed chairs began to turn. Seated here all the time, with his line of sight also turned to the fjord and the mountains beyond, was the so-called Director of the Rio de la Plata coal company's North Cape operation: Herr Otto Koch.

The bald septuagenerian faced his newly arrived guest and slowly stood. There was genuine delight in the old man's wrinkled face as he removed his monocle and straightened his black ascot and red velvet smoking jacket.

"Captain Kromer, how very good it is to see you once again. Welcome to my humble abode here on the top of the world. I do hope that your trip was a smooth one."

"It was well worth the effort, just to see your face once more, Herr Koch," returned Kromer as he stepped forward to take his host's firm, warm handshake.

As the two embraced, they were joined by a fully grown, black German shepherd. The dog seemed jealous of the attention that his master was displaying toward this stranger, and did his best to get between them.

"Come now, Beowulf," admonished Koch. "I imagine that you too would like to meet my good friend, Charles Kromer."

As the dog obediently sat, Kromer bent down to greet it. "Hello, Beowulf."

The German shepherd instantly offered its paw, which Kromer took in his hand and lightly shook.

"It's a pleasure meeting you too, Beowulf," mocked Kromer.

"How very unusual. He seems to genuinely like you," observed Otto Koch. "And don't think that Beowulf offers his paw to just anyone. On the contrary. That dog's been with me for over a decade, and I can count on one hand the number of strangers he's taken to so readily."

While playfully scratching the shepherd's ears, Kromer replied. "I once had a dog much like Beowulf, when I was a lad growing up in Munich. I called him Fritz, and we were the best of friends. What wonderful hikes in the woods we had together."

"There's nothing like a good German shepherd if you want a loyal companion," said Koch. "Old Beowulf first came to me as a pup, when I was living in Paraguay. He seemed to love the South American jungle, though this cold weather seems to suit him much better. The only trouble is that now he has no more jungle creatures to play with."

"I don't suppose that polar bears make very good playmates," returned Kromer.

His host grinned. "No they don't, Captain. Now please have a seat. Perhaps you'll be so good as to join me for some tea."

Without waiting for a response, Koch clapped his hands two times and called out lightly, "Lottie, we'll have our tea now."

By the time the two were settled in their chairs, the serving girl appeared pushing a silver cart, which she positioned between them. The cart was filled with assorted pastries and finger sandwiches.

"I do hope that you had some of that delicious black forest ham left, Lottie," anticipated Koch.

"There was just enough for two sandwiches, sir," returned the servant politely. "I also included several filled with smoked Arctic char, norwegian salmon, and of course, your favorite braunschweiger. The

157

tea is jasmine, and there's some peppermint schnapps on the lower shelf."

"Wonderful, Lottie," said Koch. "It seems you've managed to once again make do in this frozen wilderness just as if you were back home in Stuttgart. You're a gem, my dear."

The servant blushed with this unexpected compliment, and left after pouring their tea.

"If I was only a few years younger," whispered Koch as he watched the shapely woman exit. "But now it seems that the only thing which gives me real physical pleasure is my appetite. Now, I insist that you try some of that ham, and then you must take one of those pastries. They're Sacher tortes, flown in all the way from Vienna."

"You don't have to twist my arm," said Charles Kromer as he reached for a plate. "I haven't eaten since I was on the plane last night, and that was somewhere over northern Norway."

He chose a ham sandwich and one filled with bright orange salmon and creamed cheese. Otto Koch also picked the ham, though his other selection was the braunschweiger, of which he took two. One of these smoked liverwurst sandwiches he fed to Beowulf, while the other he kept for himself.

"My, this ham is delicious," admitted Kromer between bites.

"I told you that you wouldn't be disappointed," reminded his host, who was working away on his braunschweiger.

As the two ate, the boat on which Charles Kromer had arrived could be seen leaving on the waters below. Otto Koch pointed to the sturdy craft and commented.

"Ah, there goes the *Weser* back to Longyearben.

I'm afraid that's the last we'll see of her until the spring thaw."

"So I understand," replied Kromer. "The ice is already closing in, and it was a challenge just to round North Cape."

Otto Koch took a sip of tea and caught his guest's eye. "We're only expecting one more surface vessel before we close our dock for the season. This ship will be coming in from Tromso in another three days. After that, our only contact with the outside world will be by helicopter. Of course, we could always utilize the services of a vessel that could go under the ice."

Charles Kromer took this as the hint it was meant to be and put down the tea cup that he had been drinking from. "Herr Koch, please excuse me if I'm speaking out of line, but I was expecting to find much different facilities here. Has there been a change in plans of which I wasn't informed, or perhaps the pen is located somewhere else?"

"Whatever makes you say that?" asked the old man, who flashed the same devilish expression that his ex-shipmate Hans Kurtz had displayed earlier. "I don't mean to keep you intentionally in the dark, Captain. The time will soon be right for me to reveal our entire operation. But until then, relax, enjoy the food, and know that even as we speak, our great dream is one step closer to its ultimate realization."

"But where in the world is U-3313?" blurted Kromer passionately. "After all, isn't that why I've been called here?"

Otto Koch put down his plate and smiled. "I admire your straightforwardness, Captain. It is a trait that many would do well to learn. But in this in-

159

stance, I assure you that your concerns are totally unnecessary. U-3313 is closer to you than you would ever dream possible. I am proud to report that its refitting is proceeding right on schedule. The necessary parts and personnel have been arriving since summer, and by the time the final piece of the puzzle is conveyed here, your new command will be seaworthy."

"Is this missing element the gold?" guessed Kromer.

Otto Koch shook his head. "No it isn't, Captain. The gold you speak of is already safely stored within the U-boat's hull."

The look of relief that crossed Kromer's face did not go unnoticed, and his host couldn't help but gloat. "Yes, Captain, the fabled treasure of the Czars is now ours. Its salvage by mini-sub from the hull of U-3312 went off with only a single hitch. That occurred when one of our overly zealous divers apparently dropped one of the bars into the sunken U-boat's pressure hull. But that's of little concern, because the other 499 bars were successfully pulled from the wreck. At today's market price, that's the equivalent of over $62,500,000 American dollars!"

His wrinkled face flashed with excitement, and Koch added in a calmer tone. "Fifty years ago, when I was but a young SS lieutenant, who was fortunate enough to be the one who stumbled upon this treasure, little did I ever dream what would become of it. Did I ever share with you the long chain of events that followed the gold's capture?"

As Kromer shook his head that he hadn't, Otto Koch sat back and reflectively commented, "Then do bear with me, Captain, and I will tell you a story whose author was destiny itself."

Charles Kromer put down his teacup and settled into his chair. His host began the tale.

"The actual capture of the train carrying the gold, and the battle with the fanatical band of Soviet soldiers sent along to protect it has already been well documented. What has escaped the history books, though, is what happened to the treasure once it was in our hands. The SS unit, of which I was fortunate enough to be a member, was a unique squad of handpicked soldiers, whose sworn allegiance was not to the Fuhrer in Berlin, but to the very principles that created the Nazi movement. You see, from the very beginning, there were many in the military hierarchy that had serious doubts that Adolf Hitler was the right man to lead Germany onward to the thousand year Reich. In the end we were proven right, but until that time came, we were forced to play the roles of traitors.

"When the gold came into our possession, it was decided to keep its presence a sworn secret, known only to those who participated in its capture. We therefore clandestinely transferred it to a holding cache outside the occupied Russian city of Tallinin. The gold was to act as an emergency reserve that we could draw upon in the event that Hitler fell from power or was assassinated.

"You might say that we saw the writing on the wall as early as 1940, when our esteemed Fuhrer first began his lofty plans for the invasion of the Soviet Union, or Operation Barbarossa, as it was called. There were many of us in the military who knew that such an invasion had no chance to succeed and would only doom our cause. We lobbied

161

for concentrating our forces against the real enemy, Britain and its lackey, the United States. Yet on June 22, 1941, when the first of our troops crossed into Soviet territory, Germany began the long, bloody road to its ultimate defeat

"To insure that the Aryan Reich could outlive its flawed leader, we eventually moved the gold to Finland. With the invaluable assistance of a squad of Gebirgsjager, the treasure was loaded onto a convoy made of mules and reindeer. The brave men of our Alpine elite fought off cold and hunger, to finally make it to Norway. This was our true Nordic fortress, where we patiently awaited the inevitable.

"Our only hope then was that the weapon that was to be known as the atomic bomb would be perfected by our scientists in time to influence the outcome of the war. Our famed atomic physicist Dr. Bernard Kessler was the Reich's foremost proponent of this superweapon. Yet when Hitler and his twisted cronies continued cutting Kessler's research budgets, the desperate scientist came to us in Norway. We instantly gave him our support, yet the sinking of the ferry *Hydro,* and the loss of the entire existing stock of Norwegian heavy water, signalled the end of Kessler's immediate dreams. In May of 1945, he was still with us in Bergen as we set sail for South America, to plan the Reich's rebirth.

"At the same time that Grand Admiral Donitz ordered the U-boat fleet to unconditionally surrender in total shame, the two Type XXI U-boats that we had under our control set sail. U-3312 was packed with the gold and was sent off to follow us to South America. Meanwhile, U-3313 was sent in the opposite direction. Foreseeing Germany's defeat, we prepared a secret sub pen here in Svalbard. It was in

162

this ingeniously designed structure that U-3313 was subsequently hidden and mothballed, to await the call to arms once more."

Halting a moment to catch his breath, Otto Koch reached down to scratch the top of his dog's head. His rapt listener remained spellbound, and the old-timer sat back to continue.

"The rest as you say is history. U-3312 hit an old World War I mine off the Norwegian island of Utsira, and sank with the subsequent loss of most of its crew and all of the gold. Because the sub sank to a depth that was at that time deemed unsalvage-able, we decided to let it stay there. If we couldn't touch it, no one else could either, and at a depth of 283 meters it was surely safer than a Swiss bank account."

"One thing still puzzles me, Herr Koch," interrupted his guest. "Why have you waited until now to act? Surely you didn't have to wait until this moment to recover the gold and put your plan into action."

"You are correct, Captain. But the success of our dream depends on many different variables. We received our first hint that the time was upon us when the recent troubles in East Germany began. As the old communist hardliners fell from power, a more moderate group of leaders took their place. The wall that has divided East and West is no longer. Today's young Germans realize the folly of their fathers' selfish ways. Thus the fodder for the new, united Aryan nation already exists. All it needs is a spark to ignite it."

"And just what will this spark be?" quizzed Kromer breathlessly.

Otto Koch's eyes glistened as he answered.

163

"Though Dr. Kessler is long in his grave, before he died he was able to pass on the secrets of the A-bomb to a group of fellow physicists who accompanied us. These individuals have since trained a whole new generation of scientists, who have established a firm foothold in Argentina's fledgling atomic energy program. Only recently have they been able to amass enough uranium fuel to make an actual atomic weapon possible. All that they lack is the moderator to control the reaction.

"Several weeks ago, in a totally unrelated incident, a group of Norwegian divers announced their plans to salvage the heavy water that had been on its way to Berlin in January 1944 to act as this very moderator. When I learned that this same heavy water could be used to actually complete our first atomic device, I realized that this was the sign that I had been waiting for."

"But how are we ever going to be able to get our hands on such a precious substance?" questioned Kromer.

Otto Koch had tears of excitement in his eyes as he replied. "What do you think is in the hold of that cargo ship I mentioned was due here within the next seventy-two hours? Don't you see, Captain? We've already got it!"

Shocked by this revelation, Kromer sat forward. "Are you saying that the heavy water is on its way right now to Svalbard?"

"Yes, I am, Captain, and it will be stored alongside the 499 bars of gold, to be conveyed under your command to Argentina's Rio de la Plata. Here it will be transferred onto a freighter, and sent up the Parana River, to our secret jungle compound where the bomb will be constructed. Then, with

164

his weapon and a fortune in gold to finance us, the Reich shall be reborn, to cleanse a corrupt world that is destined to destroy itself."

Charles Kromer shook his head in wonder. "I had no idea that the organization was so far advanced. Why this whole thing is incredible!"

"I knew you'd be thrilled," admitted the old Nazi. "During our past meetings, your enthusiasm never failed to impress me. So Captain, do you think that you made the right choice in taking an early retirement from the navy to join us at this critical time?"

"Of course I do!" shot back Kromer. "This is the culmination of my every dream. Just to know that you are trusting me on this all-important mission makes my entire life to this point worth the effort."

Otto Koch slyly chuckled. "Don't think that it was merely the hand of fate that led you to our cause during the early days of your naval training. I had been watching you for many years before that, Captain. Of course you know of your parentage?"

Kromer hesitated a moment before responding. "I was born in Westphalia on December 12, 1945. My mother's family name was Hecht. Since I was conceived at a Lebensborne, my father could have been any number of SS officers who were sent there for the express purposes of propagation."

Otto Koch listened to these words and fought back a sudden wave of emotion. "You are the living proof that the so-called 'fountains of life' were among the noblest elements of Hitler's Germany. It is because of the state-controlled breeding establishment in which you were conceived that pure Aryan blood flows through your veins. Knowing this, we watched you since youth, and were always there in the background to subtly point you on the right

165

path when the time of choice was upon you. You can be proud to know that in your case, our interference was at a bare minimum. What you have already accomplished you have done alone. Of this fact you can be certain."

There was a truth to these words that affected Kromer deeply. And at that moment, he felt closer to Otto Koch than he had to any other male in his entire lifetime. Not the type who cried easily, Kromer nevertheless felt tears beginning to sting his eyes as he expressed his deepest thoughts.

"It is an honor and a privilege to be a part of this organization. The principles that you stand for are exactly my own. I, too, have watched modern civilization progressively edge its way to the apocalypse, and unless we Aryans take our rightful places as supreme leaders, this planet is doomed to destruction, for we are the only force pure enough to counter the corrupt Jewish/Catholic cabal currently leading this world to ruin. Their money-hungry greed must be stopped at all cost! We must also act at once to halt the deplorable mixing of the races. The blood pools of black and white must be kept segregated. Otherwise the black race will drag us down to their animalistic level, and our future generations will be no better than the savages of the jungle.

"All my life I have awaited the day when the Reich would rise once again. I always knew deep in my heart that our time was destined to be. Germany has already failed two times in this century in its attempt to lead the world to salvation. Yet we have learned from our past mistakes, and this third effort will be the one to gain the ultimate crown of power. I thus pledge my life's blood to this goal,

166

and thank you once again for giving me this opportunity to serve my people."

As Otto Koch absorbed these words, he found himself bursting with pride. Fighting an impulse to hug his guest, the old man reached instead for the crystal decanter that lay on the cart's bottom shelf. His hand shook slightly as he filled two small demitasse cups with schnapps. As he handed one of these to Kromer, he raised the other before him and toasted.

"To the Fatherland! And to the success of the Thousand Year Reich and the Aryan cause!"

His guest raised his cup and downed his drink in a single gulp. Otto Koch did likewise, and as the peppermint-flavored spirits burned his throat, he added, "Now Captain, how would you like to see the vessel that will allow our shared dreams to become a reality?"

Kromer's eyes opened wide as he replied. "I would like that more than anything in the world right now."

"Then follow this old man," said Koch as he stood stiffly.

Beowulf ran obediently to his side, and with the assistance of a hand-carved wooden walking stick, he began his way toward that portion of the room where the library was situated. Charles Kromer followed, and looked on as his host reached behind the carved coping of the bookcase set on the far right. Here he depressed a switch that caused the entire case to slide to the side with a loud hiss. Kromer was surprised to find an elevator hidden in the wall.

"Well Captain, here we go," said Koch, stepping inside the lift, along with his dog.

No sooner did Charles Kromer enter the elevator

167

when its doors shut and they quickly began to drop. Almost a full minute passed before it halted its descent.

The doors opened, and Kromer followed his host out onto an elevated platform that was attached directly into a perpendicular wall of solid rock. He was amazed to find himself inside a cavernous, hollowed out mountain. He audibly gasped upon spotting the brightly-lit object laying at the floor of this immense cavern, for sitting there in dry-dock, on a base of sturdy wooden trestles, was a Type XXI U-boat, whose streamlined surface was completely painted a glistening golden color. Dozens of workers busily milled around its sleek hull, while the blindingly bright flames of a welder's torch flashed from the vessel's stern, where its twin propellers could just be seen.

"It's absolutely magnificent!" exclaimed Kromer. "But why, may I ask, has it been painted gold? I thought the Type XXI's normal operational color was a dull silver."

"Normally it is, Captain. But recently our scientists came up with a revolutionary sonar absorbent coating, that just happened to turn this color when it was applied. So it isn't merely for the multi-million dollar treasure that's locked within U-3313's hull that the workers here call her 'The Golden U-Boat.' "

"The Golden U-Boat," repeated Kromer thoughtfully. "I like that name. Can I board her?"

Otto Koch shrugged his shoulders. "Who am I to tell this vessel's captain what he can or can not do? This submarine is under your command now, Captain Kromer. All that I ask is that she be ready for sea in seventy-two hours, when the rest of her vital cargo will be arriving. So by all means, go down and get to know her, my friend. Because it's now on your capable shoulders that the success of this entire operation now rests."

Chapter Seven

When Admiral Alexander Kuznetsov got the assignment from the Deputy Secretary General to survey the Norwegian gas pumping facility at Karsto, he could think of only one submarine to do the job. The *Lena* was a nuclear powered Alfa class attack vessel. It was small, fast, and manned by a skilled crew who wouldn't be intimidated by the dangerous penetration into shallow waters that such a mission would entail. And to insure that the job was done correctly, Alexander Kuznetsov decided to go along as a firsthand observer.

They set sail for Karsto from the Siberian naval base at Polyarny on a cold, overcast morning. Though Alexander had previously toured the *Lena* along with a group of Naval Ministry dignitaries, this would be the first time that he actually put to sea on the boat. No stranger to the workings of a submarine, the white-haired veteran had been confined to a desk for over a decade, and he looked upon this patrol as a chance to put some badly needed adventure back into a life that had become much too predictable.

As they entered the icy waters of the Barents Sea and descended to periscope depth, Alexander knew that his decision to come along had been the right one. The ship was a high-tech masterpiece, crewed by some of the most intelligent, hard-working sailors that he had ever known. This became obvious as he stood in the corner of the *Lena*'s attack center, watching its young commanding officer at work.

Captain Grigori Milyutin was only in his mid-thirties, yet had already distinguished himself as a skilled mariner. He was the type of leader that men respected. A graduate of the A.A. Grechko Naval Academy, Milyutin worked hard for his commission, graduating in the top five of his class. When asked by the examination board on what kind of vessel he'd like to serve the Rodina, the Kiev-native picked submarines without batting an eye.

Milyutin's first assignment had been as the weapons' officer of a Kilo class boat. Six months later, he was fully qualified, and his promotion to senior lieutenant was soon in coming. He distinguished himself when a fire broke out in the reactor room of a Victor class boat on which he was serving. When the captain of this attack sub was severely injured fighting this blaze, Grigori Milyutin calmly took his place in the control room, and it was said that it was because of his cool efforts alone that the crew was kept from panicking. Against all the odds, the crippled Victor made it back to port. When the naval inquiry into the incident was finally completed, Milyutin emerged with not only the Order of Lenin to pin to his chest, but a promotion to captain as well.

The *Lena* was the perfect size boat for the young officer to show Command his potential. Only eighty-one meters long and displacing a mere 2,900 tons, the Alfa class was the smallest nuclear powered sub in the fleet. Yet what it lacked in size, it more than made up for in speed, diving depth, and offensive punch.

The attack center that Alexander currently stood inside was a prime example of the *Lena*'s advanced design. In fact, the interior of this compartment looked more as if it belonged in a computer laboratory than on a warship. From their digital consoles, five senior ratings effectively ran all of the boat's operational functions. Old fashioned valves and gauges had long since been replaced by computer keyboards. Even the planesman's traditional brass wheel, by which the sub was steered, was now but a joystick.

Alexander knew that this automation was vitally necessary here, for the *Lena* only had a crew of forty-five. Over two decades ago, he had participated in the program from which the Alfa class was born. At that time, they had been looking for a submarine that could successfully penetrate an American carrier task force. To accomplish this difficult mission, a small, compact vessel was envisioned that could attain such high speeds that even the most advanced western ASW weapon couldn't touch it.

A specially designed nuclear reactor that employed a lead-bizmuth mixture as a coolant was developed, producing speeds well over forty knots. This was over ten knots faster than any other submarine could travel, and was incorporated with yet another novel feature that made the Alfa a class unto itself.

Until this time, high-tensile steel was the state of the art when it came to producing the actual pressure hull of a submarine. Such a construction method allowed depths of up to one thousand feet to be attained. But this was not good enough for the Alfa, whose hull was formed out of titanium, giving it a diving depth of three thousand feet, over three times deeper than any other sub.

Alexander had been at Leningrad's Sudomekh shipyard when the first Alfa class prototype was launched. Many of the old admirals present at the ceremony had commented on how very small and puny the vessel looked. Concerned that the billions of rubles it had cost to develop this prototype had been wasted, they anxiously awaited the results of the first sea trials.

A collective sigh of relief echoed through the halls of the Naval Ministry as the first reports from the Baltic were received. On its very first high-speed run, the boat reached 42 knots, with the captain commenting that the throttle hadn't even been completely engaged!

Unfortunately, the sub was later to experience serious cracking in its welded titanium joints, causing the trials to be abandoned. Undaunted by this failure, the engineers went back to their drawing boards, and soon the welding problems were solved. The Alfa went into full production.

Six of these capable vessels were produced, with the *Lena* being launched in 1983. As the last in its line, the *Lena* was fitted with six bow tubes that could fire a mix of conventional anti-ship and anti-submarine torpedoes. It also carried the SS-N-15 nuclear tipped anti-submarine rocket which greatly extended its ASW capability.

Because of its compact size and unique handling abilities, the *Lena* was to become the vessel of choice whenever shallow water operations were necessitated. Such dangerous missions often involved the landing of Spetsnaz commando teams onto unfriendly shores. More often than not, the successful outcome of this work depended upon careful reconnaissance and split-second timing.

Alexander remembered one such clandestine mission several years ago. He had been the senior officer of the Pacific fleet's central planning staff based at Vladivostok, and had been tasked with the job of landing a Spetsnaz team onto the shores of California's San Clemente island. Since a series of shallow shoals surrounded the island, one of the larger nuclear attack boats was out of the question and since the smaller diesel electric subs didn't have the range, Alexander picked the *Lena*, which had been assigned to the Pacific Fleet at that time.

The *Lena*'s commanding officer was a bull-necked Siberian by the name of Tartarov, who was feared by both officers and conscripts alike. A strict disciplinarian, Tartarov demanded a hundred percent from his crew and usually got it. He certainly demonstrated the *Lena*'s ability to travel at high speeds for an extended period, as they crossed the entire breadth of the Pacific in an unprecedented one-hundred and fourteen hours. Then heedless of the pair of U.S. Navy frigates that were stationed off San Clemente island's western coast, Tartarov expertly guided the *Lena* up over the shoals and practically onto the beach itself. It was said that the commandoes only had to get their feet wet as they left the *Lena* to get on with their mission. Three days later, the sub was right there to pick them up. As they initiated the sprint back to Mother Russia, they now had the additional company of the complete guidance system to an American Tomahawk cruise missile, that had been neatly plucked from San Clemente's target range.

Alexander inwardly chuckled as he once again thought about this daring caper. Though the boat's current commander was certainly not a ranting tyrant like Tatarov, Captain Grigori Milyutin could get the job done all the same, with a lot more tact and class along the way. Proud of the system that had produced such a fine young officer, Alexander looked on as a chubby, balding individual entered the attack center and headed straight for him.

"Ah, there you are, Admiral," greeted the *Lena*'s Zampolit, Felix Bucharin. "I was wondering where you ran off to."

Never a great lover of that necessary evil known as the political officer, Alexander managed a civil reply. "There are certainly no hiding places in a vessel of this size, Comrade Bucharin. Now, how can I help you?"

The Zampolit answered while patting his sweat-stained forehead with a white handkerchief. "I was wondering if you'd give us the honor of your company at tomorrow night's Komsomol meeting? We'll be discussing the role of the fleet in carrying out state policy in times of crisis, and I was hoping that you'd share some of your invaluable insights with us. After all, it's not often that we have such an esteemed passenger in our midst."

"I'd be more than happy to speak to your group, Comrade Bucharin. But I'm afraid I won't be able to stay for the entire meeting. My endless paperwork follows me even here, and I must get at it."

"I understand perfectly, Admiral," returned the Zampolit. "Be in the wardroom at eight o'clock sharp, and we'll be ready for you with open ears. Why, the men will be talking about this momentous night for months to come."

Certain that the clever political officer was only using him to beef up attendance, Alexander nodded. "Eight o'clock sharp it is, Comrade. Now if you'll excuse me, I think it's time that I had a few words with the Captain."

Alexander turned to leave, but much to his dismay, he found the portly Zampolit following him as he crossed the attack center and approached the command console. Seated here in a comfortable, high-backed leather swivel chair that was anchored directly into the deck was Grigori Milyutin. The Captain was in the process of studying a video monitor on which a miniature bathymetric chart of the entire Norwegian coastline was displayed.

"The ship seems to be running most smoothly, Captain," observed Alexander as he bent over to take a look at this chart himself. "Why, this is remarkable! I've never seen so much detail packed into so little space before. In the old days, a chart like this one would fill up the entire navigator's station."

"Would you like to see a three dimensional view of this same subterranean terrain, Admiral?" asked the Captain without taking his glance from the screen.

"Does such a thing exist?" quizzed the veteran.

With a practiced ease, Milyutin addressed his keyboard and the video screen began filling with yet another graphic. This one showed the same portion of coastline, though instead of just having soundings, an actual picture of the seafloor was displayed in graphic detail. The various trenches, rises and depressions were clearly visible, and Alexander shook his head in wonder.

"It's one thing reading about such devices in a requisition report. It's another thing altogether to actually see such gear at work. Since when have you had such an amazing capability?"

Turning to face his guest, the Captain answered. "The first software was installed three months ago. It's already been updated several times, as more accurate bathymetric data is collected."

The young officer had the look of a serious scholar. Far from handsome, his dark eyes nevertheless reflected an inner depth that hinted at an extraordinarily high I.Q.

"Sort of makes you wonder how us old-timers managed to keep our feet dry with only our periscopes and our intuition to guide us by," laughed Alexander.

"What you lacked in modern technology, you more than made up for in courage," offered the captain. The veteran seaman nodded, appreciating the grace of the young officer.

"I must admit, that it took plenty of bravado to go out on some of the submarines that I sailed on during the Great War," said Alexander. "Why in those days, we didn't even have radar installed yet, and sonar was just a dream. What we could have done with a device like this one."

"The admiral has graciously agreed to speak at tomorrow night's Komsomol meeting," interjected the Zampolit, who stood nearby, listening to their conversation. "Perhaps you would reconsider and join him, Captain. It's been much too long since you've attended one of our meetings. And your presence there, along with the admiral, would be a great morale booster."

A hint of irritation flavored the captain's tone as he responded to this. "You've already made your case, Comrade Bucharin, and as I said before, the answer is no. If I could join you, I would. But as you very well know, on a vessel this size it's imperative that either the senior lieutenant or myself be on duty here at all times. And since Senior Lieutenant Popov is scheduled to be sleeping at the time of your meeting, my duty prevents me from joining you."

"Very well, Captain. You don't have to get so upset about it," replied the Zampolit as he vainly attempted to counter the new flow of sweat that drenched his glistening forehead.

Well aware that it was time to change the subject, Alexander questioned, "How much longer until we reach our destination, Captain?"

Grigori Milyutin turned back to his console and readdressed its keyboard. On the upper left-hand portion of the video screen a number began flashing, and Milyutin was quick to interpret it.

"At our present speed of forty-one knots, we'll be reaching the waters off of Karsto in another thirty-three hours and twenty-seven minutes."

"I didn't think that we'd be able to remain at such a speed while transmitting the Norwegian coast," said the white-haired veteran. "Certainly these waters will be filled with unfriendly ASW units that would just love to tag a target such as the *Lena*."

The captain grinned. "I've already taken such units into consideration, and I guarantee you that there's absolutely nothing out there that could possibly be a real threat to us. So just relax, Admiral, and rest assured that you have chosen the right vessel for this mission."

"The *Lena* can handle it, all right," boasted the Zampolit. "Our equipment is the best. Yet what I'm most concerned with are the mental conditions of the crew. If they're not functioning properly, the highest technology in the world won't be any use to us. In a way, that's what my bi-weekly Komsomol meetings are all about. The feedback I get from the ship's Party members gives me great insights into the state of the crew's morale. Lately I've taken to videotaping our meetings. Do let me show you one of these tapes now, Admiral. It will help you prepare for tomorrow evening's speech that you'll be giving."

Alexander noted the look of pained disgust that filled the captain's face as he absorbed these words and turned back to the command console. Wishing that he had the nerve to refuse the Zampolit's invitation in the first place, Alexander reluctantly indicated for Felix Bucharin to lead the way to these precious tapes.

At the same time that the *Lena* was approaching the Norwegian Sea from the north, another submarine was headed toward these waters from the opposite direction. As was his habit on their first full day out at sea, the *USS Cheyenne*'s captain initiated his watch with a walk through of the entire sub. Steven Aldridge began his tour of inspection in the forward torpedo room.

He entered the spacious compartment and found the crew gathered around one of the flat weapons' racks. In the process of explaining the various functions of the orange-tipped, torpedo-like object secured on this rack was the stocky, crew-cut figure of Lieutenant Edward Hartman. The intense weapons' officer noted the newcomer in their midst, yet continued on regardless.

". . . thus until the new Sea Lance becomes operational, SUBROC here will have to keep doing the job. In service since 1962, SUBROC should help us hold our own with such vessels as the Soviet Alfa class submarine, that can attain a speed of over forty knots to outrun our fastest torpedoes. Once one of these very capable warships are spotted by our sensors, SUBROC will be launched. Its solid-fuel rocket motor then ignites under water, sending the spiralling missile upwards. As it breaks the surface, a booster rocket will engage, propelling it into the air at supersonic speeds. At the apex of the flight path, explosive bolts will separate the warhead from the spent booster, and the warhead will then follow its ballistic's course, eventually detonating at a pre-set depth."

"Will we be test firing one of these babies during this cruise?" asked the senior chief. "I'd sure rest easier knowing that those modifications to our Mk117 were done correctly."

Lieutenant Hartman looked to the captain for an answer.

"That depends on COMSUBLANT," said Aldridge as he walked over to join his men. "Our current operational orders don't mention anything about a test launch. But if I know Command, they'll be just as anxious as we are to know that this weapon system is truly operational. I wouldn't be surprised if we get a launch order sometime after our primary mission has been accomplished."

Aldridge touched the smooth metal skin of the rocket and added. "Right now, we're bound for the North Sea, where we'll be participating in a NATO ASW exercise. We've been tasked with the job of tagging a West German Type 206 vessel. As you well know, diesel-electric subs of this class are extremely small and hard to locate, and since our patrol quadrant is quite large, we'll really have our hands full."

"If we tag 'em, will we be launching a dummy torpedo at the Krauts, Captain?" asked Lieutenant Hartman.

"Not in this instance, Lieutenant," replied Aldridge. "Our sonar tapes will provide sufficient evidence that we've succeeded. I guess Command is taking it for granted that we're capable of following this up with a kill. So you can carry on, Lieutenant Hartman. And by the way, let me take this opportunity to convey to you and your crew a job well done with the Mk117 modification. I understand that all of you really burned the midnight oil back at Holy Loch, and your efforts haven't gone unnoticed."

"Thank you, sir," snapped the weapon's officer, who wasted no time initiating a complex explanation of the SUBROC's arming system.

Satisfied that Hartman was doing his usual first class job, the Captain began his way aft He passed by the enlisted men's quarters, and found the compartment neat and spotlessly clean. Several of the bunks had their individual curtains drawn tightly shut, indicating that the off-duty seaman inside desired his privacy. Unlike past classes of submarines, each of the *Cheyenne*'s 127 crew members had his own bed, and no one was forced to share

181

their living space, or 'hot bunk' as it used to be called.

As he proceeded into the adjoining mess hall, Aldridge spotted the *Cheyenne*'s senior sonar technician seated alone at one of the booths. Petty Officer First Class Joe Carter had a plateful of untouched scrambled eggs, pancakes and sausage in front of him, and seemed to be content merely to sip on his mug of coffee, all the while absent-mindedly staring off into space. Aldridge decided to stop off at this booth before continuing on.

"Good morning, Mr. Carter," said the captain.

Snapped from his deep reverie, the good-looking black sonar technician responded. "Uh . . . hello, Captain. Gee, I didn't even see you enter the mess."

"From that dreamy, forlorn expression on your face, it looked to me like you were thinking about something other than your immediate duty," observed Aldridge. "It wouldn't happen to be your recently concluded shore leave, would it?"

The likeable sailor grinned. "You hit it right on, Captain."

"Well, I hope yours was as good as mine was," offered Aldridge.

Carter nodded. "It certainly was memorable, Captain. This young lady that I met in Glasgow took me to Edinburgh on the train. Brother, is that ever a city! Edinburgh castle is right out of a history book, and while we were touring it, we even got to hear some of the pipes from the army music school that's located there."

"I got to hear some live pipe music myself," said Aldridge. "It really gives you the flavor of Old Scotland."

182

"I'll say, Captain. They'll never believe it back home, but I'm starting to really get into those pipes."

"You'd better watch it, Mr. Carter, or next thing you'll know you'll be coming home wearing kilts with a Scot lass on your arm."

"There could be worse ways for a guy to go," said the black man with a dreamy smile.

"How are things down in the sound shack?" quizzed Aldridge.

"Everything appears to be functioning normally, Sir. I spent my last watch doing some interface with the newly modified Mk117. I should have it completed by this afternoon."

"Good," replied the captain as he prepared to leave. "Because I'm going to need you to focus one hundred percent on the quarry that we've been tasked to tag. Do you know much about the West German Type 206?"

The St. Louisan grimaced. "That could be a real toughie, Captain. It's small, agile, and capable of extended submerged operations under battery power alone. As I used to ask my students back in San Diego, have you ever heard the sound of your flashlight operating?"

"That's true enough, Mr. Carter. But they're bound to have to ascend to snorkel depth eventually to recharge those batteries, and that's when we're going to have to nab them."

"I hear you, Captain. And we'll be ready for them down in the sound shack the moment that they switch on those diesels."

"I know that you will, Mr. Carter. Now you'd better turn your attention back to that breakfast you've got before you, or Chief Mallott is going to think that you don't like his cooking anymore."

Steven Aldridge winked and continued aft through the galley, where he soon bumped into this very individual. The portly chef was in the process of hand forming dozens of what appeared to be meatballs. As Aldridge walked by, Howard Mallott called out.

"Hello, Captain. How are you on this fine December morning?"

"It's good to be underway again, Mr. Mallott. I see that you've got your work cut out for you today. Are those meatballs?"

Halting a moment to wipe his hands on his stained apron, the bespectacled chief cook answered. "I should say not, Sir. These are turkeyballs. I'll be throwing them into the pot along with some chopped onions, celery, carrots and potatoes. Then after adding a little garlic powder and some Kitchen Bouquet, you'll be chowing down on some of the best turkey stew this side of the Mississippi."

"If it's anything like that turkey burger you served me yesterday, I'll look forward to it." Taking a second to scan the spotless galley, Aldridge added. "How's our food situation?"

"The larders are filled to the brim, Captain. Right now we could sail for two months straight and I'd never have to serve you the same meal twice."

"I don't know how you do it, Mr. Mallott. You're a real culinary magician."

"It's all in the organizing, sir. As I told you before, my father was the chef of the battleship *New Jersey*'s mess, and he's the one who taught me the importance of drawing up beforehand a comprehensive monthly menu. Then as long as you have the

184

proper provisions, the rest is a snap."

"Well, keep up the good work, Mr. Mallott. I'll be the first to let you know what I think about that turkey stew of yours."

As Aldridge turned to continue his inspection, Mallott added, "Take care, Captain, and don't be such a stranger. You're always welcome at Howard's Cafe."

Aldridge smiled, and a long cable-lined passageway took him further aft, toward the boat's reactor and engine compartments. He passed by a ladder that led directly to the control room, one deck above. Here he could visualize his XO as he stood at his customary place beside the chart table, alertly monitoring the instruments displaying their course, speed and depth. Most likely Bob Stoddard would have the well-chewed stem of a corn-cob pipe clenched in his mouth, and Aldridge could breathe easily just knowing that such a capable officer was at the helm.

A throbbing, muted hum called to him in the distance, and before going up to join his XO, the Captain stepped through a hatchway that had a sign reading, *Cheyenne Power and Light* mounted above it. The narrow, forty foot long passageway that he now transitted was completely lined with steel tubing. He could smell the wax-like scent of warm polythylene as he halted halfway down this passageway and looked at his feet. A heavy, metallic cover was set flush with the decking. Aldridge bent down, and as he lifted up this cover, he viewed a pulsating golden glow, clearly visible through the thick, lead-glass viewing port that was positioned there.

Twenty feet below him was the heart of the *Chey-*

enne's propulsion unit. The sealed nuclear reactor vessel was formed out of a grid of uranium plates, and filled with highly pressurized water that couldn't boil. A series of control rods kept the nuclear fission from occurring until the reactor went on-line. Then the rods were slowly removed, and as the uranium-235 elements began interacting, the unit went critical.

Actual propulsion was achieved when the hot pressurized contaminated water was pumped through a series of heat exchangers. A second loop of uncontaminated water absorbed this heat, which turned to steam, that subsequently spun the turbines, producing both power to drive the ship and the electricity needed to operate the rest of its systems.

Aldridge could never get over how efficient such a relatively simple process was, and as he closed the viewing port and stood, he turned to enter the space where this reaction was controlled. As he expected, he found Lieutenant Rich Lonnon seated behind the maneuvering room's central control board. The brawny Florida native was in the process of logging the data that was displayed on the dozens of gauges, digital read-out counters and dials that were spread out before him.

The two senior seamen who sat beside him also kept a close watch on this data, that showed among other things the temperature of the water flowing out of the containment vessel, its pressure, and its velocity. Only after the ship's chief engineer reached out to momentarily trigger a compact pistol switch that was directly connected to the control rods did Aldridge announce his presence.

"Good morning, Lieutenant."

Rich Lonnon alertly swung around, and as he laid eyes on his commanding officer a wide smile lit his face. "Good morning to you, Captain. Welcome to power central. Let me just get rid of this log and I'll be right with you."

Lonnon handed his clipboard to the seaman seated on his right. A brief series of instructions accompanied this transfer, after which Lonnon stood and joined the newcomer by the wall of gauges that displayed the *Cheyenne*'s internal electrical power data.

"It's really good to see you again, Sir," said Lonnon as the two officers exchanged handshakes. "I'm afraid I was forced to miss last night's briefing in the wardroom when the port turbine began acting up on us. We eventually got it squared away, but by that time it was well past midnight."

"So I understand," replied the captain, who liked the way Lonnon looked him square in the eyes when he spoke. "You didn't miss much. Ed Hartman gave us an update on the just completed modifications to our Mk117 fire-control system, and the XO briefed us on some new NavPers training courses that will be offered shortly. Then I got a chance to throw my two cents in by explaining the nature of the exercise that we're about to be involved with."

"I heard all about our little game of Kraut tag from the XO earlier this morning," said Lonnon. "When you need the speed, we'll be there to supply it. That you can bank on."

The chief engineer reached up to reset an overloaded power circuit and continued. "Since I also missed you at both lunch and dinner yesterday, I never did get to find out how your leave turned out, Captain. Did that doll of a daughter of yours behave herself?"

"Sarah was wonderful," answered Aldridge. "Susan and I kept her so busy that she didn't have the time to get into any trouble. Though she did give us a fright one time on the island of Mull when she disappeared from the yard of the B and B where we were staying. Luckily it only took us a couple of minutes to find her on a nearby pasture, cuddling a lamb that she found nestled in the grass there."

"I've been to the Highlands myself during my last tour," revealed Lonnon. "And as far as I'm concerned, it ranks a close second in raw beauty to the Everglades of my native state. Why, I bet that you could have stayed up there at least another month if you could."

"I don't know about that, Lieutenant. I kind of missed this old bucket of bolts. And besides, from the size of that stack of paperwork that was waiting for me on my desk, I got back here right in the nick of time. One more memo and I might have never been able to get back into my cabin."

The chief engineer's chuckle was cut short by the ringing of the nearby intercom handset. Lonnon alertly picked up the black plastic receiver and spoke into it.

"Maneuvering . . . why yes, XO. As a matter of fact he's standing right next to me . . . very good, I'll pass that on to him."

Lonnon hung up the receiver and turned back to his commanding officer. "The XO would like your presence in the control room, Captain. He says that those charts that you requested from the navigator are ready for your perusal."

"Good," said Aldridge. "Now I can find out more about that patrol quadrant that we've been assigned to. Will I see you at lunch, Lieutenant?"

"As long as that turbine behaves, I should be there, Captain."

"Well I sure wouldn't want you to miss out on the turkey stew that Chief Mallott's planning to serve us," said the grinning C.O.

"Not turkey again," protested Lonnon. "Why if the Chief keeps this up, not only will we have the lowest cholesterol count in the entire navy, but we'll also be the only sub crew that goes around pecking at the ground and gobbling!"

Steven Aldridge was in an excellent mood as he left the warm confines of *Cheyenne Power and Light* and climbed up to the deck above, where the sub's control room was located. He entered the familiar confines of this equipment-packed compartment and found it fully manned. Up against the forward bulkhead, the two planesmen sat harnessed to their upholstered leather command chairs. One of these seaman gripped a control stick that controlled the vessel's sail-mounted planes, while the other was responsible for activating their rudder by turning the steering column that he tightly held.

Immediately behind the planesmen, the chief of the watch guarded the complex assortment of main vent levers and air-induction valves that determined the *Cheyenne*'s buoyancy. While beside him, the manifold operator monitored the state of the boat's hydraulic and air pressure systems, ever on the ready to change the balance of their ballast should they get out of trim.

From the digital depth gauge mounted in front of the planesmen, Aldridge could clearly see that

189

they were currently sixty-five feet beneath the sea's surface. Other read-outs showed their speed to be twenty-eight knots, on a course that was taking them due northward. Satisfied that all appeared to be going well, the captain went on to join the two officers who were gathered around the chart table.

The sub's XO and its young navigator, Lieutenant Andrew Laird, were busy studying a detailed bathymetric chart of the Norwegian Basin as Steven Aldridge addressed them. "I understand that you've got the charts of our patrol quadrant ready."

"That's affirmative, Skipper," returned the XO. "And just wait until you see where they've put us."

Bob Stoddard used the stem of his pipe to point out a square portion of the Norwegian Sea laying between the Norwegian city of Narvik to the east, and Jan Mayen Island on the west.

"Our northern flank extends to the Mohns Ridge," continued the XO. "While to the south, we go as far as the Odin oil fields."

"That's quite a chunk of real estate to cover," observed Aldridge as he studied the chart. "Any ideas as to where we should begin?"

It proved to be the *Cheyenne*'s freckled-face navigator who offered the first suggestion. "I think we'll find them hidden among the seamounts of Mohns Ridge. The seafloor is extremely irregular there, with some of those ridges extending up to six-hundred feet from the sea's surface. Since that's well within the limits of the Type 206's depth threshold, the West Germans can use the natural contours of the basin to hide in."

"That's an interesting theory, Lieutenant Laird," replied Aldridge. "What do you say, XO?"

Bob Stoddard took his time responding. "The

Lieutenant might very well be correct, but since the ridge is at the northern extremity of our sector, we'd have to sprint up there directly to initiate a proper scan. If we gambled on his theory and lost, we'd have to backtrack and start all over again. Thus we'd be much better off beginning our hunt at the southern edge of the quadrant, and then continuing to work our way northward, using sprint and drift to cover as much territory as possible."

"If you think about it, those oil production platforms could offer our quarry just as much cover as that ridge could," reflected the captain. "Since our initial approach is from the south anyway, it would be to our advantage to gradually work our way to the north, rather than wasting the time rushing up there at flank speed, with our sensors all but useless. What's our ETA at the southern edge of the quadrant, Lieutenant Laird?"

The Navigator hastily calculated the shortest distance between their current coordinates and the Odin oil fields. "We're presently transitting the waters that lay between the Faeroe and Shetland islands. If our speed remains constant, we can reach the southern edge of our patrol sector in a little over thirteen hours."

"Since the exercise doesn't even officially begin for another twelve hours, that should be more than sufficient," said Aldridge. "Pull every chart that we've got on that oil field, Lieutenant Laird. And XO, make certain to inform Lieutenant Lonnon of the speed that we're going to require. The sound shack must be notified of our plans so that Chief Carter and company will be ready when called upon."

191

"I'll get on it at once, Skipper," replied the XO.

"And while you're getting this old lady ready for some action, I'll be down in my stateroom trying to put a dent in that paperwork," said Aldridge. "If I'm lucky, maybe I'll be able to find the surface of my desk by the time that Kraut sub's history."

Chapter Eight

It had been an exhausting, tense night for Mikhail Kuznetsov. Little did he realize the great distances that he would have to drive as he cautiously followed the flatbed truck away from the site where the heavy water had been stolen. The rain that continued to fall was both a curse and a blessing. The roads in this region were twisting and narrow, and the freezing precipitation only made them that much more treacherous. Yet because of this storm, traffic was a minimum, and he was able to follow at a safe distance in his rented Volvo without having to worry about losing the truck.

The route that the Nazis picked took them down the eastern shores of Lake Tinnsjo and on into the city of Konisberg. Here, the roads improved substantially, with a well lit freeway leading them all the way into Oslo. Mikhail had half expected them to stop in the capital city, but instead they drove straight through it. Thankful that he had a full tank of gas, Mikhail followed them onto Route 69. This highway led them due north to the coastal city of Trondheim, some 450 kilometers distant.

It was morning when he finally braked the Volvo to a halt beside a large wharf. Trying his best to ignore the throbbing pain that coursed through his cramped arthritic limbs, he left the car to proceed on foot.

The truck had pulled right onto one of the docks, where it had backed up to a waiting trawler. Mikhail hid behind an immense mound of smelly fishing nets and breathlessly watched as two familiar blond men dressed in black oilskins climbed out of the truck. Forgetting all about the great fatigue that had more than once almost caused him to fall asleep at the wheel, he watched as these figures proceeded to a small pierside building. The white-haired Russian would never forget the last time that he had seen this same pair at work.

He had been watching from the edge of the woods at the time as the gang initially went about stealing the thirty-three freshly salvaged cannisters. As the drums were subsequently loaded onto the truck, Mikhail could see that most of the actual heavy labor was performed by the two unlucky Norwegians who had been forced out of the salvage ship at gunpoint. No sooner was the last drum loaded, than the two blond men ordered the Norwegians to kneel on the rain-soaked ground with their hands behind their heads. Then, without the slightest hesitation, one of the Nazis pulled a gun from his jacket, put its barrel up against the back of each kneeling man's skull, and proceeded to literally blow his brains out.

All the time watching these cold-blooded murders from the cover of the pine forest, Mikhail's shocked thoughts flashed back to the last time he had seen such an atrocity. In that hell hole known as Bergen-Belsen, such shootings were an everyday occurrence. But this was a half a century later, and the war was long over. Or was it, thought the Russian. He sighed heavily.

Mikhail's first instinct was pure revenge, as he

viewed the Norwegians' blood-soaked bodies laying there in the mud. He even went as far as to finger the 9mm pistol that lay in his shoulder harness, and begged to be released on the fascist murderers. But ever mindful of his ultimate goal, Mikhail successfully controlled his fury. And thank the heavens that he had, for now he was another step closer to wiping Otto Koch, and his entire band of self-proclaimed Fascists from the face of the earth.

Stifling a yawn, Mikhail looked on as the pair of Nazis exited the dockside building along with a stout fellow who walked with a limp and wore a wrinkled blue suit. This individual was obviously a freight agent, for he hurriedly checked the truck's cargo before walking over to the nearby trawler and shouting up to its bridge.

Soon afterward, several longshoremen materialized from below deck. The truck was backed up to the very edge of the dock, and the transfer of the drums was initiated with the help of a small crane.

Mikhail intently watched this process, and knew that this could very well be the end of the line for him unless he was able to find out the trawler's destination. He decided to wait until the ship set sail. Then he would go and have a little chat with the portly freight agent. If a hefty bribe wouldn't loosen his tongue, the old veteran figured that there were always other more expedient methods to convince him to talk.

It was rapidly approaching noon when the last drum was securely stored in the trawler's hold. Mikhail wasn't the least bit surprised when the two nazis boarded the ship along with this precious cargo. The lines holding the sturdy vessel to the pier were parted, and with a single toot of its steam whistle the trawler was underway.

The blue-suited agent remained on the dock until the trawler had all but disappeared. As he turned to go back inside, Mikhail saw that he was in the process of counting a thick wad of dollar bills. Surely this was his part of the take for not asking too many questions.

Just as Mikhail was preparing to leave the cover of his hiding place and intercept the agent, a tall, muscular blond with a bandage covering part of his skull came into the picture. Mikhail cursed as this familiar giant roughly grabbed the agent by his arm and forced him inside.

"Damn it! It's that salvage diver from Lake Tinnsjo!" cursed the Russian.

Somehow the Norwegian had also found out where his stolen treasure had been taken, and now he was in the process of demanding the same information that Mikhail was about to demand!

Hoping that the agent would talk voluntarily, Mikhail shuddered to think what would happen if he didn't. Driven by the desire to revenge the deaths of his two co-workers, the Norwegian diver had every right to be furious. Taking into consideration his massive size compared to that of the portly, out of shape freight agent, Mikhail could only pray that the Viking's powers of persuasion weren't merely limited to the physical.

Back on the diving support ship *Falcon*, the other members of NUEX impatiently bided their time inside the vessel's main decompression chamber. Unable to relax, Jon Huslid anxiously paced to and iro, unable to understand how Jakob and Arne could summon the patience to just sit at the table and play chess. Behind them, the American lay in his bunk as he had done for most of their stay, reading a dog-eared paperback novel.

"I'm getting a bad feeling about this whole thing," mumbled the restless photographer to no one in particular. "I just knew that Knut wouldn't stay put."

"Maybe you should give the clinic at Rjukan one more call," offered Arne as he contemplated his next chess move.

"And what would that accomplish?" returned Jon. "He walked out of there against his doctor's orders over twenty-four hours ago, and the one thing that we can be certain of is that Knut won't be found in that hospital bed."

"Knut's a big boy. He can surely take care of himself," said Jakob, who thoughtfully moved his knight forward to do battle.

Jon shook his head. "I'm not so sure of that, Jakob. You're forgetting the type of desperate individuals that we're dealing with here. Not only are they thieves, but cold-blooded murderers as well. This is a matter for the police, not a stubborn, hard-headed diver from Telemark."

The deck below rolled under the influence of a large sea swell, and Jon had to blindly reach out for the edge of the American's bunk to keep from falling over.

"Seems like we're finally running into some of that weather that Magne was warning us about," reflected David Lawton as he put down his book and watched the photographer struggle to regain his balance.

197

The *Falcon* again canted hard on its side, this time with such abrupt force that the chess board went sliding off the table and clattered down to the deck below.

"Damn!" cursed Jakob, who had to hold onto the table to keep from falling over himself. "And here I was just setting you up for the kill."

"Like hell you were," countered Arne. "Another half dozen moves and you would have been history."

With his hands still tightly gripping the edge of the bunk, Jon addressed the bearded Texan who lay before him. "I guess you don't get many sea-states like this in the Gulf of Mexico."

"I don't know about that, my friend," answered Lawton as the *Falcon* smashed downward into a steep trough sending a bone-jarring concussion trembling through its hull. "Though it's true that a good majority of the time the waters of the Gulf are fairly stable, we get our share of rough seas. This year alone we had to ride out a trio of full-fledged hurricanes. Twice me and my boys were out on a rig when a tropical depression passed by, and even though we were on the storm's fringe, we had waves crashing into us that were a good sixty feet high. For a while there we actually feared that the whole platform would capsize, and we were even seriously considering evacuation. Yet when you're in a sea-state like that with hundred and fifty mile per hour winds whipping by, the big question is, how in the hell do you evacuate? Fortunately for us, the low-pressure system kept moving to the north, and we never had to answer it."

"For some reason I always pictured the Gulf of Mexico to be nothing but a huge, tropical lake," remarked the photographer. "With surfers and bikini-clad girls playing on its shores, and dolphins frolicking in its depths."

The Texan grinned. "Don't get me wrong, my friend. We have plenty of that too. And also some of the most beautiful beaches in all the world. Why, I guess you'll have to come down to Texas and see for yourself."

"I'd like that," said Jon as yet another massive swell sent the *Falcon* pitching to and fro like a toy boat in a bathtub.

"How's everyone doing in there?" broke a deep, familiar voice from the mounted video monitor.

The divers looked up to this screen and the rugged face of Magne Rystaad peered down at them.

"And for goodness sake, don't be too proud to shout out if you feel a bit seasick," continued Magne. "The doc's got plenty of medicine to ease any queasiness that you may experience. Because I'll warn you right now that we're in for a long, rough ride.

"We're presently just about to pass by the Odin production area. The Ice Field's rig is a good one hundred kilometers due north of us yet. She's currently floundering in the same heavy seas, and it looks like it will be another six and a half hours until we can reach her."

"Can the tugs hold the rig upright until then?" asked Arne.

Magne was quick with his answer. "Between the three of them, they should manage. The rig itself is heavy enough so that its center of gravity is close to the sea's surface, and with the additional support of those ocean-going tugs, I seriously doubt if the platform will be in any real danger.

"Now in respect to your decompression. We've got

199

you up to 155 meters. So it looks like you're right on schedule, which means that you have another twenty hours and eleven minutes to go."

As the next swell struck, Magne could be seen reaching to the console for support.

"Have you heard from the authorities in Rjukan yet, Chief?" asked Jon Huslid, whose thoughts were on other matters than the rough sea state.

"I'm afraid not," replied Magne. "The detective with whom I spoke on the telephone last night warned me that it could be some time yet until the first lead comes along. But he sounded very optimistic, and mentioned that if I didn't hear from him this morning, I was to give him a call later in the afternoon."

"Any word from Knut?" questioned Arne hopefully.

The strain in Magne's face was apparent as he somberly shook his head. "It appears as if your co-worker has managed to disappear off the face of this earth. The last I heard, he was still AWOL from the Rjukan hospital. The specialist that the company sent up from Oslo to treat his concussion has already checked out the home of Knut's parents. Our friend was nowhere to be seen, and with that the physician could only return to Oslo to wait until Knut shows himself."

"Locate those thieving murderers and you'll most likely find Knut close behind," said the worried photographer. "I know that big ox only too well. He's out there right now playing amateur detective, and nothing in the world is going to stop him from doing whatever he can do to track those bastards down."

"When Knut gets something on his mind, he's

like a one-track record," added Jakob. "He's one of the most stubborn, headstrong individuals that I've ever known. If anyone can track down those murderers, Knut's the one who can do it."

"But can he do it without getting a bullet in his skull along the way?" queried David Lawton.

The deck canted hard aport as Magne responded. "Knut's always impressed me as the sensible, practical type. If he is indeed playing detective, he'll do it discreetly. And with that said, I'll be signing off for now. Just holler if you need that Dramamine. I don't know about you fellows, but I'm feeling a little green around the gills myself, and my next stop is going to be straight to the infirmary to get some medication to counter it."

The video monitor went blank and David Lawton reached for his paperback. Jon Huslid initiated his nervous pacing once again, doing his best to keep his balance as the deck continued to roll beneath them. This left the chess players staring at each other from each side of the table.

"Well Arne, shall we give it another try?" quizzed the Lapp.

The bearded Telemark native nodded. "I'm game if you are, Jakob. And this time I'm going to beat you so quickly that there will never be any doubt as to the outcome."

"We'll see about that," replied his opponent as he bent down to begin retrieving the fallen chess pieces.

One and a half hours later they were still immersed in this same game. Though it took great effort to keep the continued rough seas from ruining this game also, they somehow managed to keep the board stabilized and the pieces in place. Behind

201

them, the American was contentedly snoring away in his bunk, and Jon was seated on his mattress scribbling away in his diary.

Through a bit of masterly deception, Jakob had just managed to pick off his opponent's queen with his rook. Arne swore for revenge, and as he began his offensive, the chamber's telephone began ringing. It proved to be Jon who answered it.

"Knut!" he excitedly screamed into the receiver. "Where the hell are you?"

These words caused both Jakob and Arne to instantly abandon their game and sprint over to Jon's side. Even David Lawton snapped out of his slumber to see what all the commotion was about. As the Texan sat up in bed, he spied Jon Huslid anxiously speaking into a black plastic telephone handset.

"I'm just glad to hear that you're safe and feeling all right, Knut . . . I believe that can be arranged. We're out of decompression in eighteen and a half hours, and if Magne can provide the transport, we'll be there. But why Tromso? . . . Okay, I can hang on until then. That's the Northern Lights Cafe, twenty-four hours from now. See you then, big guy."

The photographer hung up the handset and issued a loud sigh of relief.

"For heaven's sake, where is he?" questioned Jakob.

"Knut's in Trondheim," replied Jon. "And I'll be damned if he hasn't gone and tracked down the heavy water, along with the bastards who murdered Lars and Thor."

"All right, Knut!" shouted Arne triumphantly. "Is he going to sic the police on them?"

"Actually, he didn't say," said Jon. "All that I re-

202

ally got from him was that except for a headache, he's feeling pretty good. He said he'd explain all the rest to us tomorrow at this time in Tromso, at the Northern Lights Cafe."

"But how in the hell are we ever going to get to Tromso?" asked Arne. "That's way above the Arctic Circle."

"I'll tell you how you're going to get up there," broke a firm, deep voice from the mounted video monitor. "I'm going to have Noroil One fly you there."

As the divers turned in unison to the monitor, Magne continued. "I'm afraid I'm guilty of eavesdropping, Jon. I couldn't help but keep listening when I patched Knut through to you. It's wonderful that he's feeling good, and I'm thrilled to hear that he's managed to track down those criminals. You have my word that if the sea state allows it, the company chopper will be available to give you a lift into Tromso. I really don't understand what Knut's up to, but I'm counting on you fellows to make certain that he doesn't try to take the law into his own hands. Can I rely on you for that, Gentlemen?"

"You got it, Chief," replied the photographer. "You just get us to Tromso, and we'll get to the bottom of this mystery once and for all."

"That's what I'm counting on," said Magne, who looked visibly relieved as he signed off.

"So Knut's in Trondheim," reflected Jakob. "And next he's going to be meeting us in Tromso. I wonder what he's got planned?"

"Whatever it is, you can be sure that it involves our heavy water, and the murdering crooks who stole it," answered Jon. "Now I just pray that the big fellow can stay out of trouble for the next

203

twenty-four hours. Damn! If we could only get to him right now."

The ship rolled hard on it's side, and once more the unattended chess board went clattering to the deck. But this time both Jakob and Arne barely paid it any attention.

"Why's that, Jon?" asked Arne. "Did Knut sound like he was in trouble or something?"

The photographer took his time answering. "I can't really put my finger on it, Arne. I've just got a hunch that Knut's on the trail of a real tiger, and the sooner we're all together to give him a hand, the better it's going to be for all of us."

David Lawton decided that it was time for a little fatherly advice. "When you do get together, just make certain that the authorities know what you're up to. I mean it, guys. We're talking about cold-blooded murderers here, the type of individual who would blow your brains out just on a whim. So play it smart, and let the police do the job that they get paid to do."

A moment of contemplative silence followed as these words of wisdom were absorbed, and the ship ominously rolled in the largest set of swells yet encountered.

Chapter Nine

For the entire day Captain Steven Aldridge didn't budge from his desk. This was the only way he knew how to attack the pile of paperwork that had accumulated during the week that he had been on leave. His first job had been to properly sort through this mess, and eventually he was able to come up with several fairly neat stacks. The largest of these piles held official U.S. Navy documents that included memos from COMSUBLANT, reports from his own XO, policy updates, and various technical papers. Only after addressing this priority material would he get on to several personal letters from ex-shipmates that he would have to answer, and a request from the Naval Submarine League to write an article for their next quarterly journal.

Steven had been a member of the League almost since its inception. It was primarily made up of active and retired submariners, defense contractors, and interested civilians. The League came into being when members of the sub community realized how ill informed the American public was when it came to undersea warfare. Submariners were by their very nature secretive, yet in order to successfully compete for the funds that would guarantee the force's continued excellence, a way would have to be found to educate the public to the need of a strong underwater fleet. The Naval Submarine League filled this void with its excellent journal and its yearly Washington D.C. symposiums, that Steven made certain to attend whenever possible.

The last stack of correspondence that he would eventually get to was that which he unglamorously labeled junk mail. Included in this pile were unsolicited letters from various financial planners, insurance companies, and several mail-order catalogues.

With the initial job of sorting out of the way, he was now able to actually see his desk blotter. This was a promising sign, and he got on with the task of reading the memos that had been sent to him by an assortment of naval department personnel.

His only break was for a light lunch of grapes, cottage cheese, and oat bran crackers. He was serious about taking off the extra weight that he had recently put on, and since submariners led sedentary lives while on patrol, he would have to watch his diet most carefully.

Before getting immediately back to work, his glance caught the framed photograph that he had just mounted above his desk. This photo showed Susan, Sarah and himself during their recent holiday. It had been taken by a cooperative deckhand while they were crossing over on the ferry from Oban to the island of Mull. An ancient Scottish castle could just be seen on the shoreline over his right shoulder, and one didn't have to look close to see that they were having a wonderful time.

Susan looked especially happy. With her brown, pixie-cut hair style, freckled face, trim figure, and the University of Virginia sweatshirt that she was wearing, she didn't look much different from the young college girl that he had met and fallen in love with over two decades ago. The proof of the years passing was in the face and figure of Sarah. The six-year-old was getting to be quite the little lady now. She could ride a bike, speak elementary French, and had even had her first course in operating a computer. There was no doubt that she was the spitting image of her mother, and like her mom would be a real heartbreaker by the time she got to junior high school.

Shortly after this picture was taken, while Sarah was playing in the ferry's game room, Susan brought up the subject that between them they called "the problem." This hadn't been the first time that she had talked to him about the difficulties she faced with him gone a good six months out of the year, and it wouldn't be the last, either.

Why couldn't he transfer out of the operational end of his business, and get a position with more regular hours, she asked emotionally? In these formative years, Sarah needed a full-time father. And it was hard on Susan as well. Not only did she have emotional and physical needs that went unfulfilled by his long absences at sea, but everyday life was difficult enough for her. During his last patrol, the refrigerator had gone on the blink. And no sooner did she get a repairman out to get it working again, when the toilet backed up all over their new bathroom carpet. And wouldn't you know that all of this would occur on the same day that Sarah was to come home from school with the measles?

Steven listened to her concerns, but really didn't know how to solve them. He had told her from the very beginning that his ultimate goal was to get a submarine command of his own. And the day he was named C.O. of the *Cheyenne* was the pinnacle of his long career.

At forty years of age, Steven was at his prime. To get an attack sub of his own was all that he had ever dreamed of. He figured that he had another five years of sea duty left in him at best. During this time he had hoped to be one of the first to skipper one of the new Seawolf class attack subs. The Seawolf was the first new class of attack subs to be produced for the navy since the 688 class entered service back in the late 1970's. It proved to be an exciting, dynamic warship, and Steven wanted to be one of the first to take it to sea. Only then would he be truly satisfied with his career, and seriously think about stepping aside to let a younger man take over at the helm.

Meanwhile, Susan would just have to learn to cope with the situation. He even went as far as suggesting that they should both see a family counselor next time he was home. Susan didn't like this idea at all, and when it became obvious that he was still very serious about remaining in the operational end, at least for the next few years, Susan brought up the idea of having another child. Steven wondered if this wouldn't make her life even more difficult. Yet Susan had apparently given this matter a lot of previous thought, and explained that another baby would help fill the void in her life caused by his naval duty. As to how she would cope at home with another child to care for, she had already talked to her parents about it. They readily agreed to have Susan and the kids move in with them while Steven was on patrol.

As the only son of an only son, Steven was the last in the Aldridge line. A boy would mean a lot to him, and he accepted her offer with open arms.

In fact, they got to work on it that very evening, in the bedroom of their bed and breakfast, high in the heather-filled hills of Mull.

When they parted for this current patrol, Steven felt closer to Susan than he had in years. Their deepest concerns and dreams were out in the open now, and a new honesty prevailed between them. And, of course, there was always the hope that his seed had already taken, and a new life was forming deep inside Susan's womb. It was with this hopeful thought in mind that Steven went back to work.

At 17:00 hours exactly, an enticing aroma found its way into his cabin. Ten minutes later, there was a knock on his door and in walked Chief Howard Mallott with a tray.

"Sorry to disturb you, Captain. But it's time for some supper. I heard about that skimpy lunch that you had, and I figured that you'd be wanting to eat early this evening."

"You figured right, Chief," replied Aldridge, who cleared a place on his desk for the tray.

"I realize that you're counting those calories, Captain. And there's nothing here that's going to hurt you," said Mallott as he picked up the aluminum plate cover and added, ". . . there's the turkey stew that you saw me preparing earlier. That meat's good and lean with half the fat of ground beef. Then there's margarine for your rolls and skimmed milk to drink. Your dessert is low-fat raspberry yogurt."

Wasting no time with formalities, Aldridge picked up his fork and sampled some of the stew. "It's simply delicious, Chief."

"I'm glad you like it, Captain. It does my heart good to see someone really enjoy their chow. If only I could stick to a diet myself. It seems that I'm perpetually fighting the battle of the bulge."

Mallott patted his pot-belly and turned to exit. "Enjoy it, Captain. And if you want seconds, just give me a ring."

As the chief left his cabin, Aldridge got down to some serious eating. He found the turkeyballs moist and flavorful. The vegetables that they were cooked with complimented them perfectly. He especially enjoyed the combination of cooked carrots, celery, onions, and potatoes. He used the wheat roll to sop up the excess gravy, and didn't even have to use the margarine.

Aldridge polished off his stew, and was well into his yogurt, when his intercom rang. The handset was mounted on the bulkhead right in front of him, and he only had to reach out to grab it.

"Captain here . . . I understand, Lieutenant Laird. As OOD I'm going to let you take us up to periscope depth. I'm just finishing dinner, and I'll be right up there to join you."

As Aldridge hung up the handset he looked to his watch and saw that they were right on schedule. The *Cheyenne*'s navigator had just called to inform him that they were rapidly approaching the southern edge of the Odin oil fields. Laird had requested a quick visual scan with their periscope to confirm their position, to which Aldridge readily agreed.

Since even a routine procedure such as taking the *Cheyenne* to periscope depth was fraught with many unforeseen dangers, Aldridge hurriedly finished his dessert and proceeded to the control room. Lieutenant Andrew Laird was the ship's youngest officer and was fairly new to submarines. Though fully qualified, he lacked experience, and Aldridge vowed to give him his fair share during this patrol.

As the captain crossed the passageway that would take him directly to the control room, he remembered well his own early days as a neophyte. A decade and a half ago when he first put to sea as a raw ensign, his C.O. had been a tough old veteran, who leaned on him constantly. He was always being put to the test in pressure packed situations, and he emerged a better officer because of it.

Since that time, he had had the opportunity to break in dozens of junior officers himself, and he always made certain to give them their fair share of responsibility from the very beginning. The *Cheyenne*'s current navigator was no exception, and if he was made out of the right stuff, he'd handle himself like the professional underwater warrior that he had trained so hard to be.

Aldridge arrived in the control room just as one of the two eight inch thick, steel periscopes rose up from the deck below with a loud hiss of hydraulic oil. Several drops of water could be seen running down the shiny cylinder from its overhead fitting as Lieutenant Laird snapped down the scope's hinged handles and nestled his eyes up against its rubberized lens coupling.

"Sixty-five feet and holding," called the diving officer from his console.

The submarine began to level out and Aldridge watched as the young OOD began silently twisting the scope in a full circle. Halfway through this scan, Laird halted.

"We've got an oil platform in sight, bearing zero-two-zero," he eagerly observed. "It's lit up out there like a Christmas tree."

Instead of continuing on with **his** circular scan, Laird's line of sight seemed to be locked on the

211

platform. Steven Aldridge was about to instruct him to reinitiate his full recon of the waters above, when the young OOD did so on his own.

As he reached that portion of the sea's surface that lay immediately behind them, Laird once again briefly hesitated. Yet this was all too soon followed by a frightening cry that emanated from deep within the OOD's throat.

"Emergency deep! Surface contact headed straight toward us."

Steven Aldridge's pulse quickened as he watched his crew snap into action. With a lightning movement, the OOD slapped the scope handles to the vertical and reached over to hit the switch that would lower the periscope back into its well. Meanwhile the helm could be heard ordering, "All ahead full!"

"Full dive on the fairwater planes!" commanded the diving officer, who next instructed that the stern planes be likewise engaged.

The captain didn't have to say a thing as the chief of the watch began flooding the depth control tank, as the OOD's emergency deep order was relayed to the rest of the crew over the P.A. system. They had rehearsed this very same drill hundreds of times before, allowing them to proceed like a well choreographed dance number.

As the submarine pitched over and began its way toward the protective depths, the grinding sound of the surface ship's screws rose to a deafening crescendo, yet back in sonar this roar was soon replaced by the sound of the *Cheyenne*'s own propeller as it frantically dug into the frigid seas to move them out of harm's way.

Less than a minute later, it was all over. Having

212

no idea how close it had come to ramming them, the surface ship unwarily continued on its northward course, and gradually the sounds of its screws dissipated.

Sweat lined Steven Aldridge's forehead as he scanned the compartment, his gaze finally resting on the OOD. The young navigator looked badly shaken, and Aldridge knew very well that he was in the process of blaming himself for this near tragic incident.

"That was too close for comfort, Lieutenant Laird. But it's not unusual for these things to happen. That's why we repeat those drills over and over until you can practically perform them in your sleep."

"I . . . guess I should have completed my initial scan quicker," stuttered the navigator.

"That you should have," returned Aldridge. "But the boys down in the sound shack deserve their share of the blame also. They should have heard that contact long ago, and warned you to be on the look out for it. But we'll hash this whole thing out in detail later. Right now, how about taking us back up and taking a closer look at the vessel that almost deep-sixed us?"

Buoyed by the captain's trust in him, Andrew Laird took a deep breath and called out firmly. "Secure from emergency deep. Bring us back up to periscope depth, chief."

A sense of normalcy quickly returned to the *Cheyenne* as the control room crew pulled the sub out of its dive and guided it back toward the surface. This time though, Laird waited until sonar had the surface contact firmly fixed in the waters in front of them before raising the periscope. Only after a complete 360 degree scan with the scope was completed did the OOD concentrate his gaze on the stern of the ship that lay off their bow.

"I've got them, Captain," said the navigator, a hint of newfound confidence edging his tone.

Aldridge quickly replaced Laird at the scope to take a look for himself. Lit by the bare light of dusk, the gray seas slapped up against the lens, and the Captain had to wait until they were in between swells to spot the square stern of a yellow-hulled ship up ahead. This vessel had twin stacks set amidships, and a large crane dominating its after deck. Yet it was only after increasing the scope's magnification that he was able to read the ship's name and port.

"It's the *Falcon* out of Haugesund," he reported. "Looks to me that she's a diving support ship that's probably involved with the off-shore oil business. She sure appears to be hauling ass, completely heedless of that sea-state topside."

Even at a depth of sixty-five feet beneath the sea's surface, the *Cheyenne* found itself rolling in the under-currents produced by this swell.

"I guess those rough seas kind of take the boys in the sound shack off the hook," observed the Captain, as he backed away from the scope. "In this agitated layer, sonar would be practically useless. With all that wave action to contend with, a contact would have to be practically on top of us before they'd hear it."

"I guess that lays the blame squarely on my shoulders, Captain," offered the OOD. "It was up to me to spot that contact the second our scope broke the surface."

"That's what the responsibility of command is all

214

about, Lieutenant. But don't be too hard on yourself. You spotted that vessel in time, and that's the bottom line. Yet to make up for any guilty feelings that you might still harbor against yourself, you can wipe the slate clean by being the first to tag that West German sub that we've been sent out here to locate."

It was obvious that the Captain was giving him a second chance, and Lieutenant Andrew Laird quickly rose to accept the challenge. "I'll try my best, Sir."

"That's all I'm asking," returned Aldridge, who noted that his XO had just entered the control room. "Now I'd better go and console the XO. From that stain on his coveralls, I'd say that Lieutenant Commander Stoddard was in the midst of a little turkey stew when our little crash dive came down."

In an adjoining portion of the Norwegian Sea, yet another submarine was securing itself from periscope depth. The *Lena* was well on its way to the waters off of Karsto where its recon mission would take place, and so far their sprint down the coast of Norway had been without incident.

"She appears to be a diving support vessel of some sort," observed Captain Grigori Milyutin as he peered into his video monitor.

Looking over his shoulder, Admiral Alexander Kuznetsov also watched as the bright-yellow hull of this ship crashed into a large swell.

"I still can't get used to the idea of not having to peer through the customary cylinder-mounted viewing coupling to see such an image," commented the

215

white-haired veteran.

"Such obsolete equipment doesn't even exist on the *Lena*," boasted its Captain. "Don't forget, we don't even carry a traditional hull-penetrating periscope. Our viewing device is merely mounted into the *Lena*'s sail, where it's extended by a single push on my computer keyboard. A fiber-optic cable then relays the signal straight to this video monitor, where I can see what's going on topside from the comfort of my command chair."

"This ship continues to astound me," said Alexander.

"As she does me also, Admiral," admitted Grigori Milyutin.

The *Lena* rolled as a result of the rough seas topside, and the captain added, "It's time to return to the calm depths beneath us. Comrade diving officer, take us down to two-hundred meters."

"Two hundred meters it is, Captain," repeated the alert diving officer.

There was a slight shifting forward as the boat's plane's were engaged and the *Lena* nosed downward. Alexander tightly gripped the back of the captain's chair to keep his balance, yet soon they were running level once again, and Alexander let go of his handhold.

"I guess that I should be going to my stateroom to complete my speech for tonight's Komsomol meeting," remarked Alexander.

"I do hope that this speech isn't too much of an imposition on you," whispered Milyutin.

There was a conspirial tone to this statement, and Alexander responded accordingly. "The *Lena*'s Zampolit certainly appears to take his position on this vessel most seriously, doesn't he, Captain?"

"It's the nature of the beast," offered Milyutin.

"Why such individuals are still assigned to warships such as this one is beyond me," said Alexander quietly. "The days of political instability in the Rodina's fleet are long gone. The political officer is an anachronism."

"I agree, Admiral. Having Felix Bucharin aboard the *Lena* is a complete waste of precious space, especially with a crew of this limited size. Now if he had some sort of operational skill that we could utilize, that would be different. But as it stands now, he knows absolutely nothing about running a warship. All he does is eat our food and fill our heads with useless, boring political theories that have no practical value whatsoever."

"I must admit that I've heard similar rumblings from other officers in your position, Captain. And at long last your superiors are starting to wake up and take notice. As we in the navy increasingly have to fight for our shrinking share of the Defense Ministry budget, ways are constantly being sought to trim the fat that already exists in the fleet. Several classified reports have already crossed my desk, that question the logic behind the Party statute requiring Zampolit's on each and every one of the Rodina's warships. Millions of rubles could be saved yearly if such a nonproductive position was eliminated."

"Why not just replace them with a videotape?" offered Milyutin. "That way we could still get our dose of Party indoctrination, without having to carry the extra weight of an additional crew member to take along."

Alexander thought about this for a moment. "That's not a bad idea, Captain. Speeches could be

217

taped in advance, and distributed to every ship in the fleet. They could even be shown to the crew at meal time. At least then the Party could be certain that their audience wouldn't just sleep through the sessions. Why don't I give it some further thought, and then perhaps I'll put this suggestion in writing and send it on up the chain of command."

The Admiral looked on as the video monitor began filling with data relayed to them by the *Lena*'s fully automated sonar system. Grigori Milyutin quickly interpreted this information.

"It seems that our brief excursion to periscope depth served to degrade the ship's acoustic sensors. Our passive systems are just now coming back on-line."

"From the looks of those swells topside, I can see why our hydrophones were temporarily useless," observed the veteran. "It's good to have them back, though, because as we continue to approach our goal, we must be extra vigilant. NATO always has a ship or two in these waters, and since our mission's success depends upon absolute stealth, we must continue on with the greatest of care."

"I've already cut our speed down substantially, Admiral. As far as NATO is concerned, the *Lena* is presently all but invisible to their sensors."

"And let's keep it that way," urged Alexander. "Now the hour is getting late, and I still have to put the finishing touches on my address to the Komsomol. Perhaps I'll see you afterward."

"I'll be right here," said the Captain.

Alexander stiffly turned for the aft hatchway. The *Lena*'s cramped confines were beginning to take its effects on his arthritic knees and ankles, which badly needed a proper stretching.

"This is not an old man's business," he mumbled to himself as he painfully climbed down a steep ladder to the deck below. Politely nodding to the two officers who sat at the small wardroom table spooning in their borscht, he headed straight into his cabin.

Just large enough to hold a cot, sink, and a bulkhead mounted desk, this stateroom belonged to the *Lena*'s Captain. Grigori Milyutin graciously surrendered it to the veteran, and was currently hot bunking with the sub's senior lieutenant.

Thankful for this space to himself, he sat down before the desk. Before him now was the partially filled legal pad that he had been working on earlier. Written here were the main points that he wished to convey during this evening's speech.

He planned to start off by giving a broad overview of the Soviet Navy's ever expanding missions. He wanted to be certain to remind the young sailors that the Fleet had grown from a mere coastal defense force into a modern, ocean-going one in a matter of decades. To extend the influence of the U.S.S.R. well out into the sea, the Soviet Navy had five basic missions—strategic offense, maritime security, interdiction of sea lines of communication, support of ground forces, and the support of state policy. Since this last mission was the subject of tonight's meeting, he would dwell on it extensively.

In Alexander's opinion, the Soviet Fleet didn't have to be in a declared war to support the State's policies. Not restricted by the sovereignty of airspace over land or by territorial rights, the fleet could sail where it pleased. Comprised of a variety of warships ranging from carriers, to cruisers, to submarines, the Fleet was a flexible, mobile force able to influence events in coastal countries by extending a military threat to any level, beginning with a mere show of military strength to the actual landing of forces ashore. A strong peacetime fleet was also necessary to assert Soviet rights on the high seas, to protect the interests of the Soviet merchant and fishing fleets, demonstrate support for client states, and most importantly, to inhibit Western military initiatives.

He would end his speech by looking to the future. Alexander's vision of twenty-first century civilization was one that increasingly looked to the sea for a variety of necessities. The oceans would provide fuel, food, minerals, and even living space to a world population that was rapidly outgrowing its available landspace. And to properly police and regulate these operations, the Rodina would rely on its Fleet like never before.

Satisfied with this general outline, Alexander completed the sketch of his speech. He hoped to keep it as short as possible, and leave time for a question and answer period afterward.

Since it appeared as if it was going to be a late night afterall, he decided that a little nap was in order. He downed two aspirin to help ease the pain that incessantly throbbed in his inflamed joints, slipped off his shoes and jacket, and laid down on the cot. Sleep was upon him almost immediately, and along with this slumber came a kaleidoscope of dreams.

They started off with a train ride. He was a young soldier once again, being conveyed through the wooded countryside of his homeland along with his brother, Mikhail. An ear-shattering explosion suddenly filled the railcar that they were travelling in with smoke, and he remembered blindly reaching out in a desperate effort to locate his lost twin.

In the blink of an eye, he was transferred to a flower-filled glen in the Ukraine. A babbling brook twisted through a thick stand of gnarled oaks, and as he approached the stream to quench his thirst, he spotted Katrina Orlovski sitting on the nearby bank on a blanket, unpacking a picnic lunch. Katrina looked positively radiant with her long red hair cascading smoothly over the white lace dress that she had sewed herself. Alexander called out to the love of his youth, but Katrina seemed completely deaf to his cries. Deciding then to ford the stream and surprise her, he stepped into the icy water and to his horror, found that the stream bed was formed out of quicksand. His frantic cries for help went unanswered as gradually he sank into the swampy morass. He could feel the icy water numb the skin of his neck and arms, as his legs, waist and torso were swallowed. Just when his chin was about to be pulled under water, his brother Mikhail appeared on the nearby shoreline.

In a heartbeat, he was magically conveyed back to the smoke-filled railcar. With flames licking the car's wooden-slat walls, he continued his desperate search for his twin. His stinging eyes were all but useless, and like a blind man he extended his arms outward and groped into the smoldering flames. It was then his hand made contact. New hope filled his spirits as he grasped the hand that he had discovered veiled in the sooty haze and slowly pulled it forward. The face that accompanied this hand belonged to his brother, but how much Mikhail had changed! Gone was his wavy blond hair, smooth blemishless skin and vibrant blue eyes. From a young, handsome soldier he had been turned into a white-haired old man with wrinkled skin and dull gray eyes. It was as Alexander viewed the jagged scar that lined the entire left side of his twin's face that he awoke.

It took several confusing seconds for him to reorientate himself. With his heart still pounding away in his chest, he scanned the cramped confines of the stateroom as if seeing it for the very first time. All so gradually, elements of his recently concluded nightmare returned.

A train . . . an explosion . . . his brother lost in the resulting smoke! And there also was lovely Katrina Olovski, the one and only love of his life. How very beautiful she had looked sitting there on the stream bank. Why he could still picture her long silky red hair and the white lace dress that she had made for their wedding day. But the fates would not allow it, and when the flood surged down from the mountains and swept his beloved away, lost also was his only hope for a wife and family.

This nightmare had been a very real one, as was the scar that lined the entire left side of his brother's face. And like the painful moment when he had heard that his Katrina was gone for all eternity, Alexander would never forget his first glance of his twin brother as he was carried off the railcar.

The war had been over for several weeks before he received the official notice informing him that Mikhail was still alive. Having long ago given up any hope of ever seeing his brother alive again, Alexander cried out in sheer joy. As one of the handful of survivors pulled out of the Bergen-Belsen concentration camp, Mikhail was being treated at a Red Cross hospital and would be sent back to the

Soviet Union as soon as he was strong enough.

Fighting the impulse to go to this hospital and see his twin with his own eyes, Alexander anxiously waited for the next notice. It came three weeks later, along with the time, date and train number on which Mikhail would be arriving.

Kiev had never looked so beautiful as on that early summer morning in 1945 when Alexander made his way to the town's train station. A carnival atmosphere prevailed here as thousands of others waited for their loved ones. The train had originated in Berlin, and was packed with returning soldiers. There was many a tender moment as husbands and wives, fathers and mothers, kissed, hugged and cried, overcome with joy and relief.

It took over an hour for this riotous scene to calm itself, and only when the platform was cleared were the wounded unloaded. First came those with crutches and canes. When Mikhail wasn't spotted in this sad group, he was forced to wait until the stretchers were all carried out. There were over a hundred altogether, and Alexander had to go down the entire line twice before finally finding his brother.

Actually, it had been the other way around. Because if it wasn't for Mikhail's eyes lighting up like they did when his twin passed, Alexander would never have recognized him. Though only four years had gone by since they were separated on that fated August day, Mikhail had aged tenfold. Gaunt and almost skeletal in appearance, Mikhail was speechless as his brother embraced him. There were tears of joy running down his bony cheeks as Alexander pulled back and took his first close look at his twin. It was then he spotted the jagged

223

scar that stretched from Mikhail's graying temple to his beard stubbled chin.

Oblivious to the fact that his blond hair was now almost completely white and that even the color of his eyes had faded, Alexander reached under the sheet and picked up his brother in his arms. He was as light as a child, his once muscular frame no more. But that made no difference to Alexander, who proceeded to carry his brother all the way home.

From that day onward, Alexander centered his entire life around getting his brother well once more. It was difficult at first. Mikhail's starved body was weak, and he seemed to always have a cold or bronchitis. But Alexander persisted. He did whatever was necessary to find Mikhail nourishing foods, even going so far as giving his twin his own portion when food was in short supply. He also made certain to get his brother out in the fresh air whenever possible. Slowly but surely this therapy worked. Color returned to his once pallid cheeks, and he even began to gain weight again.

It took over a year for his body to recover. But even then there was a sallowness to his skin that never seemed to go away, and of course there were mental scars that Alexander could never begin to heal, or for that matter, even fathom.

Mikhail didn't talk much about his experiences in the death camp, but it was obvious that something hideous had taken place within the confines of that barbed-wire hell that had changed him forever. Serious and sober, Mikhail no longer knew what it was to laugh and have fun. He seemed to have been vaulted to another level of consciousness, far away from that of the mundane world.

Alexander worried that this morbid state of mind would destroy his brother, the hatred eating him up from the inside like a malignant cancer. A prominent psychiatrist was brought in, and it was this figure who suggested that Mikhail refocus this rage on an outside object. All this was taking place during the time of the infamous Nuremberg trials, and the newspapers were filled with stories telling of Nazis who had fled to Africa and South America to escape the hand of justice. When a Soviet commission was formed to investigate these reports, Alexander saw the perfect opportunity to test the doctor's theory. A quick trip to Moscow resulted in Alexander securing his brother a position in this commission. And when Mikhail was told of this, for the very first time in over a year, his face broke out in a broad smile.

Little did Alexander ever realize that Mikhail would proceed to devote the rest of his life to this cause. Even today, over four and a half decades after the war's conclusion, Mikhail was still out there on the trail of the Nazi beast.

He currently operated under the auspices of the KGB. There were many in Moscow who called his work a wasted effort, while others said that Mikhail was merely insane. Yet all of these critics were silenced time and again as Mikhail brought Nazi war criminals to justice from far corners of the globe.

Only last year, when Mikhail had returned from a three month stint in the Amazon, Alexander had asked him if he was ready to retire. His brother looked at him as if he were crazy.

"This is no ordinary job that I'm involved with," explained Mikhail passionately, "It is a lifetime quest!"

"And when will this quest end?" asked Alexander.

His brother answered bluntly. "Either when I'm dead, or after I've succeeded in destroying Werewolf."

It was at that moment that Alexander realized what was driving his twin so. Werewolf, the code name for a powerful Neo-Nazi group that supposedly had members in America, Europe, South America and Japan. Yet it wasn't necessarily the group itself that Mikhail was after, but the man who was Werewolf's self-proclaimed leader — Otto Koch, the same SS officer who had stolen the gold that they had been escorting to Leningrad — the same SS officer who had condemned Mikhail to the living hell of Bergen-Belsen.

Every morning for the past five decades, Mikhail had only to look into the mirror to be reminded of the day when Otto Koch first came into his life. Even as Alexander lay there in the stateroom of the Alfa class submarine, his twin brother was out there, somewhere in the world, devoting his every effort to bringing this demon to justice. There could be no more noble cause than this, and Alexander could only wish his brother every success in his efforts.

Having all but forgotten the nightmare that had triggered these vibrant impressions, the old veteran nervously jumped when a firm knock sounded on the cabin's shut door, accompanied by a scratchy voice.

"Admiral Kuznetsov, it's Felix Bucharin. I hope you haven't forgotten, but it's time for the Komsomol meeting."

Called thusly back to duty, Alexander replied. "I hear you, Comrade Zampolit. If you'll just give me

226

a few more minutes to get my things together, I'll be with you presently."

A familiar pain throbbed in the veteran's aching joints as he struggled to sit up. He managed to limp over to the wash basin where he washed his face in a stream of icy cold water. This served to waken him completely, and as he dried his face with a rough linen towel his thoughts were already redirecting themselves to the speech that he would soon be giving.

Chapter Ten

Petty Officer First Class Joe Carter sat in the *Cheyenne*'s mess toying with his turkey stew. Seated opposite him, Senior Seaman Sam Tabor was digging into his bowl of stew with an appetite.

"Darn it, Tabor," said Carter as he pushed away his partially eaten plate of chow. "Don't you ever get sick of this turkey stuff?"

The brawny mechanic answered without even bothering to swallow down the mouthful of food he was eating. "I like it, Joe."

"You eat anything they put in front of you," observed Carter. "First it's turkey patties, and now it's turkey stew. I'm craving for a nice juicy, medium rare steak, or maybe some crispy fried chicken and gravy. Now that's real food that sticks to a guys ribs."

Joe Carter tried a spoonful of yogurt and spat it out disgustedly. "Jesus, Mallott's even getting funny with our desserts. I want some pie or a big hot fudge sundae with peppermint ice cream."

Carter's dinner companion shovelled up his remaining stew and mopped up the plate with his roll. "Aren't you hip, Joe? This is some of that new health food. Why it's guaranteed to put five extra years on your life."

Carter sneered. "Man, if I wanted to live forever,

I sure wouldn't have signed onto a nuclear submarine. As for this health food crap, my grandpa's ninety-five years old and that guy's in better shape than half the bozos on this boat. Why he even drives himself to work everyday. And do you think that he eats turkey burgers and yogurt? Hell, no way. Old grandpop puts away a pound of bacon a week, has two eggs fried in butter every morning, and especially enjoys his fried catfish, porkchops and chitlins."

"I don't know, Joe," returned the skeptical mechanic. "My wife gets one of those health magazines and from what I read it sure sounds to me like diet plays an important role in living longer. Your grandfather must be a rare exception."

"Hell, Tabor, if you believed half the things you read in those health books you wouldn't eat red meat because of the hormones, fish because of the pollution, and fruits and vegetables because of all that bug spray that's put on them. Why they say that even the water's poison, and as far as the air's concerned, you'd better not breath it for long."

The mechanic couldn't help but laugh at this remark, and realizing how angry he had been getting, Carter joined him.

"Guess I'd better throw together some peanut butter and jelly sandwiches to take back to the sound shack with me," said Carter between chuckles. "I got a feeling it's going to be a long night."

"When's that exercise supposed to begin?" asked the mechanic as he spooned in a mouthful of yogurt.

Joe answered while standing up and stretching. "If I'm not mistaken, it already did about an hour ago."

"Then what is the *Cheyenne*'s best pair of ears doing back here shooting the stuff in the mess?" quizzed Tabor.

Joe Carter grinned. "Have no fear, my man. The captain's been saving me for the heavy stuff. And besides, we've just penetrated the southern portion of our patrol sector anyway, so the hunt is just now official."

"Well, go get 'em, Carter. I hear those Kraut submariners are tricky bastards."

"With their U-boat tradition and all, they should be," replied the senior sonar technician with a wink. "See you for breakfast, Tabor. And if you're nice to me, perhaps I'll share my turkey sausage with you."

After hurriedly preparing himself a couple of sandwiches, Carter ducked out the forward hatchway. The sound shack was situated off a long passageway that led directly to the control room. Its specially designed door was shut to protect the acoustic integrity of the compartment inside. A large hammer and sickle that had a thick red slash mark drawn over it was painted on this portal. Carter briefly touched this symbol for luck before entering.

Inside, there were three individual consoles. Each had a baffled wall between them. Only the first two stations were manned. Both of the specialists who sat here wore headphones, and had an assortment of flashing repeater screens, amplifiers, filtering mechanisms, and sound meters before them.

The room smelled of stale coffee and sweat. As Carter proceeded to his station, which lay against the far bulkhead, the figure seated in the middle position noted his presence.

"It's about time you got here, Chief," greeted Senior Seaman Vic Manning.

Carter responded while settling himself into his chair. "Why's that, Manning? Did you miss me?"

"I guess you could say that we did, Chief. Because the XO was just down here and he really read us the riot act."

"Let me guess," remarked Carter. "Lieutenant Commander Stoddard was pissed as hell because you didn't tag that surface ship that almost sliced the top of our sail off."

"You got it, Chief. But hell's bells, we've got a sea-state topside that's all full of ambient noise. And besides, the XO knows very well that even under normal conditions, whenever a submarine approaches the surface, the physics of underwater sound and the near surface effect of solar heating combine to render our sonar nearly useless."

"I understand, Manning. Just take a deep breath and relax," advised his experienced co-worker, as he draped his own headphones around his neck. "The XO knows the score. He was just doing what all officers do best, putting the fear of God in you so that you'll apply yourself even harder the next time. We're no miracle workers down here and he knows it. We can only monitor what our sensors tell us."

"And in this instance it was a big fat zero," continued the upset technician.

Joe Carter began activating his console as he replied. "I'll tell you what, Manning. When this exercise is over, I'll sit down with you and we'll go over the tape inch by inch. And if that ship's signature is indeed inaudible, I'll personally bring it up to the XO to clear the air."

"I'd appreciate that, Chief."

"Then it's settled," returned Carter firmly. "Now let's get down to work and show our NATO allies who they're dealing with out here."

Carter addressed his keyboard and initiated a broad-band passive sonar scan. Unlike the sub's active sonar that projected acoustic pulses out into the surrounding waters, the passive system involved no such transmissions that could give the hunter away. It depended upon a series of hydrophones. These ultra-sensitive listening devices were strategically set into the *Cheyenne*'s hull in various locations.

Carter began his scan to determine current sea conditions. This involved a full spectrum of incoming signals, and the senior technician did his best to separate the various random noises of the sea and its creatures from the man-made signatures that he was searching for.

In such a manner he was able to pick out the sound of the wave surge above them as it smashed into the bases of the nearby oil production platforms. Another submarine could easily take advantage of this racket and attempt hiding in it, and Carter would have to pay extra attention in monitoring it.

As he continued scanning the various frequencies, he came across a sound that seemed as if it was produced by thousands of madly clattering castenets. These musicians of the deep were shrimps. And soon they had a bass accompaniment as they were joined by a deep, drawn-out, mournful cry that sounded almost unearthly in its origin. Carter was no stranger to the monstrous creature responsible for this distinctive song, for since he was a child, whales had always fascinated him. The strange thing was that he never even knew that they could sing in this manner, until he was in basic training. This discovery inspired him to check out the San Diego seaquarium, and he wasn't the least bit disappointed. After one of the shows, a trainer let him feed a pair of small pilot whales, who responded with a series of spirited, well-rehearsed jumps.

The dolphins were extremely talkative, and there was no doubt in Carter's mind that their squeals, groans and whistles were a language all their own. Their cousins the whales also communicated in this manner, and when Carter learned that some of these songs could be heard hundreds of miles away, he decided to research this astounding subject more closely in the base library.

One of his instructors during basic was actively involved with an ongoing project that was attempting to train marine mammals for use by the navy. Carter approached him after class and practically begged him to share some of his findings. The instructor was cold to his approach at first, but after Carter continued to pester him, he finally gave in and asked Joe to accompany them on a field trip to the Channel Islands. This trip turned into a week long affair, during which time they were responsible for a pair of specially trained seals. These boisterous, perpetually hungry creatures were sent out to locate a torpedo that had been lost in the waters off Catalina Island. While the seals hunted for this object, Joe was instructed in the use of a small, bottom-scanning sonar unit that had been fitted into the hull of their boat. As it turned out, the seals found the torpedo before Joe was able to. After the seals attached a retrieval harness onto the weapon, they were gathered up and returned to San Diego.

233

By the time Joe returned to the base, he knew that he wanted to be a sonar operator. He applied himself to his studies with a new intensity, paying particular attention to his science classes. When it was discovered that he had above average hearing, he found himself one step closer to his goal. The rest was hard work and a little luck of the draw along the way.

Joe Carter was proud of his present position. As the *Cheyenne*'s senior sonar technician, he was the eyes and ears of the ship when it was underwater. Though he had been offered a permanent teaching position at the base in San Diego, he chose to go to sea instead. This had been a decision that he certainly didn't regret.

It was exciting to be a prime component of the *Cheyenne*'s attack team. Their ship was one of the best in the fleet, as was its corps of officers and enlisted men. Carter was especially impressed with his C.O. He knew Captain Aldridge was a class act from the first moment they met. Working with him was a pleasure, since he gave Carter plenty of room to do his own thing.

Sonar work was more like an art form than a regimented discipline. Though its basic premise was one hundred percent scientific, creative thinking came into play as one interpreted the data. Then there was that gray area, when the sensors showed nothing, but the intuition knew differently. Some called this nothing but pure chance or luck. Carter couldn't really say, though sometimes it was almost scary when an impulse turned into cold truth.

As the whales continued their sad song, he switched over to the narrow-band system. In an instant, the random noises of the sea were gone. He

234

was now searching for one sound only, that which would be produced by another submarine. The process that allowed such a scan was an extremely sophisticated one that required spectrum analyzers and powerful microprocessors.

Settling back in his chair, Carter isolated the *Cheyenne*'s BQQ-25 towed array. Originally stored in a long tube that lay between the pressure hull and the boat's outer casing, the array was released into the water by means of a winch set into the forward ballast tank. The hydrophones themselves were attached to a cable 2,624 feet long and .37 inches in diameter. This cable was being towed behind them in a straight line, at a restricted speed so that it would not oscillate and give their own position away. It was designed to give them a rearward-looking capability that was not available by any other means.

Carter was well into his watch, with the towed array still deployed, when the barest of flickering movements caught his eye on his repeater screen. Quickly turning up the volume gain of the hydrophone responsible for capturing this sound, he closed his eyes and focused his concentration on the steady hissing signal being conveyed into his headphones. For the briefest of seconds he picked up a barely audible pulsating noise. Yet before he could further increase the gain it was gone.

Again he carefully checked the screen, whose sensor was far more sensitive than the human ear. But just like the signal being conveyed into his headphones, it too drew a blank.

Was this distant throbbing sound the signature of another submarine? Or was it only an anomaly produced by the gremlins of the deep? With the availa-

235

ble hard data, Joe Carter couldn't really say one way or the other. He could only be guided by the pull of his instincts, that warned him that this sound was worth checking out.

Carter was in the midst of reaching out for the intercom to inform the control room of his find, when all hell broke out in the waters in front of them.

"Jesus Christ, what the hell is that?" quizzed Vic Manning as he yanked off his headphones to massage his pained eardrums.

Even without the benefits of headphones, a gut-wrenching, grinding cacophony of sound could be heard emanating from the seas beyond. Spurred on by this racket, Joe Carter turned down his own volume gain, so that he wouldn't receive a sonic lashing like his co-worker had, and tuned in the bow hydrophones.

To get the full effect, he switched to the broad band processor. As he expertly determined the noise's range and bearing, it became evident that it was originating from a portion of the sea near one of the oil platforms. It was on a pure hunch that he switched back to the narrow-band processor. It was then that he knew for certain just what had occurred out there.

Admiral Alexander Kuznetsov was in the process of concluding the speech he had been giving for the last quarter of an hour, when this same grinding noise reached the *Lena*. Even though this was the high point of his address to the eight members of the Komsomol gathered before him, the veteran immediately halted. All eyes went instinctively to the

236

ceiling, as the screeching groan of metal on metal intensified.

"Have we hit something?" cried out one of the apprentice seaman in horror.

"Good heavens, no!" retorted Alexander. "If that would have been the case, we'd all be spilled out on the deck by now, with the sea pouring in on top of us. Most likely that din is being caused by another vessel's misfortune. Why, I bet that Norwegian diving support ship that I watched pass us earlier has hit one of the oil production platforms!"

This conjecture was met by the harsh ringing of the compartment's intercom. It proved to be Felix Bucharin who picked up the handset.

"Zampolit speaking . . . why yes, Captain, he's right before me . . . I'll tell him to at once, Comrade. By the way, Captain. Captain? Captain?"

Hanging up the handset in disgust, the Political Officer looked up to address their guest speaker. "Captain Milyutin requests your presence in the attack center at once, Admiral. Maybe he'll be able to tell you what all this racket is about."

The mysterious noise had all but disappeared by now, and Alexander quickly gathered up his notes and excused himself. The attack center was lit in red light to protect the crew's night vision, and it took the veteran several seconds to be able to spot the *Lena*'s captain hunched anxiously over the sonar console. Quickly he joined him.

"Captain?" quizzed Alexander expectantly.

Grigori Milyutin looked up with a Cheshire cat grin turning the corners of his mouth. "Ah, Admiral. You'll never believe what took place in the water behind us."

"From that grinding roar, it sounded as if there's

been a collision. Was it that Norwegian ship that we watched pass on the periscope earlier?" offered Alexander.

"It's better than that," returned the excited captain. "An extensive sonar scan of the noise's source indicates that what we were hearing was the sound of a submarine colliding with the base of one of the production rigs!"

"Why that's remarkable," said Alexander. "I do hope that it wasn't one of ours."

"That's highly unlikely, Admiral. Unless there was some sort of clandestine operation going on out here that I wasn't informed of, there should be no other Soviet submarines within a thousand kilometers of us."

"Then I wonder who it was?" reflected Alexander.

Once more a broad grin turned the corners of the captain's mouth. "Shall we turn around and find out, Admiral? We could do so with the least bit of trouble. Once we identify the unfortunate vessel and determine its degree of damage, we can turn south again and be on our way to Karsto with minimum delay."

"I must admit — your suggestion sounds awfully tempting," mused Alexander.

"Just think of the wealth of intelligence such a survey will generate," added the Captain. "This will especially be the case if it turns out to be an American vessel."

It was obvious that Grigori Milyutin wanted to gloat over another commanding officer's misfortune. Such a desire was only natural, especially for a Soviet mariner. The waters off the coast of Norway had been notorious over the years as a graveyard for Soviet submarines. Three nuclear subs had al-

238

ready sunk there, while numerous others succumbed to fires and other internal disasters that sent them shooting to the surface for assistance. The Western news media had a field day with these incidents, which often made front page headlines. A proud force like the Rodina's submariners were just waiting to return the favor, and Alexander couldn't blame them. Yet was this the right time?

Back in Vorkuta, the Deputy Secretary General had stressed the utter importance of their mission, for only when their reconnaissance of the Karsto pumping facility was completed could a decision be made concerning the Soviet Union's own pipeline into the heart of Europe. Such a venture had an enormous scope, and billions of rubles were at stake. Alexander had no choice.

"I'm sorry, Captain, but we must continue on to Karsto as planned. Our mission is too important, and no such diversion can be allowed."

Disappointment was evident on the Captain's face, but his voice betrayed no emotion. He nodded curtly and said, "I understand, Admiral."

As Grigori Milyutin somberly walked back to his console, Alexander couldn't help but feel sorry for the young officer. As the first Soviet Navy representative on the scene of the collision site, he would have been an instant celebrity to his contemporaries back at Polyarny. But other duties called, and though they were less glamorous, the results of their mission could change the entire balance of power in the Rodina's favor.

Back on the USS *Cheyenne*, there was absolutely no doubt about the direction of their course. Inside the control room, Steven Aldridge looked on as his XO finished his conversation on the vessel's underwater telephone.

"It's that West German sub all right, Skipper," reported Stoddard as he hung up the handset. "Its name is the *Emden*. From what I gather, they were trying to hide behind one of those platforms, when a swell got a hold of them and smashed them up against the rig's base."

"How bad are the damages?" asked Aldridge.

"They still don't know the extent of them yet, Skipper. They've got a pretty nasty leak in the forward torpedo room, and they're operating under emergency power. But other than that, their pressure hull seems to be intact."

"Thank God for that," said Aldridge. "Any injuries?"

"A broken leg seems to be the worst of them," answered the XO. "But from what the Captain said, his crew is pretty shaken up."

"I can imagine," said Aldridge. "I wonder if they're going to need a tow into port."

The XO shook his head. "Definitely not, Skipper. That's one thing that Kraut captain was firm about. As soon as they have that leak under control, he'll be heading back to port under their own power."

Aldridge beckoned his XO to join him beside the periscope well.

"I think it's best if we stand by nevertheless, XO. Sometimes a captain can be blinded by pride. If he underestimated the initial damages, we might be needed yet."

The XO pulled his pipe out of his pants pocket, looking thoughtful as he placed its scarred bit between his lips. "I don't know about that, Skipper.

There's a full crew of Norwegians on that rig, and even though the damage to the German sub seems negligible, they've already called for a Coast Guard cutter. One's steaming out of Haugesund even as we speak."

"Then I guess that's it for our NATO maneuvers," remarked the Captain.

"Now what, Skipper?"

Before Aldridge could answer his second in command, he noted with surprise that a newcomer had just entered the control room. Petty Officer Joe Carter didn't frequent this portion of the ship often, and the black sonar technician seemed relieved when he finally spotted Aldridge and the XO perched beside the periscope well. Without hesitation, he proceeded straight for them.

"Excuse me, Captain, but I think there's something that you should know about."

"Then let's hear it, Mr. Carter," replied Aldridge, who encouraged his subordinates to be frank with him.

Joe Carter seemed a bit uncomfortable as he continued. "Right before we monitored that collision, I picked up something on the narrow-band processor. I only got it for a second, but I'm pretty sure that we just had an unidentified submerged contact pass us by. From its signature it sounded like a nuke and it was headed due south."

Aldridge looked at his XO as he responded. "Well, I'll be. If it is indeed another nuke, it's got to be the Red version. This entire sector's strictly off limits to any other NATO warship but the *Cheyenne* and our German friends out there."

"If it is Ivan, what's he doing this far east of his normal transit lane?" asked the XO.

"Maybe he's not headed out into the North Atlantic," offered Joe Carter.

The Captain's eyes lit up. "You could be onto something, Mr. Carter. Do you think that you could find them again?"

Joe Carter answered with confidence. "If he's out there and he's wet, I can find him all right."

"Then let's do it," ordered Aldridge. "And if it is Ivan, we'll secretly tail along in his baffles to see what he's up to."

Anxious to finally see some real action, the XO concurred. "You know something, Skipper? This patrol might just prove to be interesting after all."

242

Chapter Eleven

Mikhail Kuznetsov chose a hotel room that directly overlooked Tromso's main wharf area. From this vantage point he could see every single ship that entered the harbor. The docks themselves were right beneath him, four floors below. Tied up there were a number of rust-stained fishing vessels, several ocean-going trawlers, and a trio of Norwegian Navy patrol boats.

It was well past noon when he finally snapped awake. He was disoriented at first, and when he finally remembered where he was and saw the time he rushed to his room's only window. It was a gray overcast day, and snow was falling. He intently scanned the dock area, and exhaled a breath of relief only after seeing that the ship he was waiting for had yet to arrive.

Only then was Mikhail conscious of the chill in his room. He went to the fireplace and filled it with dried kindling. With the aid of a rolled up newspaper and his trusty Zippo lighter, he soon had a roaring blaze going. The heat felt good on his old bones, and he warmed himself thoroughly before turning to do his toilet.

By the time he finished his shower, he felt like a new man. He had slept for over twelve hours straight, and this more than made up for the previous evening when he was forced to drive all through the night.

Mikhail dressed himself and returned to the window to continue his vigil. He knew that the trawler was not due to arrive for at least another hour. Still, he couldn't afford to get lax now.

He sat down on the leather chair and stared out to the harbor, reaching down for the loaf of rye bread he had purchased in town last night. This, together with a tart green apple and a wheel of goat cheese, provided his breakfast. Though he craved a cup of coffee, he contented himself with a long swig from a bottle of mineral water. With his stomach filled, he turned his stare back to the gray waters below.

The snow was falling steadily, and several centimeters had already accumulated on the decks of the docked boats. Even so, the visibility wasn't that bad, and he could still see the opposite shoreline, where the rest of the sprawling city of Tromso extended well up into the snow-filled mountains. An immense, single-span suspension bridge connected this newly developed portion of the city with the older section where Mikhail was currently staying. Occasionally, when the cloud layer lifted, he could see the ultra-modern cathedral that was the predominant landmark in this newer area of town.

From what little he had already seen of Tromso, it reminded him of similar outposts that dotted Soviet Siberia. Like them, it had a young frontier spirit. Situated well above the Arctic Circle, on Norway's northern coast, Tromso was once known as the gateway to the Arctic, in reference to the many polar expeditions that used the city as their base camp on the way to the North Pole.

This was Mikhail's first visit. He only learned that he'd be going to Tromso yesterday morning, while at the docks at Trondheim. Up until then, he had followed the heavy water all the way up from Lake Tinnsjo. As he watched the thirty-three cannisters being loaded into the hold of a trawler, he waited for the vessel to set sail so that he could question the freight agent and find out where the ship was bound. Mikhail was just about to get on with his interrogation when the blond Norwegian diver unexpectedly arrived on the wharf and beat him to it.

Cursing the big-shouldered Viking's interference, Mikhail nervously waited for the diver to finish his business and leave. In actuality, he was only in the small, wooden building that acted as the freight office for a few minutes. Mikhail watched the Norwegian exit the hut and hurriedly rush off to his awaiting automobile.

Quickly now, Mikhail moved in himself. He found himself praying that the portly agent in the wrinkled blue suit would still be alive as he pushed open the door to the hut and entered. Inside, he found the room's only occupant slumped down in a chair, taking long sips from a bottle of aquavit. His hair was tousled, his clothing disheveled, as he looked up with undisguised terror at Mikhail's approach.

"Whatever do you want?" he asked anxiously.

Mikhail rounded his cluttered desk, and spotted hundreds of dollars in Norwegian kroners laying scattered on the floor.

"I want to know the destination of that trawler that just set sail from here," stated Mikhail firmly.

The agent raised his eyes in panic and confusion.

"What in the world is so special about that damn trawler? All of a sudden it seems that everybody wants to know where the *Elsie K* is headed."

Mikhail decided that a bluff would get him the quickest results. "It seems that my excitable colleague has already beat me to it. Now are you going to share that destination with me, or am I going to have to call my co-worker back here?"

"Please, I've seen enough of that brute for one day," pleaded the frantic agent. "The *Elsie K* is bound for Tromso. That's as far as I booked her, I swear. From there her skipper can take those two who chartered her all the way to Siberia, for all I care."

Mikhail had seen enough in his days to know that the terrified freight agent was telling the truth.

"How long will this voyage take?" he asked.

"At the very least, twenty-four hours. Though with the rough seas that have been reported to the north, it could take even longer."

Mikhail had heard enough, and left the hut without so much as a thank you. He returned to his car, and studied the map of Norway that was spread out on the front seat. Tromso was a good eight hundred kilometers distant by car. In no condition to tackle such a trip after his long night on the road, he decided to take a plane.

He got to the Trondheim airport just as a Braathens Safe flight headed northward was preparing to take off. He made it with seconds to spare, and an hour later was touching down at Tromso.

Suddenly finding himself with twenty-four hours to spare, Mikhail took a taxi into the town itself. When he mentioned that he had business down at the docks and was looking for the nearest hotel, his

246

driver seemed to know the perfect place for him, and it was on his recommendation that Mikhail found his present lodging.

It was only when he finally got up to his room that he realized the state of his exhaustion. Without even bothering to kick off his shoes, he collapsed onto the bed, and slept straight through to dusk.

He awoke with a ravenous hunger. At the hotel's cafe he wolfed down two orders of herring, a bowl of beets, and a double serving of boiled potatoes. Afterward, he walked over to a small roadside market and purchased a bottle of mineral water and his breakfast, which he planned to eat in his room.

There was a frigid wind blowing out of the north as he hurriedly returned to the hotel. His old bones protested at the three flights of stairs that he was forced to climb, but soon enough he was back in his room. Quickly banking the fire, he pulled off his clothes and slipped between the sheets of his bed. And here it was twelve hours later, with Mikhail feeling warm, rested, and ready for action.

As he looked out to the harbor, he could see that the three navy patrol boats were preparing to put to sea. Each of these very capable-looking craft had large search radar domes topping their masts, and were heavily armed with a cannon on the foredeck and an assortment of torpedoes and depth charges stored on the stern. The Norwegian Navy took its job very seriously, and this was most evident as the first patrol boat smartly cast off. The two others followed close behind, the three vessels looking sleek and deadly as their angled hulls cut a frothing, v-shaped swath through the gray waters of the harbor.

Mikhail looked at his watch, and noted that he had several hours yet before the trawler was due.

247

Not daring to leave his current vantage point, he would continue this vigil as long as necessary.

The only thing that could go wrong now was if the trawler known as the *Elsie K* wasn't headed to Tromso at all. Then his long wait would be in vain. But he had been absolutely certain that the freight agent had been telling the truth back in Tronheim. Mikhail had gambled that this was the most sensible course open to him, because it would have been virtually impossible to find another ship in time for him to shadow the trawler. Though it tore him apart to watch the two Nazis and their dangerous cargo slip through his hands like they did, Mikhail had no choice. If it was fated to be, he would meet with them once again in these next few hours. Then, and only then, could he continue his quest, one step closer to fulfilling his lifetime goal.

There was close to a full gale blowing when No-roil One finally lifted off from the *Falcon's* helipad. Because of the worsening weather conditions, Kari Skollevoll had full authority to postpone the flight if she so desired, yet she didn't dare disappoint the group of three young divers who were her anxious passengers.

The Bell 212 leaped off the deck and temporarily shuddered when a powerful gust of wind did its best to hurl the chopper back downward. Kari had been anticipating this downdraft, and countered it by pulling the throttle back and sending the helicopter spiralling upward.

Her crew was unusually quiet as she turned for Norway's northern coastline. The members of NUEX remained huddled in the main cabin in the

248

midst of a hushed conversation. Well accustomed to flying alone, she doublechecked her course, and then hit the 'on' switch to her cassette player. Once again it was Grieg's *Peer Gynt* that provided the spirited accompaniment as she settled back for the long flight that followed.

The tape was well into *Peer Gynt's* last act when Jon Huslid entered the cockpit and crawled into the co-pilot's seat. Kari was in the process of reaching up to turn down the volume when the photographer stopped her.

"Leave it the way it is, Kari. If I knew that you had Grieg on up here, I would have joined you much earlier."

Together they listened to Solvejg's *Song in the Hut, Song of the Churchgoers* and Solvejg's *Lullaby* before the tape came to an end.

"That was wonderful," observed Jon. "Do you mind playing the tape over again?"

"Not at all, Jon. There's so much varied music in the piece that I can never hear it enough."

"I know what you mean, Kari. I started listening to *Peer Gynt* as a kid. The music never failed to bring forth visions of trolls and fantastic forest creatures. I used to hum the melodies to myself when I was out on the fjords, with my very favorite being *In the Hall of the Mountain King.*"

"It's funny, but I always associated that particular piece with witches, warlocks and Hallowcen," commented Kari.

"From what I understand, those are the exact images that Grieg wanted to convey in that segment," returned Jon.

Barely aware of the constant background whine of the Bell 212's rotors the two continued listening to

249

the unfolding music. It was just after the haunting violin solo in the *Spring Dance* was concluding that Jakob Helgesen poked his head into the cockpit.

"It sounds pretty good up here," said Jakob. "Of course, practically anything would sound better than having to hear Arne go on about why he's the better chess player. How much longer until we touch down, Kari?"

The pilot looked up to check the clock. "We should be landing in Tromso in another half hour. Luckily, we've got a hell of a tailwind."

Jakob peered out the plexiglass windshield and could see nothing but clouds.

"I wonder what the ceiling is like in Tromso?" asked the Lapp.

Kari delicately adjusted the fuel mixture and answered. "The last I heard, visibility at the Tromso airport was down to three kilometers. They've also got some pretty strong wind gusts coming in from the west, and at last report it was snowing. But its certainly nothing that I can't handle."

"Compared to that weather that we had during take off, Tromso sounds pretty tame," said the photographer.

"You certainly did one fine job back there, little lady," added Jakob. "When that downdraft hit us, I could have sworn that Arne was going to wet his shorts."

Kari laughed. "Thanks, Jakob. Coming from you, that's a real compliment. I take pride in my job. But I still think that the work that you guys do is far more difficult."

"Perhaps you mean dangerous," said the Lapp. "It takes a real skill to fly this chopper. What do we have to know but to watch our decompression tables

250

and swim?"

"Come on, Jakob. Don't give me any of that," returned the pilot. "Nobody goes down to the depths that you guys work at without plenty of hard-earned experience. Diving might not be as technically challenging as flying, but it's a complicated endeavor all the same, that nobody walks into overnight."

"She's got you on that one, Jakob," said Jon Huslid.

The Lapp shrugged his shoulders. "I'll tell you what, Kari. I'll swap you diving lessons if you teach me to fly."

"That's a deal," shot back the pilot. "But only if those lessons take place someplace warm, like the Caribbean."

"You fly us there, and you're on," replied Jakob.

By the time Act III of *Peer Gynt* was ending, the helicopter had completed its transit of the Norwegian Sea and was flying over the rugged, fjord-filled Kvaloy peninsula. Minutes later, they were landing at the Tromso airport.

Because of the continued high winds and falling snow, Kari decided to remain in Tromso for the night. This was fine with the members of NUEX, who flagged down a cab and instructed its driver to convey them to town.

The team had been to Tromso before, while doing a preliminary salvage survey on the wreck of the German battleship, *Tirpitz*. This vessel lay on the bottom of a nearby fjord, and provided them with hours of fascinating exploration.

Since Jakob was from this region, he provided a running commentary as they approached the city center. Kari's previous visits to Tromso had been limited to the airport, and she enjoyed seeing such

251

sights as the city's new planetarium, its bustling streets, and the famous Polar museum. When they passed a statue of Roald Amundsen, Kari asked the taxi driver to stop, and she ran out in the snow to have a closer look at it. As it turned out, Kari's grandfather had once helped outfit the famous Arctic explorer, who was like a god to the people of Norway.

Leaving the statue behind, the cab headed for the nearby docks. The driver had no trouble at all conveying them to the Northern Lights Cafe, located on the bottom floor of a converted four-story warehouse. The cafe itself directly faced the harbor. In fact, Tromso's fishing fleet was docked almost right in front of the cafe's large picture window.

The raucous, electric sounds of a live rock band practicing upstairs could be clearly heard as they entered the cafe. Inside, it was warm and cozy. The majority of the clientele was students, and Jon instantly scanned this crowd for any sign of Knut Haugen. The big blond was nowhere in sight, and after choosing a round table that stood right beside the picture window, they went up to the counter to order.

"I wonder where the big fellow is?" asked Arne. They returned to the table to await their food.

"He'll show up eventually," said Jakob, who picked a chair affording him a clear view of the snow-covered wharf outside. "You know Knut when it comes to getting anywhere on time. That one's going to be late to his own funeral."

Their drinks arrived, as music blared from the cafe's p.a. system. The three divers sipped on their bug juices, while Kari contented herself with a cup of herb tea.

252

"You never did explain what Knut was doing here in Tromso," observed the pilot. "The last I heard, he was still hospitalized with a concussion back in Rjukan."

Jon took his time answering her. "Our hard-headed colleague decided to check out of that clinic early. It seems he took it upon himself to go after the men who killed his cousin and friend."

Kari winced in disgust. "I find it hard to believe that someone would actually commit homicide for a bunch of rusty drums."

"That bunch of rusty drums, as you call them, is worth its weight in gold," returned the photographer.

"I still don't understand why Knut just didn't wait for the police to find the murderers," continued Kari.

This time it was Arne who broke in. "You don't know Knut very well, Kari. We were both brought up in Telemark, where a fellow learns to take care of himself. Why, my father would never think of calling the police if there was a prowler outside. He would merely get out his shotgun and eliminate the problem himself. Knut's upbringing was no different. The big fellow's not about to just kick back and wait for the authorities to get some results. No way."

The waiter arrived with their food. Each of them had picked the daily special, which was steamed cod, boiled potatoes and peas. They were hungry after their long flight, and ate with a minimum of conversation. The food was delicious, and as they ate, a tall blond with a bandage wrapped around his head entered the cafe. He proceeded straight toward the circular table that was positioned beside the cafe's picture window.

"Hello, friends," greeted this individual casually.

"Knut!" cried Arne, who almost fell over his chair as he stood up to hug his old friend.

Jon and Jakob also stood. Each one in turn embraced the giant, whose vice-like grasp had certainly not weakened any.

"Knut, you remember Kari Skollevoll, don't you?" inquired the photographer.

"Of course I do. Although I almost didn't recognize her without the helicopter."

Kari smiled and pulled over a vacant chair. Knut seated himself in between the pilot and Arne. Their alert waiter had also spotted this newcomer, and as he came over to the table, Knut ordered the special and some bug juice. Only when the waiter turned back for the kitchen did Jon begin his questions.

"When did you get up here, Knut?"

"About ten minutes ago," replied NUEX's chief engineer. "I would have been here waiting for you, but my Uncle Karl's car had a flat outside of Narvik and I had to stop and change it."

"That's quite a drive," observed Kari.

Knut shook his head. "You don't know the half of it, Kari. In the last couple of days I've driven almost the length of this country. And I can't even tell you when I slept last."

"Well, NUEX is all together again," offered Jon. "And now we can take care of you. How's that head wound?"

Knut pointed to the bandage that encircled his skull and just covered his upper forehead. "You mean this little scratch? It's nothing. I've had hangovers that have given me worse headaches."

"A concussion is nothing to take lightly," warned Kari. "Company regulations won't even allow you to

254

fly for an entire two weeks after a serious head wound."

"Who's flying?" retorted Knut, who smiled as his food was served.

His colleagues watched as he proceeded to shovel this chow down. He stopped only to take a drink of juice and belch loudly.

"This is pretty good stuff for being only a couple of thousand klicks away from the North Pole," said Knut after cleaning up the last remaining pea. "Now, what's for dessert?"

Jon was bursting with curiosity and he sat forward to voice himself in a whisper. "To hell with dessert. What in the world are we all doing up here?"

"Why I thought that's obvious," answered Knut. "We're here to collar those bastards responsible for blowing away my cousin Lars and his friend Thor. And while we're at it, there's the little matter of those thirty-three cannisters of heavy water that they stole from us."

"But why Tromso?" asked Jakob.

"Why not?" snapped Knut. "After all, you do want to be around when the trawler holding those bastards and our treasure arrives, don't you?"

"Knut, are you saying that the ones responsible for killing Lars and Thor, and almost you as well, are on their way to Tromso?" asked Jon.

Knut nodded and pointed out the window to the snow-covered wharf beyond. "If they were able to make any time at all on the way up from Trondheim, the vessel carrying those blood-thirsty maniacs and our heavy water is due in here within the hour."

"Why that's incredible!" exclaimed the photographer.

"Do the authorities know about this, Knut?" asked Kari.

"The authorities! That's a joke if I ever heard it," spat the engineer disgustedly. "Those clowns are probably still tripping over themselves while they comb the shoreline back at Lake Tinnsjo looking for evidence. And the only way we're going to get back what's rightfully ours, and bring those murdering crooks to justice along the way, is to apprehend them ourselves.

"Now I personally saw our heavy water being loaded into the hold of a trawler by the name of the *Elsie K* back in Trondheim. The bastards who stole it from us also boarded this ship. I have it from a most reliable source that the *Elsie K* is bound for this very harbor, and is due to arrive here sometime this afternoon.

"If we go to the cops now, they're only going to screw the whole thing up. I tracked the bastards down on my own, and with your help we can collar them with the least bit of risk."

"Don't forget that you're dealing with murderers here, Knut," reminded the helicopter pilot. "This isn't some television show with a guaranteed happy ending. Most likely these guys that you're after are armed and dangerous. They've already killed once. What's going to stop them from doing it again?"

Knut raised one of his massive fists up in front of his jaw. "Those sons of bitches are going to have to get around this first."

Jon cleared his throat. "I've got to admit that I agree with Kari. This is a criminal matter now, and we should let the police handle it. After all, that's what we pay them for. What do you think, Arne?"

The Telemark native thoughtfully scratched his bearded chin and replied. "Hell, since we've come this far already, why don't we at least first see what it's all about before calling in the cops. I've seen them blow more than one bust, and this collar's much too important for us to trust to strangers."

"I agree," said Jakob. "Now if we were down in Oslo, I'd say that it would be different. But this is Tromso. The authorities up here have a whole different attitude about things. Don't forget that I grew up in these parts. Strangers from the south are looked upon with suspicion up here, and that's just who you'll be when you go marching into the local constabulary with this fantastic story. They'll never believe it. And even if they did, it would take them all day to call in the necessary backup."

"Looks like that's three against two," observed Knut calmly. "Are you with us Jon, or not?"

"Damn, somebody's going to have to be around to keep you guys out of trouble, and I guess that somebody is me," said the photographer. "But I see no reason why Kari should be dragged in on this."

"Hold on, partner!" interjected the pilot. "The way I see it, we all get our paychecks signed by the same person, and that makes me a part of this outfit too. And you're forgetting that I also have my black belt in akido."

"Then I guess it's settled," said Knut. "I think our first job should be to completely scope out the dock area. It shouldn't be too hard to find out what pier that trawler will be docking at. Then all we have to do is be waiting for them when they tie up, and surprise those bastards at the first opportunity."

There was an alien tightness in Jon Huslid's gut as he scanned the faces of his teammates, his line of sight finally coming to a halt on the picture window. Outside the snows were continuing to fall with a vengeance, and he could see a moored fishing boat, its deck completely covered in a white shroud. It was then he heard the ominous lyrics of Jim Morrison's *The End* filtering down from the cafe's stereo speakers, and the photographer knew that this dangerous game had a long way to go yet until its conclusion.

As the day continued to wear on, Mikhail Kuznetsov found it more and more difficult to stay awake. Even with his sound rest of the previous night, his eyelids were heavy as he sat beside the window looking out to the wharf below.

Since the trawler was due in any moment now, falling asleep now could be disastrous. Since he couldn't spare the time to go down and get some coffee, he decided to wash his face with cold water, and for a while, this indeed revived him. Yet all so gradually his lids once more began to fall. This time he actually drifted off into the briefest of catnaps.

He awoke with a start several seconds later, and not really knowing how long he had been out, scanned the wharf with renewed intensity. His pulse calmed down only after seeing the same collection of snow-covered vessels that had been down there all day.

Inwardly chastising himself for losing control, Mikhail yanked open the window, causing a frigid blast of Arctic air to stream inside. There'd be no sleeping on the job now, he said to himself as he slipped into his woolen overcoat and sat down to continue his vigil.

The fresh air revitalized him completely. Wide awake now, he peered down to the gray waters of the harbor, paying particular attention to the channel that led beneath the massive suspension bridge, for this was the outlet to the open sea.

Almost like a fog, the snow-laden clouds hung low, partially veiling the upper span of the bridge itself. But the visibility was still good enough for him to spot the familiar orange hull of a battered trawler headed down the channel. As this vessel passed beneath the bridge, Mikhail's pulse again quickened, and he stood, fighting the impulse to cry out in joy. Only when the ship turned for the docks was he one hundred percent positive that this was the *Elsie K*.

As he grabbed for his hat, gloves and muffler, he took one last look at the wharf to determine exactly which pier the trawler would be docking at. The *Elsie K* appeared to be headed toward the marina's central pier, where a petrol station and a small store was situated for the boaters' convenience. This portion of the pier was also accessible by automobile, and there was a parking lot beside it filled with several vehicles.

It was as Mikhail carefully examined this lot that his practiced eye picked out a group of individuals gathered behind a large van. One of these figures was a tall, well-built blond man, with a bandage peeking out from under his hat. Seeing him caused Mikhail to gasp and angrily curse.

"Oh, for the sake of Lenin, not again!"

But Mikhail knew deep inside that he was only fooling himself if he expected to be the only one here to meet the *Elsie K*. Hadn't the Norwegian

259

diver been there at the pier at Trondheim also? And hadn't the Viking beaten him to the freight agent, who was only too willing to tell Mikhail where the trawler had been bound?

The young Norwegian had every right to be here. After all, he had the deaths of his comrades to revenge. But this act would be inconsequential when compared to the type of vindication that Mikhail had in mind. Before the Norwegian and his group of cohorts moved in prematurely and spoiled the trap, Mikhail had to act quickly. Or everything would be ruined!

Knut Haugen cautiously peeked around the back end of the Volkswagen van that they were using for cover, and watched as a deckhand jumped off the orange-hulled trawler to secure the mooring lines.

"That's the vessel alright," observed Knut to his group of co-workers huddled behind the van itself.

An angry sharpness flavored his tone when two blond men dressed in black oilskins climbed onto the ship's deck from a hatchway. "And there's the bastards who killed Lars and Thor!"

The other members of NUEX were quick to peek out at these individuals themselves.

"They don't look that tough," remarked Arne. "And since there's only the two of 'em, we shouldn't have any trouble at all apprehending them."

"What's the game plan?" asked Jakob.

Knut watched as the two men he had trailed all the way from Lake Tinnsjo climbed off the trawler and disappeared inside the small dockside convenience store.

"This seems like it will be our best opportunity to

get them alone," said Knut. "All we have to do is wait for them outside that store, and when they come outside again, grab them."

"What if they're carrying guns?" quizzed the ever cautious Kari Skollevoll.

"Me and Arne will grab each one of them from behind," returned Knut. "Then once we have their arms pinned back in a firm hammer lock, all you guys have to do is frisk them real good like they do on T.V. and remove any weapons that you might find."

"Then what?" questioned Jon Huslid.

Knut looked up to meet the photographer's glance. "I guess then it will be time to call in the cops. But only after we're certain that the heavy water is all there. So if there are no more questions, let's do it."

Just as the group was about to leave the cover of the van, a deep, bass voice spoke out in broken Norwegian from behind them. "Comrades, before you go and do something that you might later regret, may I have a brief word with you?"

Surprised by this interruption, the Norwegians turned and set their eyes on the man responsible for these words. He proved to be a tall, white-haired old man, dressed in a brown woolen overcoat and a matching fedora. There was a certain intensity in his dull blue eyes that was accented by the jagged scar that lined the entire left side of his wrinkled face.

"I know that this will come as a shock to you," added the stranger. "But I too have been waiting for this trawler to arrive from Trondheim. You see, I have a personal interest in not only the cargo this vessel is carrying in its hold, but the two men who

261

are accompanying it also."

"Look Mister, I don't know who the hell you are, and couldn't really give a damn about your interests," replied Knut. "So if you'll just leave us alone, we've got business to get on with here."

"Please, comrade," implored the old man. "You must hear me out before interceding at this moment, or my entire lifetime's work will be wasted!"

This plea was delivered with such honesty and straight-forwardness that Kari dared to voice herself. "Come on, Knut. Listen to what he has to say."

Knut peeked around the van to the dockside store. "But this is the perfect opportunity to nab those two," he said impatiently.

"Those two scum mean absolutely nothing!" spat the stranger. "I know that you have personal reasons for wanting to apprehend them, and if you'll just hear me out, I guarantee you that you can have them in the end."

His tone softened as he added. "Look, it appears as if they've only stopped in Tromso for fuel and supplies. My hotel room is close by. We can talk in comfort there. From my window you'll have an unobstructed view of this wharf. If it turns out that you have no interest in the story that I'm about to share with you, then so be it. You can leave at any time and return here to get on with your little escapade."

"Come on, Knut. Let's hear what he has to say," urged Kari.

The muscular engineer looked up to get the opinions of his teammates. It proved to be Jon Huslid who was the first to speak.

"I agree with Kari. It would be different if we were under a time constraint. But so far, they've

262

made no effort to unload the cannisters. It's obvious that the two men that we're after will stick close to this cargo, and since we'll be close by and in a good position to monitor any changes that might take place down here, I say let's give our friend here a chance to properly express himself. What do you think, Jakob?"

The Lapp shrugged his shoulders. "I'm certainly in no hurry to rush into this thing. Let's hear what he's got to say and go from there."

Arne Lundstrom concurred. "I'm kind of curious to know what the hell he's doing here. And if he does turn out to be a fruitcake, there will always be another opportunity to nab those two."

It was with great reluctance that Knut backed down. "Mister, this better be good."

Mikhail Kuznetsov grinned. "Lad, the story that I'm about to share with you is way beyond good. It's amazing! So if you'll just follow me, we'll get on with it."

The trip up to the Russian's room took less than five minutes to complete. While Mikhail hastily packed the fireplace, Knut went straight to the window. The trawler was clearly in sight down below. A long black hose extended from the dockside fuel pump to the ship's engine room. Several deckhands could be seen milling around topside, shovelling snow and chipping off the heavy accumulation of ice that coated the deck.

"Well, are you satisfied that they're only using Tromso as a stopover?" asked Mikhail, putting a match to the kindling and walking over to the window himself.

"It sure looks that way," said Knut with a grunt. "But I'd still feel a lot better if we had those two in custody right now."

"Patience, lad," advised the old-timer as he sat down heavily on the chair that was positioned at the window's side. "Their time is rapidly coming. That I can assure you."

Mikhail turned his head to check on his other guests and saw that the woman was seated on his bed. The other three had seated themselves on the small sofa that was placed next to the fireplace. Beside them, the dry kindling readily took, the flames crackling and hissing. With the blond giant still standing in front of the window, the old man cleared his throat and continued.

"My name is Mikhail Kuznetsov. I am a citizen of the Soviet Union, where I hold the honorary rank of General in the People's Army. For the past forty-four years I have devoted my life entirely to tracking down and bringing to justice escaped Nazi war criminals. I have reason to believe that the two men that you were about to attempt to apprehend are members of a dangerous neo-Nazi group known as Werewolf. To the members of Werewolf, murder and theft are but a means to an end, their goal being the ultimate rebirth of the German Reich.

"As young Norwegians, you have no doubt heard the horror-filled tales of your elders as they described the Nazi occupation of your country. I personally lived through this nightmare as an occupant of a German death camp. For four long years I lived in a hell beyond description. I saw tens of thousands of innocent men, women and children tortured, starved and put to death for the mere fact that their birthright didn't fit in with the Aryan master plan. I swore to myself then that if I ever survived my incarceration, I would dedicate the rest of my life to making sure that such an evil never again walked the face of this earth.

"Over four decades have passed since then. And in that time I have watched with horror as Werewolf grew stronger and stronger, until today they are but one small step away from consolidating their power and seriously challenging the world's superpowers for control of the planet.

"You are probably asking yourselves what this has to do with the men that killed your two friends, and stole the shipment of heavy water that you worked so hard to salvage."

This comment drew Knut's immediate attention, and the engineer turned from the window to query, "How did you know about those deaths? And who told you about the heavy water?"

Mikhail looked up into the Viking's intense stare and answered him directly. "NUEX's salvage of the *Hydro* ferry and her cargo was common knowledge which I learned about in the newspapers. But I was hiding in the woods that lay near your salvage vessel on the night that the heavy water was stolen. And I saw with my own eyes as that Nazi scum ordered your friends to kneel down in the mud and then proceeded to blow their brains out."

"Do you mean to say that you just sat out there and watched my friends be murdered in cold blood?" questioned Knut passionately. "Why the hell didn't you try to save them?"

Fearing for a second that the red-faced giant might get violent, Mikhail replied firmly. "And just what did you want me to do, Comrade? It happened so fast that I hardly realized what had occurred until it was all over with. By that time it was too late."

Jon Huslid broke in at this point to diffuse this emotional confrontation. "General Kuznetsov, what do these two murders have to do with Werewolf? And what led you here to Tromso?"

Mikhail took a series of deep calming breaths before responding. "The two who are responsible for the deaths of your colleagues and the theft of your heavy water are known sub-agents of the group. I followed them all the way from Paraguay, where Werewolf has its headquarters. After they left Lake Tinnsjo, I trailed them by car to Trondheim. Knut here beat me to the agent who rented the trawler to them. It was this same agent who told me that the vessel was bound for Tromso. And here I am."

"What's so special about that heavy water?" asked Arne. "It seems that's the key to this whole thing."

Mikhail's eyes gleamed as he answered. "You are very perceptive, Comrade. Surely you know where the *Hydro*'s cargo was headed when the saboteur's explosives sent it sinking to the fjord's icy bottom."

"The heavy water was bound for Germany, where the Nazis were going to use it to develop an atomic bomb," returned Arne, who suddenly knew the answer to his original question.

Seeing this realization dawn in the bearded diver's eyes, Mikhail nodded. "Yes, Comrade. And just like fifty years ago, today Werewolf is hoping to use this very same shipment to develop their own bomb."

"Holy Mother Mary!" exclaimed Arne. "And to think that we could be indirectly responsible for putting that heavy water right in their hands."

"So just what is it that you're asking of us?" questioned Knut, who was just as affected by this shocking revelation as anyone else in the room.

Sensing that he had succeeded in swaying the

266

young group of headstrong Norwegians to his side, Mikhail decided then that they would make excellent allies, and he replied accordingly. "It's obvious that the trawler will be leaving shortly for the next leg of its voyage. I plan to follow it all the way to the nest of vipers that ordered its theft in the first place. Only when I have rooted out the entire organization will I act to crush it for all eternity."

"Well, I doubt if that trawler's bound for South America from here," offered Jon. "If that had been the case, they would have left straight from Trondheim."

"That could only mean that they're headed further north," suggested Jakob.

This time it was Kari who interjected. "There's not much further north than Tromso, gentlemen."

"Should we try to get hold of a boat and trail them?" asked Arne.

The Lapp shook his head. "Why go to all that trouble? The Tromso harbormaster is a good friend of my father's. Since no vessel is allowed out of this port without posting its intended destination before hand, why don't I just go up there and ask where the trawler's bound for?"

"That's an excellent idea," returned Mikahil Kuznetsov. "But we're still going to have to come up with a means of transportation once we learn exactly where the *Elsie K* is next headed."

A widely grinning Kari Skollevoll was quick to reply. "How do the services of an extended range, Bell 212 helicopter sound to you, General?"

Already certain that he had made a wise choice in taking these Norwegians into his trust, Mikhail answered. "My dear, such a capable vehicle would be a blessing from heaven."

267

"I don't know if my boss Magne would agree to that," said Kari with a wink. "But I'm already in this far, and if you just give me a solid place to put my chopper down, you've got yourself a ride on No-roil One."

"Then I guess I'd better be off to the harbor-master," said Jakob. "I'll meet you back here as soon as I have an answer."

The Lapp stood and turned for the door. Meanwhile Knut remained at the window, punching his balled fist into his open hand.

"I hope this still means that I get first crack at the bastards who shot Lars and Thor," asked the engineer.

Mikhail looked up to the Viking and replied. "Lad, you just help me get to where that heavy water's headed, and I swear to you that they're yours to do with as you please."

"That's all I ask," returned Knut, as he glanced down to the snow-covered wharf and pounded his fist into the flat, wooden window sill.

Chapter Twelve

David Lawton had been exploring one of the *Falcon*'s many excellent tool shops, when Magne Rystaad invited him for a tour of the ship's bridge. The Texan readily accepted this offer and soon found himself entering a spacious compartment on the vessel's topmost deck.

The night had long since fallen, and lit by a powerful bank of fluorescent tubes was an ultra-modern control room, from which almost all of the ship's functions could be run. Only a single seaman was currently on duty here. Lawton recognized this sailor as Olav Anderson, the fellow who originally greeted him when he first landed on the diving support ship several days ago.

"I thought you were taking me on a tour of the bridge, Magne," remarked Lawton facetiously. "Where's the wheel and all the controls?"

"I'm afraid this is it, my friend," replied his host. "Don't let the lack of complicated dials and stacks of equipment fool you. Everything that's needed to operate this ship is right in front of you."

Lawton took a close look at the long, waist-high console that stretched the entire width of the compartment. It was set up against a double-layered, wraparound windshield, and had surprisingly few instruments on it.

Standing at the central console, with his hand on a small joystick, Olav Anderson spoke in broken English. "Here's the wheel you were looking for, Mr. Lawton. On the *Falcon,* we do things the modern way."

"That's an understatement if I ever heard it," returned the Texan as he examined the ship's state-of-the-art radar unit. "Back home we only dream of vessels such as this one. She's sure got some fancy toys."

"Noroil is currently designing another ship that will eventually replace this one in a few years," revealed Magne. "That vessel will even be more sophisticated."

Lawton shook his head with wonder. "You Norwegians sure know how to build a boat. I guess it comes from your Viking tradition and all."

"With most of our land being mountains and fjords, we Norwegians have had to look to the sea to survive since the beginning of our history," said Olav Anderson proudly. "In fact, they say if you cut a Norwegian, he'll bleed both blood and saltwater."

David Lawton laughed at this while checking out the high-tech push button annunciator and the thruster controls, which were also operated by joystick. He reached out to steady himself when the deck suddenly rocked to and fro. The swell that caused this turbulence was far less intense than the rough seas they had encountered further south, and it soon passed. As the deck stabilized, he peered out one of the large windows that directly overlooked the empty helipad.

It was a dark, moonless night, yet he only had to look off to the port to view a wondrous sight that caused him to gasp in wonder. Rising from the sea here, like a floating skyscraper, was the Ice Field's production platform. It was a monstrous structure, lit up by a variety of colored lights and powerful spots.

The lights belonging to the three tug boats that continued towing the rig to its final resting place could also be seen in the waters beyond, and Lawton commented appreciatively, "My, that is sure some sight!"

"It even takes my breath away," reflected Magne. "She's the largest production platform ever built. And even so, the sea's almost swallowed her up."

"That sure would have been a horrible waste," said Lawton.

"We should have smooth sailing from here on up to Svalbard," added Olav Anderson. "At least we won't have anymore gales like the one we passed through down south to contend with."

"Let's hope not," said Magne. "To tell you the truth, I seriously doubted if the *Falcon* could have done much if we got up here and still found the rig floundering. At the best, we could have provided a place for the platform workers to evacuate to. Although in rough seas, even that can be a dangerous operation."

"How far will be escorting her?" asked the Texan.

"As far as I know, all the way to Svalbard," answered Magne. "The company doesn't want to take anymore chances with an investment this large at stake."

"Have you ever been to Svalbard before, Mr. Lawton?" asked Olav Anderson.

"Mister, not only is this my first trip to Norway, but it's the first time I've ever been above the Arctic Circle."

The weather-faced seaman smiled. "Then you're really in for an experience, because Svalbard is unlike any other place on this earth."

"Geologically, it hasn't changed a bit since the Ice Age," added Magne. "And except for several coal mines and our new drilling operation, man hasn't been around Svalbard long enough to damage its ecosystem much."

"Sounds interesting," said Lawton. "Will I get a chance to do some diving there?"

Magne nodded. "I believe that can be arranged, David. I might even get my feet wet this time. We'll have plenty to do prepositioning the platform and checking its base for any storm damage. And with NUEX still gone, I'm going to need every diver I can find."

"I wonder how those guys are doing," inquired the Texan.

"I got a dispatch from their helicopter pilot while you were down in the machine shop. It seems that they made it to Tromso in one piece. At last report, Tromso reported blowing snow, and Kari will be staying up there with the chopper until the weather clears."

"Did she say anything about that friend of theirs that they were supposed to meet up there in Tromso?" asked Lawton.

"You mean, Knut Haugen?" explained Magne. "No, come to think of it, she didn't. I'm going to have to call Kari back and ask her about that. I just pray that NUEX manages to stay out of further trouble this time."

"Those boys better have gone to the police if their buddy Knut had a lead on those criminals," said Lawton. "Otherwise, they could be getting into water that's way over their heads."

"NUEX might appear to be a little impulsive, but they usually listen to the voice of reason in the end," remarked Magne. "I can't wait to tell them the latest on that gold bar. You guys really came back with a piece of living history."

"You don't really believe all that stuff about it being from the missing treasure of the Czars, do you, Magne?" questioned the skeptical American.

His host looked him right in the eye and responded. "I don't see why not. That serial number that we lifted off the bar was as clear as the day that it was imprinted. The Russians sure didn't have any trouble running it down, once Oslo relayed it to them."

"But what's a piece of gold minted in the time of Czar Nicholas II, doing inside the hull of a World War II German U-boat off the coast of Norway?" quizzed Lawton.

"That, my friend, only time and a lot more investigation will tell," answered the *Falcon*'s diving supervisor.

"Do you think the boys will demand some of the reward money that the Russians are offering for the return of that gold bar?" wondered Lawton.

"It won't make much difference what they demand, David. As far as Noroil is concerned, it's now a company asset. But they know the score. They've been in this game longer than you think."

Just talking about the group of young Norwegians, that he had spent over three days cooped up with, caused a grin to etch the Texan's bearded face. "Those boys sure must have gotten an early start in life. It's hard to believe what they've already accomplished. At their age on my crew, they'd still be filling scuba tanks. But all the same, NUEX showed me that they were very capable divers. They still might be a little headstrong, but I attribute that to youth. At no time did they show signs of fear, and that's one of the main things that I look for in a young diver."

Magne slapped his guest on the back. "We weren't

any different when we first started in this business, my friend."

"I guess we weren't," reflected the American.

Magne beckoned toward the rear hatchway. "Now how about joining me for a little workout in the *Falcon*'s exercise room, David? If we're going to try keeping up with these youngsters, we sure better keep in shape."

Lawton patted his firm stomach. "After seventy-two hours cramped up in that decompression chamber, I'm ready to rock 'n roll. Lead on, partner."

There was a hushed, tense atmosphere prevailing inside the *Cheyenne*'s sound shack, as Joe Carter hunched over his console. After making a slight adjustment to his headphones, he cautiously turned up the volume gain on the sub's bow hydrophone array. A stream of hissing static met his ears, and he once more reached up to change the frequency band.

Immediately behind him, standing with their backs to the thick acoustic baffle that lined the room were the *Cheyenne*'s two senior officers. Both Captain Aldridge and his XO initiated this unusual visit soon after the sub changed course and turned its teardrop-shaped bow toward the southeast.

Oblivious to this audience, Carter's gaze remained locked on his repeater screen. The wavering lines that filled this monitor were visual equivalents of the sounds being relayed into his headphones by the hydrophones. And in this instance, the computer indeed proved more sensitive than the human ear as the barest of oscillations on the screen indicated that there was a sound source out there that Carter had yet to pick up on his headphones.

"Bingo, Captain!" observed Carter in a whisper. "I believe I've tagged 'em again."

"Is the signature strong enough to be fed through the system for an analysis yet?" questioned Aldridge.

Carter turned up the volume gain another notch and flashed a thumbs-up. Then he expertly addressed his computer keyboard with a flurry of commands.

All eyes went to the green-tinted monitor that was mounted beside the repeater screen. As it started to fill with data, it was Joe Carter who excitedly interpreted it.

"Big brother shows a sixty-seven percent probability that we've tagged an Alfa, Captain. We're picking up machinery noise and the strong cavitational hiss of a seven-bladed propellor."

"Good work, Mr. Carter," replied the Captain. "I've been waiting an awfully long time to come across an Alfa. Does he know he's been tagged yet?"

Carter shook his head. "No way, Captain. We're smack in his baffles. And since Alfas aren't equipped with towed arrays, he might never know that we're on to him."

"What would a sub like an Alfa be doing in these waters, Skipper?" asked the XO as he pulled his corncob out of his mouth. "We're way east of Ivan's normal transit lane into the North Atlantic."

"I guess we'll just have to hang around for a while and find out," returned Steven Aldridge. "Right now, they're pushing in awfully close to Norwegian territorial waters, and that tells me that they just might be on a spook mission of some sort. So don't lose them, Mr. Carter. I've got a hunch that these next couple of hours might prove damn interesting for all of us."

* * *

Totally unaware of the vessel that followed in the waters behind, the *Lena* continued on its southward course down the coast of Norway. Admiral Alexander Kuznetsov had complete confidence in the sub's ability to carry out its difficult mission, and was anxiously awaiting the initiation of the actual reconnaissance. Most of this work would be done by the trio of Spetsnaz divers that they carried along. These highly trained special forces operatives would be dropped off near the spot where the Norwegian oil pipeline made its landfall. In Alexander's opinion, this critical juncture was probably the weakest point of the network, where a saboteur only had to place a relatively small amount of explosives to shut down the entire pipeline.

The Admiral had utilized the Spetsnaz before, and they had yet to let him down. No job was too difficult for these naval commandoes, who prided themselves in creating a new meaning to the word impossible. If Alexander was fifty years younger, he would have loved to join their ranks. But this was only a fantasy of his, and he knew that he would have to content himself by merely being in their immediate presence.

The commandoes were currently staying in the *Lena*'s forward torpedo room. This was to be Alexander's first visit to this portion of the ship, and he was surprised to find the divers bunked on mattresses set right on top of the torpedoes themselves. As he entered the equipment-packed compartment, he spotted one of the commandoes doing a lightning-fast succession of one-handed push-ups on the deck before him. The lad was in superb physical condition, his muscles rippling beneath his striped blue and white t-shirt.

Another one of the commandoes was perched on his bunk stripping down his Kalashnikov assault rifle. This brute had close-cropped brown hair, steel-gray

276

eyes, and a moustache that extended well down to his chin, giving him an almost evil look. Alexander recognized him as the leader of the group and greeted him accordingly.

"Good evening, Lieutenant Kalinin. I'm sorry that I haven't had a chance to visit you until now. I do hope these quarters are sufficient."

Vasili Kalinin answered with a deep, rough voice. "Believe me, Admiral, compared to some missions we've undergone, the *Lena* is like a resort hotel. Right now, our only worry is that we'll go soft before it's time for us to go to work."

"I doubt that, Lieutenant," returned Alexander. "Anyway, it won't be long now until we reach Karsto. And then you'll be able to properly stretch those legs of yours."

"I understand that we came close to witnessing an accident back in the waters north of us," commented the commando as he vigorously polished the barrel of his weapon. "From the sound of it, some poor skipper is sure going to have all hell to pay."

"At least it wasn't one of ours, Lieutenant."

"Can you be so sure of that, Admiral? The platform it collided with would certainly make a lovely target in times of crisis. Who knows, maybe that rig was being secretly sized up for just such a future operation."

Knowing full well that the moustached commando could be right, Alexander nodded. "I guess we'll just have to wait until we get back to Polyarny to find out exactly what that racket was all about. But right now, we have different priorities."

"So I understand, Admiral. So I understand."

As the commando began reassembling his rifle, Alexander excused himself. "Please give my regards to the rest of your squad, Lieutenant. I'll be issuing

277

your final briefing when it's time to deploy."

On his way back to his cabin, the white-haired veteran's thoughts were centered on the brief encounter that he had just concluded. Lieutenant Vasili Kalinin might be a man of few words, but there could be no ignoring the fact that he was one of the Motherland's fiercest warriors. He had already proven himself time and again, having won the Order of Lenin first class for bravery under fire in Afghanistan, and yet more decorations for a clandestine operation in Central America whose details even Alexander didn't know.

The waters that Kalinin and his squad would soon be deployed in were cold, dark, and known for their treacherous currents. There was no telling what countermeasures that the Norwegians might have already placed here. Mines were their number one concern. These could be of the acoustic, magnetic, or electrical signature variety. They would also have to be on the lookout for the newly deployed Captor system, a bottom-lying mine that could even be triggered by a passing diver. By its very nature, recon work was full of dangerous surprises; that's what made duty in the Spetsnaz such a daily challenge.

Alexander was planning to return to his stateroom to get back to the paperwork that he had brought along with him, and was in the process of crossing through the wardroom, when a scratchy voice called to him from the wardroom table.

"Admiral, please come over and join me in a cup of tea. And there's also some delicious fruit compote here for you to sample. My own mother prepared it."

Finding it awkward to refuse the Zampolit's invitation, Alexander decided that he could make it through a single cup of tea. As he turned toward the table, Felix Bucharin smiled.

278

"Good, Admiral. I'm certain that you won't be disappointed with this compote."

As Alexander sat down, the political officer unscrewed the metal lid of the large glass jar that sat on the table beside him. Using a spoon, he emptied a portion of this jar's contents into an awaiting bowl. After capping the mound of fruit with a dollop of sour cream, the Zampolit pushed the bowl in front of his newly arrived guest.

"Eat, Admiral, and enjoy, for not only did my beloved mother bottle that fruit with her own hands, she grew it as well."

Alexander picked up a spoon and took a bite of the compote that was comprised of stewed cherries, peaches, plums and apricots.

"Why it's very good indeed, Comrade Bucharin," observed Alexander sincerely. "So she grows this fruit herself, you say?"

"That she does, Admiral. In fact, when my father first settled in the Ukraine, he was the one who originally planted the fruit trees. He's long cold in his grave now. But my dear mother still lives on the farm, and with the assistance of my brother Ivan, is still able to manage."

Alexander responded to this while finishing the rest of his compote. "If this dish is any example of her cooking, then I imagine it was pretty hard for you to leave this farm."

The Zampolit patted his bulging belly. "As you can see, I carry along my fair share of my mother's legacy. And yes, Admiral, it was hard for me to leave the land. But I chose my duty willingly, and have no regrets."

Alexander poured himself a cup of tea and thoughtfully stirred in a spoonful of sugar. "I'm sorry that I never got to complete my speech to the Komsomol, Comrade Bucharin."

"Your apologies aren't necessary, Admiral. All of us understand that you were called to a greater duty. Though I personally was finding your summation most brilliant. It's a shame that it was interrupted like it was. Did you and the captain manage to iron out your differences?"

"What differences are you talking about, Comrade Zampolit?"

The nosey political officer looked Alexander right in the eye and responded. "Oh come now, Admiral. You should realize by now that on a warship this size, nothing stays a secret very long, especially when it concerns our commanding officer and his superior. From what I understand, Captain Milyutin desired to change course and further investigate the mysterious collision that took place while you were speaking to us. Yet you countermanded the captain, ordering him instead to continue on with our preassigned mission."

Impressed with the Zampolit's intelligence network, Alexander was quick to set the record straight. "Comrade Bucharin, you can rest assured that I in no way countermanded the captain. When it was determined that it was another submarine that was engaged in this collision, Captain Milyutin merely voiced his desire to turn the *Lena* around and have a quick look at the parties involved. Under ordinary circumstances I would have offered this suggestion myself. I must admit that I was just as curious as the Captain, and would have loved nothing better than to investigate the collision site."

"Then why didn't we?" questioned the perplexed Political Officer.

Alexander got the impression that Bucharin was attempting to deliberately probe in an effort to find material for his personnel dossier, and he answered guardedly. "We are presently on a priority one mission, Comrade Bucharin. The Premier himself is waiting for the intelligence that we've been tasked to gather, and nothing short of a declaration of war is going to divert us from fulfilling our responsibility."

Quick to sense the veteran's sensitivity in this matter, the Zampolit backed down. "But of course, Admiral. I understand clearly now."

"It's time for me to be returning to my cabin," said Alexander as he pushed away from the table and stood. "Thanks again for the compote, comrade."

"Anytime ,Admiral. Anytime at all."

It was with great relief when Alexander finally made it to the private confines of his stateroom. There was something about the Zampolit's demeanor that grated on his nerves. Determined to stay as far away from Felix Bucharin as possible for the rest of the cruise, Alexander turned for the desk and the stack of paperwork that awaited him there.

Chapter Thirteen

Nothing filled Otto Koch's heart with pride like watching his young men hard at work at their appointed tasks. This was especially the case this evening, as the septuagenarian stepped off the elevator to initiate his nightly tour of the sub pen.

With his trusty German shepherd Beowulf at his side, Koch momentarily halted at the top of the stairway that would lead him down to the cavern's single dock. Only yesterday the penstocks had been opened to the sea, and at long last U-3313 floated on its intended medium. Lit by the dozens of powerful mercury-vapor flood lights, the U-boat's gilded hull glistened like a jewel. Several seamen could be seen working in the sub's sail, making some minor adjustments to the twin 30mm cannons that were set into each corner of the conning tower. Placed here to defend against attacking aircraft, the cannons would hopefully not see action during U-3313's upcoming trip, but they were good to have around if needed.

The U-boat's primary weapons system was its torpedoes. Because of space limitations they would only be fitted with six of these lethal fish, one for each tube. The torpedoes themselves lay on the dock, having just been brought down from storage. Among those currently gathered around the pallets holding these weapons were two of the vessel's senior officers.

Otto Koch had a particular liking for the sub's captain, and he climbed down the steps to have a word with Charles Kromer as quickly as his arthritic limbs would allow.

Koch had just managed to reach the last step, and was in the process of planting his rubber-tipped walking stick firmly onto the concrete decking below, when Beowulf began barking madly. The dog's spirited barks echoed through the cavernous pen until the reverberating sound reached almost unearthly proportions.

"Beowulf, stop that racket right now!" commanded Koch.

The dog reluctantly obeyed, and somewhat meekly rubbed up against his master's side. Only then did Koch spot the reason for his dog's unusual behavior. Sitting on a crate less than ten meters from them was a large rat. Such vermin couldn't be tolerated, and Koch pointed at the rodent and cried out.

"Sic 'em, Beowulf! Sic 'em!"

The shepherd instantly lunged forward with a snarl. The rat took one look at its attacker and leaped off the crate. As it hit the slippery decking the rat momentarily struggled to get its footing. This was all the time Beowulf needed to leap over the crate himself and crash down on the frantic rodent. Temporarily stunned, the rat now found itself totally at the mercy of his attacker, who batted it with his paw and then proceeded to snap its neck with a single bite of his vise-like jaws.

Otto Koch watched his dog stand triumphantly over its prey. Koch loudly snapped his fingers a single time and pointed toward the water. Without a second's hesitation, Beowulf utilized his jaws to pick up the rat by its tail and unceremoniously drop it into the nearby water.

An echoing chorus of applause followed this act, and Otto Koch looked up and realized that the men who had been gathered around the torpedo had also watched his dog in action. As Beowulf returned to his side, Koch reached down and heartily scratched the shepherd's head.

"Good dog, Beowulf," he proudly added as he stiffly stood upright and began limping over to join his men.

"Beowulf would probably make an excellent lookout," greeted Charles Kromer as the old man and his dog continued their approach.

"It looks like we'll soon enough find out, won't we, Captain?" returned Otto Koch, as he halted on the opposite side of the torpedo pallet. "How do these fish look to you?"

Kromer kneeled down and patted the rounded gray nose of the torpedo nearest him. "They appear to be in an excellent state of preservation, Herr Director. I personally supervised their unpacking, and like the rest of U-3313, they were stored away with great care."

"You know, you're looking at real museum pieces here, Captain," said Koch as he pointed to the stern portion of one of the torpedoes with his walking stick. "These fish were originally code named *Lerche,* and were the first operational, wire-guided torpedoes in existence."

Kromer nodded. "I realize that, Herr Director. It's incredible, but here almost fifty years later, we're still using the same basic principle of guiding a torpedo to its target by utilizing the acoustic information passed back along its wires."

"I imagine then that these fish were responsible for their fair share of damage during the Great War," offered Hans Kurtz, U-3313's second in command.

Otto Koch shook his head to the contrary. "Unfortunately they were introduced too late to play a signifi-

284

cant role in the war's outcome. Just like the Type XXI U-boat, the wire-guided torpedo was just seeing action when the Reich collapsed. Now if Admiral Donitz only had these advanced weapon systems online a couple of years earlier, there's no telling what may have happened."

"I once heard that the plans for the Type XXI vessel were introduced as early as 1941, with the first prototype set to be launched less than a year later. Yet it wasn't until 1944 that this prototype went to sea, and by then the war was already lost. What took so long?" asked Hans Kurtz.

"Senior Lieutenant Kurtz," said Koch with the air of a strict school teacher. "It's obvious that you haven't read your history books closely. Any real student of the war knows full well that it was because of one man alone that the Type XXI project was shelved. But now is not the time to get me started on the shortcomings of the Bavarian paperhanger who led the Fatherland astray with his blind ego and arrogant pomposity, for we still have much work to do down here."

Taking this as his cue, Kromer interjected. "We've completed the hull integrity test, Herr Director. U-3313 passed with flying colors."

"Did you expect any differently?" retorted Koch.

Kromer stood firm. "You never know for sure how a hull will hold up to a protracted state of dry-dock, Herr Director. We've also just finished tests of the boat's electrical, hydraulics, and fire-control systems. We've taken on a full load of diesel fuel and are close to a hundred percent charge on the batteries. Once these torpedoes are loaded, all we'll need are the fresh foodstuffs and we'll be ready to set sail."

"But aren't you forgetting one more critical item, Captain?" quizzed Otto Koch. "And I can finally report that the thirty-three drums of heavy water are at long last on the final leg of their journey to Svalbard. The trawler that's carrying our treasure should be arriving at North Cape within the next twenty-four hours. Only after those drums are safely secured in U-3313's storage compartment will we be ready to set sail for the Rio de la Plata."

The sound of an engine starting up nearby interrupted the elder, who turned to see where this commotion was coming from. It was the truck that had just delivered the torpedoes. Koch watched as this vehicle began its way down a long asphalt driveway that was situated next to the narrow inlet of water that supported U-3313. The truck appeared to be headed straight for the side of the mountain itself, when a huge steel door that was set into the hollow rock here began lifting upward. The rumbling of the vehicle's diesel engine soon faded when the truck passed under the cavern's entrance and disappeared into the night beyond.

As the doorway began to close, Beowulf once again began barking. Otto Koch looked down to see what was bothering his dog this time, and found Beowulf pointed toward the submarine's conning tower. Here, at the forward edge of the sail, a seaman had just climbed out of the hatchway. This individual was a hefty character, whose one distinguishing feature was the fact that he was covered from head to toe in black grease.

"Beowulf, mind your manners!" scolded Koch.

"Take it easy on him, Herr Director," advised Kromer lightly. "Our chief engineer isn't known as the king of rats for nothing. Just like a rat, Chief Dortmund seems to be perpetually covered in greasy slime, and we hardly ever let him up to see the light of day."

Looking up to the conning tower, the Captain

added, "Siggy, quit scaring this poor defenseless creature so!"

Chief Sigmund Dortmund stiffly saluted and proceeded to do his best to wipe the black grease off of his face with a stained rag. He only needed to expose his forehead and eyes for the German shepherd to finally stop his incessant yelping.

Kromer couldn't help but laugh as he looked back to Otto Koch. "I guess poor Beowulf didn't know what to make of our esteemed chief engineer. I've got to admit that I sure was pleasantly surprised when I learned that Sigmund Dortmund had signed on with us. We sailed together on many a patrol, and they don't come any better than good old Siggy."

"I was hoping that you'd be satisfied with our selection," said Koch. "Actually, you can thank your senior lieutenant for going out and recruiting Chief Dortmund for us. He's been a hard worker, and already seems to know every square inch of U-3313, from her bow to her stern."

Siggy managed to have his whole face wiped clean by the time he climbed off the gangplank and joined them beside the torpedoes. Even then, Beowulf snarled at the newcomer.

"Beowulf, behave!" chided the dog's master.

Siggy wasn't the least bit intimidated by the snarling German shepherd, and as he got within touching distance of the dog, he kneeled down and held out his hand. Beowulf cautiously sniffed the stranger's skin, and after determining that this creature was human after all, returned to his master's side and obediently sat down.

"I'm sorry to have scared your dog, Herr Director," apologized Siggy. "But in a way I can't blame him. Once after a hard day working in the bilges, I passed by a mirror and when I accidentally caught my reflection, I even managed to scare myself!"

The group laughed and even Otto Koch managed a grin, as Siggy continued.

"I was just coming up to get some fresh air after patching up that little hydraulics leak that we found during this afternoon's test. As I was passing the radio room, I was asked to pass the following news to you, Herr Director. Several minutes ago, a helicopter belonging to the Norwegian state oil service contacted the harbormaster's office requesting permission to land here at North Cape. Apparently they're having some sort of engine trouble, and don't have enough fuel to reach Longyearben."

Otto Koch thought a moment before replying. "Well, under the circumstances, I guess the only thing we can do is let them land here. After all, we can't go and get the landlord mad at us, can we?"

"By all means not," concurred Kromer. "To deny them access would immediately arouse their suspicions. And before we knew it, they'd have that Coast Guard cutter that I saw back in Longyearben snooping around up here."

"So get on with it, Chief," ordered Koch. "And make sure that the harbormaster treats our new guests cordially."

As Siggy turned back for the sub to inform the radio operator of this directive, he asked one more question. "What if the repairs on this helicopter require parts that are not available here?"

"Then those parts will just have to be flown up here as soon as they can be found," returned Otto Koch. "Meanwhile, the crew can have the services of one of our dormitories. But they'll be under surveillance twenty-four hours a day, and under no circumstances will they be allowed near this mountain."

"I understand, Herr Director," said Chief Dortmund

as he climbed up onto the sub's deck and headed for its sail-mounted forward hatchway.

It was as Siggy disappeared inside the conning tower that Beowulf started barking again.

"Good heavens, Beowulf! What's gotten into you this evening?" asked the dog's irritated master.

"He probably just misses his new friend," offered Charles Kromer.

"Or maybe he has something against our new Norwegian visitors," joked Hans Kurtz, who eventually turned his attention back to the torpedoes, and the briefing their captain had been in the midst of when they were initially interrupted.

Noroil One swept in low over the waters that bordered Svalbard's North Cape, its course rough and erratic.

"Hang on tight, guys!" warned Kari Skollevoll from the cockpit. "I'm going to put us into a tailspin just as we cross over the coast. If they're watching down below, that will really convince them that we're in trouble."

Beside the pilot, Mikhail Kuznetsov warmly grinned. "That was some idea that you came up with, Miss Skollevoll. And of course, this whole ride is most appreciated. Why I even enjoyed hearing *Peer Gynt* once again. It's been much too long since I've sat back and really listened to a piece of music."

"Well, after all this is over, you've got to make a promise to yourself to take some time out of each day just to sit down and listen to some music. As far as I'm concerned, there's no better relaxation in all the world. And please, call me Kari."

"Very well, Kari," returned Mikhail with a smile. "I promise to give your therapy a try. You know, when I was a boy growing up in Kirov, my father used to take me and my twin brother Alexander to the symphony, whenever his naval duty allowed. My, those were magical moments. I enjoyed the works of Tchaikovsky the best, though both Borodin and Rimsky Korsakoff were my second favorites."

"Is your twin brother still alive?" asked Kari as she forcefully pushed the Bell's control stick hard to the side, causing the helicopter to veer off abruptly to the left.

Holding onto his harness for dear life, Mikhail held back his answer until the helicopter stabilized. "Alexander is an Admiral in the People's Navy. The ministry has been after him to retire for the past five years now, but he won't even think about such a thing. His whole life's been his work, and without it he'd probably shrivel up and die."

"It sounds like you and your brother have a lot in common in that respect," observed Kari, who sighted the flashing lights of the coastline up ahead, and proceeded to rock the helicopter back and forth with a wild, vibrating gyration.

"You are most observant," managed Mikhail as he regripped his harness and did his best to ride out the series of aerial acrobatics that soon followed.

For a sickening moment, the helicopter seemed to lose all power, and it plummeted downward. The flashing lights of the small Arctic outpost down below grew larger with an alarming swiftness, and Kari waited until the very last moment before engaging the throttle and regaining control.

Only when this maneuver succeeded in restabilizing them did Mikhail manage to find his tongue once more. "Not only are you observant and have excellent taste in music, but you are also one of the most daring pilots that I have ever met. And I've been up in

MIG's!"

"Hey hotshot, enough of the amateur theatrics!" cried a voice from the main cabin. "Arne's turned white as a ghost after that last maneuver, and even Knut's starting to look a little pale."

Kari recognized this voice as belonging to NUEX's photographer. "But I haven't even attempted the tail spin yet, Jon," returned the pilot.

"The hell with that tailspin, just get us down!" screamed the shaken photographer.

"You asked for it," muttered Kari as she pushed down on the stick and sent the Bell 212 on its steepest dive yet.

Mikhail could actually feel the harness as it cut into his shoulders, so steep was their angle of descent. Just when he was about to call out to the young pilot to pull up, he spotted the bright circle of lights down below, belonging to the outpost's helipad. A flashing strobe lay in the center of this circle, and Kari put the helicopter down squarely on top of it.

They landed with a jolt, and Kari quickly switched off the engines and then bent over to reach under the dashboard. Seconds later, she re-emerged with a tiny fuse in one hand and a devilish gleam in her eyes.

"This should keep those engines from turning over until I want them to," said Kari as she securely buttoned away the fuse in the breast pocket of her jumpsuit.

"Jesus Kari, are you trying to get us all killed?" rasped Jon Huslid as he poked his head into the cockpit.

Kari replied nonchalantly. "Come off it, Jon. I was only trying to make that little air emergency look authentic."

"Well, you did that all right," returned the pale-faced photographer. "And poor Arne's still puking his guts out for the sake of authenticity."

"I told him not to eat those two raw herring and onion sandwiches when we were leaving Tromso," said Kari as she helped Mikhail unbuckle his harness.

Knut Haugen's deep voice broke from the main cabin, "Hey Jon, our reception committee is on the way. Wait until you get a load of these goons. They look like a bunch of Swedish dockworkers with toothaches."

"Now what?" asked Kari a bit apprehensively.

Mikhail Kuznetsov was quick to take over. "We've accomplished our first goal, and we've made it to North Cape. If Jakob's source proves to be accurate, and I hope to God it does, the trawler with the heavy water on board will be docking here in another twenty-four hours. We've got to extend our welcome at least that long, so that we can follow those cannisters to their final destination."

"Hopefully, this is it," remarked the photographer.

"I'm not so sure of that, comrade," returned the Russian. "But I do think that we're getting close."

Jon shook his head. "Well, you can't go much further north than Svalbard. From here, practically everywhere's south, even Siberia!"

Mikhail noted a little tension in the young Norwegian's voice and he spoke compassionately. "I owe all of you so much already. A few hours ago, we were total strangers. Now the hand of fate has brought us together, and our destinies are one. I can only hope that the black cloud that has followed me all of my life will spare you the bitter rains of sorrow."

Kari already felt close to the white-haired Russian and softly caressed his weathered neck. "Don't worry about bringing down troubles with NUEX around. They're very adept at doing just that all on their own."

Jon took a deep breath and squared back his shoulders. "Here it goes, kids. I'll go and see what our greeting party has to say and see about getting us some accommodations for the night. We can work on extending our stay tomorrow."

"Thank you, Jon Huslid," said the old Russian almost tenderly.

The photographer winked and turned for the main cabin. As it turned out, the reception committee that was waiting for Jon outside the helicopter proved to be most cooperative. A van and driver were provided for them and they were soon whisked off up into the black hills.

They spent the night in a cold, drab dormitory building. Constructed much like an Army barracks, the structure had a large common room filled with dozens of empty bunks. Adjoining this area was a communal bathroom. For safety concerns, a guard was stationed in the hallway that led to the building's only exit. This individual curtly explained that lights out was at ten p.m. sharp, then left them alone to get settled.

It was Arne who pointed out the large black and white pennant that was mounted on the wall at the head of the room. It showed the earth with a golden star crowning the North Pole.

Kari did a swift inspection of the barracks, and mentioned that from the dust that had accumulated inside, the room hadn't been occupied for quite sometime. Because of the late hour, and the sentry that remained stationed outside, they decided to wait until morning to initiate their investigation. The bunks were cramped and far from comfortable, but they were tired after their long day of travelling and all slept soundly.

The group awoke at seven a.m. when the sentry came into the room, turned on the lights, and blew loudly on a small plastic whistle. This shrill blast served to get everyone's attention, and as they groggily stirred, the guard announced that breakfast would be served in the mess hall in one-half hour. This left them little time to tarry, and as they slowly climbed out from under their blankets, they graciously allowed Kari the first use of the bathroom.

The mess hall turned out to be in a large wooden building directly across from their barracks. As they were escorted to it, they were greeted by a frigid gust of Arctic air. It was a gray, overcast morning, that fit in well with the bleak range of black mountains that encircled them. As they crossed the narrow asphalt roadway, each of them got a brief glimpse of the bay that the outpost was built around. It lay to their right, approximately three kilometers distant.

The bay was a desolate body of water that was ringed by a collection of glacial mountains. A small wharf could be seen on the shoreline, along with several other low-lying structures. The helipad was also situated here, and Kari could just view the array of antennaes that she had spotted last night as she was preparing to put the chopper down.

Except for their escort, who remained with them while they ate, the mess hall was completely vacant. A cold buffet table had been set up inside this barn-like room that was filled with several rows of spartan wooden tables and chairs. Their meal was as simple as the furnishings that surrounded them — cheese, bread, liver spread and tea, yet they were hungry and ate heartily.

Exactly a quarter of an hour after they had sat down to eat, a tall, middle-aged, blond man dressed in a brown suit entered the mess hall. He carried an air of military authority that caused their sentry to stand stiffly at attention as the newcomer stood before the buffet table and addressed them.

"On behalf of the Rio de la Plata consortium, welcome to North Cape. I am Klaus Dietricht, the settlement's associate director. I was informed last evening of your arrival, and regret that business matters kept me from paying my respects until now. Please excuse these humble facilities. As you can imagine, we have few guests, and we are not usually accustomed to uninvited visitors. I have made a van available to convey you down to the helipad so that you can initiate repairs on your helicopter. If you'll just follow me, I'll accompany you to this vehicle."

Before any of the group stood up to obey this directive, Jon Huslid spoke up. "Excuse me, Mr. Dietricht. Would it be possible if four of us have a look around the settlement while our pilot and chief engineer work on the chopper? I'm afraid that all we'd do down there is get in the way."

The outpost's associate director carefully studied the individual who made this request and replied. "To whom do I have the honor of speaking?"

"I'm sorry, sir. I'm Jon Huslid. I'm employed with Noroil as an underwater photographer."

"Mr. Huslid," returned Klaus Dietricht coldly. "Unfortunately, insurance concerns force me to deny this request. Because of the dangerous state of the coal reserves we are presently working, you are confined to either the helipad or your barracks."

"But we won't be going into the mines, sir," responded Jon. "Actually, we're much more interested in just seeing how your settlement operates."

The associate director impatiently looked at his watch. "I would love to give you such a tour, Mr. Huslid. But today I just can't spare the time. So if you'll just follow me, you can either accept a ride down to the helipad or remain here at the barracks under the watchful eye of Karl here."

The sentry alertly nodded in acknowledgement of this mention and Jon could only shrug his shoulders.

"Come on, gang," said the irritated photographer. "Let's all get down to the helipad and see what we can do to patch up the chopper and get to someplace a bit more hospitable."

Seemingly ignoring this hostile comment, Klaus Dietricht led the group outside. The van was a nine seater. Dietricht and a driver sat in the front, while the members of NUEX, Kari Skollevoll and Mikhail Kuznetsov piled into the back.

The road that they were soon travelling followed the floor of the valley. On both sides of the narrow thoroughfare rose a desolate, mountainous plateau, whose black basalt rock was streaked with snow. They passed by several more dormitories that were conspicuously empty of any occupants. It was only as they got closer to the shoreline that they spotted several men gathered before a small corrugated steel warehouse, in the process of loading what appeared to be food into a compact delivery van.

The helipad lay on an isolated clearing near the wharf area. As they exited the vehicle, two large panel trucks whizzed past them, headed toward the road that followed the coastline up ahead. Curious as to where these vehicles were headed, Jon tapped Dietricht on the shoulder and pointed.

"Mr. Dietricht, where are those two trucks off to in such a hurry?"

"To the mines," spat the associate director, who was obviously pressed for time himself. "I've got to go now," he added. "Two of my men are waiting for you down at the helicopter. Consider them at your disposal. They have been instructed to do whatever is necessary to help you get airborne once again. With that, I wish you good luck and good flying."

Klaus Dietrich turned back for the van, which wasted no time speeding off in the same direction as the two trucks. This left the group temporarily alone on the clearing.

"General Kuznetsov, do you think he's one of your Nazis?" asked Arne.

The Russian thoughtfully replied. "It's obvious he's been trained in the military. And of course, there's no doubt that he's a German. As to being a Nazi . . ."

Mikhail was cut short by Knut Huagen. "Excuse me, sir, but we've got visitors coming our way."

The two dour looking brutes who had originally greeted them last night could be seen quickly approaching.

"Damn!" cursed the photographer. "We've got to find someplace where we can talk."

Kari pointed toward the nearby helicopter. "I happen to know the perfect place to hold a private conversation. Follow me, gentlemen."

The pilot led them into the main cabin of the Bell 212. Since their two escorts remained right outside, Kari turned on the cassette player, and soon the rousing refrains of Grieg's Peer Gynt all but guaranteed their privacy.

"All that you need up here is barbed wire and this place would be the perfect prison camp," observed Arne.

"Who needs barbed wire on Svalbard?" returned Knut. "It's not as if there were anywhere close by to escape to up here."

"I think that you're being too critical of the place," interjected Jakob. "Don't forget where we are. The nearest settlement is Longyearben, and that's not saying much. Svalbard's coal outposts are notorious for being among the most isolated in all the world. These

297

people up here are not used to strangers, especially uninvited ones. Why the only visitors they get are coal ships in the summer, and themselves in the winter."

"I'm not so sure that the coal mines up here in North Cape are even active anymore," offered Jon. "Did any of you see any miners or their families around? And where's all their equipment?"

"We did see those two trucks, that Dietricht said were going to the mines," answered Arne.

"I've been around long enough to know that those vehicles certainly weren't coal trucks," said Jon. "Around Oslo, panel trucks like that are used for light delivery purposes."

"What do you think is going on up here, General?" asked Arne.

Mikhail leaned up against the cabin's forward bulkhead and thoughtfully answered. "I agree with Jon that coal is not the purpose of this settlement's current existence, though it most probably was at one time. As I was saying before, the few individuals that we've managed to meet have all the trappings of being military trained. And of course, then there's the matter of that pennant that was hung on our barracks' wall. A similar one flew from a flagpole outside that warehouse we passed. I have seen this design before, in Argentina. The black and white globe with the gold star above the North Pole is the standard of the Rio de la Plata coal company. I know for a fact that this supposed consortium of German and South American investors is nothing but a front for the Neo-Nazi organization I have spent the better part of my life trying to destroy — Werewolf!"

"But if that's the case, why bother shipping the heavy water up here?" asked Kari. "Svalbard is hardly a practical place to start a Fascist revolution."

"Right now, I'm just as perplexed as you are, my

298

dear," replied the Russian. "If only we could remain here long enough to do some further investigation and monitor the heavy water once the trawler arrives."

"I believe we can arrange that," said Kari, who reached into the breast pocket of her jumpsuit and pulled out a single fuse. "This chopper's not going anyplace until this fuse goes back in place."

"Then all we have to do is figure out a way to stall for some more time," added Arne.

"That shouldn't be too hard to accomplish," said Knut. "Kari and I will start stripping down the engines. And we'll make such a mess out of things that it will take a good twenty-four hours to put it back together again."

"That should give us plenty of time to do some snooping," remarked the photographer. "And I think that the perfect time to get on with it will be this evening."

"I'd like to have a closer look at where those two panel trucks were off to in such a hurry," offered Jakob.

Mikhail added. "That sounds like a good place to get started. But how will we manage to do all this exploring on foot?"

The photographer's face broke out in a sardonic smile. "Who says anything about travelling on foot? We'll figure out a way to get us some wheels. Don't forget, General. You're in the capable hands of NUEX now."

Much to the consternation of the two men that had been assigned to assist them with the repairs, Kari and Knut spent the day tearing down the Bell's engines. It was evident that the helicopter would never get off the ground in the immediate future, and one of the sentries left to inform the associate director of this fact.

Klaus Dietricht paid them a visit soon afterward. He was noticeably upset when he saw for himself the work that yet had to be done on the helicopter, and pressed them for a completion time. Kari casually mentioned that twenty-four hours seemed like a reasonable estimate. Only after getting her to definitely commit to this time frame did Dietricht reluctantly offer them the use of their dormitory for yet one more night. He left them with an angry scowl, and a warning that if they weren't ready to go as promised, a helicopter would be chartered at their expense to convey them out of North Cape by the next sunset.

It was pitch black outside by the time they returned to the dormitory. Before even having the opportunity to properly wash up, they were rushed off to the mess hall where a meal of canned sardines, cheese, stale bread, and liver spread was served. Their guard watched them poke at this food somewhat amusedly before escorting them back to the dormitory.

Kari and Knut had formulated a plan to effect their escape while working on the engine. The success of this scheme all depended upon how much sex appeal the pilot could summon, and just how amorous their young guard was at the moment.

It was well past lights out, when Kari climbed from her bed and slunk out into the hallway. Fortune was with her as she caught the wide-eyed sentry immersed in a dog-eared copy of Playboy. He did a double-take when Kari seductively smiled, pulled down the shoulder of her blouse, and beckoned him to come closer. He swallowed heavily, stood, and almost tripped over his feet as he moved forward to obey her silent command.

Kari was enjoying the role of a seductress. Besides, her young victim wasn't all that bad looking, though he was at that age when his complexion was giving him problems. Thankful that he was a man of a few words, she easily lured him away from the entrance to the bunkroom. She didn't even have to make skin contact with him as she stepped aside, forcing him to turn along with her. No sooner was his back toward the doorway when Knut appeared in the shadows behind him. Knut innocently tapped the young guard on the shoulder. He obediently turned his head and was met by a hammer-like fist blow directly on his jaw. This was the only punch needed to send him to the floor for a ten count and much more.

From the same shadows that Knut had come from, the other members of NUEX emerged, along with Mikhail Kuznetsov. They were fully dressed and even had the pilot's parka in hand as they proceeded straight to the dormitories exit.

"Nice job, Kari," complimented Jon. "Now let's see about getting those wheels."

Outside, the intense cold hit them like Knut's fist on the young guard's jaw. Luck was once more with them as their desired course put the biting wind at their backs. They walked quickly and silently, their way lit solely by the waning moon.

When they finally spotted the corrugated steel warehouse that they had seen from the road earlier, Knut and Arne broke out into a trot. By the time the rest of the group caught up with them, Knut had succeeded in forcing the lock to the structure's garage with a tool he had brought from the helipad for just this purpose. As Arne slid the garage door upward, a relieved sigh was shared by all as they set their eyes on a mud stained compact delivery van. Not only was this vehicle unlocked, but the keys were still dangling from the ignition.

"Get in," commanded Knut. "I'll drive."

Both Karl and Mikhail scooted in next to him on

301

the front seat, while the other members of NUEX climbed into the back where they sat on the cold steel floor alongside several shrink-wrapped cases of canned goods. It proved to be Arne who identified the contents of these cans.

"Somebody sure must like their beans. There's got to be well over five hundred cans of the stuff packed back here. Anyone hungry?"

No one took up his offer, and Knut turned over the ignition and rammed the gears into reverse. They transitted the road down to the bay in a matter of minutes, and were soon speeding over the narrow asphalt thoroughfare that followed the coastline for the first couple of kilometers. At no time during this entire journey did they pass another moving vehicle.

With the flickering lights of North Cape now well behind them, the road began gradually turning away from the water. Slowly they began gaining elevation, the black mountains looming before them like giants from another realm. Knut downshifted as the road began snaking up a series of switchbacks. He was in the process of steering the van around a tight corner, and was reaching over to downshift, when he suddenly slammed on the brakes. Everyone in the van was thrown violently forward by this unexpected stop.

"Hey, Knut! What the hell's going on up there?" quizzed Arne angrily."

This question was met by a moment of silence that was broken only by the confounded voice of Kari Skollevoll. "What in the world happened to the road? It couldn't just end here."

Arne, Jakob and Jon peeked over her shoulder to see what she was carrying on about, and set their combined gazes on a confusing sight. Only a few meters away from their current location, the asphalt pavement terminated in an abrupt dead end, replaced by the sheer rock face of a mountain.

"Now hold on a minute," remarked Jon. "Knut, did you see any turnoffs on the way up from the coast?"

As NUEX's chief engineer shook his head that he hadn't, Jon continued. "Then where did those trucks that we saw this morning end up?"

On pure impulse, Kari snapped open the van's glove compartment and removed a plastic garage door opener. She held it up before her and depressed its trigger mechanism. Slowly, the unthinkable started to happen—the solid rock face that lay before them started to slide upward! In its place shined a blindingly bright bank of flood lights.

A voice cried out from this void. "Hey, you! Quit sleeping and get that crate inside. You know the Director's rule about leaving the entryway open."

Spurred into action by these words, Knut started up the van and drove cautiously forward.

"Get a load of this place!" exclaimed Arne as he wondrously peered out the van's side window.

The immense cavern which they now entered seemed dimensionless, especially since the majority of the flood lights were focused downward, toward the cave's floor. Before being allowed further access, a burly guard sauntered up to the driver's window and peeked inside.

"Kind of late for a delivery, isn't it fellow?" he questioned.

Knut's ad-lib skills were put to the test as he calmly answered. "I guess that depends on who you're working for. When the associate director found out that these supplies hadn't been delivered he threw a fit and sent us, his very own staff, to complete the job."

The guard snickered and examined the van's passengers with the help of his flashlight. "Well I'll be. Herr Dietricht's really getting everyone involved now.

303

Why I've never seen any one of you around here be-fore."

"You should come visit us over in administration someday," offered Kari with her sexiest smile. "It can get awfully lonely over there."

"I wish I had the time," replied the guard. "But like everyone else, they've got me working double shifts. It seems I never get out of this damn pen."

Deciding that they had exchanged enough small talk, Knut got down to business. "Where do we drop off our load, my friend? This delivery stuff's a little new to us."

The guard grinned. "It's about time you pencil pushers saw the operational end of our little project. Have you gotten a chance to see the boat as yet?"

Not having any idea what he was talking about, Knut shook his head. "Like yourself, we've been chained to the office. This will be the first time for all of us."

"Prepare yourselves, then, for the thrill of a lifetime. Just follow the yellow line that's painted on the cav-ern's floor to the pen area. You can park in front of the forward gangway, but for only as long as it takes to carry the supplies into the boat. What are you deliver-ing anyway?"

"Beans," revealed Jon from the back of the van.

"I should have known it," returned the guard. "No wonder Herr Dietricht sent you out here at this late hour. How can we send our brave sailors to sea with-out their precious beans!"

The van filled with forced laughter, and Knut sa-luted and put the vehicle into gear. The yellow line led them up a ramp and then down onto the floor of the cavern itself. And it was then that they saw it. Floating on a pool of water, and glistening under the glare of the overhead flood lights, was a golden submarine!

"As Lenin is my witness, it's a German Type XXI U-boat!" exclaimed Mikhail Kuznetsov.

With a reverent slowness, Knut guided the van closer to the gilded vessel. The Norwegians were stunned into silence, and had to rely on the white-haired Russian to make some sense out of this surprise discovery.

"So this is the real purpose of this settlement. I bet this vessel was purposely mothballed in this hollowed-out mountain at the war's conclusion. And all these years Werewolf was just waiting for the need to deploy it."

"And what need is that?" asked Kari.

"Why the heavy water, my dear child!" revealed the enlightened veteran. "What better vessel to utilize to convey this priceless treasure to the Rio de la Plata. From here, the cannisters will most likely be shipped up the Parana River by freighter to the lab where the bombs will be assembled. And God only help us if they succeed in this endeavor!"

The gangway that the guard had mentioned came into view, and Knut slowly continued their approach.

"What do we do now?" asked Arne.

"Right now, I'd say that our best bet is to complete the delivery and get the hell out of here," said Jon, who continued looking at the submarine and softly mumbled. "You know, that sub looks awfully familiar."

"I was thinking the same thing," remarked Jakob, whose eyes opened wide with astonishment upon viewing the white numerals now visible on the vessel's sail. "Jon, do you see what I see?"

The photographer gasped in wonder. "Oh my God, Jakob! It's the sister ship of the one we boarded off of Utisra!"

"Do you mean the sub where you found the gold brick?" queried Kari.

"What gold brick is that?" questioned Mikhail as he turned his head to await a reply.

"It's a long story, General," returned Jon. "While surveying the projected route of an undersea gas pipeline, the company we work for discovered a sunken submarine. We were called off of Lake Tinnsjo to take a closer look at it, and as we entered its rusted hull, Jakob found the gold bar. You know, come to think of it, didn't Magne say something about it being Russian, from the time of the Czars?"

This revelation caused Mikhail to sway back dizzily, and for a few seconds he thought that he might actually faint. A thousand questions came into his mind. But before he could express himself, Knut pulled up to the gangway.

"Here we are, ladies and gentlemen," he said lightly. "The faster we get this over with, the quicker we can get out of here. So I don't want any shirkers."

As the Norwegians assembled outside the van, Mikhail remained seated to sort through his reeling thoughts. So much had happened in so little time that he had temporarily lost his objectivity. But it only took one look at the streamlined vessel that lay floating beside him to fine-tune his focus. And in that instant he knew what had to be done. The time of waiting was over. The time for action was at long last upon him!

Somehow, someway, the U-boat had to be stopped before it completed its mission. He could think of but one individual to accomplish this task—his twin brother, Alexander.

"Come on, General. I said there'd be no shirkers in this outfit," prompted Knut from outside.

"Very well, comrade," replied the veteran as he stepped out of the van.

Their cargo turned out to be twenty-five cases of Heinz pork and beans, packed twenty-five cans to the case. Knut managed to lift three of these shrink-wrapped cases at one time, while his teammates attempted only two. Both Kari and Mikhail were content to carry one apiece.

As they made their way up the gangway they were intercepted by a sailor who had just emerged from the aft hatch. This hefty individual was completely covered in grease and he spoke out with a friendly tone.

"Ah, now we're truly ready to go to sea. Every sailor's best friend has finally arrived. I was wondering when our beans would get here. Like I once told Captain Kromer, there's more power packed in those cans than a hundred liters of prime diesel fuel. To hell with uranium-235. Somebody should attempt tapping the power of the bean!"

Knut made a feeble attempt at laughing, yet the load he was carrying diverted his thoughts elsewhere. "Where shall we store these?" he asked, his face red with strain.

The grease stained seaman answered apologetically. "I'm sorry, my friend. Here I am spouting my big mouth off while you're earning yourself a hernia. If you'd like, you can convey them through the forward hatchway. Be careful going down that ladder. Once you're below deck, just tell the first sailor that you see that Siggy instructed you to store these precious valuables in the safest portion of the boat. He'll know what I'm talking about, and will show you the way."

"And make certain that none of those rascals try to talk you into giving them some free samples," added Chief Sigmund Dortmund as he watched the motley assortment of workers head toward the forward portion of the sail.

Mikhail Kuznetsov was last in line. With Kari's assistance, he passed on the carton that he had been carrying and began his way below deck. The scent of

307

diesel fuel and machine oil met his nostrils as he climbed down into the sub's control room. This compartment was in an unbelievably superb state of preservation. The dozens of pipes, gauges, wheels and levers looked as if they were brand new. And even the brass fittings shined as if they had been installed just yesterday.

Having only seen such a vessel in books before, Mikhail knew that the Type XXI was a revolutionary breakthrough in submarine design. Produced by the Germans in the closing days of World War II, it was the world's first real submersible warship. As such, it could operate beneath the sea's surface for extended periods of time, allowing it to avoid detection by spotter planes, surface ships, and radar. It was the same model that the present batch of diesel-electric powered submarines were patterned after, and if properly crewed could hold its own even in today's high-tech battlefield.

Mikhail shuddered to think what Werewolf could do with this boat. It could be quite an effective pirate, and haunt commercial shipping worldwide. Even more frightening was that scenario in which Otto Koch and his band of demented fanatics used this platform to deliver an atomic weapon. Able to silently penetrate even the most sophisticated harbor defenses, this U-boat could deposit a nuclear device in places such as Upper New York Bay and hold the entire island of Manhattan hostage!

Knowing full well that he had to do everything with in his power to stop this machine, Mikhail listened as Knut began conversing with one of the vessel's crew members. It was this same sailor who volunteered to lead them to the storage compartment.

With his case of beans in hand, the white-haired Russian followed his Norwegian friends down a nar-

308

row, cable-lined passageway. There were several compartments adjoining this corridor and one of them had its door open. As he walked by, Mikhail peered into this vacant room and viewed the bank of equipment belonging to the U-boat's radio compartment. He spotted an old-fashioned Morse code transmitter on the counter and could visualize the dispatches already relayed to South America on this ancient, yet still effective, set.

They continued down the main passageway until it ended at a sealed hatch. Their guide opened the steel dogs that would keep this hatch watertight in the event of flooding, and pointed inside.

"You can stack the cases on the left side of the room, next to the other canned goods."

Anxious to get rid of his load, Mikhail followed the group inside. He handed his case to Arne, and was just about to return to the passageway when the glint of a light on shiny metal caught his eye from the room's opposite corner. Whatever was responsible for this reflection was locked behind a sturdy wire mesh cage and Mikhail walked over the investigate.

The old-timer almost fell to his knees. Not knowing if this all was but a cruel hallucination, he looked on with unbelieving eyes at the stack of rectangularly shaped, golden bricks that were clearly lit by several overhead flood lights. He saw the distinctive Romanoff Imperial crest that was carved into the surface of each bar, and knew that there were most likely five hundred of them locked away here. Tears began falling down his leathery cheeks. After a half century, he had been strangely reunited with the treasure that had been stolen from him soon after the Nazi invasion of the Motherland!

Mikhail hardly noticed it when this glittering stash drew his companion's attention as well.

"Oh my God, Jon!" whispered Jakob. "These bricks appear to be identical to the one that I picked out of the pressure hull of U-3312."

"I can see that," responded the astonished photographer. "Magne's never going to believe it!"

The stern voice of their escort interrupted them. "Hey you, get away from there! That portion of the ship is off limits per express orders of the Director."

Though Kari and Knut were dying to find out more about what Jon and Jakob were talking about, they wisely held their tongues. The group reluctantly returned to the passageway to retrieve the rest of the cases. Tailing behind them, Mikhail shivered with heightened awareness. U-3313 would not only be carrying the precious heavy water southward, but a fortune in gold also! Werewolf would be virtually unstoppable once this cargo reached the Rio de la Plata. Now, it was solely up to him to insure that it didn't.

To call in his brother at once, he slipped into the still vacant radio room. His heart was pounding madly in his chest as he scanned the collection of vacuum-tube operated transmitters and receivers that now lay before him. Thankful for his previous military training on just such gear, Mikhail Kuznetsov switched on the transmitter. While he waited for it to warm up, he located the transmitter's frequency knob. This would allow him to isolate a channel that would convey his signal directly to KGB headquarters. Then it would be up to his comrades in Red Square to pass this urgent message on to his twin brother.

Otto Koch was having after dinner drinks with U-3313's two senior-most officers, when he received the emergency call from security informing him that something was seriously wrong down in the sub pen. The Director immediately passed on this upsetting news to his guests, and they headed quickly for the elevator. The ride downward seemed to be taking unusually long, and even Beowulf sensed his master's relief when the doors finally slid open.

Waiting for them on the landing was Koch's assistant, Klaus Dietrich. A young, blond security guard stood beside Dietrich, and one didn't have to look very close to see that his jaw was broken.

Dietrich's tone was urgent as he initiated a rushed briefing. "Herr Director, the Norwegians who landed here by helicopter yesterday have broken out of their dormitory. We believe they have stolen a van and have succeeded in penetrating the pen."

"And where are they now?" asked Koch impatiently.

Dietrich turned around and pointed toward U-3313.

"Oh, no!" cried out the furious Director. "Captain Kromer, we must act to protect the ship at once!"

Already well on his way to doing just that, Charles Kromer and his senior lieutenant sprinted toward their threatened command. An empty van with its cargo door wide open lay parked beside the sub's forward gangway. Strangely enough, their grease-stained chief engineer could be seen sitting on the deck before this ramp, calmly puffing away on a cigarette.

"Siggy!" shouted Charles Kromer. "Where are the individuals who belong to that van?"

"Oh, you mean the delivery crew," returned the Chief, who was puzzled by his captain's frantic state. "There's no need to get upset, Skipper. They're securely storing away the last of the beans in the forward storage compartment."

Kromer raced up the gangway and cursed. "Damn it, Siggy! We must get down there and round them up

311

at once!"

"Yes, sir!" snapped the confused engineer as he stood and looked on as Senior Lieutenant Kurtz followed the captain up the ramp.

It was the sudden barking of a dog that drew the chief's attention back down to the dock. And he knew then that something was seriously wrong, for even the Director himself was headed toward the boat with a bone in his teeth.

Otto Koch accepted the chief's grease-stained hand as he hurriedly stepped off the boarding ramp.

"Where's the captain?" breathlessly quizzed the old-timer.

As coolly as possible, Siggy replied. "The last I saw he was running for the forward hatchway. If you'll just come with me, I'll escort you, Herr Director."

Otto Koch anxiously beckoned the chief to lead on. Siggy did so, and was genuinely surprised when the Director ordered him to carry the snarling German shepherd below deck with them. Somehow the chief managed this task without falling off the ladder or having the dog bite him.

Once in the control room, Beowulf continued his incessant barking as he took off running for the forward passageway.

"Beowulf, where in the hell do you think you're going?" shouted Otto Koch, who scrambled after his dog as fast as he could manage.

Siggy was totally confused by the turn of events and took off in the Director's wake. It was the angry growl of the German shepherd that drew him into the radio room. As Siggy cautiously poked his head inside this compartment, he witnessed a bewildering tableau. Standing in the middle of the room was the Director, his hard gaze locked on the dull blue eyes of a white-haired old man, who was seated in front of the radio

312

transmitter. This same stranger had a long scar lining the entire left side of his wrinkled face, and looked at the Director as if he were seeing a ghost.

With Beowulf still snarling away at his side, Otto Koch's face lit up with a wicked grin as he spoke. "So we meet again, Mikhail Kuznetsov. Don't think that I haven't been following your exploits these last fifty years. For an old man, your resiliency astounds me."

"The feeling's mutual," returned the intruder, who bitterly added. "I've been praying for this day to come, Koch, and by the grace of God, I've managed to find you before you were able to launch yet more evil into the world."

The Director stifled a laugh. "Ah, that's a good one. General Mikhail Kuznetsov, the faithful Party watchdog, imploring the divine assistance of a God his Communist forefathers long ago refuted. The next thing you'll be telling me is that you go to church on Sundays."

"Shut up, Koch!" spat the stranger, who struggled to stand on his trembling limbs.

Beowulf reacted to this movement with a renewed fit of angry barking, that was only interrupted by the sudden reappearance of U-3313's Captain.

"It looks like we've got all of them, Herr Director," revealed Charles Kromer. "There were five of them altogether, four men and a woman. They all appear to be Norwegians, and I don't think they were able to do any damage to the ship. We've got them confined in the forward storage compartment."

"Here's one more for you, Captain," said Koch triumphantly. "You can go ahead and lock up this old bag of wind with the others."

As Kromer beckoned his Chief Engineer to carry out this directive, the radio room's intercom activated

313

with a loud buzz. It was U-3313's C.O. who answered it.

"Captain here."

"Captain," broke a hoarse voice from the wall-mounted speaker. "This is Seaman Frank in radar. I've got the *Elsie K* on the screen, Sir. The trawler's approximately ten kilometers out of North Cape, and should be arriving within the half hour."

"Thank you, Seaman Frank," said Kromer as he switched off the transmitter and looked at the bald figure who still stood in the center of the room.

"That's wonderful news, Captain," observed Otto Koch, who noted that the Chief had yet to remove Mikhail Kuznetsov as ordered.

"Chief Dortmund, are you going to stand there all night? Remove the prisoner at once! And when he's securely locked away with the rest of his pathetic comrades, perhaps you'll join us at the wharf, so that we can get on with transferring the liquid treasure that awaits us there."

As Siggy reached out to take the thin arm of his white-haired prisoner, he momentarily caught this stranger's icy glance as he stared at the Director. If pure hatred had a look, the chief knew that this was it.

Chapter Fourteen

RED BANNER FLASH DISPATCH
To: Admiral Alexander Kuznetsov.
Message relayed via: Northern Fleet Headquarters,
Murmansk
START . . . FOUND GOLD ABOARD U-3313 . . .
KOCH CLOSE . . . URGENT SEND HELP . . .
SVALBARD NORTH CAPE . . . MISHA . . . END

From the private confines of his stateroom, Alexander reread the dispatch that he had just been handed three times before fully understanding it. There could be no doubting its authenticity, or the message's underlying meaning. His brother had made a fantastic discovery, and was in desperate need of Alexander's assistance.

The gold could only be in reference to the five-hundred golden bars that had been stolen from them fifty years ago. Alexander still had nightmares about that fated August day back in 1941, when he had thought that he had seen his beloved brother for the very last time. To this very day railroad trips triggered a stream of unpleasant memories ranging from dive-bombing Stukas to the sickening smell of burning human flesh.

The mention of U-3313 was a bit puzzling. He could only assume that his brother was referring to a

German submarine. Because of the high sequence of I.D. numbers, it was most likely a Type XXI vessel, the world's first true fully submersible warship and one of the most capable fighting vessels ever made. Only its late introduction kept it from turning the tide of the war. It was common knowledge that several of these subs had been unaccounted for after the war's conclusion. Could his brother have been referring to one of these mystery boats?

There was no need to ponder the next portion of the dispatch. Otto Koch had led the raid on their train, and was responsible for Mikhail's scar and his four year internment in Bergen-Belsen. His twin had dedicated the next fifty years of his life to tracking this fiend down. Yet until this time, Koch had been but a shadow that Mikhail could never pin down. Not the type to exaggerate, especially when it came to Otto Koch, his brother wouldn't say that he was close to capturing the Nazi unless he was serious.

And then there was his brother's urgent plea for help. This was totally out of character for Mikhail. Not once in the years since they were reunited had Mikhail asked for his assistance, not even in those confusing, bitter days following his release from the death camp. Alexander genuinely feared that his twin was in a desperate situation.

This was a sobering realization. He had almost lost Mikhail one time before, under circumstances that were totally out of his hands. How could he ignore this desperate plea, knowing full well that by doing so he could be condemning Mikhail to a certain death?

Alexander needed an atlas to clarify the last portion of the dispatch. He eventually found North Cape on the extreme northern coast of the Arctic island of Svalbard. No stranger to this desolate, isolated land mass that was so strategically critical in times of crisis,

Alexander hastily calculated that the *Lena* was approximately eight hundred kilometers away from Svalbard. Even at flank speed, it would take some twelve hours to reach. But could he abandon his duty and divert the *Lena* for this purpose?

The dispatch had ended with his brother using the nickname Alexander had been so fond of when they were children. As far as he knew, no one else called his twin Misha. And Mikhail had purposely utilized this nickname to underscore the legitimacy of his plea.

Alexander heavily put down the dispatch and considered his options. For all his efforts, he could think of only two. He could ignore the dispatch and continue on with the plan of the day, or immediately order the *Lena* to change its course for Svalbard.

Their current mission was a critical one, there could be no doubt in this. The intelligence that they would soon be collecting would be channeled to the highest echelons of government. The General Secretary himself was depending upon this data to decide the fate of a multi-billion ruble project which could alter the state of the Rodina's stagnant economy.

But it was still only a reconnaissance mission, one that they would have another chance to complete in the future. Could he say the same for the life of his brother? And what of the criminal that Mikhail had sacrificed his life to track down, and the organization that Otto Koch headed? Werewolf was just as much a threat to the Motherland as economic collapse or the hordes of capitalism were. In many ways it was even more so, especially if the neo-fascist cause was infused with a fortune in Russian gold to support its evil doings.

In the century that was just passing, the Motherland had only one true enemy. Hitler's Germany was the antithesis of every principle in which the founding

317

fathers of Socialism believed. To the Nazis, communism was abhorrent, and could be dealt with in only one manner—total annihilation of the U.S.S.R. Why, in the siege of Leningrad alone, one million, three hundred thousand brave Russians lost their lives. If one were to add up Russia's total losses during the war, Leningrad would appear to be a mere skirmish!

Mikhail had proved time and again that the fascist cause was still alive and growing. The new bases of nazism might be hidden deep in the jungles of South America or the isolated foothills of the northwestern United States, but their reach could extend far and wide, especially if they were to get hold of a nuclear or biological weapon and a reliable system to deliver it. A Type XXI U-boat was just such a platform.

The time for second guessing was over, and Alexander knew that he had but one choice. By the authority invested in him by the Supreme Soviet, he would order the *Lena* to turn northward, to counter the evil that had gathered there.

A quick phone call found the *Lena*'s captain on duty in the attack center. Without a moment's hesitation, Alexander left his cabin to personally explain to the submarine's commanding officer the nature of their new duty.

The attack center was bathed in red light as Alexander entered. Hardly giving his eyes time to adjust, the white-haired veteran went straight to the central command console. Grigori Milyutin was here, along with one other member of the *Lena*'s crew, the Zampolit, Felix Bucharin.

"Captain, there's been a change in the *Lena*'s operational orders. You are hereby instructed to turn immediately on course zero-one-zero. We're going to need flank speed for the next twelve hours."

Caught completely off guard by this incredible directive, Grigori Milyutin asked for a clarification. "Did you say course zero-one-zero, at flank speed for the next twelve hours, Admiral? Why, that would put us somewhere in the Arctic."

"Our destination is the island of Svalbard to be exact," added Alexander firmly.

"But we still have our mission at Karsto to complete," countered the confused Captain.

Alexander's voice rang true and clear, his tone commanding. "Are you challenging my authority in this matter, Captain? As your superior officer, I'm ordering you to change this vessel's course as instructed, at once!"

"Excuse me for interrupting, Admiral," interjected the Zampolit. "But we weren't informed by Northern Fleet headquarters of any such change in the *Lena*'s mission."

"These orders don't originate from Murmansk," explained Alexander. "As a senior fleet officer, I have initiated this change on my own."

"But isn't such a thing highly irregular?" observed the Zampolit.

"I don't really give a damn, Comrade Bucharin!" shouted the angry old man. "And if you continue with this unnecessary line of questioning, I'll have you arrested for mutiny, and that goes for you as well, Captain Milyutin. Chart the new course that I ordered!"

Still hesitant to relay these changes to the helmsman, the Captain looked to his political officer for support. Perspiration beaded the Zampolit's forehead as he dared to express himself.

"Let me assure you, Admiral, that our actions are definitely not mutinous. As fellow officers we're only questioning the reason behind your sudden change of mind. Only a few hours ago, you were adamant about how vitally important our mission to Karsto was. Why ·

319

you wouldn't even allow the Captain to turn around and investigate that collision that we monitored."

"I've never heard such impertinence in my entire naval career!" spat Alexander. "How dare you question my command authority, Comrade Bucharin. My superior rank allows me to do with the *Lena* as I please, and I certainly don't have to clear all my decisions with the likes of a mere political officer!"

Cut down to size, the sweating Zampolit looked meekly back to the captain. Grigori Milyutin hadn't risen to his current rank by being a troublemaker, and the young Captain graciously bowed to the will of his superior officer.

"Helmsman, make our new course zero-one-zero. Engineering, all ahead flank speed."

With a single twist of his joystick, the helmsman engaged the Lena's tail-mounted rudder. As this device bit into the surrounding water, the submarine began a tight U-turn. Meanwhile, back in maneuvering, the chief engineer hit a single pistol switch that would further heat the reactor vessel's lead-bizmuth coolant mixture. This would, in turn, raise the temperature of the steam generator, the force responsible for turning the vessel's seven-bladed propeller.

Tightly gripping the back of the captain's command chair to keep from falling during this high speed turn, Alexander Kuznetsov took a series of deep calming breaths. For better of for worse, he had made his decision. Heedless to the fact that his entire career would be ruined if his brother's fears proved groundless, Alexander felt strangely relieved. He could only wonder what awaited them on the edge of the ice pack, for this was the direction that their destinies now lay.

Captain Steven Aldridge was huddled over the chart

table with his XO, trying to figure out the Alfa's ultimate destination, when word arrived from the sound shack that the Soviet vessel was in the process of initiating an abrupt change of course. The *Cheyenne* had been silently following in the Alfa's unsuspecting baffles until this point. Fearful of being tagged themselves, Aldridge ordered an immediate drop in speed to loiter velocity. A state of ultra quiet prevailed as they anxiously waited for the Alfa to play its hand. As it so happened, it wasn't long in coming.

"Our contact's new course is zero-one-zero," revealed senior sonar technician Joe Carter. "And from the way they're churning up the water, Ivan is sure in a hurry to get wherever he's bound for."

"What in the world do you make of that, XO?" asked Aldridge.

Bob Stoddard peered down at the chart of the Norwegian coastline that they had been studying and replied, "It sure beats the hell out of me, Skipper. One minute they had all the makings of a spook mission — low speed and a course that was taking them directly to one of Norway's most inhabited regions. Now they go and turn almost due northward, not giving a damn how much of a racket they're leaving behind them."

"Maybe this is Ivan's way of clearing his baffles," offered Lieutenant Andrew Laird. The ship's navigator pointed to the Alfa's last position on the chart and added. "He might have suspected that he was being tailed, and is making all this noise to lure us into showing ourselves."

The Captain nodded. "Interesting thought, Lieutenant. But there are a lot less drastic ways for a sub to clear its baffles, and this certainly isn't one of them. No, I say our Alfa just got an unexpected change of orders. Most probably there's been an emergency of some sort. That would account for

321

their sudden course and speed change."

"It sure would be interesting to know what it's all about," prompted the curious XO, as he softly tapped the empty bowl of his pipe against the edge of the chart table.

"Then what do you say if we just go and find out ourselves?" offered Aldridge with a grin.

"But how will we ever catch 'em, Captain?" asked the freckle-faced navigator. "After all, that's an Alfa we're talking about."

Steven Aldridge looked at his young navigator like he hadn't heard him properly. "Come now, Lieutenant. I hope you have a little more faith in the *Cheyenne*'s capabilities than that. This old fox might not be a rabbit like that Alfa, but in the end, we'll be right there at the finish line."

"Captain, sonar reports that the contact's new course is remaining constant. Estimated speed is thirty-three knots and still gaining."

Aldridge absorbed the quartermaster's report with an exaggerated grimace. "Well XO, I guess it's time to get those cobwebs cleared out. Ring up Lieutenant Lonnon, and let him know that *Cheyenne Power and Light* is about to get a chance to show what it's made out of. Because I've got a hunch that this is going to be a race that's right down to the wire."

It took the rest of the night and most of the next day to get the heavy water unloaded from the trawler, transferred up into the sub pen, and then secured inside U-3313's forward storage compartment. Once this was accomplished, though, the Golden U-boat was ready to set sail.

It was late afternoon when the massive camouflaged door that was set into the seaward side of the mountain was raised. With a minimum of fanfare the vessel's diesel engines were started. The final mooring line was disconnected, and slowly the sub nosed its way out of the pen where it had been stored for over four decades.

They would travel on the surface until reaching the preselected diving area. Only when there was plenty of water under the boat's hull would the diesels be shut down and the battery-fed motors engaged, as the submarine descended below the surface into its intended medium.

Otto Koch was beaming with pride as he stood on the exposed bridge that was set into the top of the streamlined sail. Beside him, Captain Charles Kromer was also satisfied, knowing that he had once again managed the impossible by helping get his present command ready for sea so quickly. Two young seamen were also on the sail, their binoculars trained on the seas before them for any signs of ice.

The gray, overcast sky was rapidly darkening. The air was cold and fresh with the salt spray that whipped over the bow and flew as high as the bridge. Soon the whole deck was dripping with salt water, which was already beginning to freeze.

"The engines sound good," observed Kromer in response to the steady throbbing sound that emanated from below deck.

"They'll work themselves in nicely enough," said Otto Koch as he wiped some spray from his eyes.

Kromer quickly scanned the horizon with his binoculars before checking his watch. "I'll still feel better once we're under, Herr Director," he commented. "An iceberg can end this mission long before we can even get to the open seas."

"How much longer to the diving point?" asked Koch.

323

"Another quarter of an hour," answered the Captain. "We could go under earlier than that, but I want plenty of water beneath us for that first dive."

"She'll do just fine, Captain," offered Koch as he turned and viewed the shoreline still visible behind them.

The hollowed out mountain from which they had emerged was hardly recognizable. It seemed to have long since blended in with the desolate, snow-capped mountain ridges. Only a single blinking beacon indicated the location of the outpost known as North Cape. Several dozen hearty souls would remain there, keeping the facility habitable for the next time that it would be needed.

The sound of a barking dog diverted his attention to the open hatch set at his feet.

"Beowulf, behave yourself down there!" shouted Koch.

Almost instantly the barking stopped, only to be replaced by the shrill voice of a young woman. "Herr Director, are you certain that you are dressed warmly enough? I have another muffler with me in case you need it."

Otto Koch looked over to the captain and winked before replying to this offer. "Thank you, Lottie, but I'm doing just fine."

"Well, your tea is ready whenever you'd like it, sir," added his faithful servant.

The old man chuckled. "That one is a real gem, Captain. She takes better care of me than my own mother did."

"Are your quarters comfortable, Herr Director?" questioned the captain.

"They're more than sufficient, Captain. Lottie even got down there beforehand and did a little decorating. Right now the bulkheads are covered with my Bavar-

324

ian prints and my favorite cuckoo clock."

U-3313's hull bit into the gathering swell and as Kromer reached out to steady himself, he asked guardedly, "Herr Director, I've been meaning to ask you, could you explain to me why we're taking those prisoners along with us? Wouldn't it be better to just throw them overboard and be done with them? They would certainly be a lot less bother to us."

"I understand your concern, Captain. But please bear with me just a bit longer. The young Norwegians will make excellent hostages. Should the need arise, we can use them for blackmail purposes. As for the old Russian, I'll deal with him myself when the time is right."

"I gather that you knew this man previously," probed Kromer.

"Let's just say that we're old acquaintances from the war, Captain."

The excited shouts of one of the lookout's interrupted Koch. "We've got ice dead ahead of us, Captain!"

"More ice off to the port, Sir!" screamed the other seaman.

Kromer raised his binoculars and quickly sized up their situation. "I was afraid of this, Herr Director. The winds have apparently shifted and sent this pack ice down from the north. If we don't want to risk a collision, we'd better think about going under."

"Then let's do it, Captain," urged Koch. "I'd much rather take my chances with the bottom of the sea, than take on one of those floating menaces."

Even without the benefit of binoculars, the ice was clearly visible. It seemed to cover the whole horizon, and came in a varied assortment of shapes and sizes.

Kromer looked at his watch, then barked into the waterproof intercom box. "Rig for diving!"

As this order rang through the boat, Kromer ordered the lookouts below. As they scrambled down the conning tower ladder, the captain helped Otto Koch climb through the hatch. After taking one last look at the sea in front of them, Kromer descended the ladder himself.

Below deck, the warmth was most noticeable. As an alert seaman took Kromer's parka, hat and gloves, the captain looked over to the diving station. Standing there, before the collection of vent and hull opening indicator boards, diving rudder indicators, and trim indicators, was Senior Lieutenant Hans Kurtz.

"The boat is rigged for diving, Captain," informed U-3313's second-in-command.

"Very good, Hans," replied Kromer. "Stand by to, dive! Sound the alarm!"

The compartment filled with a blaring klaxon. And as Kromer readied his stopwatch to record their diving time, he momentarily caught the glance of the bald old man who was responsible for this mission. Standing calmly beside the vacant fire-control panel, with his dog Beowulf faithfully seated beside him, Otto Koch returned the captain's glance with the barest of supportive nods.

"Open all main ballast valves!" orded Kromer. "Open vents of bow buoyancy. Open vents on number one ballast, number two ballast, and the safety tanks. Bow planes at hard dive!"

"All engines stopped and valves closed, Sir," reported the Senior Lieutenant.

Charles Kromer knew that the moment of truth was finally upon them. In a few more seconds, U-3313 would start to plane below the water's surface, driving forward with the push of its electric motors.

Back in the engine room, he could picture Chief Dortmund at work making absolutely certain that the hull and engine induction valves were securely closed off against the sea. It was through these valves that the diesel engines were vented and got the enormous amounts of air that they needed to breathe. In the watery realm that they now entered, the diesels would be useless, with the U-boat depending upon its battery-powered engines for propulsion.

"Main inductions closed," informed the quartermaster.

Kromer felt an alien pressure on his eardrums as pressurized air was bled into the boat. His eye went to the aneroid barometer, and as it gradually rose and the needles held steady, he was positive that the hull was airtight from within.

"Take us down, Hans," ordered the captain tensely.

This was all the senior lieutenant needed to hear to move the levers of the main ballast tanks. The compartment filled with the loud hiss of the air being vented through the tops of these tanks, followed by the onrushing surge of seawater that poured in to replace this air from the bottom valves.

"Pressure in the boat, Captain. Green board," reported Hans Kurtz.

Kromer walked over to the diving station to note the time it took for them to reach a depth of 35 feet. Next he studied the bubble angle indicators, that showed them down by the bow at about eight degrees. This meant that the top deck was thoroughly submerged now, with the sail soon to follow.

At forty feet, Kromer ordered the bow buoyancy vents closed. At forty-five feet, he instructed Hans Kurtz to close all vents, informing the planesman to level them off at a depth of sixty-five feet. Only then did the captain look at his stopwatch and exhale a long breath of relief. A hand gently touched him on the shoulder, and he turned to be greeted by a warm, almost fatherly voice.

"Nice job, Charles," complimented Otto Koch. "You have made this old man very proud."

This was the first time that the veteran had ever called him by his first name, and Kromer felt the bond between them further tighten.

"Thank you, sir," he humbly replied. "But it's this crew of ours that deserves the job well done. They handled themselves like true professionals."

"Sonar reports ice dead ahead, Sir," relayed the quartermaster.

Called back to duty, Kromer turned to his second lieutenant.

"It's time to see how tough this old wolf really is, Hans. Take us down to 450 feet. All ahead full. We've only got the Kongsfjord Strait to transit now, and then it will be nothing but open sea all the way to the Rio de la Plata!"

Throughout the boat, the crew began settling in for their long voyage. Electricians crawled into the dark pits that stretched almost the entire length of the hull, monitoring the vessel's hundreds of batteries, while other seamen focused their attentions on the minor leaks and other petty mechanical difficulties that were an inevitable part of any such submerged run.

In the forward storage compartment, the only indication of the great depth in which they were now travelling was the ominous creaking of the outer hull. Locked inside a wire mesh cage that was previously utilized to store foodstuffs, the U-boat's six prisoners tried to make the best of their captivity.

The cage itself was barely large enough to permit all six of them to lay down on the cold metal decking at one time. Each of them had been permitted the luxury of a single woolen blanket. The toilet facilities consisted of two metal buckets, one of which held foul-

328

tasting, tepid drinking water, and the other to be used for bodily eliminations. This spartan arrangement was particularly distressing for the only female present, and it had been Knut who had suggested rigging up a blanket to give Kari a bit of privacy.

Since their capture, they had been fed only a single time. This feast consisted of a can of cold pork and beans, that had to be eaten with the hands as no utensils were provided.

Adding to their mental discomfort was the view that they were forced to endure. Secured to the deck immediately in front of them was the heavy water that only a few days ago lay on the bottom of Lake Tinnsjo. The precious fluid had been transferred into several dozen heavy plastic carboys that looked temptingly close, but for all effective purposes were miles away.

Just visible on the opposite side of the room was the locked cage in which the gold was stored. Mikhail Kuznetsov found this particularly ironic. Here it had taken him fifty years to track this treasure down, and now it appeared that his life would end with the gold within his sight, yet still completely out of his reach.

The white-haired Russian was taking their incarceration particularly hard. Since being locked inside the cage, he had done little but sit in the corner, his blanket wrapped tightly around him. He seemed completely deaf to whatever conversation was going on around him. Instead, his attention was focused inward.

Haunting Mikhail's inner vision was the face and figure of a single man. It had been half a century since he had last laid his eyes on Otto Koch. Though the years had aged him considerably, Mikhail knew who he was the instant he came hobbling into the radio room. It had been his eyes that had given him away. The cold, steel-gray orbs flashed with the same vicious cruelty that had characterized them fifty years ago. They were a direct channel into hell, and Mikhail would never forget staring into their evil depths on that fated August day in 1941, when Koch physically and mentally scarred him for life.

And now . . . it appeared that the evil would triumph again. Koch's gloating grin had sickened Mikhail's very soul. It was the German who would get the last laugh, as he once more ordered Mikhail to be imprisoned, to await a sentence that would have only one outcome. And with his death, Mikhail's entire life would have been completely wasted!

He had managed to tragically drag in the innocent group of young Norwegians. They, too, were condemned to suffer Koch's wrath, all because the cruel hand of fate had brought their young lives together with his.

Mikhail's only hope was that somehow his brother had received his desperate call for help. Being a realist, he knew that the odds were slim that the message had even reached its intended party. Even if it did, would Alexander have the courage and foresight to heed his plea, and act?

At stake here was not only Mikhail's life and those of his young Norwegian allies, but something much, much bigger. If the U-boat was to reach its goal, with the heavy water and the gold safely delivered into the clutches of Werewolf, the entire world would be faced with its greatest threat since Adolf Hitler.

Over forty years ago, shortly after Mikhail had been released from Bergen-Belsen, he was faced with a crisis of faith. At that time his broken body and spirit stripped him of his very will to go on living. It had been Alexander who had given him the priceless gift of renewed purpose, and as Mikhail's body grew strong once again, he focused his energies on one purpose only — to insure that the Nazi demon would never again run rampant on the planet.

The saddest part was that he had actually fooled himself into thinking that his efforts were succeeding in this task. He had been responsible for bringing dozens of escaped Nazis to justice, and had even managed to infiltrate several of the most prominent neofascist organizations. But all this meant nothing now.

Infused with new capital, and bolstered by the nuclear weapons that it would soon be producing, Werewolf would rapidly grow into a powerful force, one to be reckoned with. Its growing ranks filled with the twisted slime of the earth, the new Reich would continue where the old one left off, with a new and even more dangerous leader at its helm. Though old in years, Otto Koch was still an effective organizer, as this current operation proved.

It was evident that Koch would be able to give Werewolf its initial direction, until a younger, more dynamic leader was found to guide the fascist cause into the twenty-first century.

Mikhail had come so close to ridding the earth of this cancer once and for all. Yet his best efforts had been in vain, and soon millions of innocent men, women, and children would pay the price in tears and broken dreams. This was the ultimate injustice — that evil should prevail over good, death over life, and hatred over love. Soon the scourge of world war would once more be unleashed, this time with the horror of a nuclear apocalypse only a heartbeat away.

Chapter Fifteen

The Norwegian Coast Guard was a relatively new service. Established by an act of Parliament in December 1976, the Coast Guard became a fully integrated part of the Norwegian defense command. As such it had a wide variety of missions. These included sovereignty patrols, fishing enforcement, search and rescue, and coastline defense in times of war. It was this latter mission that the cutter *Nordkapp* was practicing during its current deployment.

The *Nordkapp* was the lead ship in a new class of vessels. Appearing more like a frigate than a mere cutter, the ship was 105 meters long and displaced some 3,240 tons. Four diesel engines propelled it up to speeds of 23 knots, with a range of over 7,500 nautical miles. As the first ship in the Royal Norwegian Navy to carry a helicopter, the *Nordkapp* currently deployed a Lynx Mk86.

One of the ship's distinguishing features was its 57mm Bofors gun that was mounted near the bow. The *Nordkapp* was also armed with a 20mm cannon, six torpedo tubes, and a full load of depth charges, making it an excellent vessel for anti-submarine warfare purposes. Currently assigned to Squadron North, the *Nordkapp* could most often be found patrolling the waters around Svalbard.

Commander Gunnar Nilsen was the ship's present

C.O. The forty-six-year-old Bergen native enlisted in the Coast Guard in 1977. Before that time he worked for Noroil as a diver. He still had many good friends at Noroil. In fact, he had only just gotten off the radio-telephone with one of them.

Magne Rystaad was currently diving supervisor aboard the support ship *Falcon*. If all worked out as planned, they would be having breakfast together the very next morning.

The *Falcon* was presently less than forty miles away from the *Nordkapp*, supervising the placement of the first Ice Field's gas production platform. This would be a valuable new Norwegian asset, and Commander Nilsen was anxious for the current exercise to end, so that he could have a look at the monstrous platform himself.

Gunnar Nilsen stood inside the *Nordkapp*'s glassed-in bridge, watching as the deck crew lowered what looked to be a weighted steel cable down into the gray waters of Kongsfjord Strait. This was actually a prototype hydrophone array that they were in the process of testing for the Defense Ministry. Such a portable system was designed for the detection of enemy submarines, a threat that was taken most seriously, especially because of the unique shape of the Norwegian coastline with its deep fjords, jagged inlets, and thousands of small islands.

This particular array could perform both active and passive searches. In the active mode, a surge of acoustic sound would be shot out into the surrounding water. This distinctive ping would then reflect off any object that happened to be passing at the moment, giving the operator a sonic picture of any unwanted trespassers. The passive mode depended upon the hundreds of hydrophones placed inside the cable itself.

These ultra-sensitive listening devices could pick up the sound of an approaching submarine. This signature would then be analyzed, and the class and nationality of the vessel determined.

The array would give ships of the *Nordkapp* class an exciting new capability. Already equipped with a full load of ASW weapons, the cutter now wouldn't have to rely on platforms such as the P-3 Orion to do the hunting for them.

He could see from the awkward movements of the deck crew that the array was a bit bulky to handle. Eventually it would be deployed by means of a mechanical winch, but before it went operational, it had to be thoroughly tested. For the moment, it would have to be lowered into the sea by hand.

To best test its capabilities, Gunnar picked the waters of the Kongsfjord Strait. This natural choke-point would be a typical transit route for a submarine that desired to reach Svalbard from the open sea. The relatively shallow waters of the strait would force such a vessel to stick close to the central channel, thus making it an easy target for the active and passive sensors around which the array was designed.

Though Gunnar was certainly not expecting to detect any submarines during this particular exercise, he always found it beneficial to make his training missions as authentic as possible. Once the array was fully deployed, they would test it on the special monitors that had been set up in the *Nordkapp*'s operations room. If all checked out, it would be pulled in, and they could be off to their rendezvous with the *Falcon*.

Gunnar sincerely hoped that all would go smoothly. He hadn't seen Magne Rystaad in almost a year. As young men they had been inseparable. Both had gotten their diving certificates together, along with their very first professional jobs. Gunnar had been there on the night that Magne initially met his wife-to-be. Anna was a real knockout, and Magne pursued her with that easy-going charm of his resulting in a long marriage and two wonderful boys.

While on the radio-telephone, Magne had mentioned that he had a guest with him visiting from Texas. Also a professional diver, this individual was making his first visit to Norway, and Magne was hoping that he would be allowed to visit the *Nordkapp*. Gunnar didn't foresee any problems granting this request. The *Nordkapp* held no secrets, and if anything, the crew would be glad to show her off.

Commander Gunnar Nilsen was thus most satisfied when the deck crew notified the bridge that the array had been deployed without complications. Now the damn thing only had to work properly, for his reunion to go as planned."

Alexander Kuznetsov was on his way to the *Lena*'s attack center when he heard the steady throbbing whine, which had been with them for the last twelve hours, suddenly lessen. Someone had just cut back on the massive steam turbines that had produced this noise, signalling that they were close to their destination.

The white-haired veteran had been anxiously waiting for this moment to arrive. Though, now that they had reached Svalbard, he really wasn't sure what would happen next. He could only trust in his brother and continue on to North Cape, which was on the island's northern shore. Hopefully, once they arrived at this isolated outpost, their next move would be obvious.

By the time he reached the attack center, the whine of the turbines had stopped completely. He found the sub's two senior officers huddled beside the sonar console and quickly joined them.

"Why have we stopped?" asked Alexander breathlessly.

The captain took his time in answering. "We were preparing to enter the Kongsfjord Strait, to complete our transit to North Cape, and had just slowed to initiate the standard sonar sweep when another contact was made. Would you like to hear for yourself, Admiral?"

Not waiting for a reply, Milyutin handed Alexander a set of headphones. He heard the familiar pinging sounds almost immediately.

"Is there a surface vessel up there responsible for this active sonar search?" quizzed Alexander.

The captain nodded. "It appears that way, Admiral. They must be anchored over the very center of the transit channel, which means that it will be almost impossible to penetrate the strait without being detected."

"That is a dilemma," concurred Alexander as he handed the headphones back to the captain. "Is there another way to reach North Cape?"

This time it was Senior Lieutenant Popov who replied. "Not from this direction, Admiral. We'd have to back track, circle Svalbard, and approach from under the ice from the north. Because these waters are poorly charted, such an alternative route would take us approximately five hours."

"But that's nearly half the amount of time it took to get us all the way from the Norwegian Sea!" countered Alexander.

"There will be no sprint speeds up here, Admiral," informed the captain firmly.

336

Not about to override Milyutin in this matter, Alexander wondered if the surface vessel up ahead had anything to do with his brother's dispatch.

"Is there anyway for us to find out the identity of the ship that's blocking the channel?" he quizzed.

The *Lena*'s C.O. thought this over a moment. "We could go to periscope depth and give it the once over with our see in the dark unit. But that would momentarily leave us open to detection by radar."

"Then that's a chance we'll just have to take," said Alexander.

"Very well, Admiral. Periscope depth it is."

While the captain went over to his command console to carry out this procedure, Alexander remained beside the sonar operator. He was so wrapped in thought, that he didn't notice the arrival of the boat's Zampolit until hearing his gravelly voice close behind him.

"May I ask why we've stopped?" questioned Felix Bucharin.

"There's a surface ship blocking the channel up ahead," answered Alexander. "We're presently going to periscope depth to identify it."

The sound of venting ballast accompanied this response, and the now-lightened submarine began slowly ascending.

"We certainly handled ourselves well on that run up here," continued the Zampolit. "It's a tribute to the crew and the individuals who designed this craft, that we were able to travel at such incredible speeds without interruption."

In no mood for idle chatter, Alexander muttered. "Yes it is, comrade."

Suddenly the voice of the captain cried out from his

337

command console. "I've got it! I'm taking us back down."

The ballast tanks were once more flooded, and as the *Lena* began sinking back into the protective depths, the captain revealed his findings. "The computer enhancement shows our contact to be a Norwegian *Nordkapp* class Coast Guard cutter."

Alexander ingested this information and doubted that such a vessel would be a part of his brother's warning. Most likely this was but a routine patrol that had nothing to do with gold-filled U-boats or neo-Nazis. He was just about to suggest that they try waiting for the cutter to move on, when the sonar operator announced yet another contact.

"I'm picking up strong screw sounds, Captain, from the opposite side of the strait. It sounds as if its coming from another submarine, though it's unlike anything that I've ever heard before."

This was the type of contact that Alexander had been waiting for, and he excitedly addressed the seated technician. "Run it through the signature I.D. program, comrade. I must know what type of submersible that we're dealing with here."

The sonar operator expertly addressed his keyboard. Seconds later, his monitor screen began filling with the requested data. Alexander bent over to read this information himself.

. . . contact unknown . . . signature not on file . . .

Not satisfied with this answer, Alexander ordered the sonar technician to run the signature through the computer once again, this time requesting that it list any other submarines with similar sound emissions. This did the trick, and the monitor began filling with hard data.

. . . See file — Whiskey Class . . .

338

"Shall I access that file, Admiral?" asked the sonar technician.

"No, that's alright, comrade. I've seen enough," managed Alexander, as he thoughtfully backed away from the console.

The Zampolit noted an unusual expression cross the old veteran's face as Kuznetsov vacantly looked off into space, as if seeing some sort of apparition. It was obvious that whatever he had just read on the screen had been the cause of this dreamy state, and the political officer bent over to have a look at the monitor himself.

"Comrade sonar technician, would you mind accessing this file on the Whiskey class for me?" requested Felix Bucharin softly.

The seated operator responded by hitting a single key. This caused the monitor to suddenly fill with a screen full of information. Carefully, the Zampolit read each and every word.

. . . attack submarine Whiskey Class . . . displacement — 1,050 tons surfaced — 1,350 tons submerged . . . Length — 75 meters . . . Propulsion — Diesel-electric . . . Main Armament — torpedo tubes — Developmental History — The design of the medium range Whiskey class was based exclusively on German blueprints captured in the closing days of World War II. Almost an exact duplicate of the German Type XXI attack submarine, 236 units of the Whiskey class were built during the 1950's in the largest submarine construction program of the post-World War II period . . .

The report went on, and as the political officer continued his extensive study of it, Alexander found his limbs trembling with the realization that this new contact was none other than U-3313, the vessel his brother had warned about in his dispatch. But if this was indeed the case, now what was Alexander supposed to do? The *Lena* could easily destroy the Type XXI U-boat with the launch of a single torpedo. Yet what if Mikhail was somehow aboard this submarine? Could he risk taking his own brother's life?

Closing his eyes in an effort to solve this dilemma, he found himself wishing only one thing. If he could only see what was going on inside that vessel, then he'd know how to proceed!

—

Otto Koch was in the midst of having Lottie give him his customary evening rubdown, when he was informed that he was wanted on the bridge at once. Taking only the time to throw on a long, red velvet robe and some slippers, he left the cramped confines of his stateroom, and began his way down a passageway so narrow that Beowulf had to follow on his heels.

He entered the control room and found the boat's captain bent over the periscope. This in itself did not look alarming, and Koch casually announced his presence.

"Whatever is so terribly important out there, Captain? Surely the Arctic night can't be conducive to star gazing at this hour?"

"It's not the heavens that I'm looking at, Herr Director," returned Charles Kromer as he stood and stepped back from the periscope well. "Have a look yourself, if you'd like. There's not much moonlight to speak of, but it's enough to give you an idea what we're up against."

Curious now as to what the captain was referring to, Koch stepped up to the periscope and peered into its lens. At first he could see nothing but blackness.

But then gradually the sleek outline of a warship took form in the distance.

"I know that vessel. It's the *Nordkapp*," revealed Koch calmly. "She's only a Norwegian Coast Guard cutter and will do us no harm."

"I beg to differ with you, Herr Director," countered Kromer. "I too saw this same vessel while passing through Longyearben, and I remember thinking at the time how heavily armed she seemed for a mere cutter. But I never dreamed that she'd also be equipped with a fully operational sonar suite."

"Why that's pure nonsense," retorted Koch. "I've personally toured that warship, and I can assure you that the *Nordkapp* has no active or passive sonar capabilities."

Not even bothering to respond to this, Kromer turned to address his sonar operator. "Frederick, relay that signal that our hydrophones are picking up from the waters ahead of us through the compartment's P.A. system."

As this directive was carried out, the room filled with the deafening hollow ping that every submariner in the world had bad dreams about sometime in his life.

Otto Koch's expression filled with astonishment as he nodded. "Well, I'll be. So the *Nordkapp* indeed has an array working out there. I doubt if the Norwegians would appreciate finding us in their territorial waters. Since the only way to the open sea is through that strait they're blocking, I guess we don't have much of a choice."

"Then we'll be returning to North Cape, Herr Director?" assumed Charles Kromer.

"Returning to North Cape!" repeated Koch. "Why in the world would we want to do that, when we're

341

carrying six fish that can easily solve the problem."

"You don't mean that you want me to torpedo them?" questioned Kromer with a tone of utter disbelief.

Otto Koch's face reddened as he forcefully responded. "And why the hell not, Captain? This isn't some Bundesmarine exercise that we're dealing with here. This is war! Since there's no way for us to reach the open seas without going through that channel, we must negate the obstacle at once. In other words, Captain Kromer, open those bow torpedo caps and sink the Norwegian bastards!"

At long last their mad dash beneath the Norwegian Sea was over, and Joe Carter could initiate a proper sonar scan. For the past twelve hours, the *Cheyenne* had been running with its turbines wide open. This corresponded to a speed of thirty-seven knots, an unprecedented velocity for a 688-class vessel. Along with this tremendous speed came the inherent noise that went with it. The whining turbines, the surging grind of the reactor's coolant pump, and the cavitational hiss of the propeller, all served to severely limit the effectiveness of Carter's sensitive equipment. Now all this racket was gone, and the senior sonar technician gratefully went back to work in an effort to determine the exact whereabouts of the Alfa.

Amazingly enough, he found the Soviet sub on his very first scan. The Alfa had also halted its sprint, and was quietly loitering dead ahead of them, less than a mile distant. In an effort to determine the reason for this abrupt decrease in speed, Carter increased the range of his sweep and opened up the frequency band. That's when he heard the pinging of an active sonar unit, that appeared to be coming from a surface warship. Knowing now why Ivan had put the brakes on, Carter was in the process of reaching for the intercom to inform the captain of this find, when yet another alien noise filtered in through his headphones. This brief grating sound had originated in the waters far beyond the surface ship that he had just tagged, and had a disturbing quality to it. This was a signature that he had been trained to listen for from his very first day at sonar school, the opening of an unknown submerged contact's torpedo doors!

Carter relayed this shocking information to the captain. He wasn't at all surprised when the *Cheyenne*'s C.O. immediately directed him to interface this data into the newly modified Mk117 fire-control system. In the forward torpedo room, Lieutenant Edward Hartman was directed to prepare a conventionally armed SUBROC, in the event that a worse case scenario was to prevail.

There was a hushed, somber atmosphere prevailing inside U-3313's control room. After taking a final look into the periscope, the U-boat's captain backed away from the lens and turned to face his superior.

"The final coordinates are locked into the fire-control computer, Herr Director," revealed Kromer heavily. "Since the cutter remains at anchor, I feel that a two shot salvo should be sufficient to break the cutter's back."

Otto Koch stood beside the weapon's console, and anxiously rubbed his liver-spotted hands together. "Then let's get on with it, Captain. We're losing precious time here."

Kromer hesitated and Otto Koch exploded in rage.

343

"Oh for heavens sake, Captain! I see that you still don't comprehend the fact that we have declared war on the world!"

Disgustedly looking down at U-3313's second in command, who was seated before the weapon's console, Koch forcefully ordered. "Senior Lieutenant Kurtz, fire one! Fire two!"

With shaking hands, Hans Kurtz carried out this directive. Without a second thought, he hit the two red launch buttons, and the compartment filled with the bubbling hiss of compressed air as the pair of wire-guided torpedoes shot out from their tubes.

Oblivious to this racket, Otto Koch reached down to pet his dog's head. "Beowulf understands what it means to be the hunter, don't you, boy?"

Seemingly in response to this question, the German shepherd barked two times, and Otto Koch grinned.

"That's right, boy, one for each torpedo. Why, I should have made you captain of U-3313. You'd certainly show your enemy no mercy."

Commander Gunnar Nilsen's first impression, when he heard the frantic report of his sonar operator, was that this was all some sort of sick practical joke. After all, a torpedo attack was about the last thing he would have expected. Having a good mind to go down into the operation's room and castigate the senior chief responsible for this convincing warning, the *Nordkapp*'s C.O. ambled over to the bridge's wrap-around windshield and looked out in the direction that this supposed attack was coming from.

What Gunnar Nilsen saw in the moonlit waters caused shivers to run up and down his spine. The pair of narrow, spiralling white wakes was headed straight for them. Feeling as if he were in the midst of a horribly realistic nightmare, Gunnar knew that any evasive actions on their part would be impossible. In fact, he only had time to brace himself as the first of the torpedoes smacked into the *Nordkapp*'s hull with a loud, metallic bang. Only then did Gunnar realize that this weapon hadn't detonated, leading him to believe that this surprise attack was all part of the exercise.

It was at that moment that the second torpedo struck with an ear-shattering blast. The resulting concussion shattered the glass windshield and sent Gunnar crashing to the deck. An emergency klaxon began whining in the background, and Gunnar could smell the acrid scent of smoke as he struggled to stand once again. He ignored the cuts to his face, neck, and hands, instead going right to the damage control telephone. There was a bit of confusion on the other end, but finally he got a hold of a second lieutenant who seemed to be fairly well composed.

The torpedo had caught the *Nordkapp* amidships, doing most of the damage to the engine room. There appeared to be several fatalities, and many more wounded. The damage control party was already on the scene, their big concern being fire and the hole that had been blown in the cutter's hull just above the waterline. The lieutenant's bottom line assessment was that the *Nordkapp* could be saved, only if the fires were extinguished before they reached the fuel tanks and ammunition bins.

Relieved that they still had a fighting chance, Gunnar Nilsen hung up the handset and decided his next call would be an SOS, that would be solely directed to a single vessel. If anyone could get there in time to help them in this desperate struggle, it would be Magne Rystaad and the *Falcon*.

345

* * *

No one was as shocked as Steven Aldridge when informed of the attack on the surface vessel. Having only learned the identity of this warship seconds before the first torpedo smashed into the cutter's hull, Aldridge could only pray that the damage to the *Nordkapp* wouldn't be fatal.

The *Cheyenne*'s C.O. was at a complete loss as to who the attacker might be. At first he assumed that this was all some sort of realistic exercise that had gone tragically wrong. But only seconds ago, Joe Carter had informed them that the mystery vessel responsible for the salvo had opened yet another torpedo door.

Not about to stand by and watch the defenseless Norwegian cutter be hit once again, Aldridge decided that there was but one option available to him. Nevertheless, it was with grave reluctance that he ordered the weapon's officer to launch the conventionally-armed SUBROC.

From the attack center of the Alfa class attack submarine *Lena*, Admiral Alexander Kuznetsov monitored these same proceedings with horror. He was absolutely sickened when the U-boat launched its initial salvo, for if he hadn't hesitated, the *Lena* could have taken out the German submarine long before its first torpedo was fired.

Now there was no doubt in his mind that these fascist pirates had to be exterminated, regardless if his brother was a prisoner on board the U-boat or not. Surely Mikhail would want him to act in a decisive manner. Yet all of this had to be temporarily thrown

346

aside when the frantic cries of the *Lena*'s sonar operator informed them of a more immediate threat.

"There's another torpedo launch, Captain. But this one's emanating from an unidentified submerged contact that's been lurking in the waters behind us!"

Shocked by this announcement, Alexander hurried over to the captain, who was seated before his central command console. Arriving here at the same time was the Zampolit.

"In the name of Lenin, who could these new attackers be?" quizzed the sweating political officer.

Grigori Milyutin managed to answer while addressing his keyboard with a flurry of requests. "At the moment, their identity is irrelevant, Comrade Zampolit, though most likely they're Americans. My number one concern is escaping this unprovoked attack and then answering it with one of our own!"

Alexander had to reach out to steady himself as the *Lena* began picking up forward speed once again. The deck canted hard to the right as the vessel initiated a sequence of computerized evasive actions.

"The torpedo continues its approach in our baffles, Captain!" revealed the sonar operator. "It seems to be travelling at an incredible speed, and at this supercharged velocity it will surely hit us in a matter of minutes."

"Damn it! Where is that speed?" cursed Grigori Milyutin as he furiously attacked his keyboard.

"Easy, Captain," advised the white-haired veteran who stood close at Milyutin's side. "No torpedo on earth can keep up that frenzied pace forever. And as it eventually decelerates, we'll have our opportunity to outrun it."

"I wish I could share your optimism, Admiral," nervously retorted the Zampolit. "And to think that we still don't know who this phantom attacker is."

Grigori Milyutin seemed to have the whole thing figured out as he expressed himself. "It's only too obvious that we've been lured into some sort of Yankee ambush. I never did understand what we were doing up here in the first place, and I hope we'll all be alive so that the Admiral can explain it to us one day."

The *Lena* rocked hard on its left side as the sub began a tight preprogrammed turn. Not anticipating this abrupt change of course, Alexander momentarily lost his balance and went crashing into the Zampolit. Felix Bucharin's palms were cold and wet as he grabbed the veteran's forearm and helped steady him.

Having regained his balance at this point, Alexander replied to the captain's request. "You have my sworn word that I'll explain everything at the proper time. If I'm indeed guilty of falling for an American trick, no one is sorrier than I."

"Now that's more like it," observed Milyutin as he watched the speed indicator begin a steady climb upward. "There might be some light at the end of this tunnel yet," he added.

This did little to relieve the Zampolit's anxieties. "And to think that we could all die without ever getting a chance to revenge this cowardly attack."

Grigori Milyutin's eyes were glistening as he passionately reacted to this pessimistic statement. "I wouldn't go that far, Comrade Zampolit. Because with Admiral Kuznetsov's permission, I'd like to launch a little salvo of our own. That will give those Imperialist pigs something to think about."

"By all means, permission granted!" replied Alexander, who only hoped this attack would be a quick and successful one, for they still had another adversary waiting in the wings.

348

It seemed to take an eternity for the SUBROC to complete the underwater portion of its flight path and break the water's surface. But when it eventually did, its solid-fueled rocket motor engaged with a vengeance. This deep, resonant roar was music to Joe Carter's ears.

The senior sonar technician visualized the rocket as it shot up into the heavens at supersonic speeds. Any moment now its reverse thrusters would activate, and as the spent thrusters separated, the encapsulated torpedo would follow its ballistics course to a splashdown in the waters directly above their unwary target. As the torpedo sliced into the frigid sea, its self-contained sonar unit would guide it the rest of the way. In this manner, SUBROC would draw its first blood.

Joe Carter found it hard to believe that this wasn't just an exercise. Most likely men had already died aboard the unlucky cutter and more men would meet their Maker once SUBROC did its thing. Though he had trained a good portion of his life to be ready when this moment came, he somehow never thought that he would have to utilize his skills in a real underwater battle.

Equally as shocking was the fact that they didn't even know the true identity of their current enemy. Carter had always taken it for granted that the Soviet Union would be the most likely opponent if hostilities were ever to break out. But for some reason, he had a gut feeling that their target was not of the Red variety.

As he prepared himself for the moment when the SUBROC was due to hit the water, Carter adjusted his sensors to get a quick update on the Alfa's status. Even with the broad-band processor, he couldn't fail to hear the familiar whine of the Soviet sub's turbines as the vessel unexpectedly shot off in a series of steep, twisting turns. Yet then there was also a secondary signature, that brought a lump to Joe Carter's throat. Having heard this dreaded sound only during trial firings and exercises, the senior sonar technician frantically grabbed for the intercom to inform control that they now had an incoming torpedo salvo headed their way!

"What do you mean that torpedo wasn't meant for us?" quizzed the furious captain of the *Lena* to his sonar operator. "I thought that you had a definite lock on it as it was headed in from behind us."

The red-faced technician vainly tried to explain himself. "That's indeed as it first appeared, Captain. But then the torpedo abruptly altered its course and shot up to the surface, leading me to believe that this is an anti-submarine rocket not meant for us, but for the vessel that fired on that cutter."

"Why not just cut the wires on our torpedoes and utilize the underwater telephone to inform the Americans that our attack was a mistake?" offered Alexander Kuznetsov.

The *Lena*'s Captain rubbed his forehead and replied. "I wish it were that simple, Admiral, but we launched acoustic-homing torpedoes that can't be recalled."

The white-haired veteran winced as if he were in pain. "Then I guess unless that Yankee skipper pulls a miracle of some sort out there, that we've got a major international incident on our hands."

"I knew we should have never abandoned our primary mission," said the Zampolit. "My career will be ruined, even though I wasn't to blame."

"To hell with your career!" shouted Alexander. "Here we've got an incident that could very well push the two superpowers into a nuclear confrontation, and all you worry about is yourself. Shame on you, Felix Bucharin! You disgust me, and are an insult to the great Party that gave you the honor of representing it."

"The submarine seems to be reacting to our attack, Captain," interrupted the sonar operator. "They're picking up speed and initiating evasive actions. The computer indicates that this is indeed an American vessel of the 688-class."

Seriously doubting that it would do the doomed Yanks much good, Grigori Milyutin instructed sonar to scan the waters where the vessel responsible for attacking the Norwegian warship had been situated. He obediently carried out this directive and was able to monitor the exact moment when the rocket-borne torpedo plunged back into the water and began the final phase of its attack with an angry, buzzing whine.

Chapter Sixteen

It proved to be a simple electrical short that prevented U-3313 from launching a second salvo and finishing off the crippled cutter. Otto Koch angrily paced the crowded control room, all the while cursing their misfortune. He had hoped to break the warship's back with the initial torpedo attack, and sink them quickly. But this was not to be, and now the Norwegians had plenty of time to inform command of their situation, and most likely help was already on the way. Such notoriety was not in the least bit desirable, and Koch knew that they had to get out into the open seas with all haste.

"Incoming torpedo round!" cried out the sonar operator. "Somehow it just came out of nowhere, in the waters right above us!"

Koch absorbed this shocking report and his first impression was that it had to be an anomaly of some sort. Surely the Norwegian cutter never had a chance to launch a weapon at them. Or did they? And it was then that he heard the distant buzzing whine that seemed to get increasingly louder and louder with each second's passing.

This dreaded noise was audible throughout the U-boat, and even the vessel's captain was temporarily stunned into inaction by it. With not even the time to order evasive action, Charles Kromer could think of only a single warning.

"Brace yourselves for an explosion!" he shouted, seconds before all hell broke out inside U-3313.

First there was an ear-shattering explosion, followed by a powerful, jarring concussion that sent all those crew members not restrained by safety harnesses tumbling to the rocking deck. This included Otto Koch, who ended up on his back beside the periscope well. The lights flickered off and then on again, while the frenzied voice of the quartermaster relayed the message that had just been passed on to him through the sound-powered telephone he was responsible for monitoring.

"After engine room is flooding!"

Even though he found himself sprawled on his side against the chart table, Captain Kromer reacted instinctively. "Blow the main ballast! Blow safety tanks! Blow bow buoyancy!"

No one stopped to question these orders. All were aware that the sea was pouring into U-3313's stern, and the only thing that mattered now was getting the boat safely to the surface.

Senior Lieutenant Kurtz had been harnessed to his chair at the diving console and he automatically pulled down the levers of the air manifold. This caused a burst of highly pressurized air to roar into the tanks, expelling the seawater ballast with a mad whirl.

"Hard rise on the diving planes!" ordered Kromer unnecessarily, for the men responsible for this task had already initiated it.

As Charles Kromer painfully got back to his feet, his eyes went to the depth gauge and the inclinometer. Oddly enough, the boat seemed to hang for a moment at even keel at a depth of eighty feet beneath the sea's surface. But it was pure instinct that told him that his command was waterlogged beyond her buoyancy.

Seconds later, U-3313 began to sink rapidly by the stern. This drop was so sharp that many of the men, who had just picked themselves off the deck, lost their footing again and went sprawling toward the aft bulkhead. Accompanying them were coffee cups, manuals, navigation instruments, and other loose gear.

With his palms biting into the steel edge of the chart table, Kromer could see that there was no chance of raising the boat now. Their only hope was if the U-boat could make it to the bottom in one piece. But any further pondering on his part was cut short by a new menace, as water began pouring in from the ventilation pipes leading from the aft bulkhead.

It showered down with an incredible force, knocking Kromer to his knees, and completely soaking him in bitterly cold salt water. This meant that the concussion had damaged the boat's air induction system, and the only way to stem this flow would be to get to the valves and seal off the ventilation flappers.

With a superhuman effort, Kromer dragged himself, hand over hand, up the slippery deck, whose angle was now as steep as forty degrees. His chilled skin was already numbing, but unless he got to those valves, they would be doomed.

A young seaman cried out in horror behind him. The lights were flickering once again, and the hull plates were beginning to creak in protest of the tremendous pressure that the depths were now applying. Doing his best to ignore all of these things, Kromer inched himself forward with only one goal in mind.

Having lost all the feeling in his hands by now, he desperately lunged for the valve cover, and by sheer tenacity alone he was able to hold on. With a pained grunt, he pulled up his soaked body. Not even taking the time to wipe the stinging salt out of his eyes, he went to work tightening the valves, and soon the onrushing roar of water faded to a trickle.

As Kromer caught his breath and turned around, he viewed yet another frightening scene develop at the aft hatchway. Two men were in the process of pulling themselves out of the knee deep water that filled the passageway leading to the engine room. The terrified seamen were scrambling for their very lives, for if they didn't get into the control room they would be trapped like their shipmates back in engineering. Any second now, the water would begin flooding over the stoop and the hatch would have to be sealed. With this realization the two sailors literally threw themselves forward into the control room. With great difficulty the hatch was then closed and its handles dogged tight.

Gradually, the U-boat's steep angle of descent lessened. Kromer was able to get to his feet, and as he scanned the compartment, he spotted Otto Koch seated in his red robe with his back up against the periscope well, with his soaked German shepherd faithfully at his side.

Kromer really wasn't certain when the actual grounding came. All that he was aware of was a slight bumping sensation, and the fact that the depth gauge was remaining constant now at 407 feet, just within their hull's crush limit. But before anyone could celebrate, the lights flickered and then went out for good, leaving them in total darkness.

Someone managed to get a hold of a flashlight, and began distributing the emergency supply of battery-powered torches that had been stored beneath the

355

weapons console. Kromer got hold of one of these torches and initiated a quick inspection of the compartment's valves. For the moment they were holding, and this allowed him to move across to the quartermaster.

"Any word from the men back aft?" inquired the captain anxiously.

The quartermaster somberly shook his head. "I'm afraid not, Sir."

Unable to accept the fact that over half of his fifty-man crew were dead, Kromer grabbed the quartermaster's telephone set. Hurriedly adjusting the headphones, he shouted into the transmitter. "Hello, engineering, do you hear me? Engineering, this is the captain. Do you hear me? Siggy!"

Kromer was cut short by a firm hand on his shoulder.

"Let it be, Charles," advised Otto Koch compassionately. "You must accept the fact that they most likely died instantly, and concentrate on more important things such as our own survival."

Knowing that the old man was right, Kromer turned his attention to the forward portions of the boat and found them almost completely undamaged. This included the torpedo room, where ten men waited for further orders, and the main storage compartment, where their foodstuffs were stored along with the gold, the heavy water, and their six prisoners. Also located in this compartment was the forward escape hatch, which right now looked to be the only way out of this fix.

"Good heavens, my dear Lottie!" exclaimed Otto Koch, who suddenly remembered that his servant had been in his stateroom when this tragedy befell them.

The Director's cabin was located in the forward portion of the U-boat, and Lottie was eventually found bruised and shaken, but otherwise in good health. With this concern out of his mind, Koch began the grim task of sizing up their situation.

For the moment, there was air to breath, and plenty of food and water available. The cold would be a factor though in the next few hours, especially in their soaked conditions. So one of the first priorities would be to dry themselves off as best they could and find as many blankets and spare clothing as possible. Then the long wait would begin for their rescue.

There was no doubt in Otto Koch's mind that this moment would come. For even though the Golden U-boat would no longer be of service to them, surely there were other vessels capable of fulfilling their mission. The mere fact that they were still alive filled him with a renewed sense of hope.

Yet another drama was unfolding on the opposite end of the Kongsfjord Strait, as the *USS Cheyenne* valiantly attempted to shake the pair of torpedoes that the Soviet vessel had fired at them. Orchestrating this effort, Steven Aldridge stood with his hands tightly gripping the edge of the chart table as the *Cheyenne* initiated a tight, high-speed turn.

"Both fish are still on our tail!" exclaimed the voice of Joe Carter, which was now being broadcast over the control room's P.A. system. "Bearing is zero-two-zero, relative rough range 3,700 yards and still closing."

"Is that MOSS decoy ready to fire yet, Lieutenant Hartman?" quizzed Aldridge.

The stocky, crew-cut weapons' officer answered from his console. "We'll have a green light any second now. Hold on, Captain. My boys won't let us down."

Designed to simulate the signature of the *Cheyenne* and lure an attacking torpedo away from the boat, the MOSS decoy was an invaluable asset that Aldridge was counting on. Yet if it wasn't ready to launch shortly, it would be useless.

In the meantime, Aldridge was trying his best to lose the torpedoes by leaving what was known as a knuckle in the water. This maneuver depended upon a series of tight, high-speed turns that would leave a hissing vortex of agitated sea water in their wake.

"We're at 380 feet, Captain," observed the diving officer coolly.

Because of the relatively shallow depths of this portion of the strait, Aldridge had little water beneath him to play with, making his already difficult job even harder.

"Range is down to three thousand yards," revealed the tense voice of Joe Carter.

The digital knot indicator that lay mounted on the forward bulkhead before the harness-restrained helmsmen registered twenty-eight knots. Yet the turbines were just getting warmed up, and if they hoped to outrun their attackers, they would have to increase this velocity dramatically.

"XO!" shouted Aldridge. "Get Lonnon to open up those throttles. We need more speed and we need it now!"

The captain turned to the helmsman. "Pull us up to 300 feet, Mr. Murphy. Make our new course two-eight-zero."

The boat canted hard on its right side as this turn was initiated, and it seemed to shudder as it also began to nose upward.

"We've got a green light on MOSS, Captain!" revealed the weapon's officer joyously.

358

"Then fire away, Lieutenant Hartman," returned Aldridge.

An exploding blast of compressed air indicated that the decoy had been launched, and the deck quivered as the now empty tube began filling with water to compensate for the great weight it had just lost.

"MOSS appears to be running true, Captain," observed the weapon's officer. "We've got her sprinting off on course one-four-zero."

Aldridge's eyes flashed to the knot counter. "Damn it, Bob! Where's that additional speed?"

The XO had the intercom handset cradled up against his ear, and could only hunch his shoulders as the digital indicator seemed to be locked on twenty-eight knots.

"Helmsman, swing us around to bearing two-two-zero, and make it crisp," ordered Aldridge.

As the *Cheyenne* turned hard on this new course, Joe Carter excitedly reported. "We've lost one, Captain! It looks like MOSS has a taker."

Aldridge accepted a brief thumbs-up from his weapons' officer, but was quickly brought back to earth as Carter added.

"Range of the remaining torpedo is twenty four hundred yards and still closing. Bearing zero two zero."

Having utilized their one and only decoy, Aldridge now had to come up with yet another way to lose the persistent fish that remained on their tail. Briefly glancing down at the bathymetric chart of the strait they were in, he could see that it wouldn't be possible to outdive the torpedo. There was, at the very most, another two hundred feet of water beneath their keel before they would strike bottom. But could they use this unique bathymetric feature to their advantage in

359

this instance? Aldridge certainly didn't think that there would be any harm in trying, and he shared this novel maneuver with the planesman.

"Mr. Murphy, take her up to ninety feet, on bearing two-six-five. Then take us down hard to 460 before bringing us back up to ninety feet again."

"Prepare yourselves for a little roller coaster ride, gentlemen," added the captain, who noted with satisfaction that the speed indicator rose one, two, and then three complete digits before halting at thirty-one knots.

The sail-mounted planes bit into the surrounding sea water and the *Cheyenne* angled up sharply toward the surface. Steven Aldridge could feel the resulting g-forces pull his body backward, and he had to tightly regrip the chart table to keep from being flung back to the aft bulkhead. Several coffee mugs and other loose equipment had already clattered to this portion of the deck, and the captain bided his time by keeping his stare locked on the depth gauge.

At 180 feet, Joe Carter broadcast another update. "The torpedo's is coming on up with us, at a range of eighteen hundred yards."

This would be one instance when Aldridge wanted this fish to get as close as possible to them, for this would give his daring tactic a better chance to succeed.

The *Cheyenne* gained another knot of forward speed and was soaring upward like a sleek jet fighter of the sea. As they broke the 125 foot barrier, the helmsman readied himself for action. As it turned out, his timing was superb, and he was able to pull the *Cheyenne* out of her sharp climb only a few feet short of his goal of ninety feet. Remaining at this depth for brief seconds, he pushed down on his steering yoke, reversing the direction of the planes and sending the sub spiralling down into the black, frigid depths.

Now Aldridge and the rest of the crew found themselves being pulled forward, along with the assortment of loose gear that had already clattered onto the deck and now smashed into the forward bulkhead. Once again, he tightly re-gripped the edge of the chart table, and anxiously listened as Joe Carter's voice boomed out loud and clear.

"Torpedo has just broken the thousand yard threshold, and it's continuing to come down on our tail."

Separated now by the equivalent of ten football fields, the torpedo was rapidly closing in on them, and Aldridge found his pulse quickening in anticipation. At a depth of three hundred and fifty feet this distance was almost halved, and sweat started to mat the captain's forehead and palms. They were hurtling downward now at a speed of thirty-three knots, and as the floor of the fjord rapidly approached, Aldridge momentarily found himself thinking about his family. Yet he forcefully pushed the images of Susan and Sarah out of his mind, concentrating instead on the rapidly falling depth gauge that had just passed 430 feet.

"Mr. Murphy, pull us up, now!" ordered the captain, who could visualize the hard rocky floor of the fjord waiting to greet them in an embrace of instant death.

The helmsman yanked back hard on his steering yoke, and the *Cheyenne* slid to a depth of 457 feet before the dive was reversed. Upward they climbed now, and Aldridge knew that this was the moment of truth, for he was gambling that the torpedo wouldn't be able to pull out of its dive as quickly as the *Cheyenne* had managed, and that he hadn't underestimated the depth of the fjord in this portion of the strait.

361

This time, as they shot to the surface, he allowed his thoughts to return to his family. His fate and that of his crew were in Another's hands now, and if this was to be the moment when he would be sent to meet his Maker, he wanted to go with the vision of the two people he loved most on this earth firmly implanted in his mind.

He could picture Sarah playing on the heather-filled hills of Mull, with hundreds of sheep milling around her, while his lovely Susan waited for her on the sun-drenched hilltop, with a picnic lunch spread out on a large checkered quilt. This was his vision of paradise, and he knew that he had been very fortunate to have experienced it, even if for but a few fleeting hours.

Aldridge was snapped from his brief reverie by a deep, thundering explosion. The deck beneath him madly shook and trembled, and for a second he thought the worse, that the torpedo had struck them. Expecting next to hear the loud whine of the collision alarm, he looked to the helm and noted that the turbines were still managing to grind out a steady thirty-two knots, while the depth gauge was smoothly displaying their continued ascent. Yet it was only when Joe Carter's joyful voice broke from the P.A. speakers that Aldridge realized that his gamble had paid off, with the most valuable jackpot of all—their lives.

"Scratch one more Red fish," observed the ecstatic senior sonar operator. "From that concussion, you can rest assured that this portion of the fjord is now a couple of feet deeper."

"I'll note that on my bathymetric chart," replied Aldridge, who caught his XO's relieved glance and added, "Bob, I think it's time to give Ivan a little dose of his own medicine. I'm not too sure what the hell is

362

going on around here, but the *Cheyenne* has more than paid her dues, and now's the time to even the score.

"Lieutenant Hartman, load up four wire-guided Mk48's. And keep a couple of SUBROC's closeby for good measure. It's time to reverse roles, with the hunted becoming the hunter!"

Chapter Seventeen

In his long naval career, never before had Alexander Kuznetsov witnessed such superb seamanship. In a matter of minutes, the American 688-class vessel went from loiter speed to almost thirty knots, as their desperate dash to escape the *Lena*'s mistakenly fired torpedoes was initiated. One of these torpedoes was drawn off by a decoy, while the other continued its relentless pursuit. That's when the American vessel really started to put on a show. They inaugurated a series of intricate highspeed turns in an effort to free themselves. When this didn't succeed, the 688 began an amazing maneuver that took it shooting upward, practically to the surface, then crashing back down into the depths. The *Lena*'s torpedo had just surged forward in a final burst of attack speed, when the 688 abruptly pulled up, only a few scant meters from the bottom of the fjord. Unable to change its course as quickly as the submarine, the torpedo proceeded to shoot downward until it smacked into the sea floor with a resonating explosion.

As Alexander stood in the hushed attack center, beside the *Lena*'s captain and Zampolit, he listened as their sonar technician monitored the 688's new course, that was bringing them right back to the center of the strait. It didn't take much imagination to figure out what the American sub was planning to do, and Alexander knew the time for the *Lena* to act was now.

"Captain Milyutin, I feel that it's imperative that we amend this situation at once," said Alexander. "We must make contact with the 688 and explain that our attack was a mistake, and implore them to keep from answering our blunder with a salvo of their own."

"Do you really think that the Yankees would be receptive to such a plea at the moment?" countered the Captain. "Revenge will be in their hearts, and our only hope is to launch another attack now, before they beat us to it."

The Zampolit vainly tried to halt the flow of sweat dripping off his brow with a soaked handkerchief as he expressed himself. "I think that all of this talk about attack and counterattack will only get us an early grave. We must flee from this cursed strait while we still have the chance, and rely on the *Lena*'s superior speed to see us out of this mess."

Alexander absorbed these opinions and thoughtfully shook his head. "No, Comrades, I still feel that by launching another salvo ourselves we'll only be needlessly risking the *Lena*. And running away will accomplish us absolutely nothing. In this instance, honesty is the best policy, and if we direct our appeal properly, the Americans will understand and call off their attack."

"The 688 is continuing its rapid approach, Captain," interrupted the concerned sonar technician. "They are just about to break our defense perimeter."

Grigori Milyutin still appeared to be deliberating his alternatives, and Alexander spoke out forcefully. "You've already seen how that 688 negated our first attack, Captain. Do you seriously think that a second salvo on our part will be any different? Come to your senses, Comrade, and show me how to operate our underwater paging system this instant!"

"Do it, Captain!" urged the panicky political officer. "Since we have no time left to flee, this is our only chance."

Grigori Milyutin looked Alexander directly in the eye and firmly offered. "I'll agree to your request only if you'll explain to me the exact reason you've diverted us to these waters."

"You've got it, Captain," returned Alexander. "As soon as I've contacted the Americans, I'll give you a full briefing."

A look of relief painted the Zampolit's chubby face as he watched the two senior officers cross over to the communications console. Quick to join them himself, Felix Bucharin listened as the white-haired veteran lifted up the red telephone handset that was handed to him, and spoke out loudly in excellent English into its transmitter.

"American 688 class submarine, this is Admiral Alexander Kuznetsov of the People's Navy of the Soviet Union. I am currently aboard the Alfa class attack sub *Lena*, in the waters directly in front of you, and I'm calling to negotiate a truce . . ."

Steven Aldridge, along with the other members of the *Cheyenne*'s control room crew, listened to the Soviet Admiral's emotional plea as it was conveyed to them over the compartment's elevated P.A. speakers. This was an unprecedented moment, and came just as the *Cheyenne* was preparing to launch a trio of Mk48 torpedoes at this same Alfa class submarine.

Clearly affected by the Russian's words, Aldridge allowed Admiral Alexander Kuznetsov to finish his statement before seeking the opinion of his second in command. "Well, what do you think, Bob? Is Ivan

366

trying to pull a fast one on us? Or is the Admiral talking turkey?"

The XO pulled his pipe from his mouth and answered. "I think he's telling the truth, Skipper. And if you look at it from their perspective, it makes sense. After all, how would we react if we monitored a SUBROC launch in our baffles from a contact we didn't even know previously existed?"

"I imagine we'd shoot first and ask questions later," replied Aldridge. "And that's precisely why I'm willing to give Ivan the benefit of the doubt on this one. But I want to keep those Mk48's on-line just in case. My gut tells me that something's still not right out there, and it would be foolish to let our defenses down prematurely."

"Then we'll be surfacing and proceeding to check out that damaged Norwegian cutter, and what's left of that mystery sub that our SUBROC k.o.'d?" asked the XO.

"You've got it," returned Steven Aldridge, who was already anticipating his first close up view of one of the long-fabled Alfa class attack submarines.

Inside U-3313's forward storage compartment, the penetrating chill was even more noticeable because of the constant blackness that prevailed here. Without even a single torch to provide them light, the six prisoners huddled closely together in their makeshift cell, with their blankets wrapped tightly around them.

Ever since the U-boat had presumably been hit by a torpedo and sunk to the bottom, they had had a minimum amount of contact with the crew. From what they gathered, over half of them had perished when the aft compartments flooded. The surviving members were gathered in the control room, and visited the storage compartment only to pick up the food that was kept here.

The members of NUEX had held up pretty well during this confinement. As divers, they were used to extended stays in cold, wet environments. Kari Skollevoll had trouble adjusting to the numbing chill at first, and her companions did their best to warm her up by sharing their spare clothing and body heat.

All through their ordeal, the old Russian sat in the corner continuing-to blame himself for their misfortune. Often they could hear his teeth chattering. And when the old man did manage to sleep, he did so restlessly.

Cold beans were still the extent of their meals. They dared not complain, or even this pittance might be taken away from them.

To pass the time in the perpetual darkness, they took turns telling stories. Whenever their spirits sunk particularly low, Jon Huslid would remind them of the time he accompanied a Norwegian Navy surface flotilla while it was participating in a NATO submarine rescue exercise. As long as the hull remained dry and the air breathable, they still had a chance, emphasized the photographer, while it was Knut who reminded them that one of the best features of the compartment in which they were held was that it contained the very hatch through which such a rescue would be carried out.

The dim Arctic dawn provided just enough illumination for Magne Rystaad and David Lawton to view an incredible scene unfold up ahead on the waters of Kongsfjord Strait. From the ultra-modern confines of the *Falcon*'s bridge, they gazed out at the three incongruous warships at anchor there. All of these vessels

368

were approximately the same size, though the two submarines seemed to be dwarfed by the *Nordkapp* class cutter that they were floating beside.

"Considering that hit the cutter took, she doesn't look too bad," observed the Texan.

"The *Nordkapp* is very fortunate," replied Magne. "They were able to shore up the hole in their hull before their watertight integrity was seriously threatened, and from the report that commander Nilsen shared with me, his fire-control teams extinguished the fires just as the flames were lapping at the ship's fuel tanks. If they had gone up, the only view we'd be seeing of the *Nordkapp* would be from our bottom scanning sonar unit."

As the *Falcon* continued to close in on the center of the strait, the damages to the cutter were more obvious. Its gray hull was stained with black scorch marks, especially amidships on the port side. The ship's Lynx helicopter could be seen on the helipad, apparently unaffected by the flames.

"Thanks to that chopper, all of the *Nordkapp*'s seriously wounded have been transferred to the hospital at Longyearben already," remarked Magne. "And it's a good thing that they weren't relying on us to provide the transport, because Noroil One is still AWOL."

Lawton knew that Magne was referring to the *Falcon*'s own helicopter. "Kari Skollevoll sure didn't seem like the irresponsible type."

"She's not, and that's what scares me," said Magne. "The last report she filed at the Tromso airport showed her returning to base, and since then, no one's heard a thing from her."

"Maybe she's just shacking up with a beau," offered Lawton.

"I hope that's the case, David. Because otherwise, it doesn't appear too promising."

A strained silence followed as the *Falcon* completed its approach to the wounded cutter. As the diving support ship dropped anchor, David Lawton got his first good view of the two submarines sharing the waters with them. The largest of these submersibles had the Stars and Stripes billowing from its sail. Three sailors were visible on this structure's exposed bridge, in the process of scanning the *Falcon* with their binoculars. Less than one-hundred yards away, the other submarine displayed the crimson red hammer and sickle banner of the Soviet Union from its streamlined sail. This vessel was smaller than the American sub, and also had three sailors perched on the conning tower, looking over the *Falcon*.

David Lawton found himself wishing that he had brought his camera along with him so that he could document this amazing sight. Surely such a photo would make front page newspaper copy worldwide.

It had been previously agreed over the radio-telephone that the command staffs of all four vessels would initially meet in the *Falcon*'s galley. The Texan was quite pleased when Magne invited him to join this meeting as his guest.

An hour after the *Falcon* dropped anchor, this conference was called to order. Lawton was genuinely moved as Commander Gunnar Nilsen provided a blow by blow description of events aboard the *Nordkapp* immediately before, during, and after the torpedo strike. Captain Steven Aldridge, C.O. of the *USS Cheyenne*, then introduced himself. He explained how his vessel sank the mystery sub responsible for this unwarranted attack with an amazing weapon by the name of SUBROC.

At this point Magne asked if the wreckage of this still unidentified craft had been found as yet. Standing up to answer him was a white-haired old man in a well-tailored blue uniform. Lawton was surprised to hear that this individual was an Admiral in the Soviet Navy. As senior officer aboard the Alfa class attack submarine *Lena*, he had ordered a sonar scan of the waters in which the mystery vessel had presumably gone down. In this manner, the vessel was located on the bottom of the strait, 407 feet beneath the surface. This site was only two and a half kilometers due north of the *Falcon*'s current position. When Admiral Alexander Kuznetsov mentioned that the wreck's hull still appeared to be intact, Magne immediately offered the services of the *Falcon*'s two diving bells to check for any survivors.

The white-haired Russian seemed genuinely thrilled by this offer. Quickly he asked the others present if they could initiate this rescue effort at once. There were no objections, and while the submariners returned to their vessels to monitor the proceedings, the *Falcon* moved into position.

Solo, the diving support ship's ROV, was launched. Through the magic of fiber-optics it was soon relaying back to them the first video pictures of the vessel that had attacked the *Nordkapp*. Both Magne and Lawton were staggered to learn that this submarine was a German Type XXI model. Even more shocking was the fact that it carried the markings U-3313 on its gilded sail, making it the sister ship of the U-boat that they had previously explored off the coast of Utsira!

That such a vessel could still be in working order was simply unbelievable. The only damage to the U-boat seemed to be confined to its aft portions, and when a standard-sized rescue hatch was found intact on the boat's forward section, both agreed that it appeared to be readily accessible from one of the *Falcon*'s diving bells.

There was no question in their minds about who

371

would man this bell. While the crew readied it for action, both veteran divers went off to don their heavy neoprene wet suits.

The descent to 407 feet went off without a hitch. With *Solo*'s continued assistance, a guide-wire led them straight down to the U-boat's forward escape hatch.

"We're going to have to see about putting you on the company payroll," joked Magne as the bell attached itself onto the hatch and began to pressurize. "You're starting to become a regular around here with Noroil."

Lawton grinned and picked up a wrench. "Nothing against Norway, partner, but I'm starting to get a little homesick for Texas already."

As the pressure in the bell equalized to that of the U-boat's escape hatch, Magne reached down and pulled up the bell's bottom hatch. A slight fluttering sensation in the ears accompanied this process. Facing them now was a circular, heavy iron wheel.

"Here goes nothing," said Magne as he bent over and gripped the wheel.

It wouldn't budge, and as Magne backed out of the way, Lawton violently rapped on it with the side of the wrench. This time both of them gripped the wheel.

"Okay, we'll give it all we've got on the count of three," instructed the Texan. "One . . . Two . . . Three!"

Both of the brawny divers strained with all of their combined might, and the wheel gave with a loud, grating squeal. Yet before opening it all the way, Magne reached for their masks.

"We'd better keep these on, David. If salt water mixed in with the boat's battery acid, that hull will be filled with lethal chlorine gas."

Lawton slipped on the mask that covered his entire

372

face and fed him a constant stream of pure air through an umbilical. He flashed Magne a thumbs-up, and reached down to finish opening the wheel.

It took both of them to break the seal. They yanked the hatch backward, and were met by a dark stairwell leading down into the sub itself. It was completely dry inside. Before either one of them could reach the battery powered torch that they carried along with them, the beam of a flashlight cut through the blackness. This was all Lawton needed to see to rip off his mask.

"Hello, down there," he called out excitedly.

Strangely enough, this greeting was answered by the angry barking of a dog.

The Texan bent down to have a closer look inside and was met unceremoniously by the long barrel of a pistol. As he cautiously backed away from the stairwell, the individual who carried this weapon climbed up into the bell to join them. This no-nonsense, middle-aged figure sported a graying crew cut, pale blue eyes, and a square jaw. When he addressed them, his English was heavily flavored with a German accent.

"If you'll just proceed down into the interior of the submarine, my superior officer would like to have a word with you."

David Lawton could tell from the way that he held the Luger that he was trained in the handling of firearms, and the ex-SEAL decided that now was not the time to test his reactions.

"That's a hell of a way to greet the people who just saved your lives," managed the Texan as he reluctantly began his way down the tubular steel ladder.

The darkness quickly enveloped him. Yet as Magne joined him on the deck below, Lawton's eyes gradually began to adjust to the poor lighting. He could barely make out the dimensions of the large compartment where they found themselves when the blindingly bright shaft of a flashlight hit him full in the face. A dog could be heard growling closeby, only to be over-ridden by the cold, deep voice of a man.

"Welcome aboard U-3313, gentlemen. Whom do I have the honor of addressing?"

Still shielding his eyes with his forearm, Lawton exploded in rage. "Listen, buster. You certainly have a lot of balls. Here we go risking our necks to save your lives, and you greet us with a Luger and twenty questions."

"My, aren't you the angry American," observed the stranger calmly. "Perhaps your associate will be a bit more cooperative, and I won't have to order Captain Kromer to show you what an excellent shot he is."

Magne sensed that this character wouldn't hesitate to give such an order, and he responded with no show of emotion. "My name is Magne Rystaad, and I'm diving supervisor of the Noroil support vessel *Falcon*."

"Magne!" cried an assortment of voices from the blackness.

The confused Norwegian looked into the black void, desperately trying to see where these familiar voices were emanating from.

"It's Jon Huslid, Chief!"

"Shut him up!" ordered the stranger.

The dog began barking once again, and the sound of muffled footsteps could be heard in the background. This didn't deter Magne Rystaad from replying.

"Jon, I don't know what the hell you're doing down here, but hang on, my friend!"

At this point the blinding beam of light was redirected, and both Magne and Lawton looked on as the face of the stranger who had been talking to them materialized out of the void. It proved to be a face that neither one of them would soon forget—wrinkled skin,

374

cruel gray eyes, bald head.

"So, it seems that you know my guests," reflected Otto Koch with a sardonic grin. "It's a small world all right, one that seems to be getting smaller everyday. But it's such coincidences that makes life interesting, and I shall look forward to hearing all about your relationship together at a later time. But right now, we must organize our priorities, the first being to get all of us safely to the surface."

Anxious to get out of this cold, damp environment himself, Lawton turned to address his host. "It doesn't sound like we have much of a choice, do we, partner?"

Magne grunted. "No, David, I'm afraid we don't."

"Then shall we proceed," prompted the forceful voice of Otto Koch.

There were twenty-seven individuals and a German shepherd to convey topside. This included the members of NUEX, Kari Skollevoll, and Mikhail Kuznetsov. Magne was truly shocked to find five of his employees among the crew, yet had to wait to get a report on how they managed to end up here, as his services were needed in the bell.

The first trip was accomplished with just Magne and seven heavily armed seamen, including the U-boat's captain and senior lieutenant. Magne was warned not to inform the *Falcon* that anything out of the ordinary was taking place, or Kari Skollevoll would be the first hostage to die.

After reluctantly dropping the submariners off in the *Falcon*'s moonpool, he turned the bell back to the U-3313. During this descent he shuddered to think what was taking place on the *Falcon* as these desperate, armed men spread through the ship to wrest control of it.

It took four more trips to get everyone evacuated, and when Magne eventually returned to the *Falcon* for

375

the final time, his worst fears were realized. He found himself escorted into the galley where the rest of the ship's complement was seated on the floor. Three of the Germans watched over the crew, with Uzi submachine guns held threateningly in front of them.

Magne was led into the adjoining wardroom, and it was here Otto Koch issued his demands. In exchange for the safe release of all the hostages, Magne was to return to the sunken U-boat and retrieve two portions of the vessel's cargo. Once this material had been brought topside, all personnel not vital to the actual running of the ship were to be released on life boats. Then the skeleton crew, together with the German submariners and their cargo, would initiate a voyage to South America's Rio de la Plata. At the conclusion of this trip, the *Falcon* and its remaining crew would be free to go where they pleased.

If Magne refused to meet all of these conditions, the penalty was to be deadly simple. Every five minutes until he changed his mind, a member of the *Falcon*'s crew was to be executed, beginning with Kari Skollevoll. To show that he meant business, Otto Koch pulled out his pocket watch, and informed Magne that he had four minutes and fifty-nine seconds before Kari would be shot. A bare thirty seconds later, Magne gave in, and agreed to immediately return to the moonpool to initiate the remaining salvage effort.

This operation proved to be an enormous one. Even with the use of two bells, the transfer of the 499 gold bricks took most of the day. This left seventy-two carboys of heavy water, each holding twenty-five gallons to convey topside.

It was while this task was being carried out that the commander of the *Nordkapp* contacted the *Falcon* to get the results of their initial investigation into the condition and identity of the sunken submarine. The captains of the American and Soviet warships that were anchored nearby also desired this information, and Otto Koch made the difficult decision to inform them that the *Falcon* and its crew were now under his control. Koch left the Norwegian commander with a stern warning that if any attempt was made to interfere, he would not hesitate to begin carrying out the executions of his hostages.

The final carboy of heavy water reached the deck of the *Falcon* at 4:30 a.m. Fifteen minutes later, the diving support ship weighed anchor and began transitting the waters of the Kongsfjord Strait, headed south for the open sea beyond.

The departure of the diving support ship did not go unnoticed. Neither did the two hyperbaric lifeboats that the *Falcon* left behind in its wake. Inside these small all-weather craft were the thirty-two non-essential hostages that Otto Koch had promised to release. These fortunate individuals were subsequently debriefed aboard the *Nordkapp*.

At 5:45 a.m., a strategy session was called to order in the cutter's wardroom. In attendance were Commander Gunnar Nilsen, Captains Steven Aldridge and Grigori Milyutin, and Admiral Alexander Kuznetsov. It was during this session that Gunnar Nilsen revealed a portion of what he had learned as a result of interviewing the freed hostages. Alexander Kuznetsov was particularly interested in the cargo that the Germans ordered brought up from below. This supposedly included a large stash of gold bullion and several dozen, plastic containers of a substance known only as heavy water. Yet it was as the Norwegian mentioned the prisoners that had also been brought up from the U-boat's hold that Alexander's eyes opened

377

wide and his pulse quickened. For one of these individuals was described as an old, white-haired Russian, with a scar lining the side of his face. Alexander knew in that instant that he had found his brother Mikhail!

Knowing full well that his twin would never survive the sea journey if Otto Koch escaped, Alexander decided that the only way to stop the *Falcon* was by a united effort. Since even Grigori Milyutin still didn't understand the full scope of this incident, Alexander stood and told everything he knew about Werewolf, the gold, and his brother's involvement in these matters.

By the time he completed this impassioned discourse, his rapt audience was ready to act.

"But how can we stop the *Falcon* without bringing harm to the hostages?" asked Gunnar Nilsen, whose good friend Magne Rystaad was among those still on board.

"I believe that my ship could stop them," offered Steven Aldridge. "All the *Cheyenne* would have to do is hit the *Falcon*'s stern with a non-detonating, wake-homing torpedo. That will put them dead in the water soon enough. But that still leaves us with having to get a rescue team on there."

"You could use the *Nordkapp*'s helicopter," offered Gunnar Nilsen.

"I'm afraid such a delivery system is too dangerous, Commander," returned Aldridge. "The kidnappers would know that a chopper was coming long before it got there, and would be ready for it the moment it landed. We need something more clandestine. We need a group of professionals trained for just such a risky mission."

"I happen to have both of those things, Captain!" revealed Alexander Kuznetsov. "Currently deployed aboard the *Lena* is a three man Spetsnaz unit. These naval commandoes have been specially trained in all facets of counter-terrorist operations, including the rescue of hostages. As the fates so have it, they are also fully equipped with weapons and other necessary gear."

"But how will they get onto the *Falcon*?" quizzed the Norwegian Coast Guard officer.

Alexander's eyes gleamed as the vision came to him. "I'll tell you how, Commander Nilsen. The moment the *Falcon* goes dead in the water as a result of the American torpedo, the *Lena* will surface beside the diving support ship and our commandoes will board her. This transfer can be accomplished in a matter of seconds, with the *Lena* diving back into the depths long before Koch and his gang of Nazi pirates have a chance to spot our vessel."

"If these commandoes of yours can handle it, I believe such an operation might work," observed Aldridge.

Alexander smiled. "Don't worry about the Spetsnaz not being able to handle this job, Captain. There's no better trained group of warriors on this planet, except perhaps for your SEAL's."

Steven Aldridge nodded in reference to the U.S. Navy's special warfare unit, and listened as the Soviet admiral emotionally continued.

"So it seems that we've gone from adversaries to allies overnight, Captain Aldridge. I thank the fates that you had the wisdom to listen to my humble plea earlier, and now we go out to attack a common enemy as a team. Isn't it ironic that our foe in this instance is once more the nazi beast?"

"It's just too bad that it always seems to have to be some kind of threat that brings our two nations together," said Steven Aldridge, who picked up a legal pad and began sketching out a preliminary attack plan, with the able assistance of his contemporary in the Soviet Navy.

It took almost the entire morning for the members of NUEX to explain to Magne and his American friend the sequence of events that led to their eventual imprisonment aboard U-3313. Of course, David Lawton was particularly interested in the fortune in gold bricks that was presently locked away in the *Falcon*'s hold, for he had participated in the exploration of the U-boat's sister ship, and had been there when Jakob chanced upon a brick from this very same shipment.

Kari Skollevoll was somewhat embarrassed as she explained how she came to be involved in this whole mess. Her boss, though, was very understanding, and Magne revealed that he would have probably done much the same thing if he had been in her position. This made Kari feel better, and she tried hard to get the old Russian general to brief Magne on all he knew about their kidnappers.

Unfortunately, Mikhail Kuznetsov was in no condition for talking. His encounter with Otto Koch and his subsequent imprisonment had injured his psyche. In a way, he felt like he did on that day when he was at long last released from the death camp—empty, with no goal, and psychologically raped.

All that Mikhail could see before his mind's eye was the gloating image of his arch-nemesis the moment Koch discovered him in the U-boat's radio room. Was he condemned to go to his grave with this sickening picture engraved on his soul, to haunt him for all eternity? Was evil destined to ultimately win out over good, as it had done in this instance, and so many times before throughout human history? These were the questions that raced through the veteran's mind as he sat there in the corner of the *Falcon*'s galley, waiting for Otto Koch to come and end his misery with a bullet into the back of his skull.

Knut Haugen had yet to give up hope and he found an unlikely co-conspirator in David Lawton. The Texan seemed to be a man of action like himself, and Knut sensed that this rugged fellow diver had seen his share of bloodshed in his day. Both of them seriously doubted that their captors would keep their bargain in the end, and with this in mind, they began plotting to overpower the three armed men who presently stood at the head of the galley with Uzis in their hands. They had just come up with a plausible plan, when the doors to the galley swung open, and in walked the man known as the Director.

Otto Koch was dressed in a black velvet smoking jacket and gray slacks. He looked a bit like a character from an old-fashioned movie with his bald shining scalp, monocle, and carved walking stick that he carried at his side. Arriving along with this imposing personage was a large, black German shepherd, and two tall blond men carrying combat shotguns.

"Excuse me, ladies and gentlemen," greeted Koch, after he loudly cleared his throat to draw everyone's attention. "But it has come to my attention that there are several among you that are plotting to disrupt this voyage. Such insubordination will not be tolerated! To stem it right now, I've decided to pull from your ranks a select few who will be placed in isolation. If any subterfuge is subsequently attempted, these individuals will be shot immediately. Will the following please stand and come with me. Kari Skollevoll . . ."

No sooner was the helicopter pilot's name out of Koch's mouth when the deck beneath them briefly shuddered. This unusual vibration was enough to divert Koch's attention, and cause his dog to suddenly start barking.

"Beowulf, behave yourself!" ordered Koch forcefully. The dog continued his mad yelping despite this command, and did so even when his master raised his stick overhead and prepared to strike the German shepherd. Yet once again Koch found his attention drawn away, this time by the urgent buzzing of the bulkhead-mounted intercom.

"One of you morons get that telephone!" demanded Koch to his sentries. A young seaman moved to the bulkhead and lifted the receiver.

"It's Captain Kromer, Herr Director. He's calling from the engine room. It seems that we've hit something that's damaged the ship's prop. At the moment, the vessel is incapable of any forward velocity."

"What?" cried Otto Koch in utter disbelief. "What nonsense is this? " he spat out as he hurried over to have a word with the captain himself.

Just as Koch put the receiver to his ear, the door to the galley burst open and in strode a single figure, dressed in black fatigues. With his right hand, Lieutenant Vasili Kalinin raised his Kalashnikov assault rifle and cooly put a bullet into the foreheads of the two sentries standing nearest him. Before the others could react, he tossed a stun grenade into the startled bunch of remaining guards. This device detonated with an ear-shattering blast that sent up a wall of thick white smoke. Veiled in this choking mist, a dog could be heard barking, along with the deafening crack of a pistol firing.

All the while, watching this drama unfold from the back corner of the galley, were the equally startled hostages. David Lawton alertly ordered his fellow prisoners to hit the deck. They did so at once, and were soon enveloped in the roiling white smoke that filled the entire room in a thick shroud.

The sound of exploding gunfire was everywhere as Alexander climbed onto the diving support ship's deck from the sail of the *Lena*. He was determined to be instrumental in bringing his brother's tormentor to justice, and he ordered Captain Milyutin to supply two armed men to accompany him onto the *Falcon*. With their help he made it onto the vessel just as the Spetsnaz team began its well-coordinated attack.

While one of the commandos secured the bridge, the other took care of the engine room and the adjoining compartments. This left the squad's leader free to penetrate the galley, where the hostages were last reported to be held. It was to this section of the *Falcon* that Alexander hurried.

As he frantically rushed down the passageway that led him further into the ship's interior, the crack of exchanged gunfire triggered memories long since forgotten.

Had it really been fifty years since that fated train ride so changed the lives of him and his twin brother? Excited to be this close to the monster who took Mikhail from him and scarred his very soul, Alexander took a deep breath and readied himself for the inevitable confrontation.

He located the galley and saw the smoke that was pouring from its open doors. With no thought for his own safety, Alexander entered the compartment and found himself engulfed in a blinding veil of white mist. His stinging eyes were all but useless, and like a blind man he extended his arms outward and groped into the roiling haze. Suddenly he flashed back to the nightmare that he had experienced several days ago back on the *Lena*, and just like in that terrifying vision, his hand made contact. New hope filled his spirits as he grasped the hand that he had just discovered in the blinding haze and slowly pulled it forward. And out of the smoke, like a ghostly apparition, emerged his twin brother.

"He's dead!" cried Mikhail joyfully. "The bastard is finally dead!"

2/95

Dear Doug,

This is written by a woman - but maybe you'll find something here to help you with your journey & growth. As you read this, keep in mind what I said about "husbands" needing a guide for living with an alcoholic wife.

Take what you need & leave the rest.

Love Always
Kay

When Someone You Love Drinks Too Much

When Someone You Love Drinks Too Much

A Christian Guide to Addiction, Codependence, & Recovery

Christina B. Parker

1817

A Ruth Graham Dienert Book

HARPER & ROW, PUBLISHERS, San Francisco

New York, Grand Rapids, Philadelphia, St. Louis
London, Singapore, Sydney, Tokyo, Toronto

FIRST EDITION

Library of Congress Cataloging-in-Publication Data
Parker, Christina B.
    When someone you love drinks too much: a Christian guide to addiction, codependence, and recovery/
Christina B. Parker.—1st ed.
        p.   cm.
    "A Ruth Graham Dienert book."
    ISBN 0-06-252019-9
    1. Codependence—Religious life. 2. Alcoholics—Religious life. 3. Alcoholism—Religious aspects—Christianity. 4. Codependence (Psychology)—Religious aspects—Christianity. I. Title.
BV4596.C57P37   1990
261.8′32292—dc20   89-45892
                                                                          CIP

90 91 92 93 94 RRD(H) 10 9 8 7 6 5 4 3 2 1

*Lovingly dedicated
to Corinna and Nora,
the jewels of my life,
and to John,
who made them
(and this book)
possible*

Contents

Acknowledgments

I owe a great debt of gratitude to many. I hesitate even to mention gratitude to God in this context, for fear of trivializing a relationship so sacred I don't fully comprehend it. Yet I find He must come first on this list.

Many friends have helped and encouraged me both as a writer and in my personal growth. Although this is not a complete list, the ones that come to mind are Terry Bennett, the Caravan family—especially Ronald Caravan—Mary Dixon, Nellie Eggleton, Jeri Foster Cole, Linda Finck, Carolyn Hendrickson, Eileen Silva Kindig, Carleen Lovelcss, Elaine Miller, Katherine Rose, Judith Scrudato, Helen Thompson, and Janet Snow.

For giving me a good grounding in God's Word, I am deeply thankful to pastors John W. Fogal, S. Glenn Thomas, and Dennis McKenna; and also to my favorite radio teachers, Drs. Charles Swindoll and James Dobson.

Some of the first and best friends to believe in my potential were my parents, Dorothy C. and the late Robert O. Brown. They also gave me two excellent friends: my sisters Judith Brown and Janis Avery, who have been wonderfully supportive through everything.

Ray, Ann, Bill, and Ann Parker, along with Deborah and Al Carpenter, also deserve thanks for their love, kindness, and understanding.

Special thanks go to the members of my local Al-Anon and Families Victorious groups for helping to keep me honest and pointed in a constructive direction.

I am very thankful to Ruth Graham Dienert, the first editor to believe in the possibilities of this book, and to Noreen Norton and Lonnie Hull for polishing it and helping me through the publishing process with a minimum of anxiety.

Finally, I'd like to thank Harry Lorence, author of *Hay, How's Your Lawn?* Having a cousin write a book when I was young helped me to place authorship within the realm of possibility.

Introduction

Does your life revolve around a loved one who drinks too much or abuses other drugs? Mine did for many years.

In fact, my life is still deeply affected by someone else's alcoholism and probably always will be. In spite of that, God has given me more serenity and peace within myself than I ever again expected to have.

Are you suffering through sleepless nights—worrying when your loved one isn't there or enduring pointless arguments and terrible domestic disruptions when he or she is around? I've had many nights like that. If you have too, then this book is for you.

Do you feel that your life isn't your own—that you're always dancing to someone else's tune, reacting to one crisis after another rather than acting on your own goals and ideas? Do you feel trapped in a bad situation over which you have no control? So did I, but I want you to know you have more power in your situation than you think.

Do you take over responsibilities that shouldn't be yours in order to fill gaps created by your loved one's drinking or drug abuse? Have you put your own life and goals "on hold" until you can get this person straightened out? I did that too, but I found out that I had other choices.

At first, I didn't realize that alcohol was a big factor in the problems my young family was experiencing. Part of that was denial, but some part of it was also naiveté. Unlike many spouses of alcoholics, I hadn't grown up with the disease. My parents were regular, moderate social drinkers, so to me drinking was normal for adults. I hadn't much taste for it myself, but I had no idea how to recognize the destructive effects of excessive drinking. *Alcoholic* was an extreme and shocking word that had little to do with anyone I knew personally.

In my adult home, though, things were different. Finally, the domestic discord grew too terrible to be written off as "normal," and the ties to alcohol too obvious to ignore. After one horrendous night, I packed two toddlers and all their favorite toys into a station wagon and drove four hundred miles to my parents' home without telling anyone I was going. It was a "permanent" move that lasted one week—not a very mature solution.

Afterward, I began attending an Al-Anon group, because I was now convinced I needed it. I expected a heavy dose of sympathy from the group, along with some helpful bits of specific advice. Neither was forthcoming; instead, I encountered a whole new philosophy.

I quickly "bought" the Al-Anon program, read all the literature, and stored up much "head knowledge." Among the things I learned were these:

- Alcoholism is a disease.
- I didn't cause it, can't cure it, and can't control it. (That came as a relief from a great psychological burden.)
- I too am sick, because becoming "addicted to the alcoholic" is a disease in itself.
- Though I can't change or control the drinker in my life, I can make myself happier by changing my own attitudes.
- I am responsible for my own life and happiness, and the drinker for his. The Twelve Steps of Alcoholics Anonymous (AA) and Al-Anon can help me practice a healthy responsibility.
- The attitudes I need to cultivate include acceptance of the situation, emotional detachment from the alcoholic, and recognition of the limits of my own power.
- If I allow myself to be abused, that is a symptom of my own illness.

I found that "head knowledge" wasn't enough, though. It took practice, years of it, to internalize these ideas and put them to work.

But they did help. My relationship with my husband became more peaceful and less destructive, at least for a time. The Al-Anon philosophy was not the only reason, but it was definitely a factor. There were cycles—good times and bad—but in general, I was able to live more productively by detaching myself from a problem that was not truly mine.

But I had reservations about what I heard at Al-Anon. I was also a new Christian attending an evangelical church, reading popular Christian literature, and listening to radio preachers. I was learning many sound and enduring truths, but they were put in different terms and had a different sound from the ideas taught at Al-Anon. Also, I was picking up some ideas I identified as "Christian" that caused me some doubts and conflicts:

- Real love is unconditional and does not concern itself in any way with the behavior of others.
- Having a "servant's attitude" (being like Jesus) means you allow others to treat you any way they please.
- It is "un-Christian" to take any thought for one's own rights, desires, or needs.
- Forgiveness means being willing to take the consequences of another's wrong action upon yourself.
- A wife's attitude toward her husband should be one of un-critical adoration and nearly unconditional submission. A wife must never leave her husband for any reason.

When pressed, most ministers would say that a wife is justified in separating from a husband who physically abuses her. But they don't discuss that problem unless someone else brings it up. They seem to consider it very rare.

I was confused. Were these two belief systems basically incompatible? Did the Al-Anon philosophy express a lack of Christian charity? Or were the teachings of Jesus sometimes being presented in an off-center, one-sided way?

Al-Anon principles were "working" for me. I had largely overcome my debilitating fear and self-pity, increased my self-esteem, and cut down on arguments and violence at home.

But it wasn't enough to know the program "worked." I had to know whether it squared with God's Word, on which I planned to base my life. Everything I had learned that was truly biblical also turned out to be wonderfully practical. (I believe we have a practical God.) So there was no alternative but to study the issues for myself.

Here are some things I wanted to know:
- Is it good, or bad, to set limits on the treatment I will accept from others? Does this constitute "judgment"?
- What does forgiveness really mean?
- Is it always a sin to be angry?
- Is alcoholism really a disease, or is it a sin?
- Is unconditional acceptance the highest form of love?
- Is it wrong to love myself?
- When, if ever, is marital separation a positive step?

Meanwhile, during my times of prayer, the Holy Spirit was urging me to write a book on living with alcoholism. I felt unqualified but decided to begin with research, since I still had so many unanswered questions.

I read dozens of secular and Christian books on alcoholism and related issues, took piles of notes—and became more confused. Each book gave me some useful ideas, but their overall points of view showed great diversity. None of them had a basic philosophy that made me completely comfortable. Some had good advice for the alcoholic that was useless to me without his cooperation. Some wanted me to follow a step-by-step program of specific actions, as if I were not an adult who could decide what to do once I understood the principles (and as if everyone's situation were the same.) Others advocated a "get-tough" stance without explaining where the concept of love fit in. In contrast, some books for Christian wives seemed to advise me to cultivate a soft heart and a softer brain.

Finally, I turned to the Bible, as I should have done in the first place. In my study of Proverbs, I found a wealth of relevant material to add to my notes, all of it eminently practical. Now I felt "at home." Later I found more, equally useful ideas in many other books of Scripture through studies of individual words and concepts.

This book details the answers I found and the conclusions I believe God gave me through my study of His Word and my personal experiences. It is the result of my own journey toward recovery—a journey that still continues. (At this writing, my path has led to separation from my alcoholic husband, but I don't believe the final chapter has been written on that subject.) Others might read the same Bible and draw conclusions different from mine. That's fine; I don't believe God intends us all to think exactly alike.

By now it should be clear that this book was written to myself as much as to anyone else. I do, of course, hope it will be as helpful to one who reads it as it has been to me to write it. If you are still recovering from the effects of someone else's dependence on alcohol or other drugs—or if your journey has just begun—come, take my hand. Let's walk together.

All names used in this book have been changed to protect the privacy of individuals. All incidents presented as fact are true stories—events that happened either to me or to someone I know personally.

You will note that much of my material pertains to white middle-class and working-class Americans. Much of it also deals with the situation of a male alcoholic and a female codependent rather than the reverse. This is unavoidable, given the nature of my own background and experience. I have tried to not exclude anyone in this book, but I believe much more needs to be written, especially by Christians, about chemical dependency and codependency among people of both sexes and various races, nationalities, and ethnic groups. I regret that I cannot "be all things to all people" in this way, and I challenge other Christian writers with backgrounds different from mine to begin filling the gap.

Part 1 Defining the Problem

1 Why Can't We Live Like Normal People?

> I tried cheering myself with wine, and embracing folly—my mind still guiding me with wisdom. I wanted to see what was worthwhile for men to do under heaven during the few days of their lives. ECCLESIASTES 2:3

Evie's Story

Evie's stomach hardened into a tight knot as she heard Ted's car pull in, two hours late. It had been such a nice, peaceful week. She'd thought maybe she and Ted had turned a corner and finally left their recent problems behind them.

One look at Ted's glazed, vacant eyes told her this evening wasn't going to be a good one. When he looked at her and read the worry and disappointment in her face, his own expression turned to one of defiance, as if silently daring her to say anything about his lateness or condition. The battle lines were already drawn, and no one had spoken a word.

The children acted upset at the supper table, reacting to their parents' moods and to the long delay before eating. Joshua burst into tears when Evie said he had to finish his peas. Then Ted told him, "Shut up, or I'll give you something to cry about!"

This statement—which never in the history of the world has gotten a child to stop crying—didn't work with Joshua either. Both children ended up running off in misery to their rooms.

"This is the toughest, driest roast I've ever seen," Ted complained. "I work all day to put food on this table, and you can't do any better than this?"

"It looked plenty tender enough at five-thirty," she answered.

3

"You can't just keep a roast hot forever, you know. Why can't you at least call when you're going to be late?"

Ted came back with an angry reply, and another rip-roaring argument was off and running. By the time it was over, Ted had dumped the remaining contents of his plate on the floor and called Evie an obscene name; Evie had been afraid he would hit her. When she attempted to leave for a while to cool off, he wouldn't let her go. First he refused to give her the car keys, and then he barred the door with his body to keep her from leaving on foot. She responded with some choice, angry comments she would never have made under other circumstances.

After Ted finally fell asleep in his chair, Evie's tears fell on the food she scraped off the floor. Later, she stared out the window at the house across the street, which always seemed so peaceful. She had never heard a raised voice from over there. "Why can't we be as happy as Barb and Mac seem to be?" she wondered. "Why can't we live like normal people?"

Then guilt and self-doubt set in. "What am I doing wrong, that my husband wants to get drunk before he comes home at night? If I were a good enough wife, wouldn't he want to come straight home?"

Although her guilt isn't appropriate, Evie has already taken the first step toward a better life, by admitting that her family has a problem. Her situation has gotten so out of hand that she can no longer tell herself things like, "This is normal. Everyone has an argument or a bad day now and then. I shouldn't expect anything different." Owning up to a serious problem is progress, even though it doesn't feel good at the time.

Our Alcohol-Saturated Society

Did Evie's domestic tale of woe ring any bells with you? Did it remind you of your own family, or that of a friend or relative, or perhaps the home in which you grew up? Alcohol abuse has touched practically everyone in our culture in one way or another.

Drinking goes back almost to the Flood in biblical times. In Genesis 9:20–27 we learn that Noah got drunk and became estranged from one of his sons because of it. (Noah may not have known what would happen, if he was in fact the inventor of wine.)

There is hardly a country in the world today that doesn't have an alcohol problem to one degree or another, but the United States is said to have the second-highest rate of alcoholism in the world. Only in France is the rate of alcoholism higher. No one knows exactly how many alcoholics we have, but estimates range between ten and fifteen million. Two-thirds of all American adults—and a majority of our teenagers as well—drink alcoholic beverages. Of these many millions of "social drinkers," one expert says that about 10 percent will become addicted, compulsive drinkers, or alcoholics.

This simply means that though alcohol abuse should never be accepted as normal, it is extremely common in our society. Ironically, this is one reason an addicted drinker can continue for a long time to excuse his or her irresponsible behavior as "normal."

The reasons the majority of people drink are easy enough to understand. Drinking is a deeply ingrained social custom, and in many circles alcohol acts as a social lubricant. To some hosts and hostesses, it's a symbol of their hospitality—something they routinely offer all guests, in the same class with food, coffee, or a place to hang one's coat.

Then there are those who like the taste of alcoholic drinks, or the status appeal of a fine wine or expensive liquor. Some people use it as a sleeping aid or a tranquilizer; alcohol's advantage here is that it is more easily available and more socially acceptable than other drugs. It does have the predictable effect of taking one's mind off one's problems for a period of time. Then there are people who use alcohol as a painkiller, for anything from a toothache to a chronic bad back.

But the high rate of addiction to alcohol turns any possible advantages into disadvantages. Its relative cheapness, easy availability, and social acceptance just make it easier for more people to become hooked. Who would knowingly, voluntarily become a slave to a drug for any of the above reasons? No one would. Instead, each drinker insists, "I'll be careful and drink wisely. I'll be among the majority of drinkers who don't become alcoholics."

There currently is no sure way to predict which drinkers will keep their habit under control and which will lose that control. "Problem" drinkers come from both sexes and all social classes, races, religions, and ethnic backgrounds. They start out with all sorts of personalities, although they tend to become a great deal alike in their behavior as the disease progresses.

Many researchers now believe that a tendency toward alcoholism can be inherited. Some are trying to find a "genetic marker" or a physical test that would determine who is likely to have a problem.

But, we already know that a child of an alcoholic is more likely to develop the condition than anyone else, even if the child is adopted and never knows the alcoholic biological parent. It's also true that some nationalities and ethnic groups have a more pronounced problem than others, probably because of cultural as well as genetic factors; drunkenness and heavy drinking are much more acceptable in some cultures than in others.

Many people fail to recognize alcoholism in friends and family members because of certain common, preconceived ideas. We tend to think of an alcoholic as an unshaven, filthy man living in the streets, sipping cheap wine from a paper bag. (Actually, only about 5 percent of alcoholics ever are reduced to living on skid row.) Or, we think of a man whose behavior is violent and unpredictable. We always think of a *man*, though, don't we? So it takes us by surprise when a *woman* friend turns out to be a closet alcoholic, drinking all day from supplies kept under the kitchen sink with the bleaches and cleansers. And we are equally surprised when a nice, decent family man with a good job turns out to be committing slow suicide by ruining his liver with excessive drinking.

A drinker can cross the line into alcohol addiction during childhood or the teen years, during retirement, or at any age in between. Some young people seem to become hooked with their first drink and never drink "normally"; others become addicted only after many years of moderate drinking.

Some longtime members of Alcoholics Anonymous say that there are no "pure alcoholics" under age twenty-five. By that they mean younger problem drinkers usually abuse other drugs as well. They may combine illegal drugs with alcohol, use them at different times, or take whatever they can get when their "drug of choice" is unavailable. In this way they only compound their legal and financial problems and increase their confusion, their erratic behavior, and their likelihood of brain damage.

Left untreated, alcoholism, sooner or later, ends in death. And it also contributes to just about every social evil there is. It seems strange, then, that drunkenness is often treated as a laughing matter by the entertainment industry. A comedian can usually get a good laugh with a drunk act, and some have built their careers on it. It seems that our society just doesn't want to see that its "harmless diversion" has severe and devastating consequences for many people.

Moreover, the consequences of alcohol abuse are not confined to the drinker. We all suffer from it—even people who never touch a drop. Anyone who lives with an abuser of alcohol is profoundly affected. That is why alcoholism is called "the family disease." But even outside the immediate family, there are others whose lives are disrupted or inconvenienced to some degree: relatives, employers, employees, co-workers, neighbors, and friends.

It is quite likely that you have been affected by someone's excessive drinking. Have you lost a loved one in an accident caused by an intoxicated driver? Has your house been broken into by kids under the influence? Have you ever been asked to cover for a colleague who was in no condition to do his job? Have you waited in vain for an electrician who never came back from lunch, or given breakfast to a neighbor child whose mother would not wake up? And all of us pay a great deal more for our car insurance than it would cost if everyone drove only when sober.

Yes, all of us have suffered one way or another from the dread disease of alcoholism, and with the psalmist we cry out, "You have shown your people desperate times; you have given us wine that makes us stagger. . . . Save us and help us with your right hand, that those you love may be delivered" (Ps. 60:3, 5).

2 *The Consequences of Alcoholism*

Abusers of alcohol harm themselves and those around them in many ways. The brief list I offer here, which is not all-inclusive, will set forth four main categories of harm.

Physical Harm

Alcohol acts as a depressant on the central nervous system. It is a poison: a fifth of a gallon of whiskey in an hour can paralyze the brain stem, causing coma and death. The liver can process and break down about one-half ounce of pure alcohol in an hour, which is the amount contained in an average drink: one to one and a half ounces of liquor, five ounces of wine, or twelve onces of beer. When a person has more than one such drink in an hour, the rest of the alcohol circulates in the bloodstream "waiting its turn" to be broken down. So the number of drinks taken determines the approximate number of hours the drinker will be under the influence. While it's in the bloodstream, the circulating alcohol affects every organ and system of the body.

Probably the best-known physical consequence of heavy drinking is cirrhosis of the liver—a buildup of excess connective tissue caused by slow poisoning, which often leads to death. The "beer belly" so often joked about is frequently a sign of a swollen liver and the water retention that goes with it. Kidney disease of various kinds, pancreatitis, ulcers, and diabetes can all be made much worse by drinking.

Alcoholics have a greatly increased risk of getting tuberculosis, even now when we think of TB as a conquered disease. But the alcoholic has a lowered resistance to infections in general.

A person in the late stages of alcoholism often forgets to eat or is unable to keep anything down. The resulting malnutrition can cause brain damage severe enough to land the person in a nursing home, permanently. This happened to a man I knew who was barely fifty years old.

At the same time, withdrawal from alcohol is also dangerous for an addicted drinker and should be done only with medical supervision. Delirium tremens, or *d.t.*'s, can cause very realistic and frightening hallucinations; sudden withdrawal can also lead to convulsions and even death. However, for a drinker with a milder dependency, withdrawal usually results in "the shakes" and excessive perspiration.

These so-called natural causes of death are not the only way alcoholics shorten their life expectancy by an average of ten to twelve years. Accidental deaths claim many drinkers and the people around them. (Such drinkers don't have to be alcoholics, of course, but alcoholics can be expected to be under the influence more often than others.) The number of traffic deaths caused by drunken driving has hovered around twenty-five thousand annually in the United States for many years, with many thousands more injured. Fortunately, tougher enforcement of the law has begun to make a dent in this terrible statistic. For many years, our courts and legislatures didn't seem to regard intoxicated driving as a real crime, but dedicated groups of concerned citizens have been working to change their minds and to change public behavior.

But there is another important question. What about accidental deaths that do not involve highway vehicles? A great many home and industrial accidents are said to be alcohol related, and no one knows how many fires, drownings, hunting accidents, falls, electrocutions, and so on have alcohol as a contributing factor. In the city where I live, for example, a fisherman who had consumed several beers fell to his death from a stone stairway on the riverbank.

Alcohol abusers can die from their condition in more ways than we can think of. A woman I knew was drinking one cold night and wandered outside to the family swing set, where she was found in the morning dead of hypothermia. A close friend, a man in his fifties, died at home one Sunday afternoon after drinking a great deal of alcohol, passing out, and inhaling his own vomit.

Experts have estimated that 35 to 40 percent of suicides are alcohol related, and that in half of all homicides, the assailant and/or the victim has been drinking. Alcohol is also a large factor in child abuse and family violence. And, of course, no one can even guess how many days and hours are spent in unproductive misery because of hangovers.

Financial Harm

"For drunkards and gluttons become poor, and drowsiness clothes them in rags" (Prov. 23:21). Spending more than one can afford on liquor is merely the beginning of the financial consequences of alcohol abuse. These can include the loss of a job due to poor performance, or the failure of a self-owned business because of poor management. A drinker's judgment is just as likely to be impaired in financial as in other matters, but he or she doesn't realize it at the time. Heavy drinkers may miss appointments, make poor decisions, enjoy playing the "big spender" with associates, make unwise loans, or invest in foolish schemes. Drinkers who work with their hands, whether repairing computers or performing surgery, will lose judgment and coordination and make costly mistakes.

Alcoholics in business will insist that they have to spend a great deal of time in bars to make contacts. They surround themselves with others who live in the same state of mental fog, and they are oblivious to the fact that nondrinkers who see their cars always in the tavern parking lot tend to avoid doing business with them.

Abusers of alcohol are liable to have to pay for property damage caused by alcohol-related accidents of various kinds. In the later stages, they may run up preventable medical bills or become unable to get health or motor vehicle insurance. Traffic violations or bad business decisions can lead to substantial legal expenses.

Mental and Emotional Harm

The problem drinker in your life is most certainly going through terrible anguish and suffering in spite of making a valiant effort to conceal it. In various ways, the drinker tries to "pass on" that misery to you and other close associates, rather than suffer it alone.

Alcohol abuse is a vicious cycle, emotionally. First a person discovers, perhaps by accident, that a drink seems to improve his or her mood, causing an emotional lift. But unfortunately, the effect soon wears off, and another drink is needed to regain that good feeling.

Eventually, drinkers develop increased tolerance, or the need to drink a greater amount of alcohol before experiencing the "lift" that was so easily obtained at first. Tolerance enables them to hold more alcohol without appearing to be drunk. But now when the mood returns to normal, "normal" is lower than it used to be. They feel increased anxiety and guilt when sober, especially about the drinking and any bad behavior that went along with it. So they drink even more, or more often, to ward off these painful feelings. This chain of events marks the gradual beginning of addiction.

We can know for sure that a drinker has crossed the line into alcohol abuse when he or she has to drink ever-increasing amounts just to feel normal. (In the late stages of alcoholism, when there is severe physical damage, tolerance drops again, and the drinker acts "drunk" after consuming very little alcohol.) And as alcohol becomes increasingly important to drinkers, they will not admit to a drinking problem. Deep inside, they are aware that this is a way of life with no future, that they are slaves to something outside themselves, and that they are committing a slow form of suicide. They consume more and more alcohol in an effort to drown feelings of anxiety.

There is an old Chinese saying: "First the man takes a drink, then the drink takes a drink, and finally the drink takes the man."

Then, as if that unhappiness weren't enough, the drinker starts to experience blackouts—chemically induced periods of amnesia. Blackouts are not to be confused with passing out. During a blackout, the drinker will look quite normal (or normally drunk)—walking, talking, and doing things—but later won't remember any of it. A blackout can last minutes, hours, or days.

At this stage, the drinker is paying a very high emotional price for those fleeting "good times": guilt, depression, anxiety, lowered self-esteem, hostility, defensiveness, self-pity, and the sneaking suspicion that life has gotten out of control. Rather than face all this, the heavy drinker practices denial: a refusal to admit to anyone the truth about loss of control.

At this stage, too, heavy drinkers are liable to turn their anger at themselves on others—a process called projection. They often lash out at others, especially those who are closest, claiming that others' faults and failures are responsible for their drinking and poor behavior. Irrational outbursts of bad temper at the slightest sign of imperfection in a spouse or family member are commonplace. And irrespective of the drinker's own faults, imperfection in others cannot be tolerated. No matter what happens, there must be someone else to blame.

Spiritual Harm

No matter what their religious background, addicted drinkers suffer grave spiritual emptiness in addition to all their other problems.

Alcoholics who have known God's grace in the past feel keenly aware of all that they are missing in terms of communion with the Lord and true fellowship with other believers. Former Christian friends have likely backed off, not knowing how to handle their current behavior and attitudes. Hurt by this, the alcoholic condemns them as hypocrites and eventually stops going to church. Then if the pastor or someone else tries to help, the drinker often explodes with anger—a cover-up for a deep-seated inner fear.

The alcoholic who knows the Bible at all cannot doubt that drunkenness is against the will of God. And this knowledge leads to a heavy load of guilt. There is no way a person can be filled with alcohol and with the Holy Spirit at the same time, as is confirmed in

Ephesians 5:18: "Do not get drunk with wine, which leads to debauchery. Instead, be filled with the Spirit."

Debauchery, the corrupt or immoral behavior that the drinker falls into, causes even greater guilt. As drinkers struggle against the knowledge that they have violated their own system of values, and choose to bury that knowledge rather than deal with it, they slip into a carnal, double-minded spiritual state. Such people are among the unhappiest in the world, even though they may appear carefree and concerned only for their own pleasure.

Even a person who has never had a personal, saving relationship with God still knows deep inside that drunkenness and its accompanying bad behavior are wrong. This feeling may keep that person from even approaching God. For at such times the Enemy works subtly to convince the alcoholic that God can't and won't forgive anyone so low and unworthy.

As the apostle Paul said, "Christ Jesus came into the world to save sinners—of whom I am the worst. But for that very reason I was shown mercy" (1 Tim. 1:15–16). Absolutely no one is beyond God's grace.

The drinker may also be afraid that a close relationship with God would call for an end to drinking, and that is correct. Yes, such a step would be bone-breakingly hard, but no one is expected to do it without help. Jesus assures us, "What is impossible with men is possible with God" (Luke 18:27).

The person who continues to make an idol of alcohol will most certainly suffer grave spiritual consequences, perhaps for eternity. In writing to the Corinthian Christians Paul made it clear that not "thieves nor the greedy nor drunkards nor slanderers nor swindlers will inherit the kingdom of God" (1 Cor. 6:10). And centuries before that the wisdom writer gave us these wise words:

> Do not gaze at wine when it is red,
>   when it sparkles in the cup,
>   when it goes down smoothly!
> In the end it bites like a snake
>   and poisons like a viper.

Your eyes will see strange sights
    and your mind imagine confusing things.
You will be like one sleeping on the high seas,
    lying on top of the rigging.
"They hit me," you will say, "but I'm not hurt!
    They beat me, but I don't feel it!
When will I wake up
    so I can find another drink?" (Prov. 23:31–35).

3 *Sin, Disease, or What?*

Wine is a mocker and beer a brawler; whoever is led astray by them is not wise.
PROVERBS 20:1

Have you noticed that, so far, we have described alcoholism quite a bit but haven't defined it? Writing a definition of alcoholism is such a thorny task that many books on the subject never attempt it at all. We're told what to do about the condition without being told what it is. The reason for this is that when we try to define alcoholism, we run into certain controversies that may become roadblocks for you, the spouse or close associate of a problem drinker, in your quest for a better life. However, as we take a closer look at the problem, we'll see this need not be the case.

A Tricky Question

First comes the question, is alcohol abuse a disease or a sin? In response, the medical profession, Alcoholics Anonymous, and many Christians say, "Alcoholism is a disease. Nobody chooses to have it, and those who do need compassion and professional treatment."

By contrast, there are those Christians who say, "Nuts to that! Drunkenness is a sin; that's all there is to it, and we shouldn't condone or excuse it by making up this so-called disease of alcoholism!"

Now, no matter which of these two responses (if either) is acceptable to you, it is important that this question not become a stumbling block in your path toward personal growth. Your plan of action for improving the quality of your life remains the same! Your primary focus should be on your own life and how you choose to live it. If you do further research into the subject you may even conclude, as I have, that drunkenness is a sin *and* alcoholism is a disease. The two ideas really are not mutually exclusive. Let's see why.

Drunkenness Is a Sin

There is no doubt that both the Old and New Testaments classify drunkenness as a sin and the drunkard as a sinner. From Noah and Lot to the later kings of Israel and Judah, drunkenness was a condition that led to incest, murder, military defeat, and other disasters (in a word, debauchery, as we saw in Ephesians 5:18).

Without question, drunkenness in ancient biblical days was seen as a sin in itself. In Deuteronomy 21:18–21, parents of a rebellious, habitually drunken son are instructed to take the boy out and have him stoned to death. (Even the threat of such a solution must have been very sobering. Let's hope that parents used this idea in motivating more than in actual practice.)

Jesus himself condemned those who get drunk and neglect their responsibilities, saying they deserve "a place with the unbelievers" (Luke 12:42–46). And drunkenness is high on the lists of sins spoken against in the writings of Paul and Peter. In writing to the Christians in Galatia, Paul said, "The acts of the sinful nature are obvious: sexual immorality, impurity and debauchery; idolatry and witchcraft; hatred, discord, jealousy, fits of rage, selfish ambition, dissensions, factions and envy; drunkenness, orgies, and the like" (Gal. 5:19–21).

In other New Testament writings such acts are called "deeds of darkness" (Rom. 13:12–13) and a "flood of dissipation" (1 Pet. 4:3–4).

It is true that many nonaddicted drinkers choose to get drunk as a recreational activity. But to make such a choice is to expose oneself to the possibility of committing every other sin on the list through lowered inhibitions. It also shows indifference to the real possiblity of accident, injury to others as well as oneself, and future addiction. To make such a choice is to consciously thumb one's nose at God and the world and say, "I don't care."

But then comes the question, Is the addicted drinker capable of making this choice, or is it out of his or her hands? Certainly the alcoholic's capacity for free choice is reduced. My own opinion, though, is that alcoholics usually know deep down, that they are out of control. Generally, addicts also know that treatment is available. If a person chooses not to take the treatment, that is also a choice. Drunkenness is still a sin.

Alcoholism Is a Disease

The Bible presents drunkenness as a deliberate act of disobedience. By contrast, medical definitions of alcoholism revolve around loss of control on the part of the drinker.

This definition comes to us by way of the American Medical Association: "Alcoholism is an illness characterized by preoccupation with alcohol; by loss of control over its consumption, such as usually leads to intoxication or drinking done by chronicity; by progression and by tendency to relapse. It is typically associated with physical disability and impaired emotional, occupational, and/or social adjustments as a direct consequence of persistent and effective use."

"Loss of control" means that alcoholics cannot predict with any reliability whether a particular drinking episode will be "normal," that is, whether they will be able to stop when they choose, or "abnormal," resulting in drunkenness in spite of their best intentions.

For example, let's say that on Monday Donna decides to have two drinks with her co-workers on the way home. She does just that and arrives home in time to fix a good supper. No problem. Then on Wednesday she decides to do the same thing. But suddenly, hours later, she is drunk and honestly doesn't know how it happened. Donna is an alcoholic.

"Progression" means that without treatment, the condition gets worse until the patient dies. It never improves or goes away on its own. In AA, one hears stories of alcoholics who went back to drinking after being dry for more than twenty years and found themselves "right back where they left off"—their symptoms as severe as ever. In no way were they "starting fresh," as if they had never had a drink before.

This is why an alcoholic can never become a "normal" social drinker, in spite of extensive treatment or a well-adjusted emotional life. Several years ago, some researchers claimed that their therapy had helped some "former alcoholics" become able to drink responsibly and moderately. Later investigation showed that their data were flawed, and that most of their patients had relapsed into active alcoholism.

Members of Alcoholics Anonymous recognize the progressive, incurable nature of their condition by referring to themselves as "recovering alcoholics," never "former alcoholics." Some recovering Christians choose not to call themselves alcoholics any longer, because they are "new creatures in Christ." They, like the AA members, have no intention of becoming social drinkers.

Progression occurs in certain recognizable stages. According to one expert, the first of three stages is marked by drinking for emotional relief and by the first incidents of drunken driving and blackouts. The second, or crucial, stage is marked by poor work performance, absenteeism, and financial and family problems. Medically, it may also include sexual impotence and liver disease. In the last stage, the sufferer probably has permanent liver and brain damage and may even have lost home and family.

Without treatment, alcoholism is fatal. If appropriate treatment begins in the crucial stage, the recovery rate may be as high as 80 percent. Even at the latest stage, as many as 25 to 30 percent of alcoholics can recover, according to some experts, enough to become employable and live a normal life.

It is possible that the majority of alcoholics also abuse sedatives and tranquilizers, which they often get by prescription. They have no more control over these than over alcohol, and will often substitute one drug for the other. This is called "cross-addiction." In such cases recovery cannot begin until they give up all such mood-altering drugs, according to knowledgeable doctors. Moreover, it is dangerous to combine pills and alcohol because each can multiply the effects of the other, and an accidentally fatal overdose has often been the result.

Born to Be Drunk?

Genetic predisposition is a concept that helps us understand why alcoholism is progressive and incurable. It has been discovered fairly recently by the researcher Virginia Davis in Houston that alcoholics actually process alcohol differently in their bodies than do nonalcoholics. For example, when the alcoholic is drinking there is a significant buildup in the brain area of a highly addictive chemical called THIQ (tetrahydroisoquinoline). However, the nonalcoholic is able to break down this chemical and dispose of it.

Apparently this chemical causes a craving for alcohol. When it is injected into the brains of laboratory rats that would normally be repulsed by alcohol, it actually makes them prefer vodka to plain water.

Furthermore, studies on monkeys have shown that THIQ stays in the brain for life once it is there. No wonder an alcoholic can stay dry for decades but still be incapable of so-called normal social drinking.

THIQ could account for the tendency of alcoholism to run in families, which is well documented. A Swedish study of adopted sons placed at birth in nonalcoholic homes showed that sons whose natural fathers were alcoholics were nine times more likely to become alcoholics than sons whose natural fathers were not alcoholics.

It seems likely that some children inherit a genetic predisposition to build up THIQ—more addictive than morphine—in their brains when and if they drink. This does not mean they are alcoholics from birth. They still have to drink to develop the condition. But if they ever start drinking, they run a high risk of addiction simply because their body chemistry is different from that of a person who can drink moderately and keep it under control.

So far, there is no test to determine whether a person carries this genetic factor. Obviously, anyone with an alcoholic parent or grandparent should be very cautious, and it would be safer not to drink at all.

However, even in the absence of a genetic predisposition, a drinker can become addicted after drinking heavily over a number of years.

Even a level of drinking that most would call moderate can be dangerous: "A person who drinks two to three drinks three or more times a week is setting him- or herself up for trouble" in an average of seven to ten years, according to Dr. Anderson Spickard, Jr., a professor of medicine at Vanderbilt University Medical Center.

Other research has suggested that allergies or blood sugar problems may also play a role in alcoholism. But to date the evidence is inconclusive. In most instances men and boys have been the subjects of the studies that have been done. Because recent investigation suggests there may be as many female as male alcoholics, it is important to find out whether the process works differently in women.

God's Word on Sin and Disease

As Christians, we need to examine all the important questions in life in a scriptural light. A careful reading of the Bible shows us that the dividing line between sin and disease can be rather fuzzy to our limited human sight. Let's look first at three of Jesus' many miracles of healing.

In Mark 2:2–12 we learn of a paralyzed man whom Jesus enables to get up and walk. The Lord's first words to the man were, "Son, your sins are forgiven." When criticized for assuming the authority to forgive sins, Jesus replied, "Which is easier: to say to the paralytic, 'Your sins are forgiven,' or to say, 'Get up, take your mat, and walk?' "

Of course, Jesus cured the man of both his sin and his disability, but we can certainly conclude that the two were related, at least in that case. The Lord again combined the two ideas in his later metaphor, "It is not the healthy who need a doctor, but the sick. I have not come to call the righteous, but sinners" (Mark 2:17). This story and comment can be found in three of the four Gospels.

Turning next to John 5:1–14, we have the story of Jesus healing another paralyzed man—this time at the pool of Bethsaida. After the man was healed, the Gospel writer says, "Later Jesus found him at the temple and said to him, 'See, you are well again. Stop sinning or something worse may happen to you.' "

It is also worth noting that Jesus had previously asked this man, "Do you want to get well?" as if he had some doubt about the man's motives. Perhaps there had been some "rewards" for him in becoming or remaining a long-term invalid. In each case, though, we see that Jesus never rebuked or condemned the sick and disabled; he treated them with great compassion.

However, before we start thinking that all infirmity is somehow related to sin, let's turn to the story of the blind man in the Gospel of John to whom Jesus gave both his sight and some remarkable spiritual insight: "His disciples asked him, 'Rabbi, who sinned, this man or his parents, that he was born blind?' 'Neither this man nor his parents sinned,' said Jesus, 'but this happened so that the work of God might be displayed in his life' " (John 9:2–3).

The Old Testament also shows us that sin and disease are connected in some cases, and not in others. In Psalm 38, David clearly blames his failing health on God's anger against him because of his sin. Yet in the case of Job, who was covered with painful boils from head to foot, we are told directly that no sin of his was responsible; rather, Satan was being allowed to afflict and test him to prove his faith (Job 2:1–8).

Sorting It Out

So, if sin and disease are related in some cases and if calling alcoholism a disease does not rule out the concept of sin, are we justified in referring to it as a disease? I think we are. Alcoholism affects the whole person: body, mind, emotions, and spirit. The physical component of the disease does not in any way absolve the alcoholic of moral responsibility for his or her choices, though. It isn't a case of, "Oh, the poor guy, he has a disease; he can't help anything he does."

With our emerging knowledge of the genetic factors in alcoholism, we must give up the traditional idea that the condition is caused by a weakness of character. When two new drinkers each pick up their first beer, they are morally just alike. Neither is violating a clear command of God, since nowhere does the Bible condemn all drinking of alcohol—only drunkenness is forbidden.

Suppose, though, that one of these new drinkers has a genetic predisposition to build up THIQ and the other does not. Neither one knows or believes that he or she is in danger of addiction. But one of them becomes an alcoholic even though he does not "bring it on himself deliberately." The loss of control is gradual, inconsistent, unpredictable, confusing, and clouded by denial. The alcoholic makes the same early choices as the social drinker, but with far different results.

The budding alcoholic, however, can choose to stop drinking at any time—not after having a drink or two, because loss of control occurs then—but by not picking up a drink in the first place. And if that budding alcoholic is unable to choose abstinence on his own, there is help available from God and from other supportive human beings. He generally knows this, and he also senses that he is in trouble as he gets increasing negative feedback from others and from his own feelings of guilt. Confusion and denial, as powerful as they are, are not excuses for falling deeper into trouble.

Alcoholics Anonymous has helped more alcoholics get well than any other agency on earth, and they recognize alcoholism as a disease. At the same time, though, they hold their members to a very high standard of moral responsibility for their own recovery, apparently seeing no conflict between that and the disease concept. Though not specifically Christian, its Twelve Step program emphasizes dependence on God.

We often think of "disease" as something that strikes us out of the blue, something over which we have no control. This is sometimes true, but more often it isn't. Some of the most common degenerative diseases that plague us—heart disease, strokes, hypertension, most forms of cancer, diabetes—may be at least partly preventable through good nutrition, weight control, regular exercise, and refraining from smoking.

All these conditions are said to involve some genetic predisposition—like alcoholism. And also like alcoholism, they can often be prevented, overcome, or kept under control by self-discipline in changing one's lifestyle.

To put it bluntly, sin is involved in the development of many of our diseases. Gluttony (excessive or unhealthy eating), sloth (lack of exercise due to laziness), and the deliberate pollution of our bodies with poisons such as tobacco are all acts for which we are morally accountable. Yet we don't judge or condemn our loved ones when they bring illness on themselves by such acts. We treat them with compassion, the way Jesus treated the sick.

We also don't deny that a person has a disease on the grounds that his or her behavior was a contributing cause. I've never heard anyone say, for instance, "Lung cancer is not a disease, because Uncle Joe brought it on himself by smoking cigarettes." Yet this sort of reasoning is often applied to alcoholism.

Alcoholism is different only in that it always involves the spirit, mind, and emotions in addition to the body. Treatment in these areas is helpful in any disease or disability, but it is absolutely essential in alcoholism.

So we conclude that alcoholism is a disease, but the alcoholic is still morally accountable for choosing to drink or not or to accept or reject help in overcoming the problem.

Now, it is most important for each of us who is related in any way to a problem drinker to arrive at a good understanding of the "what" and the "why" of what is happening. But the important thing to *you* is that you don't let anything hinder your own recovery from the effects of your loved one's drinking. On the other hand, don't let anyone tell you that your alcoholic husband is not responsible for his behavior because he has a disease. (Would they say that if he were a diabetic who ate pounds of candy every day?) On the other hand, though, don't reject the very real help offered by AA and Al-Anon, among other agencies, just because you think they are "tainted" by viewing alcoholism as a disease, which some of your friends may believe is false.

You and you alone must choose the path to a better life that the Lord shows you, and it will not necessarily be exactly the same as someone else's path. By all means don't let someone else's confusion and misunderstandings hinder your progress.

For Further Reflection

On health, sin, and accountability, read Psalm 38 and 1 Corinthians 3:16–17.

On drunkenness, read Isaiah 5:11–12; Habakkuk 2:15–16; and Romans 13:12–14.

4 Who Is an Alcoholic?

It is not good to have zeal without knowledge,
nor to be hasty and miss the way.   PROVERBS 19:2

How can you tell if your loved one has crossed the line between social drinking and chemical dependency? He may say that he has control over his drinking, but has he really? I have two short answers for you and one long one. One short one is, "By the time you have to ask, he has probably been an alcoholic for some time." The other is, "It doesn't matter as much as you think. If your life is being ruined by someone else's drinking, it's more important for you to save yourself—and improve his chance of sobriety in the process—than to fool around with definitions."

When I took my friend Julie to an Al-Anon meeting after the alcohol abuse in her family had brought her to the end of her rope, she told the members, "I'm really not sure I belong here. I don't know whether my husband is an alcoholic."

"Yes, you do belong here," several group members told her in various ways. "If someone else's drinking is messing up your life, it doesn't matter whether you call him an alcoholic or not. You are not calling him one just by being here. What you are saying by your presence is that *you* have a problem with his drinking, and *you* need some help in handling that problem."

Anyone who looked objectively at Julie's life at that time would have seen severe alcohol-related problems, not only in her husband but in their young adult son, too. Yet she was reluctant to call either of them alcoholics. She loved them! How could she label them with such a nasty name?

Who's an Alcoholic?

To begin the long answer, we need to get back to the problem of defining alcoholism. We have seen the medical definition in the last chapter. One less technical idea on the subject suggests that a person has an alcohol abuse problem when he or she continues to drink even though drinking diminishes the quality of life, whether socially, financially, physically, or mentally. The idea here is that if the drinker were not chemically dependent, he or she would consider the problems alcohol brings to be reason enough to quit.

To put it simply: How important is alcohol to this person? There is a well-known saying that "if you need a drink to be social, you're not a social drinker."

Physical symptoms are usually a reliable sign of growing alcohol dependence, notably buildup of tolerance and the presence of withdrawal symptoms when alcohol is no longer taken.

Tolerance has increased when it takes more alcohol to get an individual drunk than it used to. Some drinkers become proud of their capacity to "hold their liquor," rather than recognizing this as the danger signal it is. A drinker who is criticized for consuming too much, may turn into a secret or private drinker.

Withdrawal symptoms do not have to mean delirium tremens or convulsions. There are milder symptoms like trembling hands, profuse sweating at night, anxiety, and irritability.

In more advanced cases, there are physical signs that do not depend on withdrawal: nausea, vomiting, loss of sexual potence, "beer belly," chronically shaky hands, and a tendency to look older.

Then, too, personality changes are common as the disease progresses. Some of the more common ones are the following:

- A damaged relationship with God and the church, if the person previously was interested in spiritual things.
- Rationalization—always having a good reason to drink.
- Projection—turning self-hatred outward to those closest, with inappropriate anger, bitterness, and far-fetched accusations.
- Mood swings and unpredictable behavior even when not drinking. An alcoholic can go from euphoria to rage without warning

or provocation. Some seem to have a whole different personality when drinking.

- Blackouts—a defect in memory storage in which a person forgets everything that happened during a given period of time.
- Deterioration in job performance—absence, lateness, taking shortcuts, inefficiency, poor judgment. (But the job is sometimes the last thing to go, family life having taken a nosedive long before.)

Twenty Questions

Here is a list of questions widely used by alcoholism counselors. Anyone who answers yes to three or more of these is an alcoholic. Even one or two positive answers spell trouble. Read them, and answer as your loved one might if he or she were being totally honest.

1. Do you lose time from work due to drinking?
2. Is drinking making your home life unhappy?
3. Do you drink because you are shy with other people?
4. Is drinking affecting your reputation?
5. Have you ever felt remorse after drinking?
6. Have you gotten into financial difficulties as a result of drinking?
7. Do you turn to lower companions and an inferior environment when drinking?
8. Does drinking make you careless of your family's welfare?
9. Has you ambition decreased since drinking?
10. Do you crave a drink at a definite time daily?
11. Do you want a drink the next morning?
12. Does drinking cause you to have difficulty in sleeping?
13. Has your efficiency decreased since drinking?
14. Is drinking jeopardizing your job?
15. Do you drink to escape from worries or trouble?
16. Do you drink alone?
17. Have you ever had a complete loss of memory as a result of drinking?

18. Has your physician ever treated you for drinking?
19. Do you drink to build up your self-confidence?
20. Have you ever been to a hospital or institution on account of drinking?

A drinker may try to prove he is not an alcoholic by stopping all drinking for a certain number of days, weeks, or months. Most alcoholics can do this, but it proves nothing. If your spouse wants to test himself this way, give him a real challenge: set a daily limit of not more than two drinks a day for three months. A drinker who can live successfully with that challenge for an extended period of time is probably not an alcoholic. As a rule, an alcoholic loses control after that first drink or two and cannot help drinking more.

Your loved one probably won't agree to try this test just because you ask him to. Or if he does, you may never find out the result.

This Test Is for You

Here is another twenty-question test, but this one is for you rather than the drinker. If you can answer yes to three or more of these questions, your life has been altered enough by someone else's drinking that you should get some counseling for yourself or join Al-Anon or a similar group.

1. Do you spend a significant amount of time worrying about someone else's drinking?
2. Do you lose sleep waiting for the drinker to come home?
3. Do you have health problems related to emotional stress?
4. Is it an unspoken rule in your house that the drinker can do whatever he or she wants, but your needs and desires don't matter?
5. Do you sometimes think you are to blame for the drinking?
6. Do you argue, accuse, or nag about drinking?
7. Is nothing you do ever good enough for the drinker?
8. Has your standard of living been lowered by drinking or related financial problems?

9. Has your social circle narrowed to include only heavy drinkers and their families?
10. Have you missed work or have children missed school because of an alcohol-related crisis?
11. Are you or the children afraid to invite friends home because of possible embarrassment?
12. Has the condition of your home or the level of housekeeping suffered because of drinking?
13. Has the drinker subjected you to verbal abuse, unfair accusations, or irrational anger?
14. Have you been a victim of physical abuse or intimidation by the drinker?
15. Have you taken on responsibilities that properly belong to the drinker?
16. Is your family unable to celebrate a holiday happily or take an enjoyable vacation together?
17. Does the entire mood of the household depend on what is happening with the drinker?
18. Do you think the drinker couldn't get along without you?
19. Do you think your life would be vastly different without him or her?
20. Do you wonder how others manage to live normally?

To Use the Term or Not

Now that you have the two short answers and the long answer, you probably have formed a tentative opinion as to whether anyone close to you is an alcoholic. If not, that's good. But if it seems to be true, it probably is. You are showing courage and honesty in facing this painful fact when it is so much easier to deny it. Please don't feel guilty, as if it were your admission of the fact that made it true. You know that isn't the case.

Next comes the question, should you—now or ever—tell your loved one that you think he or she is an alcoholic? Should you use the word with others outside the family?

Some people feel that the term *alcoholic* is more trouble than it's worth because it is so loaded with negative connotations in our society and arouses so many defensive feelings. They prefer terms that are more emotionally neutral such as "alcohol-troubled person," "problem drinker," or "chemically-dependent person."

I still plan to use the term *alcoholic*, among others, throughout the rest of this book because it has the advantage of being recognized and understood by the majority of readers. I don't believe, as some do, that it is judgmental to label someone else an alcoholic. To me, that is just "calling it as I see it," providing, of course, it's not done in a spirit of anger or blame. Since I believe in the disease concept of alcoholism and genetic predisposition, I don't blame anyone for becoming an alcoholic.

Again, that doesn't mean that any kind of drunken bad behavior is excusable or that you are wrong to get angry over it or that you have to continue living in unacceptable circumstances. Bad behavior can be dealt with separately from alcoholism, and it is not judgmental to recognize it when you see it.

The time may come, however, when you decide to tell your loved one you think he or she is an alcoholic as a means of emphasizing the seriousness of the problem. (Read chapter 7 first.) But make sure you do it gently and in love, not in anger. Know your own motives, for the wisdom writer once said, "All a man's ways seem innocent to him, but motives are weighed by the Lord" (Prov. 16:2).

No matter what words you use to describe the problem in your family, the important thing is to recognize its seriousness and resolve to make some changes in your life that will enable you to be a happier person. It is important that you do this for your own sake, but paradoxically, whatever is good for you is also good for your alcoholic. One expert writes that when the spouse of an alcoholic gets help, the alcoholic has an 80 percent better chance of eventually getting help and becoming sober.

This way, everyone benefits and is happier. The Proverbs writer expressed it well when he said, "A happy heart makes the face cheerful, but heartache crushes the spirit" (15:13).

5 Getting Started in Your New Life

I have set before you life and death, blessings and curses. Now choose life, so that you and your children may live and that you may love the Lord your God.

DEUTERONOMY 30:19–20

Have you become alarmed at the grim future that lies ahead for your problem drinker and your family if things don't change? Did you pick up this book hoping to find the answer to the question, What can I do to make him stop drinking? Please don't give up on me when I answer, "There is nothing you can do to make him stop drinking!"

The chances are that you already know that a frontal assault is futile. Let's face it. How many of the following ways have you already tried?

- Getting rid of all the alcohol in the house
- Begging, nagging, complaining, yelling
- Logical reasoning
- Making "deals" or trade-offs
- Asking friends or relatives not to serve drinks
- Threatening to leave
- Calling or going to bars to coax the drinker home
- Marking bottles, keeping track of consumption
- Searching for hidden bottles
- Taking control of the purse strings
- Getting drunk yourself to "show him how it looks"

Did any of these methods work? For how long? If there were short-term results, were they worth all the trouble?

31

I just have to say at this point that the only "direct" method that has any effect at all is prayer. As you turn the situation over to the Lord, he will give you guidance and good judgment. Remember the old saying, "You can do more than pray, but you cannot do more than pray until you *have* prayed."

The Serenity Prayer used constantly by AA and Al-Anon members, says, "God grant me the serenity to accept the things I cannot change, the courage to change the things I can, and wisdom to know the difference."

There are some things I can change, but there is only one person I can change. That's myself.

"But I'm not the one who needs to change," you may be saying.

With all love and compassion, because I've been there and said that too, I ask you to look again. Haven't some of your own attitudes become bent out of shape through years of living with alcoholism? Weren't there actions you took and decisions you made, at times, that didn't make a whole lot of sense but were reactions to the craziness that was going on around you? Aren't there some positive things you could have done if you weren't feeling too paralyzed and helpless to do them?

Co-alcoholic or *codependent* are terms for someone whose personality has been deeply affected by living with alcoholism or drug abuse. We don't like them, any more than an alcoholic likes to be called an alcoholic. But it isn't a judgment or condemnation, and it doesn't mean we started out different from anyone else. People just change and adjust when living with an alcoholic, because sometimes it seems to be what a person has to do to survive. This is the reason alcoholism is called "the family disease."

It's like a dance. Your partner makes a move, and you move in a way that responds. Then your partner takes another step, and you follow. All of this is beautifully illustrated in the 1954 movie called *The Country Girl*, with Grace Kelly and Bing Crosby. I suggest if at all possible that you obtain a video of this picture, for in it is a classic portrayal of how a "co-alcoholic" acts. In watching it, you may get the feeling they are telling your story.

So, How Do I Change Myself?

In order to change you need to "stop dancing backward!" that is, stop centering your life around your reactions to the actions of the drinker. Since you can't control the drinker, concentrate on regaining control over yourself and taking responsibility for your own actions, decisions, and happiness. To use a different metaphor, you need to drop the reins of your loved one's life and pick up your own.

The important fact is that you can teach yourself to live like a normal person again, whether your loved one stops drinking or not! This may be hard to believe, but it's true. The positive changes you make in your own life may very well be a good influence on your alcohol abuser, but that *must not* be your primary goal. God gave you one life to live on this earth, and your obligation is to live that life before him in a healthy, constructive manner.

In doing this, you will have to make some changes in your underlying attitudes as well as in your actions. It will take time, patience, and self-examination. But the attitudes don't have to come first—your can act your way into better attitudes, and you can start now. These negative forces—denial, obsession, fear, guilt, and so on—are like the "giants in the land" that made the Hebrews afraid to enter Canaan. But of this you can be sure—when you approach them boldly, you'll find the giants aren't as scary as they looked at first, and God will help you conquer them!

Above all, don't waste time blaming yourself for letting your life get sidetracked along with the alcoholic's. If you had known how to prevent it, you would have. Remember, you are smart and you are strong—that's why your alcoholic relies on you so much! So start today to pick up those reins and live your own life. Only you can decide exactly *how*. You and your situation are unique, but in the remaining chapters of this book you will find some specific principles and examples that may be helpful.

Why Should I Be the One to Change?

Maybe you're still asking, "Why me? He's the one with the problem." Here are some of the reasons for you to change.

Change for your own sake. Even if the drinker never changes, there is no sense in two of you going down the drain. If you are a wife, it wouldn't make you a "good wife" to do so. You can become happier, wiser, and more spiritually mature through this experience, but only if you are willing to grow and learn from it. It is true, of course, that there are some people who just wallow in misery and let their problems destroy them—but you don't want to be one of those, do you?

Change to follow the example of Jesus. Jesus was badly mistreated; but instead of showing spite, he set an example of humility and forgiveness that still shines for Christians and non-Christians alike. He didn't just say, "Love your enemies, do good to those who hate you, bless them who curse you, pray for those who mistreat you" (Luke 6:27–28); he *did* it.

*Change as an investment in the future of your family.*Remember the story Jesus told: you want to build your house upon a rock, not on the sand (see Luke 6:46–49). The emotional interactions learned in an alcoholic family make it more likely that the children will grow up to have troubled families themselves, possibly including marriage to an alcoholic. But when you learn to live in a more stable, positive way, your children will learn too by your example. Even if they are grown, your influence is still stronger than you may think.

Change because you have been given the light. "You are the light of the world. A city on a hill cannot be hidden. Neither do people light a lamp and put it under a bowl. Instead they put it on its stand, and it gives light to everyone in the house. In the same way, let your light shine before men" (Matt. 5:14–16). Right now you may be the only one in your household with enough faith and perspective to be capable of self-improvement. When the others see that you are happier with your new way of thinking and of doing things, they may follow your example.

Elyse's Story

Although Elyse was intelligent and a full-time homemaker, her home was in a constant state of disorganization. Because she had lived with a highly critical and manipulative alcoholic husband for many years, she had almost no self-esteem left. In fact, Max had her halfway convinced that she was "the crazy one." She spent most of her time and energy reacting to him and his demands—dancing backward.

Elyse had come to think she was not, in her words, "a regular person who deserves to live a normal life." She was also ashamed of feeling that way. It was confusing, because she had started out as a very confident and dignified young woman. But when she decided she could no longer continue to live the way she did, Elyse came to realize that you can get to *be* a normal person by *acting* like one, and that you don't have to feel like a normal person to *start* acting like one. You can start with an action and let the feelings follow along later.

Elyse chose the way she was handling the supper hour as her first target for change. It was a time of tension for the whole family, as Max had begun coming home later and later, usually looking for an argument—and he could usually find someone to oblige him. Dreading this time of day, Elyse had taken to starting supper quite late, but this was hard on her hungry teenagers. Then on the occasional day when Max came straight home from work, he was upset because nothing was ready.

One day, she announced to the family that from then on, she would have a well-planned meal ready every evening at 5:30, and she would serve it then regardless of who was at home. After a few weeks, she found that the new system worked very well. It was much easier on her nerves; the children were happier; and most food could easily be kept warm or reheated in the microwave oven for Max or anyone else who was late.

This change worked out so well that a month later she decided to take a further step. When Max came home late, it had been her habit to hover around him, making sure his supper was piping hot and urging him to eat. Somehow she didn't feel her day's work was done until Max ate, even if it was past midnight.

One morning when Max was sober she told him, "I feel too tired at night to stand around, reheat, and serve your supper when you are late. So when the kids and I have finished our dinner, we will leave the food in the kitchen, and you are welcome to help yourself when and if you feel like eating." (Notice that she put this in terms of her own needs. She didn't make a moral issue of it or accuse him of anything. Neither did she ask permission.)

To her surprise Max said, "Fine." Right away she felt happier, more like her old, more confident self. Sometimes she also felt guilty and had to force herself to stay out of the kitchen while he reheated his meal, but she reminded herself that it was alcoholism that made him late, and that she wasn't really doing him a favor by catering to his disease.

One night, though, he tested her and said, "Do you mind getting me something to eat?"

It was very late and she was ready for bed. "Yes, I do mind," she responded. He then went to get a plate, grumbling loudly about "what kind of wife would deny such a simple and basic duty as to feed her man." But the attempted guilt trip didn't work; she felt at peace. She knew that when Max was in a mood to complain, nothing would hinder him from finding something to complain about.

By refusing to make that one small adjustment to her husband's sickness, Elyse had allowed him to behave in a slightly more grown-up and responsible manner. She had given him back a small part of the consequences of his drinking. Ironically, she had done him a favor by doing less for him.

The new system was good for her, too. She had taken up sewing, an old hobby, now that her evenings were more free. Consequently she was happier, and they argued less often. Her new way of life reflected her love for Max—even though she didn't always *feel* loving—better than her insecure hovering had. By helping herself toward happiness, she was hopefully helping him toward recovery.

In thinking about Elyse, ask yourself now what your first change will be. Do something nice for yourself today just because you are important! Stop catering to alcoholism in some small way, and you'll be less angry and self-pitying because you'll have less to be angry about and less to pity yourself for. And in making yourself a little happier, you will be doing something good for that special person you love, too.

Changes That Don't Change Anything

Warning: *superficial changes in your circumstances will have no effect at all on alcoholism!* Regardless of what your alcoholic says, it will not help him quit drinking if you move to the country, if he changes jobs, if you have a child, if you allow your children to live with someone else, if you quit your job (or take one), if you stay away from certain friends or relatives, if you change cities, and so on and on. These kinds of things are called "geographic cures" (humorously) by members of AA and Al-Anon. They know by long experience that they really aren't cures at all.

Though any of these changes might be a good idea for one reason or another, none of them will have any effect on the disease as such. Your drinker doesn't abuse alcohol because of any of the external pressures in his life, no matter what he says. His reasons are deep inside and will remain there irrespective of geographic location.

Wherever you go, there will be liquor. You can't get away from it. Neither can you get away from "those evil companions who are such a bad influence." There are alcoholics everywhere too, and your drinker chooses them as friends because they're his type of people and the kind he wants to be with.

It is also important that you not be isolated from people who are supportive of you, and this could happen if you move away or stop seeing your friends. Far from helping your loved one, isolation helps the disease!

The trouble with so-called geographic cures is that they are an attempt to run away from the problem rather than deal with it. They waste time and their inevitable failure increases your sense of hopelessness. Instead, concentrate on making a change within your own relationship; that's the only kind of change that will lead you to a better way of life.

Expect Resistance

Now, it is important to realize that you are involved in spiritual warfare, and it is serious business. Your enemies are powerful: a disease that has crept into every corner of your family life, and Satan, who wants to keep it that way. But "our side" is even more powerful. First, there is God, and we are assured that "the one who is in you is greater than the one who is in the world" (1 John 4:4).

In addition to God's great power for good, you have more power in this situation than you think! Alcoholic behavior is especially designed to cover up this truth, but it's still true that *your drinker needs you more than you need him!* You not only do a good bit of caretaking, but you may also be your loved one's strongest link with health and sanity. And this is not something taken lightly, because in reality your alcoholic spouse would be thrilled to escape his or her drunken prison. (If there was a decent human being in there before alcoholism, there still is.) So there are three allies: God, you, and the better side of that person you love.

Remember, though, when you start making changes that attack the disease's progress, that part of your alcoholic that is in bondage will panic. He may use a variety of manipulative tricks:

- Respond with great anger to your small changes. (But listen carefully; the anger has a hollow ring.)
- Attack your self-esteem by saying anything he can think of to hurt you. (He knows you so well that he knows just which strings to pull. If you see through this, it will hurt less.)
- Become more arrogant and tell you he doesn't need you, that he could do fine on his own or with someone else.
- "Punish you" by getting drunk more often or at carefully selected times, such as on your Al-Anon night.
- Double up on whatever bugged you most in the past.
- Express a syrupy false sympathy for the "problems" or "illness" troubling you. (The implications are that it's all in *your* head, of course.)
- Stop drinking.

Stop drinking? "Oh, wonderful," you say. "Now I can relax." Not likely; not when it's done without his getting into a recovery program. It will probably be temporary, one more sick game to try to get you to stop whatever you are doing. No matter what—just keep right on with your positive changes. If he really does never drink again, both of you will need some emotional and spiritual recovery just the same. It's okay to be happy that the drinking has stopped; just don't give up your own recovery as part of any related "deal." If your alcoholic is sincere, he'll want you to do what's best for you.

It's important to be patient and move ahead slowly. Your life didn't get off track overnight, and you won't get everything fixed overnight either. Just start with one little step and expect resistance and set-backs, but *don't ever give up!* Each day is a fresh new start, and you can reach your goals because *you are going to regain control over your own life and you are going to become a happier person!* In writing to the Christians in Ephesus, Paul said, "For you were once darkness, but now you are light in the Lord. Live as children of light (for the fruit of the light consists in all goodness, righteousness and truth) and find out what pleases the Lord" (Eph. 5:8–10).

For Further Reflection

On freedom, choice, and responsibility, read Deuteronomy 30:15–20; Psalm 92:12–15; John 8:31–32, 36; 10:10; Ephesians 5:15–17; 1 Peter 4:1–5; and 2 Peter 3:17–18.

On God as your helper, read Exodus 15:13; Psalms 30; 46; 121; Isaiah 41:10–13; and Ephesians 3:12–21.

Part 2   Through Denial
to Truth

6 *Denial: Sweeping It Under the Rug*

Surely you desire truth in the inner parts; you teach me wisdom in the inmost place.   PSALM 51:6

Denial is a psychological defense mechanism in which we pretend that an unpleasant truth isn't so. We know, deep down, that it is true, but we are just not ready to face the pain of it. Perhaps you've experienced momentary denial when you were told that someone you cared about had died. "Oh, no!" you said. "It can't be true."

In the case of a death, we soon have to face the truth and get on with our grieving. With alcoholism, it is common to keep on denying for years that the condition exists. Denial is practiced by the problem drinker and by family, friends, even doctors. Alcoholism comes on gradually; its symptoms can be misinterpreted; and heavy drinking is well tolerated in our society. All of these factors make it easier to deny.

Because of denial, alcoholism usually goes unrecognized and un-treated until the late stages. The subject is taboo in many homes; many people have grown up with an alcoholic parent and don't realize it until well into adulthood. "I knew my family wasn't normal, but the problem never had a name," they say.

Isn't it odd that families who suffer so deeply from alcoholism are willing to deny the existence of their problem? But it isn't, really. To admit there is a problem is to release all kinds of negative emotions we wish we didn't have. Also, once we "know" such a thing, we are going to feel obligated to do something about it, and we aren't sure what. So for the time being, it's safer "not to know."

How the Alcoholic Denies

Much of the typical alcoholic's denial system is built around exclusionary definitions. In other words, "I can't be an alcoholic because . . .

I don't drink in the morning."
I don't drink every day."
I drink only in bars."
I never drink in bars."
I never drink alone."
I drink only beer [wine, good Scotch, etc.]."
I never drink wine [hard liquor, etc.]."
I drink only with business associates."
I drink only at parties."
I never miss a day of work."
I have friends who drink more than I do."
I've never had a ticket for drunk driving."

All these things are irrelevant. None of them proves that a person is not an alcoholic. Here are some other ways in which alcoholics deny reality:

1. Making excuses for drinking rather than taking responsibility for it. They blame job pressures or a bad marriage or some tragic event in the past. If these reasons were valid, everyone with the same problems would be drinking heavily.
2. Believing they are unloved and unworthy of love, while their thoughts and actions are totally self-centered.
3. Acting in ways that go against their own basic values.
4. Saying they don't need alcohol while centering their entire lives around it.
5. Lying about the amount they consume, sneaking extra drinks when others aren't looking, hiding bottles at home.
6. Failing to recognize that many of their problems at work and at home are caused by heavy drinking, rather than the other way around.
7. Believing a "geographic cure" of one kind or another will help them stop drinking.

8. Believing that "I can stop whenever I want," even after they make sincere efforts to stop and can't.

In the advanced stages, denial may actually take the form of "double-think," or totally irrational and contradictory thoughts. The author Jean Kirkpatrick illustrates this kind of unreal thinking from her own drinking days: "Taking the bottle with me, I went back to the bedroom and drank leisurely, for I had decided that I wouldn't drink that day."

In her book *Turnabout: Help for a New Life*, she also describes deciding never to drink again while taking a few shots as a hangover cure, buying liquor "for guests," and deciding to have "just one" after going cold turkey for days. These are all manifestations of denial.

The alcoholic hangs on tightly to denial because he or she is scared to death of giving up alcohol. It is virtually the sole means of coping with stress and tension.

How You Deny

Congratulations if you have given up denying that you have an alcoholic family member! (I am assuming that everyone reading this book has at least one such person among family or friends. If not, maybe you will be able to help a friend face the disease, and that's good too.) However, don't be hard on yourself for denying in the past; it's normal. We're told that the average family takes seven years to recognize alcoholism after solid evidence exists—and then, usually another two years go by before they seek help.

Here are ways the typical family helps denial along:

1. Believing the alcoholic's denial system. It can be easy to buy your loved one's excuses and rationalizations.
2. Covering up or making excuses to others. "Jim won't be in today. It's a touch of the flu." "Dad is too busy to come to your game tonight, honey. He had to work late." "Don't bother Mom, kids—she's very tired today." "If Lisa acts strange, it's this prescription medicine she's on."
3. Minimizing the problem. "It isn't really so bad. He's such a nice

guy when he isn't drinking. He wasn't always like this. Other people have problems as bad or worse."

As spouses and others who are very close to alcoholism, we have forms of denial that are all our own.

1. We blame the drinker for everything that goes wrong and for his crazy behavior, without taking responsibility for our own sometimes irrational behavior.
2. We think life would be perfect if only he would stop drinking. Look around you carefully—whose life is perfect? Don't wait for sobriety; make improvements now.
3. We think we are controlling the alcoholic.
4. We believe the alcoholic can get better on his own. Almost no one ever does. It takes divine intervention and human help.
5. We think we don't need any help. We think we are superman or superwoman and can handle everything just fine. But there is plenty we can learn from people who have been here before us; besides, it's a blessed relief to find out others understand. Are you reluctant even to bother God with your problems?
6. We think we are already doing as well as we can. Once you take your focus off the drinker and put it back on yourself, you'll be able to recognize your priorities and get back to fulfilling some of your lost dreams.
7. We believe we deserve mistreatment. False, false, false—nobody deserves to be abused in any way. But abuse is so degrading to the spirit that we come to believe it on an unconscious level.

Why You Deny

We have already seen that giving up denial releases negative feelings and forces us to face the question of "what to do about it." But there are other reasons why denial lingers for years beyond its time. One reason has to do with cycles.

Alcoholism tends to get really bad for a while, then better for a time before getting worse again. These cycles are partly a result of the drinker's efforts to clean up his own act. Each new low in behavior shocks and frightens him, so he decides to "get hold of himself," and stop drinking or cut back. And with even limited success comes a feeling of relief that possibly he or she isn't an alcoholic after all. Then after the drinker's guard is let down there comes the danger of lapsing into the old habits.

During the good times, the drinker's false sense of security extends to those close by. Just when you were getting really worried—or angry—the drinker straightens up and looks good for a while. With a sigh of relief you say, "Things will be okay now." But then when the downward spiral begins, you don't want to see it. The disappointment is too bitter.

Rather than send your emotions on a roller coaster ride, try looking at these cycles with a realistic kind of hope. Yes, the good times are a false calm and the bad times get worse. But it's all progress! Your loved one is proving to himself and to you that he can't overcome his condition on his own.

As a spouse, another reason you may not want to face alcoholism in your marriage is the fear that you or the dynamics of your marriage brought on the condition. But alcoholism cannot be caused or prevented by the drinker's relationship with any other person. You never had that kind of power, so let go of that guilt right now.

Another question: Have you denied the disease because you didn't want the humiliation of being pitied? People may offer you pity, but you can refuse to accept it or wallow in it. Walk in dignity, and others will respect you as you respect yourself.

It is important that you let go of others' opinions completely. You may be afraid that people will expect you to do something drastic that you are not prepared to do, like leaving your husband or wife. Or maybe you think people will feel contempt for you if you stay with the alcoholic. Remember, though, that it doesn't matter what they think. It is God you want to please, not people.

At the same time, ignoring a problem doesn't make it go away, even as acknowledging a problem doesn't make it any worse. But giving up the denial tendency can make you *feel* worse temporarily, as you experience the negative feelings you've been sweeping under the rug. The important thing is to get your feelings out in the open. Then they will lose their power over you.

Denial on the Part of Others

After you have coped with your own denial you may still have to face the denial of others among your family and friends. Be patient, however, as you remember that it took time for you to acknowledge the truth.

It's especially difficult when someone else's denial system includes blaming you for the alcoholic's actions. ("Lynn sure makes a mountain out of a molehill." "Dexter must have a lot of trouble at home; otherwise he wouldn't spend so much time in that bar." "My son never drank much before he married that woman." "Mom may drink too much, but she's fun. It's Daddy who acts so weird.") The important thing is not to internalize the feelings and attitudes of others.

Now congratulations on breaking free from denial. In arriving at this place you have taken a huge step in your own recovery. When Jesus said, "The truth will set you free," he was talking about the truth of who he is. But all truth sets us free—free from illusions, from inappropriate guilt, from many kinds of unproductive emotional baggage, free to be whole, healed, and happy. Remember the words of Jesus, "If you hold to my teaching, you are really my disciples. Then you will know the truth, and the truth will set you free" (John 8:31–32).

For Further Reflection

On truth and lies, read Psalm 34:11–14; John 8:44; 14:6; 1 Corinthians 13:6; 2 Corinthians 13:8; and 1 John 1:5–7.

7 Confrontation: Speaking the Truth in Love

Speaking the truth in love, we will in all things grow up into him who is the Head, that is, Christ.
EPHESIANS 4:15

Confrontation is speaking the truth—especially an unpleasant truth—in love. Notice in this verse from the book of Ephesians the two essential ingredients: truth and love. Truth without love is cruel. Love without truth is mindless. Both, of themselves, do more harm than good.

Maybe your mother taught you the same expression mine taught me, "If you can't say something nice, don't say anything at all." Mothers teach this because they don't want to hear their children asking old Mrs. Murphy, "Why does your dog smell so bad?"

But while this principle is all right for casual acquaintances, it's a poor idea to "say nothing at all" when there are problems in our intimate relationships. It is impossible to have closeness without communication, and real communication is not always nicey-nice. To love someone deeply, I have to understand who he is, what he thinks and feels and needs, and how my behavior affects him. In order to love me back, he needs to understand the same things about me.

And to understand, we usually have to be told. Too often, we expect the other person to be a mind reader: "He ought to know how I feel." But how should he know? Not everyone reacts to the same treatment in the same way. We have different temperaments; we come from different backgrounds; and there are basic differences between the sexes. Also, we aren't as sensitive as we could be to body language and other nonverbal signals. We need the words.

Confrontation helps crack through the denial of alcoholism. This may seem hard to believe, but your problem drinker truly doesn't know how his behavior hurts you unless you tell him. Even the average person has to be told, and alcoholics are far more wrapped up in themselves and their own anxieties than the average person. Sometimes they don't even remember what happened after they started drinking on a given day (because of the periods of amnesia called blackouts).

When the drinking problem and all its fallout become unmentionable topics in your home, you are conspiring to protect the disease. Alcoholism thrives in darkness, on all that hush-hush secrecy. Bringing the truth out into the open in a matter-of-fact and loving way can help the alcohol abuser face the fact of the disease and its effect on the family. He or she may eventually become worried enough to want to do something about it. Even without sobriety, you can insist on—and get—better treatment.

Confrontation Isn't Judgment

The Gospel writer gave us these important words, "Do not judge, and you will not be judged. Do not condemn, and you will not be condemned. Forgive, and you will be forgiven" (Luke 6:37). Some people feel that to call anyone else's behavior into question is to "judge" in this negative sense of the word. But I don't think so. I think what the Lord is telling us here is that we are not to condemn anyone as unworthy, inferior, or "no good." When we attack another's basic worth as a person, or declare that we know where he is going when he dies, we are playing God in the most presumptuous and destructive way. Such things are not for us to decide.

It isn't judgment, in that sense, to recognize an obvious sin when you see one. Jesus, Peter, Paul, and all religious leaders down through the ages have done so. In 1 Corinthians 5, Paul advised a congregation to shun a member who was engaged in incest. How could they possibly do that without pinning a label on the sin when it came to their attention? Furthermore, we have already established that drunkenness is a sin, and a grave one at that.

The important thing is to condemn the drunkenness rather than the person who gets drunk. We are to "hate the sin and love the sinner" as the popular expression says. And certainly, a person doesn't have to be blind to sin in order to love.

Judgment interprets the sinner's relationship to God. Confrontation deals with our own relationship to the one who is hurting us.

Judgment blames. Confrontation points out facts.

Judgment assassinates character and denigrates a person's worth. Confrontation deals with behavior, while recognizing the value of the person in God's eyes.

The motive of judgment is to express anger. The motive of confrontation is to express hope for improvement. Judgment throws love away. Confrontation tries to salvage love, heal it, and help it grow.

Forgiveness is a major element of confrontation. After the church member gave up his incest, Paul told the Corinthians to forgive him and reaffirm their love for him (2 Cor. 2:5–11). Jesus gave the woman caught in adultery a second chance, telling her to "go now and leave your life of sin" (John 8:11), while also exposing the hypocrisy of the other, more self-righteous sinners who wanted to put her to death. He did not excuse her wrongdoing in exposing theirs, though.

In Luke 6:42, Jesus says, "First take the plank out of your eye, and then you will see clearly to remove the speck in your brother's eye." Notice the word "first." We are to deal with our own sin first and foremost—and we all have some to deal with. But Jesus never said, "and forget about the speck in your brother's eye." He was warning against self-righteousness, not forbidding his followers ever to deal with someone else's wrongdoing.

How to Confront

Confrontation, when done right, can be a form of peacemaking. It seems ironic, but it's true—when we express our feelings honestly, it becomes possible for us to adapt to one another and live together in greater harmony. We can't change our ways to please our loved ones if we don't know they are being hurt.

When anger and resentment are "swallowed" by one person and allowed to grow and fester in silence and darkness, they can lead to a sudden and total rejection of the other. Many a husband and many a wife have found themselves suddenly alone and said, "I don't understand what happened. Up until the day he [or she] left me, I thought everything was fine between us." How much better to deal with problems as they arise than to have a marriage explode from built-up pressure. Actually, confrontation leads to a real marriage, one with a better chance of survival no matter how severe the problems.

Here's how to go about it:

1. Confront as often as necessary. Deal with important issues as they arise—as soon as you recognize a pattern of behavior that offends you.

2. Pay attention to timing. Morning is usually the best time to confront an alcoholic, as there will be less of the drug in his system. It's useless to talk to a person under the influence of alcohol; he won't really hear you.

3. Stick to the facts. Tell your alcoholic spouse what he did while drunk and how it made you feel. Skip the moralizing, preaching, and predictions of the future. Be specific. Say, for instance, "Last night at Jim and Laura's, you slurred your words, stumbled when you walked, and stepped on their baby's hand. You told Laura her teeth made her look like a rabbit. I felt terribly embarrassed, and also angry with you."

By all means don't say, "Last night at Jim and Laura's you acted like a jerk. I doubt they'll ever invite us there again. Decent people don't want to associate with a drunk." Those aren't facts; those are opinions and conclusions that leave plenty of room for argument. Present the facts, and let the other person form his own conclusions.

4. Make it short and to the point. Say what you have to say in two or three short sentences, at most, and then drop it. Don't repeat yourself or make a long speech. The alcoholic will hear you better

that way, believe it or not. If he acts as if he didn't hear you, he still did.

5. Watch your tone of voice. Keep your voice cheerful and your emotional setting as close to "neutral" as you can. You don't want to sound unduly worried; let the other person decide if there is something to worry about. Don't sound fearful, and by all means, don't vent your anger. You can tell him you're angry, if you are, but an excessive show of emotion might cause your anger to be mistaken for the problem itself: "She's just exaggerating because she's down on me." In fact, any strong emotion from you at this point is likely to harden the position of the other person.

6. Concentrate on "I" messages. Emphasize the effects of his behavior on you by starting your sentences with "I"—for example, "I felt very much alone when you yelled at me and slammed the door."

7. Don't be drawn into an argument. Don't offer a reply if the person disputes your facts or throws counteraccusations at you. It's good to have an "escape route" planned, such as a trip to the supermarket, so you don't have to continue the discussion unduly. Give the other person a chance to think about what you said.

8. Mention any promises he made as if you expect him to remember and keep them: "Oh, don't forget you said you'd take all the kids fishing today" or "How nice of you to offer to install your mother's new roof."

9. You can suggest AA or professional counseling, but don't push for it often. Then, if he agrees, let him make the phone call if possible.

10. Confrontation can be nonverbal. If you find a hidden bottle by accident, put it out in the open. This neutralizes the attraction to "forbidden fruit" and lets the other person know he's not fooling anyone.

11. Praise him, too. Be as free with compliments as you are with confrontation, or more so. Look for something you can truthfully praise, and slip it into casual conversation. If you've gotten out of the habit of doing this, make a point of doing it once a day for the next week. You don't want all your messages to be negative ones.

12. Don't interfere with confrontations by others. Don't be a "big

brother" or "big sister" and jump in to defend your loved one when the drinking behavior causes a conflict with someone else. You may be surprised to catch yourself doing this. Your loyalty is a good trait, but don't misuse it by defending the disease. Such encounters are a natural consequence of the drinking, and it is better to let them take their course. It's healthy for the drinker to face the consequences of his or her own behavior.

How Not to Confront

1. Don't defend or explain any changes you are making. A short, simple statement is enough: "I need all the grocery money for food and cleaning products. From now on, I won't buy beer. If you want it, you'll have to buy it yourself." At the same time, there is no need to analyze your whole decision-making process for him. Let the other person wonder about what is going on in your head. In the same way, don't go into detail about what was said at your Al-Anon meeting or counseling session.

2. Don't try to be the other person's therapist. It's a waste of time to carry on long, late-night, "meaningful" talks about philosophy with a drinker. If you enjoy it, fine. But don't take the "insights" you gain too seriously. And by all means don't try to come up with deep, psychological reasons for the drinking—it only encourages denial.

3. Don't ask why. To ask the alcoholic why he drinks or why he did certain things is to invite excuses and rationalizations. If you are trying to check out facts, ask "what" rather than "why," but even then don't expect the facts to be straight.

4. Don't get involved in disputes about how much he drank or whether he was drunk. You can't win unless you're prepared to do a blood test. Concentrate on the facts you observed for yourself. You can end such a discussion by saying, "Okay, if you had three beers, I guess that's more than you can handle, because you were swerving all over the road."

5. Don't pour out bottles, whether hidden or kept openly. An alcoholic will just find a way to replace them and is sure to rebel

against your attempt to control him or her. And don't play mind games such as searching for hidden bottles or marking bottles.

6. Don't make ultimatums unless you really will follow through. An ultimatum is a strong confrontation that states what the consequences will be if certain conditions are not met. For example, "If I even see you with a drink again, I'm moving out." "If you're not home by seven, I'll go without you." "If you take that child out on the road now, I'll call the police and report you as a drunken driver."

There are times when ultimatums are necessary, but don't overuse or misuse them. First, don't give one unless you are doing it for your own sake (or for a child's sake) and will need to follow through for your own peace of mind. And don't put yourself on the spot by saying you'll do something you aren't prepared to do. But if you do give an ultimatum, don't back down.

Guided Intervention: The Big One

Jesus said, "If your brother sins against you, go and show him his fault, just between the two of you. If he listens to you, you have won your brother over. But if he will not listen, take one or two others along, so that every matter may be established by the testimony of two or three witnesses. If he refuses to listen to them, tell it to the church" (Matt. 18:15–17).

Guided intervention, a technique currently popular among alcoholism counselors, works quite a bit like what Jesus said here. If an alcoholic refuses to listen to the individual confrontations that come his way, he is treated to a carefully planned, "surprise" group confrontation by several of the most important people in his life.

The group can include some combination of the drinker's spouse, children, doctor, minister, relatives, employer, co-workers, and best friend. Participants are chosen for their ability to bring off the confrontation without being judgmental or overly vulnerable; young children should not necessarily be left out, as they can be very effective. The group prepares and rehearses with a professional counselor, who will also be present at the intervention.

When the time comes for the confrontation, each group member in turn speaks to the alcoholic, giving three or four colorful, specific, recent examples of the drinker's behavior that hurt that person. Then following such a confrontation, the alcoholic is asked to enter a treatment program for which arrangements have already been made.

Participants should also tell the alcoholic about any consequences that will occur if he or she refuses treatment. Will she lose her job? Will there be a marital separation, or will a child leave home? Will an old friend decide not to see him anymore? These things should be carefully thought out ahead of time.

Guided intervention is said to have a surprisingly high success rate. Even drinkers who don't immediately accept treatment often change their minds in a day or two. But if that doesn't happen, the intervention shouldn't be considered a failure. It can be a healing and unifying experience for the family because they are freed from the burden of denial—truth has prevailed.

Confrontation is scary. It's frightening to bring hidden feelings out into the open and put them into words. I know. But I believe the benefits outweigh the risks. Speaking the truth in love is tremendously liberating: it will always give you greater inner peace and serenity. Then, too, your loved one's response may be better than you expect. So start in a small way—but do start. The ancient wisdom writer expressed it well: "A truthful witness saves lives" (Prov. 14:25).

For Further Reflection

On confrontation, read Proverbs 12:18; 24:23–26; 27:5–6; Ecclesiastes 3:7; John 8:3–11; Ephesians 4:25; and James 5:19–20.

Part 3   Through Fear
to Faith

---

8 *Be of Good Courage*

Have I not commanded you? Be strong and courageous. Do not be terrified; do
not be discouraged, for the Lord your God will be with you wherever you go.
JOSHUA 1:9

The Lord told Joshua not once, but three times, to be strong and
courageous as he was preparing for a series of tough battles. Joshua
had already shown himself to be exceptionally brave, but the Lord
knows that even the most confident of us tend to start trembling when
the going gets tough. God's Word is for us, too. The spiritual warfare
of living with alcoholism is enough to wear down anyone's fortitude
after a while.

How many of the following fears have been yours?

1. That your loved one who drinks might die from it or commit
   suicide or leave you
2. That you might lose your home or go bankrupt
3. That the alcoholic will embarrass or disgrace you
4. That others will think less of you because you let someone treat
   you so shabbily
5. That if you try to break free and live a happier life, you will "pay
   for it"
6. That the alcoholic, in a rage, might hurt you or a child
7. That the general, paralyzing anxiety you feel from time to time
   means you are going crazy
8. That you will ruin your health through nervousness and worry
9. That something terrible will happen to the alcoholic if you quit
   rescuing him or her from the consequences of drinking

The first step in getting a handle on your fear is to admit that you have it. If you can identify with one or more of the statements above, welcome to the club—it has a very large membership.

If you do struggle sometimes with fear, anxiety, and worry, be sure to remind yourself—as I do—that courage is not the absence of fear but the wise handling of fear.

Here are some tips for coping that have helped me and others:

1. Take violence seriously. If you or your children are in any real physical danger, remove yourself and them to a safe place as soon as possible. Read the chapters in this book on abuse before going any further. Taking steps to protect yourself doesn't imply personal failure or a lack of trust in God.

2. Turn it over to God. Confess you fear to the Lord as often as you need to, and ask for his help. As you do so, let your feelings of free-floating anxiety come to the surface and wash over you like a crashing wave; don't try to hide from it. Experience the anxiety fully; it may make you shudder, but it won't hurt you. Then say something like this: "Lord, you see what kind of feeling I'm dealing with today. Please remove it from me now and help me to find out where these feelings are coming from and to eliminate the causes."

No, your heavenly Father will not get tired of hearing from you. He wants to help you deal with this and anything else that keeps you from walking fully in his light.

3. Think through your fear. One thing that God will then lead you to do is to cut your fears down to size by examining them completely. Ask yourself, "What is the worst that could happen?"

For example, if you are afraid of going broke and losing your home, you can imagine begging for bread from your former neighbors and sleeping in their toolsheds. Take your scenario to the most ridiculous extreme you can think of. It might make you laugh. Then again, some things will be too grim to laugh at, such as the idea of your loved ones dying. Read the twelfth chapter of Luke, and claim the Lord's promise that he will take care of you no matter what, if you depend on him. In this process you have to give up some of your expectations, but you can trust God to take care of you.

When you have answers for all those pesky "what-ifs," you won't have to dwell on them so much anymore. Your life can only be lived one day at a time, and fears about tomorrow take away from your focus on today. You won't need to picture these "worst-case scenarios" very often, but when you do, remember that that's what they are. They aren't what's going to happen, they're only the worst that could possibly happen.

4. Take action. Sometimes we think we need to have positive feelings first, then do positive things. This is the natural, worldly way to look at it, but God's way is the reverse. We often need to step out in faith—it may feel like "blind" faith, but that's okay—and do some physical thing before God steps in and helps us get the result we want. Good feelings are the eventual result, not the cause or motivation. If Joshua had stayed on the hill overlooking the Promised Land, he could have wallowed there in fear all his life.

Several years ago, an article in a secular magazine for women told of a woman who got through a difficult time in her marriage by "acting as if" she loved her husband. Eventually, not immediately, her love for him returned.

In the same way, you can "act as if" you are not afraid of your alcoholic loved one, of anything he might do, or anything that might happen to him. When you "act as if" you expect that person to take on normal responsibilities, it's more likely—not guaranteed, just more likely—that it will happen.

"Acting as if" can take as many different forms as you have fears. You can "act as if" you hope for your loved one's recovery by praying for her daily, even when she seems to be beyond even the help of God. You can go to bed calmly at your usual time, "acting as if" the missing drinker's whereabouts don't cause you much concern.

5. Don't display fear to the alcoholic. This suggestion is like the last one, because you're going to act as if none of the alcoholic's threats or manipulations affect you in any way. For example, if your alcoholic spouse hints that he'll leave you, don't indicate that you can't get along without him. Or if he says he'll kill himself—wanting you to hover over him—be careful to show no strong reaction. You might say something like, "That would be too bad, but it's your

decision. I can't force you to live. Your life is valuable to me, but it's in your own hands."

Even if the alcoholic threatens your life, it is possible to keep your verbal response calm and neutral. This is not to say that you should take any kind of threat casually. But in any kind of verbal attack, your confident attitude will increase the drinker's respect for you, and threats will grow less frequent. A whipped-dog response on your part just invites more of the same abuse.

"Acting as if" is not being phony or denying reality. You are changing your reality, that's all. Threats are sick, pathetic behavior, and you don't want to motivate the alcoholic to continue to dump verbal garbage on you.

6. Keep busy. Fear is less likely to overtake you when you are engaged in some constructive activity that occupies both your body and your mind. Don't give worry much room in your life. The superwoman described in Proverbs 31:10–31 almost seems too good to be true, but as we read those verses, there's one thing that stands out clearly—she worked too hard to have time to worry.

One evening Brenda decided to clean out, dust, and rearrange her bookcases rather than stew and fret about where her drinking husband was. When Doug came in hours later, she found herself thinking, "Oh, is he home already?"

7. Drain away tension with exercise. Fear, worry, and anxiety build up physical tension in the body. If not released, the tension can make you physically ill. Aerobic exercise is the best kind of tension relief because it accelerates the heartbeat. You can choose any one or more beneficial exercises such as brisk walking, jogging, swimming, cross-country skiing, an exercise or dance class, bicycling, singles tennis, or others. The important thing is to exercise three to five times a week for at least half an hour. But always check with your doctor.

You may also want to drain tension by learning some form of Christian meditation, or conscious relaxation, such as you might learn in a class for prepared childbirth.

8. Watch your diet. Severe panic attacks call for the attention of a doctor. They are sometimes related to the ups and downs of blood sugar—try eliminating sugar and caffeine and eating a nourishing, well-balanced diet.

Dig Out the Roots of Fear

Once you start turning your fears over to God, he may point out errors in your thought life that have caused you to become afraid needlessly. Some of these are listed here.

Thinking It's Up to You to Run the World

Anxiety often comes from taking upon yourself emotional responsibilities that properly belong to God or to others. Remember, you cannot control the actions of others and will never be answerable to God for what anyone else does. It's the same old story—picking up someone else's reins. If you think you *have to do* what you *can't do*, no wonder you feel a little crazy sometimes. Spouses of alcoholics tend to think this way a lot—not only about the alcoholic, but about the world in general. "Let go and let God," as the Al-Anon slogan says.

Overcommitment

Your overdeveloped sense of responsibility may have caused you to take on more jobs than you have the time or resources to do well. Anxiety can come from trying to squeeze twenty-five hours of work into a sixteen-hour waking day. Is this the way you are? How many hats are you wearing: worker, home maintenance, parent, gardener, spouse, volunteer worker, church leader, caretaker of older relatives, foster parent, pet owner, counselor to troubled friends? Stop now and ask God which hats you can hang up for a while. There is just no way you can do it all!

Misdirected Love

The Bible says "perfect love drives out fear" (1 John 4:18). I don't understand exactly how that works, but I think it has to do partly with the fact that perfect love lets go, trusts God, and doesn't try to control anyone else.

Perfect love doesn't demand that my loved one do things *my* way. We can learn this from Jesus. He told—and showed—his listeners how to live abundantly, but he never tried to make them do it right. He wept for them and sacrificed for them (and us) but never did for other people what they were able to do for themselves.

Living More Than One Day at a Time

Regrets about the past and worry about the future cause more unnecessary anguish than almost anything else on earth. "One day at a time" is a slogan central to the philosophy of AA and Al-Anon, but they did not originate the concept. It was Jesus who said, "Therefore do not worry about tomorrow, for tomorrow will worry about itself. Each day has enough trouble of its own" (Matt. 6:34). This does not exclude planning for the future, since the Savior also said to "count the cost" of what we plan to do (Luke 14:28–30). Instead, it is an injunction against stewing about future calamities that may or may not ever happen.

That kind of worrying is called "projecting." I'm sure you've heard about crying over spilt milk; projecting is crying over milk that is still sitting in the pail but might be spilled. A wise person once said, "If you see ten troubles coming down the road, nine of them will hit the ditch before they ever get to you." That is so true. How many things have you worried about that never happened? And, as for those worries that did come true, was your advance worrying of any help?

The only day that truly exists is today. It's up to us to accept this gift with joy and do the best we can with it. And as for the past, it can't be called back or changed. When you have regrets, remind yourself that God's forgiveness is real and permanent. Make amends to anyone you've hurt, if possible, and then put it behind you. Today is the one that counts.

People Pleasing

The fear of "what people will think" is one that often leads to denial of alcoholism. Yet we don't need the approval of people; God is the One who counts. So there's no need to play up to people or put on a show for them.

If you do what is right, your reputation will take care of itself. But if you are sometimes misunderstood, remember God's promise that "an undeserved curse does not come to rest" (Prov. 26:2).

Misunderstanding God

How can God help us conquer fear if we are admonished throughout the Bible to "fear God"? In the first place, it is important we understand that the word *fear* means "to have awe or reverence." In some modern-language versions of the Bible, it is translated "honor" or "respect." This kind of godly fear is not only appropriate, it can even help insulate us against ordinary human fears. If we have the proper awe and reverence for the power of the heavenly Father, and also experience his love, we will have no greater desire than to trust him with full control over our lives. And then, what will be left for us to fear? The psalmist understood this when he said, "When I am afraid, I will trust in you. In God, whose word I praise, in God I trust; I will not be afraid. What can mortal man do to me?" (Ps. 56:3–4).

For Further Reflection

On fear, read Psalms 16; 23; 27; 91; 112; Proverbs 3:5–6; 10:24; 29:25; Isaiah 41:10–13; Luke 12:1–34; Romans 8:15–39; 2 Timothy 1:7; Hebrews 2:14–15; and 1 John 4:16–18.

On living one day at a time, read Exodus 16:1–31; 1 Kings 17:7–16; Psalms 68:19; 90:12; 118:24; Proverbs 27:1; Matthew 6:11, 25–34; 11:28–30; James 4:13–15; and 2 Peter 3:8–13.

9 *Keeping the Faith*

I have been crucified with Christ and I no longer live, but Christ lives in me.
The life I live in the body, I live by faith in the Son of God, who loved me and
gave himself for me.   GALATIANS 2:20

Possibly by now you are saying, "Okay, I won't be guilty of denial, and I know I've got to make some changes in my life. But it's so hard, because I'm afraid and confused. I feel alone, and it's easy to slip back into old ways."

Yes, it is too hard for us alone, but there is help. You cannot eliminate any negative habit or pattern in your life without substituting something positive for it. Otherwise, you just leave a large "hole" in your life and remain vulnerable to the same old problems. Faith in the living God is what we all need to plug that hole. Faith is the opposite of fear, and it can occupy the spiritual space that your fear takes up now.

What is this faith? And how can we get it and keep it while still living with the chaos and uncertainty that alcoholism brings?

Faith is the belief that God is telling the truth when he says he will always be with us (Matt. 28:20) and that we don't have to go through life totally under own own power. Faith is our confidence that God always keeps his promises. It is trusting the heavenly Father enough to turn ourselves, our loved ones, and everything we care about over to him.

The Bible calls faith a gift of the Spirit (1 Cor. 12:9), a shield (Eph. 6:16), and a grafting of our branches into a holy Root (Rom. 11: 17–20).

To have authentic faith, we must take eternal life into account (Titus 1:2) because God looks at things with a much longer perspective than we do. We not only live for now but for that future time. In the words of the author of that marvelous "faith chapter" (Hebrews 11), "faith is being sure of what we hope for and certain of what we do not see" (verse 1).

What a relief it is to know that God's faithfulness to us doesn't depend upon our perfection. The life of David as we trace it through his story in 2 Samuel certainly proves that point. In spite of his gross lapses into sin, when he repented, God was faithful in forgiveness. In recording David's dying words, the writer refers to him as "the man exalted by the Most High, the man anointed by the God of Jacob" (2 Sam. 23:1). Yes, our faith is strengthened as we reflect on God's faithfulness.

But faith doesn't just emerge full-blown out of nowhere; it is built up by degrees, step by step. The more knowledge of God's Word we have, the more faith we will have. Then, too, our faith is strengthened as we share what we know with others. You will find it helpful to follow a daily program of Bible reading. And it may help to join a Bible study group and attend an adult Sunday school class. As you become increasingly active in your search for truth, your faith will be strengthened, and you will find it easier to share what you have learned with others.

And, as much as we might hope otherwise, even our problems test and try our faith and make it stronger, if we respond to them correctly (James 1:3–7; 1 Peter 1:6–7). After all, if our faith were never put to the test, it wouldn't mean much. Each problem we face, including those in a difficult marriage or family relationship, should be considered an opportunity for growth and a chance to show the Lord that our love for him is unconditional and cannot be shaken.

How You Can Have It

Wouldn't you like to have the peace and happiness that faith can give you here and now? This is immediately possible, for as we read our Bibles we learn that through Christ's death and resurrection, his salvation is ours as a free gift. All we have to do is accept it. If you have never done so, you can accept Jesus' sacrifice on your behalf right now by saying a simple prayer like this: "Lord Jesus, I know I am a sinner. Thank you for dying on that cross to save me from my sins. I accept your gift of eternal life. Please come into my life, take charge of it, and show me how I can live it for you. Amen."

Possibly, though, you committed your life to Christ long ago but haven't been living like a Christian. If so, now is the best time to rededicate yourself to the Lord. (No matter what you have done, there is no end to his forgiveness.) In taking this step you will find it helpful to read chapters 3 through 8 of the book of Romans.

What Faith Does for You

In addition to overcoming your fears, you will find that your faith in God helps you to live an authentic spiritual life, using your spiritual gifts—special abilities and strengths you didn't have on your own that enable you to help and encourage others.

You will discover that faith is strengthened through use, like a muscle built up by exercise. When your faith is strong and mature, no situation can knock you down for long. You will be always conscious of God's nearness, and his ability to protect you from evil (2 Thess. 3:3). The greatest power in the universe is always with you and in you. The writer of 1 John gave us this promise: "The one who is in you is greater than the one who is in the world" (4:4).

How Faith is Misused

It is important, however, to remember that faith is misdirected whenever it is based on anything other than God. For example, your faith is working against you, not for you, if it depends on any of the following:

- Your own ability to "fix" the alcoholism
- "Wishful thinking" that you can ignore the disease
- The ability of a pastor, therapist, or any human being
- A "geographic cure"
- Your trust that the alcoholic will keep his or her promises

Foolish hopes such as these will set you up for repeated disappointment. And eventually, you will react to the crushing blows by forming a shell—becoming hardened. Perhaps you've already learned, as I did, to protect yourself by deadening your feelings in this way. But how much better it is to trust only God and be open to his miracles.

Yes, God can and does work miracles; he has even sometimes raised the dead. This means there is always hope—hope for a miracle. There are times when the Lord needs our faith to work miracles, although I'm not sure why. We learn in Mark 6:1–6 that Jesus was not able to heal in his own hometown because the people there lacked faith in him. To them he was just "the carpenter."

Sometimes, too, there is some practical thing we need to do before a miracle can take place. When the Hebrews under Joshua were ready to cross the Jordan into their Promised Land, priests had to step into the river before the water would stop flowing and the people could cross safely. And there will be times in your life when it will take a step of "blind" faith to get your miracle.

Faith, Hope, and Love

If faith is our belief in the truth, then hope is the basis on which that belief rests. Nowadays we water down our concept of hope until it means something like "wishful thinking," as in "I hope it won't rain." But the biblical concept of hope is much stronger; it is the confident expectancy, or the active looking forward to *what we firmly believe is going to happen*.

Hope, by definition, is for something we do not yet have (Rom. 8:22–25). Hope is a chance to wait patiently, to prove to the Lord the reality of our faith. Hope is patient but never passive. To hope for your alcoholic loved one's recovery is an act of true love, irrespective of the cost.

Now if faith rests on hope, what does hope rest on? It rests on nothing less than the Lord himself, "Christ Jesus our hope" (1 Tim. 1:1). It rests on his identity and integrity; he always keeps his promises.

Love is said to be greater than either hope or faith (1 Cor. 13:13). But in practice, there is little separation among the three. Faith builds up love, and love helps us to put faith into action. Loving someone who cannot love us back in the way we'd like—someone like an alcohol abuser—helps us understand God better. He loves us unconditionally despite our failures and faults. How can we fail to have faith and hope in the face of such love? In the sixth century before Christ the Old Testament prophet caught the spirit of this when he wrote, " 'The glory of this present house will be greater than the glory of the former house,' says the Lord Almighty. 'And in this place I will grant peace,' declares the Lord Almighty." (Hag. 2:9).

For Further Reflection

On building your faith and hope, read Psalms 31:24; 33:12–22; 119:89–90; Proverbs 3:5–6; Matthew 8; 9; Romans 4:18–22; 5:1–8; Ephesians 2:8–9; Hebrews 6:10–11, 19–20; 11; 1 Peter 1; 3:15; and 2 Peter 1:5–9.

10 *Living the Faith*

Pursue righteousness, godliness, faith, love, endurance and gentleness. Fight the good fight of the faith. Take hold of the eternal life to which you were called.   1 TIMOTHY 6:11—12

It seems odd to think of faith as a muscle that has to be exercised regularly, because it is spiritual and not physical. But faith isn't a passive state of being. We don't just sit around and think "faith" to make ourselves feel better. No, when faith is real, it leads to action. Faith becomes faithfulness, or loving action, as naturally as the dawn flows into the day, and we become more like Jesus as we exercise our faith.

Faith starts with the belief that God loves us and is with us always. Jesus would have died for you if you were the only person in the world he could save. We know this because of the story Jesus told of the shepherd and the one lost sheep (Luke 15:3—7). Because this is true, it follows that he wants us to have a decent and productive life filled with dignity, sanity, and healthy, loving relationships. He wants good things for us just as we do for our own children (Matt. 7:7—11).

Faithful people ("full of faith") are godly, loving, humble, open in sharing their beliefs, able to handle responsibility, and willing to serve others. They all serve in different ways because of their unique gifts and abilities. And as you grow spiritually, you will become more faithful and will serve in your own special way.

The book of James, though short, has a great deal to teach us about the way faith expresses itself in action. Above all, it assures us that "faith without deeds is dead" (2:26) and urges us to rejoice in our trials, to love others without prejudice, to tame our tongues, and to do good works. "I will show you my faith by what I do" (2:18).

Good Works

What are good works? They are the things we do that show love to others and meet their needs, whether the needs are physical, spiritual, or emotional. It doesn't necessarily mean giving others everything they want. If your toddler wants to meander into heavy traffic, do you let him do it just because he wants to and is having fun? Of course not! That wouldn't be very loving and it certainly wouldn't be very consistent with the baby's needs.

The love involved in good works sometimes has to be tough love, or love that is motivated by the other person's highest and best good, regardless of what he or she wants at the moment. I firmly believe that tough love, when the motive is right, is a good work. When you enable a person dependent on drugs or alcohol to go right on depending, you are not doing a good work, because you are not considering his or her best interests. (You *enable* when you do anything that makes it easier for the drinker to continue drinking.) It is true, of course, when you refuse to be an enabler, he or she won't be particularly happy about it for a time, but you will be acting out of the very highest form of love.

Suppose that Michelle's husband, who is already quite drunk, asks her to go out and buy him another bottle. On the surface, at first, it might seem like a good work—a good idea—to do what he asks. "After all," she reasons, "that way I can keep an intoxicated driver off the road. And putting myself out to do him a favor shows that I care about him."

But is Michelle really doing her husband a favor? If she consents, here are the results: a few more dollars are spent on liquor; he gets drunker; he is aware that he has asserted an unfair kind of power over Michelle by causing her to go against her own principles; and he loses a little of the respect he has for her.

At such times Michelle needs to examine her motives a little more closely. Is she really making this unscheduled late-night trip out of love, or is it because she wants to avoid the temper tantrum her husband is going to pull if she says no? Could she also be looking for a few extra "moral brownie points" toward her martyr complex?

To use a different sort of example: Ron has decided that a guided intervention is best for his family, and he's in the planning stages. He suffers an agony of guilt because what he is planning doesn't feel very loving at gut level. (Sometimes our gut feelings are wrong.) After all, he is sneaking around behind Tanya's back, planning to say things that will hurt her even though they're the truth, and lining up other friends and relatives to do the same. It doesn't fit with what he's always been taught about a husband's protective role.

Yet look at his motives. He loves Tanya and wants her to recover from the fatal disease of alcoholism. Ron wants to save their marriage and to build a strong family. And although he can't quite *feel* it yet, he knows he is displaying a high form of love, as well as commitment to his wife's best interests.

It may seem paradoxical, also, that our faith requires that we be willing to surrender our loved ones completely if necessary, as Abraham was willing to sacrifice Isaac in obedience to God's instructions (Gen. 22:1–18). For example, Michelle has to "let go" enough to risk her husband's displeasure by not going as he asks. And Ron has to cope with his fear that the intervention will make Tanya so furious that she'll leave him. Love has its risks. We have to be able to pray, "Father, I want that special person healed, and I want us to be happy together. But whatever you decide, no matter what, it's okay with me."

This kind of faith is what it takes for a miracle to happen. There are many people alive today who have seen their loved ones healed and delivered from all sorts of "hopeless" conditions after praying that way. Even if there is some reason why our desire can't be granted, our prayer strengthens our relationship with our Father.

Two Warnings

Two warnings come to mind at this point. One has to do with the currently popular teaching called the "prosperity doctrine." According to advocates of this idea, if your faith is strong enough, you should be able to get anything you want automatically—healing, miracles, wealth, or whatever. According to this theory, only a lack of faith can keep your prayers from producing spectacular results. But to accept this false idea is to treat God like some kind of giant vending machine in the sky! We are to conform to *his* will, not the other way around.

Sometimes God wants us to wait and lean on him more. There are times when he may say no, although our pain hurts him, because of some larger plan he has for us. God sees beyond the immediate moment.

The other possible danger lies in letting our "head knowledge" get too far ahead of our ability to put what we believe into action. There are times when we want to soak up all the knowledge we can from Scripture, sermons, books, tapes, seminars, and other sources. But doing it without putting into practice what we already know can lead to discouragement. It's like trying to lose weight by reading lots of diet books (my former practice).

It is important that we balance our learning with *doing*. This means that when you come across a biblical teaching that looks as if it may be helpful, make plans right away to apply that idea to your own real life situations. Our best help for daily guidance comes through reading God's Word—the Bible—and praying. The Holy Spirit will guide us into the truth.

How Should We Pray

The importance of prayer as an exercise of faith cannot be overestimated. Along with your other prayers, you should pray especially for your alcoholic loved one every day. Sometimes it will be the only constructive thing you can do.

Choose a daily quiet time when you can be alone and undistracted. Early morning is often good, or naptime if you have small children. In my experience, bedtime is not good because sleep comes too easily. But it can be a good time to touch your sleeping spouse and pray for him or her. In addition, use odd moments for prayer during the day—while driving, doing physical work or exercise, in line at the supermarket, or when waiting for someone. And at times you may find it helpful to pray with a partner, especially someone more mature in the faith.

Here are suggestions on what to pray for and how to do it:

1. Start with praise and thanksgiving. Praise God for who he is and for all he has done for you. Praise him for protection, personal growth, material things, health, family, friends, and small everyday pleasures.

2. Confess your sins and ask forgiveness. Accept God's ready forgiveness. Ask him to bring to mind any wrongdoing you may not be aware of, as well as any amends you need to make to anyone. (Amends are anything you can do to help make up for the hurt you have caused another; see Matt. 5:23–24). Unconfessed sin is a barrier between you and God.

3. If you want to be forgiven, you in turn have to forgive anyone who has hurt you, including your alcoholic loved one. Ask for enough faith to be able to forgive (see Matt. 6:12 and Luke 17:3–5).

4. Now, and only now, are you ready to start asking favors. It's appropriate to ask for healing for a loved one on the basis of your own faith, not necessarily his. (See Matt. 8:5–13 for an example.) Rely on the Holy Spirit to guide you in what you ask for. You don't always have to be saying words when you pray (Rom. 8:26–27); sometimes you'll be listening. Answers will come through the Spirit, usually as distinct impressions on your mind rather than as an audible voice.

5. Whatever you ask for, ask "in the name of Jesus Christ the Lord" (see John 16:22–27). Jesus intercedes with God the Father on our behalf and wants us to ask for good things in his name.

6. It is essential to ask with the right motives—for the glory of God and the enhancement of his reputation on earth. The writer of the book of James tells us that we won't get an answer if our purpose in asking is for our own selfish pleasure (4:3).

Of course, there is nothing wrong with asking for a person or a marriage to be healed. Spiritual growth in a person is always gratifying to God. Your motives make a real but subtle difference.

7. Pray that the strongholds of Satan will be torn down in your alcoholic's life, even in his thought life (2 Cor. 10:3–5).

8. If your alcoholic has never accepted Jesus as Lord and Savior, make that a primary focus of your prayer. Other good things will follow from that. Pray that all the little spiritual "seeds" that you and others have planted will sprout and grow.

9. Pray for more love for your alcoholic loved one and for appreciation of his or her better qualities. If your love is not strong, read John 15:9–17, and ask for God's love to abide in you.

10. Pray with faith, knowing that "all things are possible with God" (Mark 10:27). And pray that your faith will be increased day by day.

11. Pray boldly and don't be afraid to claim the promises of God for your situation. Claim the promises in God's Word. There are hundreds of such promises; a good one to start with is found in Luke 11:9.

12. Pray persistently. Sometimes we may feel we are "nagging God" when we keep asking for certain things over and over again. But we read in Luke 18:1–8 that God wants us to keep asking. It's not that he needs to be convinced of what's right; he just wants to know how serious we are.

In God's wisdom, the Almighty wants us to help accomplish his plan here on earth through prayer and good works. And in fulfilling his purposes for us we will grow spiritually as we strive with his help to defeat the Enemy. Jesus asks in Luke 18:8, "when the Son of Man comes, will he find faith on the earth?" It is important that we do our part to make sure he does!

For Further Reflection

On faith and faithfulness, read Proverbs 3:3–8; Matthew 8:5–13; 25:14–30; Luke 8:40–56; 1 Thessalonians 5:23–24; and James 1:2–8, 22–27; 2:14–26.

On God's promises, read Psalm 37 and Matthew 5:3–12; 7:7–12; 11:28–30.

On prayer, read Matthew 6:5–15; Mark 11:22–25; Luke 6:27–28; 1 Thessalonians 5:16–18; James 5:13–18; and Revelation 5:8.

Part 4 Through Obsession
to Detachment

11 *Let Go and Find Peace*

Great peace have they who love your law, and nothing can make them
stumble.
                                                                PSALM 119:165

Do you "stumble" over references like the one above in Psalm 119
that speak of the peace of God? "How can I have peace," you wonder,
"when my life is inextricably bound up with that of someone who
wants nothing to do with peace? I'm always picking up the pieces
after some crisis."

Yes, the daily, petty irritations of living with an alcoholic can seem
like the slow drip, drip, drip of some kind of torture. Then when the
big blowouts come, you have no reserves of emotional strength and so
are completely drained. And possibly you feel unhappy and trapped
even though you can still find things to love about your drinking
loved one. Could it be that your preoccupation with him or her
borders on obsession?

Consider the lyrics of the popular love songs we have heard all of
our lives. They say things like, "Oh baby, I can't live without you. I
think of you all day long. I'm nothing without you, and if you were to
leave me, I'd just curl up and die." This attitude elevates romantic
love to a form of idolatry, and seems actually to invite cruel treatment. Yet, this is the way our culture teaches us to think.

Well, here's the good news: the hold your alcoholic loved one has
over your mind and emotions is potentially under your control. You
can, and must, cut it down to a more manageable size, and the process
of doing this is called detachment.

Now, detachment doesn't mean that you stop caring about your
loved one. Instead, it means that you hold your emotions back from

overinvolvement. You give him or her the proper amount of time and attention, but not a lot more.

If you are the wife of an alcoholic, call to mind some woman you know in a good, "normal" marriage. (If your alcoholic is your grown child, think of some parents of "normal" kids, and so on.) Then ask yourself if these "normal" people appear to spend all their time worrying about their loved ones and what they're going to do. Do they appear to be obsessed about the meaning of every little action and comment? No, of course not! They live their own lives, and you can too!

"That's easy to say," you may be thinking, "because these normal people are more secure in their relationships. They haven't been put through the wringer the way I have." True; but you too can live more normally. Affirm this truth every day.

How Obsession Develops

The manipulations and power games that are part of alcoholism are designed to keep the thoughts and energies of loved ones confused, focused exclusively on the drinker, and dedicated to enabling the drinking.

The abuser of alcohol typically uses anger and intimidation to keep the spouse and other family members in line. These ploys are especially effective with wives—although they are successfully used on husbands, parents, and children of drinkers as well—because the wife is culturally conditioned to want to please her husband. She tries to do whatever her husband wants and to avoid the angry outbursts of verbal (even physical) abuse that come when he is displeased. But because his desires are unpredictable, it becomes more and more difficult to please him. Family members keep trying, though, believing, hoping that "If only I could meet his needs perfectly, maybe he wouldn't drink."

Then, too, the alcoholic plays on the family's guilt and fear. Eventually the unwritten rule of the family becomes "Daddy's every whim is our law." Everything revolves around the moods of the drinker; no one can make plans, because they may have to be changed at the last minute. At the same time the alcoholic's attitude becomes "I'll do whatever I want, and you'll do whatever I want, too."

When the husband and father is the alcoholic, this domination goes far beyond what God intended for him as the spiritual head of the home. Loving, sacrificial, Christ-like leadership is God's standard for a husband—not a petty tyranny that confuses the husband with God himself.

Children with an alcoholic parent either keep trying to be perfect or they give up and withdraw from family relationships, becoming "invisible." Another response of children is to rebel, perhaps taking on drinking, drugs, and delinquent behavior themselves.

Guilt and fear can lead one to ridiculous extremes in trying to please a drinker. Connie's husband told her he drank because there was never good food on the table. In response to that accusation Connie resolved to always have a good meal ready whenever Dave was hungry.

Like a petty tyrant Dave set the time when he wanted his dinner. And the menu had to be adjusted to fit his moods. If a roast was half cooked and Dave wanted pork chops—goodbye roast. Or if he decided he'd rather eat out at a restaurant, they'd leave dinner in the oven.

Do you think this "demand feeding system" helped Dave to drink any less than before? Hardly. There was never any shortage of reasons why he needed a drink.

This type of husband does whatever he can to make his wife feel insecure. He often flirts openly with other women and threatens during an argument to walk out and not come back. Then, too, this kind of husband plays up his wife's faults in an effort to make her feel small and inadequate. By contrast, a "normal" husband wants his wife to feel beautiful, secure, and loved.

Sometimes, though, the domineering alcoholic husband will unpredictably treat his wife like a queen for no apparent reason. He buys her an expensive gift and praises her, saying, "You're wonderful to put up with me the way you do." This is even more addicting to her, of course. "He really does love and appreciate me," she thinks. But deep down, it doesn't satisfy. She wants to be treated decently on a regular basis and loved for who she is, not for what she "puts up with."

This sort of thing happens when the drinker is the dominant personality in the family. On the other hand, sometimes the alcoholic is the marital partner with the more gentle temperament; in that case the dynamics are different, although not any healthier. The alcoholic just becomes sneakier about the drinking. Many a quiet alcoholic housewife keeps liquor in bottles that look like a household cleaner or medicine. And she cuts down on other expenses to disguise the amount spent on alcohol.

When the drinker is a mild-mannered man, the wife may similarly feel that she is in sole charge of the family, although she is just as obsessed with her husband's comings and goings as her meeker counterpart. She is also just as likely to take over his responsibilities. Consequently, when he gets drunk or she discovers his hidden bottles, he takes on the air of a "bad boy" rebelling against a strict mother. And her anger and scolding absolve him of his guilt feelings.

In almost all alcoholic families, there is a warped sense of who is responsible for what. Danny gives Margaret his entire paycheck every week. She, the sober one, is supposed to pay the bills and hide the rest of the money so that he can't go out drinking. If he finds the cash and blows it, that is her fault, they both think, for not hiding it well enough.

Serenity Through Letting Go

Even as faith and hope are antidotes to fear, they should also dispell any ideas we might have that we can control another person's destiny.

There is powerful truth in the prayer-petition "God grant me the serenity to accept the things I cannot change." One of the primary things you can't change is your alcoholic's freedom of choice. You cannot have a healthy relationship without accepting the fact of the other person's free will. Even child rearing is a process of gradually releasing control over the child's life and decisions. If we cannot—and should not—dominate the lives of even our older teenagers, how much less can we expect to make choices for another adult?

The other side of the coin is that if we can't make decisions for another person, neither can we be held accountable for his or her actions. It is obvious this truth isn't understood when we hear a person say, "Don is in rough shape. You just must do something about him!" But true acceptance means knowing in your heart where your responsibility begins and ends—what you can and can't do. When you accept, you can see things as they are.

Not only are we to accept the things that cannot be changed, but as the prayer urges, we are to have the "courage to change the things we can." What you can change is your own reaction to your circumstances. You are responsible for your own life, including your thought life. Your happiness doesn't depend on your spouse or any other person; you aren't being disloyal if you reach out for a little happiness of your own. You don't have to wallow in your alcoholic's misery.

The prayer concludes with this significant petition for "wisdom to know the difference." If letting go boils down to "minding your own business," it takes special insight to determine what is your business. Letting go doesn't mean just giving up in apathy and defeat. Rather, it means taking action only after we have thought through a problem, asked God for guidance, and determined what is the best and most loving thing to do. God wants us to use the brains, free will, and wisdom he give us.

How to Detach

"Detachment" means disengaging your emotional overinvolvement with your alcoholic and the situations he or she gets you into. It means not becoming obsessed, and it means making your own decisions calmly. Of course, it's one thing to talk about detachment and quite another to practice it in the heat of a crisis—when the drinker has wrecked the car, failed to show up for an important event, or spent two straight hours telling you how worthless you are.

At such times it will help to get alone even for a minute or two and repeat to yourself the Serenity Prayer, a favorite hymn or Bible verse, or an Al-Anon slogan such as "Let go and let God," "Easy does it," "First things first," or "One day (hour, minute) at a time."

Try to respond calmly even when the alcoholic and others are angry or upset. Don't let anyone coerce you into making a decision you're not ready to make. If someone is trying to manipulate or bully you into something, say, "I'm not ready to talk about that right now. I'll get back to you when I've had a little more time to think."

If verbal abuse is getting you upset, remember to mentally label it for what it is: "This is the alcohol talking. I won't take it personally."

Or, take some mental "time out" to admire something in your immediate surroundings that is beautiful: the shape of a baby's head, a single flower, the pattern of clouds in the sky. No matter where you are, there is beauty.

Above all stop keeping track of your drinker's consumption of alcohol. Counting his drinks and looking for hidden bottles are acts that help keep you obsessed. Remember, he isn't "getting away with it" if there are drinks you don't know about. Consequences have a way of showing up on their own.

However, detachment doesn't mean maintaining a grim silence. There are times to be quiet and times to confront. Detachment is just a calm state of mind that helps you decide wisely which is which.

Once when I was waiting outside a tavern for my husband—a situation that would sometimes make me angry and resentful—I just put my head back, looked up through the windshield, and watched the sunlight filtering through a thick screen of maple leaves. The play of light and the various shades of green were so beautiful, they truly made me forget to feel bad. When someone came out to ask me to "join the fun," I replied that I was happy where I was. And it was true.

Remember, though, that you have to give freedom in order to get it. Part of my serenity at that moment came from the knowledge that I could leave anytime I got tired of waiting. My husband could have found another way home. This thought relieved me of any pressure I might have felt to make him come home with me.

Your mind is the key to abundant life. As we read in Philippians 4:8, "Whatever is true, whatever is noble, whatever is right, whatever is pure, whatever is lovely, whatever is admirable—if anything is excellent or praiseworthy—think about such things." Your mind is under your control, and if you choose to think about positive things *most of the time*, you will have happiness and peace. You won't be obsessed with a problem over which you have no direct control.

But God cannot take control of your problems while you are still tightly grasping them. Turn them over to him, and he may come up with solutions you could never have thought of on your own. One thing's for sure—the Lord wants you to have the serenity that comes from letting go of what is not yours. Only then can you think clearly about what, if anything, you need to do. Let go, and accept your serenity as a precious gift from him. Fix your thoughts on these words of Jesus, "Peace I leave with you; my peace I give you. I do not give to you as the world gives. Do not let your hearts be troubled and do not be afraid" (John 14:27).

For Further Reflection

On peace and freedom, read Psalms 85:7–13; 146:7; Proverbs 14:30; Isaiah 26:3; Romans 12:18; 2 Corinthians 3:17; and Galatians 5:22–23.

12 *Let Go of the Consequences*

The soul who sins is the one who will die. The son will not share the guilt of the father, nor will the father share the guilt of the son. The righteousness of the righteous man will be credited to him, and the wickedness of the wicked will be charged against him. EZEKIEL 18:20

Just as each of us makes decisions, we must also take responsibility for what we do and live with the consequences of our actions. If the results are good, we're more likely to make similar decisions in the future. If the consequences are not good—if we are "punished" in some way for what we do—we learn to avoid that kind of behavior in the future. Either way, we learn from our own past conduct. The wisdom writer said it well: "If a man digs a pit, he will fall into it; if a man rolls a stone, it will roll back on him" (Prov. 26:27).

Yes, other Bible verses say that the consequences of sin can remain with a family for three or four generations. This is just something that happens naturally and is not a deliberate punishment inflicted by God. The person committing a wrong act is the only one to be held morally accountable for it, although innocent parties sometimes suffer along with him or her.

This natural order of things becomes distorted in the alcoholic family, as other family members begin to try to assume the drinker's negative consequences and shield the drinker from the pain caused by his or her behavior. But when this happens the drinker doesn't learn anything from the mistakes, doesn't come to realize how harmful his or her actions have been.

By "rescuing" the alcoholic from the consequences of drinking and poor behavior, we actually get in God's way; we interfere with the drinker's relationship with God and help keep his conscience from functioning properly. When others suffer all his pain for him, he has no motivation to change.

So, do we need to "punish" the alcoholic to get him to learn what he is doing wrong? No. All we need to do is step out of the way and let things take their natural course. The important thing is to avoid jumping in and rescuing the alcoholic.

For example suppose that Fred has been out drinking one summer night and he doesn't quite make it into the house but passes out on the front porch. His wife, Janet, could haul him bodily inside, clean him up, and put him to bed. But that isn't something a wife should have to do. If Janet does look after him that way, she is suffering for his decision to get drunk. How about Fred, though? Is *he* inconvenienced or suffering? No—he wakes up warm and dry in his own bed, just as if he'd behaved responsibly. He hasn't learned a thing from his previous night's episode that would keep him from getting drunk again.

On the other hand, suppose Janet lets him spend the night out on the porch sleeping it off. In the morning when Fred comes to, he hurts all over, smells bad, and is self-conscious knowing that his early-rising neighbors have seen him stretched out grotesquely on the porch. Now he has learned what can happen as a result of his picking up that first drink. It is true he may be angry at Janet for not rescuing him, but he has no legitimate gripe with her. It was his actions, not hers, that caused him to sleep on the porch. Although he may accuse her of being cold and heartless, she has actually acted lovingly. She loves him enough to want to help him get well.

What Kind of Love Is Tough Love?

We defined tough love in chapter 10 as love that is motivated by the other person's highest or best good. In practice, tough love often means allowing the loved one to suffer the consequences of wrong actions. You don't take on the other person's punishments. You don't accept unacceptable behavior, but instead you hold him accountable.

Does that sound mean and cold? It isn't. It doesn't involve "giving up" or washing our hands of our alcoholic loved one, and it certainly doesn't mean we no longer care what happens to him or her. Rather, it means we care enough to let go and respect that person's individuality and freedom of choice. Tough love isn't easy; we suffer quite a bit of emotional discomfort in learning to practice it, as we work through the crippling guilt and fear that have kept us in the role of rescuer.

Ironically, the practice of tough love can make the alcoholic begin to want to get well. When the family stops centering around the drinker and constantly taking his pain for him, a kind of pressure builds up in him that may evoke a desire for sobriety. Tough love raises the drinker's self-esteem to a healthier level as he takes on more personal responsibility. Also, when you appear to quit worrying about his health and welfare, he may develop more concern for it himself. At the same time, he will respect you more as you show more self-confidence and stop hovering over him.

In addition, your good feelings about the alcoholic will increase when you develop a healthy amount of detachment. You'll have less reason to resent him or her when you are taking better care of yourself, and you'll be able to better appreciate your loved one's good qualities. Sometimes we hover and rescue because we feel guilty about our resentment of the drinker and are afraid we don't love him or her anymore. But as a more normal balance is restored to your relationship, you'll find the alcoholic actually doing things to try to please you.

Tough love is biblical, godly love. God gave us free will—he takes the risk that we will make bad decisions. He could have made us totally controllable, like robots, but then our love wouldn't mean much to him, would it? In the same way, we must give those we love their freedom even though we risk losing them.

Jesus also "let go" lovingly. Did he prevent the rich young man from walking away? (see Mark 10:17–23). No, the man was allowed to decide for himself and to live with the consequences of his choice. Jesus didn't do for others what they could and should do for themselves. The only reason he died on the cross for us was that we were totally incapable of atoning for our own sins. Even now we read that he "stands at the door and knocks" (Rev. 3:20). He doesn't barge into our lives and take over, although it's a fact that he could manage things better than we do.

Watch your motivation as you practice tough love. You should want the best long-term benefit for your alcoholic loved one—if you just want revenge or to "demand your rights," that isn't love. The difference is subtle but very real. Think about what you would want your loved ones to do if you were the one engaging in self-destructive behavior. Even as you take tough actions, or refuse to engage in rescuing, you can maintain an attitude of forgiveness.

How Does Tough Love Work?

It isn't the purpose of this book to tell you exactly what to do. You are capable of making your own decisions, and you know your situation better than anyone else. Also, you may not be emotionally ready to take a certain action that you believe is right. That's all right; give yourself time. However, here are some things "tough love" has meant to others:

- Let the drinker find his or her own way home at night.
- Refuse to call in sick for a worker who is hung over.
- Stop paying bills that are the alcoholic's responsibility.
- Stop interfering in the drinker's arguments or misunderstandings with other people. Stop apologizing for him, since an apology implies that you are partly responsible.
- Let a drunk driver spend a night in jail rather than putting up bail immediately.
- Tell the truth about the source of an injury rather than protecting a physically abusive alcoholic.
- Confront the drinker about the drunkenness, using a guided intervention if necessary.

Yes, it's true that an alcoholic may make mistakes—even very serious and costly ones—when you reduce your caretaking activity and start letting him make more of his own decisions. But don't let guilt get to you. Any bad decisions are his, not yours. After all, your hovering hasn't prevented mistakes in the past. His mistakes may cause him to "hit bottom" and want to get sober. Remember, caretaking and rescuing will prolong the disease.

Don't be threatened by feelings of fear either. Are you afraid your alcoholic spouse will leave you or cut off his or her ties to you if you stop rescuing? If that were the case, you might well be better off without him. But generally it doesn't work that way. He will respect you more as you respect yourself more.

Question: If alcoholism is a disease, doesn't that mean that the person who has it needs extra loving care and protection? No. More personal responsibility is a better prescription for an alcoholic who is not doing anything to try and recover. Tough love does protect; it protects against the harm that can come to a whole family when alcoholism is allowed to flourish unchecked.

For a sense of balance, frequently read the Bible's great "love chapter" (1 Cor. 13). There you will be reminded that love is patient, kind, and humble. It is not envious, boastful, rude, self-seeking, easily angered, or unforgiving. You can cling to these positive attitudes even as your love takes on the "toughness" it didn't have before.

As your alcoholic loved one sees you becoming less and less involved in your rescuing behavior, it is possible he or she might conclude that you simply don't care anymore. If this happens, I urge you to continue to find ways to express your love without violating your tough love principles. You can do it by learning to hear and speak your dear one's own "love language."

Actions that say "I love you" vary from person to person. One man "hears" his wife say "I love you" when she irons his shirts to perfection, while another man doesn't care so much about shirts but hears "I love you" when his wife wears her hair the way he likes it. One woman hears "I love you" when her husband uses his vacation time to paint the house. Another woman feels love when her husband makes her a special cup of hot tea when she is suffering from a cold. Whatever seems to make your loved one especially happy and grateful—flowers on the table, a home-cooked meal—that's what you can do to make him or her feel loved, even as you take a tough stand on drinking.

Tough love is a lot of work, spiritually, but you can do it—you can keep the toughness without losing the love. Remember the Apostle Paul's words to his Christian friends in Rome. "Love must be sincere. Hate what is evil; cling to what is good" (Rom. 12:9).

For Further Reflection

On love, read Matthew 5:43–48; 22:37–40; John 15:9–17; Romans 12:9–21; 13:8–10; 1 Corinthians 13; and 1 John 4:7–21.

On responsibility, read Ezekiel 18.

13 Anger: Detoxify the Poison in Your System

> In your anger do not sin. Do not let the sun go down while you are still angry, and do not give the devil a foothold. EPHESIANS 4:26

If you had asked me two years ago, I would not have admitted that I was angry with my husband. I was putting up with some treatment I didn't like, but I seldom told him how I felt about it. After all, he should know, shouldn't he? I sometimes confided my troubles to close friends, and I attended meetings of Al-Anon and a Christian self-help group. In all these discussions, I tried to remain upbeat and positive in all I said. I had to show everyone what a "good Christian" I was and how self-controlled. I was so busy being "spiritual" that I couldn't allow myself to be real.

Then one day while out walking with a friend, I surprised and upset myself by "blowing my cover." I complained long, hard, and bitterly to this dear woman. Why her? Why then? I knew her own background, and I suppose I sensed, correctly, that she would understand and not judge me.

After that I had to admit to myself that I was sitting on a lot of bottled-up anger. I knew that wasn't good; a spirit that holds in a negative emotion for a long time is like a body that is constipated. The waste products are a burden on the system and need to be eliminated. But I didn't know what to do about it.

This is what I wrote at that time on an index card that I put in my Bible, "What is the correct thing to do with anger so I am not 'stuffing it' inside? Does turning it over to God mean expressing it only to him, or does it mean he will show me what to do with it? Is it a sin to get angry because my own high hopes and expectations are violated?"

After some thought and prayer I decided to confront my husband with my anger. He was so hard to pin down, I had to make an appointment with him at his place of business. I told him how some of his recent actions had hurt and angered me, and I suggested that we both get some counseling. After doing this I felt better immediately, even though his first reaction was anger.

In the following weeks, he referred to that conversation several times and made some positive changes. I thought it was wonderful just knowing he had heard me.

Deal with Anger Constructively

My prayer and reading—in the Bible and other sources—has convinced me that anger is not wrong in itself, and it certainly is not wrong to express it in a good confrontation. When anger becomes long-term, inward rage, it poisons both body and soul. It blunts our capacity for more desirable feelings, like love, joy, and peace, and it causes us to be alienated from the very ones with whom we want to be close. It is important that we learn how to neutralize this poison.

As Christians, we often ask ourselves whether we have "the right" to feel certain negative emotions, and we tend to go off on guilt trips over feelings we see as "wrong." But I now believe that our feelings at any given moment are not moral issues in themselves. They are not right or wrong, they just are, and God accepts us as we are. But because anger and other negative feelings are harmful to us, we have to learn how to deal with them constructively.

However, anger is not all bad. It can be useful when it helps us face a bad situation and make necessary changes based on scriptural standards. Constructive anger can help us take a stand against a wrong, defend an innocent victim, protect a child from danger, or begin to reject the consequences of someone else's bad behavior. (Anger *could* be a sin if it served only our own convenience or selfish desires.)

We read in the Gospels that Jesus was angry at times. In the Old Testament, we see God the Father getting especially angry at the sins of the people he loved best. He describes himself as "slow to anger" (Exod. 34:6), and the condition is temporary, "For his anger lasts only a moment, but his favor lasts a lifetime" (Ps. 30:5).

We need to accept our anger (not deny it, as I did) and learn how to express it appropriately. Before confronting the alcoholic loved one or anyone else, consider carefully your true feelings. Sometimes we are angry at someone and take it out on "innocent bystanders," especially children. It is sometimes true that we give others angry messages "in code" because we haven't accepted our real motivation. For example, Gail kept telling her husband, "You don't spend enough time with the children," when she really meant, "I need to know whether you still care about me."

As you already know, I'm sure, confrontation is not the same as "ventilating" your anger. Shouting, arguing, name-calling, and stony silences do more harm than good. They make the recipient angry at *you* and invite retaliation. Then instead of the two of you being reconciled, your position as "enemies" becomes more fixed. Also be careful how you involve a third party. You may have a legitimate need for some counseling in dealing with your anger, but indiscriminate complaining and sarcastic "joking" to others are absolutely out, of course.

Acceptance Reduces Anger

It's good to acknowledge and deal with anger, but it's even better not to let it get a hold on you in the first place. Acceptance is the key to prevent this from happening.

Acceptance is the recognition that "what is, is." It means letting go of your ideas about "the way things should be" and yielding to the way things really are. It is submission to reality.

So your loved one is an alcoholic—that's a fact. Acceptance means you don't waste time and energy denying that or stewing about the unfairness of it all or indulging in escapist fantasies. In acceptance, you don't butt your head against a brick wall, demanding that another person be someone he's not. Let's face it, we believe most of life's problems would be solved easily if we could just change other people. But it doesn't work that way. We can influence others only by changing ourselves.

At the same time acceptance doesn't mean putting up with abuse or unacceptable behavior. Neither does it mean treating an alcoholic exactly like a nonalcoholic or writing off a drinker as someone who will never change. People do change, and sometimes it happens in response to our own changes.

Acceptance just recognizes that the behavior of other people is normal *for them*, given their own circumstances, personalities, and values. Getting drunk, for instance, is normal behavior for an alcoholic. So is arrogance. How angry can you get at normal behavior?

Then, too, anger is always at least partly directed toward God for allowing the conditions to exist that we find so unacceptable. When we accept that there is a purpose in whatever God allows, it should put things in perspective for us and help diminish our resentment. But that doesn't mean you should judge and condemn yourself for feeling angry. Instead, we are to accept ourselves as normal, human, and imperfect. Just remember that anger is a normal reaction, and anyone who lives with alcoholism usually has ample reason to get angry.

Then, too, you need acceptance in order to forgive and to love. Forgiveness is essential to your own happiness, and you can't forgive until your anger is neutralized. And you can only love others as they are, not as you wish they were. Authentic love doesn't demand that others devote themselves to making us happy. That's possessiveness, not love.

Acceptance is necessary for self-love, too. When you realize that no one exists for the express purpose of making you happy, you will take more responsibility for getting your own real needs met. If you are angry at your spouse for not spending time with you, for instance, you can fill some of those free evenings with a night-school class or good times with friends.

Anger or bitterness only helps keep you focused on and obsessed with your alcoholic, so it robs you of joy and peace. In this way you are giving the alcoholic enormous power to control your moods. It can be incredibly liberating to take back that power. When you say, "I have the right to be angry" you are really saying you have the right to be unhappy. And you do, but is that what you want?

Your Mind Is the Key

God's Word tells us, "Be made new in the attitude of your minds," and as part of this process, we are to "get rid of all bitterness, rage and anger, brawling and slander, along with every form of malice. Be kind and compassionate to one another, forgiving each other, just as in Christ God forgave you" (Eph. 4:23, 31–32).

From this we see that our emotions are under the control of our minds. We *can* "help it." No one really "makes" us angry; we make ourselves angry by our reactions to what happens. Here are some of the errors in our thinking that cause these faulty reactions:

1. *Labeling* others as "jerk," "idiot," "no-good," "stupid," or "creep." Let's face it, people aren't all good or all bad; they're just human like you and me. To label them is to assassinate their character and dismiss their value to God. Jesus had some pretty strong things to say on this subject. Read what he said in Matthew 5:21–22.

2. *Blaming*, or having to assign fault for everything that goes wrong. Some things are no one's fault. And sometimes it doesn't matter whose fault it is. People may be weak and imperfect but are often doing the best they can. Acceptance is better than blame. There are even times when we want to blame everything on alcoholism, but this just isn't realistic.

3. *Mind reading*. We invent motives for those who hurt us. We say, "He doesn't love me." "She doesn't think I'm important." These motives are strictly from our own imaginations. Just for the moment, pretend you are the person at whom you are angry and say, "Now why did I do what?" Try to see things from his or her point of view. It is even possible the other person's reactions had nothing to do with you. An alcoholic is seldom drinking *at you* and probably has no desire to hurt you.

4. *Exaggerating* the importance of some event that ticks you off. If your alcoholic loved one makes a crude joke in front of your church friends, remember the Al-Anon slogan "How important is it?" Few things are worth blowing your serenity.

"All-or-nothing thinking" is a form of gross exaggeration. When you hit a red light, you think, "I *always* get the red lights," but is that really true? And when you say to your drinker, "You're *never* around when I need you," you forget the times he or she has been.

5. *Maintaining unrealistic standards.* Most of us have a lot of rules for the way we think the world should function. And so often other people fail to live up to *our* high ideals. But is is important to accept the way things are. Husbands and wives are sometimes thoughtless and even cruel to each other. Babies don't always sleep the whole night through. When you catch yourself fussing and fuming about what should be, try to substitute the phrase, "It would be nice if . . ." You may find it helpful to write down your angry thoughts and consider them thoughtfully and prayerfully.

God's Word acknowledges that we all become angry from time to time, but it also reassures us that we can use our minds—at the point of our anger—to put out the flames. The often repeated injunction "Do not let the sun go down while you are angry," means that we are to deal with our anger as soon as we become aware of it. The writer of the book of James cautions us, "Everyone should be quick to listen, slow to speak and slow to become angry" (1:19). We are to remain cool and not jump to conclusions. An explosive temper tantrum harms both you and your victims.

Jesus said, "Anyone who is angry with his brother [some versions add "without cause"] will be subject to judgment" (Matt.5:22). It seems to me that the judgment will be invoked for the way the anger is handled rather than for the anger itself. Just as temper tantrums are wrong, so it is also wrong to deny anger and bottle it up until it becomes silent rage or hatred.

Finally, become aware of your anger. Accept it, and accept the person or situation that triggered it. Pray about it and talk it out with someone you can trust. Then forgive and forget. The wisdom writer called it right when he said, "A fool gives full vent to his anger, but a wise man keeps himself under control" (Prov. 29:11).

For Further Reflection

On anger, read Exodus 34:5–7; Proverbs 20:3; 22:24–25; 29:22; Matthew 5:21–26; 1 Corinthians 13:5; and James 1:19–21.

14   *More Kinds of Poison*

Hope deferred makes the heart sick, but a longing fulfilled is a tree of life.
PROVERBS 13:12

Have you been waiting and hoping for a long time for your loved one to stay sober without seeing any progress? Of this you can be sure—God understands that this can make you "sick at heart."

Anger is one very basic heartsick emotion that is directed outward toward those you hold responsible for your unhappiness. In this chapter we'll look at some other forms of heartsickness (or what I call poison) that are mostly directed inward. Acceptance helps neutralize these poisons the same way it does anger—acceptance of yourself and others just as you are.

Self-Pity

The "poor me" attitude of self-pity is the flip side of anger even though it is more passive than anger. This attitude is expressed in words such as, "Poor me; life just isn't fair and there's nothing I can do about it!"

My own tendency toward self-pity surfaced years before my anger. I suppose it helped me deny my anger for a time. It took Al-Anon to shake this attitude loose.

I went into an Al-Anon group thinking I would tell my sad story and they would pat me on the shoulder and say, "Poor Chris!" Imagine my surprise when they didn't, and when they told me instead that my life was in my own hands.

At one particular meeting, I was all upset because of a terrible

99

scene at home that involved a struggle in the driveway over the car keys. I was crying and hardly noticed the plain-looking, thin woman on my right. Finally someone asked her how things were with her. "Oh, not bad," she replied. "I'm getting my feet back under me now, but it was rough when I returned from my mother's house a few weeks ago, after recovering there from my surgery. I'd told my husband I was coming, but there was no one to meet me at the airport. So I had to find another way home. When I got there, no one was at the apartment, but it was a terrible mess and all the furniture was gone. He had apparently moved in a half-a-dozen drinking buddies, and they'd sold all my family antiques for the money to buy more booze."

"Poor Chris" shrank to about two inches tall. I had not only a house full of furniture, but a husband who was a good provider and two lovely daughters. Thank you, dear friend, wherever you are, for teaching me that night to count my blessings.

Thankfulness is the main medicine for self-pity. God has given you your life, now and forever, as well as every good thing you have. Failure to appreciate it is an offense to him. But as the apostle Paul wrote, "Thanks be to God! He gives us the victory through our Lord Jesus Christ" (1 Cor. 15:57).

Envy

Envy is a close relative of anger and self-pity. To be envious means that we resent someone else who appears to be better off than we are. Like the other forms of nonacceptance, envy is a waste of precious time and energy, and it hurts you more than the person at whom you direct it.

Envy is similar to the other spiritual poisons in important ways. It is unloving (1 Cor. 13:4) and bad for the health, "A heart at peace gives life to the body, but envy rots the bones" (Prov. 14:30). Envy is based on unrealistic thoughts—if you think someone else's life seems ideal, you probably don't know that person well enough to be aware of his or her problems. After all, everyone has problems of one kind or another.

Sometimes we may also envy "sinners"—including the alcoholic—who seem to do whatever they want and get away with it. Feeling sorry for ourselves, we say, "God will forgive him when he gets around to asking, so why am I knocking myself out to do what's right?" Many of the psalms and proverbs in our Bible deal directly with this problem, and they assure us that the score will be settled someday. In Jesus' parable of the prodigal son, the older brother has this kind of envy (see Luke 15:11–32), but he shouldn't have. Even after his brother had returned and been forgiven, there were consequences for the young man: his share of the estate is still gone, and the older brother will inherit whatever is left.

The consequences of wrongdoing are inescapable no matter how much rescuing anyone does. And it isn't likely "their fun" is quite the way it appears to be.

Self-righteousness

The attitude that says, "I know it all and I'm always right, so I have the right to be angry at you" is self-righteousness, a form of pride. It, too, is based on a warped view of reality. None of us is that good, "for all have sinned and fall short of the glory of God" (Rom. 3:23).

It's easy for the close associate of an alcoholic to fall into this know-it-all trap, because you look so good by comparison. But it's not that black-and-white. In spite of what you may think, your alcoholic loved one is not wrong all the time about everything.

Actually, it may well be that your alcoholic uses your self-righteousness to justify bad behavior. Isn't that reason enough to stop pretending to be perfect?

We all need a healthy dose of humility. And that means knowing we need God, that we can't make it on our own. Just remember how often you have tried unsuccessfully to break a bad habit. Reflecting on your own failures will make you far less judgmental of someone else.

Lack of Forgiveness

If you are unable to forgive the alcoholic or others, it is likely you don't understand your position with God. Jesus said, "For if you forgive men when they sin against you, your heavenly Father will also forgive you. But if you do not forgive men their sins, your Father will not forgive your sins" (Matt. 6:14–15). That's a sobering thought, isn't it? God has much to forgive each one of us for, even if we are what the world calls a good person or a good Christian.

To forgive someone isn't to say that his or her sin was "all right," though. Forgiveness means you are willing to put it behind you, accept what happened, yield your anger, and not hold a grudge. It means you'll accept and love the person as if the offense never took place.

A wrong is still a wrong, though, and it's all right for the "guilty party" to take responsibility and accept the consequences. If a friend breaks something of yours, you can forgive her and still accept her offer to pay for it. In the same way, it's all right to allow an alcoholic to assume the consequences of his or her drinking.

Jesus said that if someone wrongs us and repents, we should be willing to forgive even seven times a day (Luke 17:3–6). And when the disciples said, "Increase our faith," it showed they understood the great emotional cost of such forgiveness. Let's face it—it is hard to give up our anger, because sometimes it feels so good. But the rewards are great: peace of mind and serenity.

But there's more. If it's hard to forgive someone who repents and asks forgiveness, what about someone who doesn't believe he has hurt you or doesn't care? It's harder to forgive that kind of person than someone who has expressed sorrow and regret, but you still need to do it for your own sake. May God increase *our* faith, too.

Guilt

Guilt is usually a real "biggie" for those who live with alcoholism. I'm not talking about genuine remorse for something we did that was wrong, which of course is constructive. Realistic remorse convicts you of sin while still allowing you to feel loved and forgiven by God when you ask forgiveness and make amends. No, what I'm referring to here is irrational or excessive guilt, which strikes at the very core of your being and makes you feel "rotten and just no good."

Irrational guilt makes you unable to forgive or accept yourself or believe that God forgives you. This is called condemnation, and there is nothing constructive about it. Condemnation is no more appropriate when directed toward yourself than toward anyone else. The apostle Paul reassured us when he wrote, "Therefore, there is now no condemnation for those who are in Christ Jesus" (Rom. 8:1).

Verbal abuse and rejection are the main reasons for excessive feelings of guilt and self-condemnation. If you were neglected, ignored, or made to feel worthless in early childhood, such feelings are deeply ingrained in your mind. An alcoholic will likely build on these feelings by heaping abuse on you as an adult. He or she may harp on all your real or imagined faults by saying, "Who wouldn't drink with a wife [husband, child, etc.] like you?" After a time that kind of abuse gets to you until you come to believe that you are worthless, even as you argue back and try to prove the drinker wrong. But the truth is that you are a precious and valuable person in God's eyes. And anyone who puts you down does so because of his or her own spiritual problems.

Then, too, errors in thinking also contribute to irrational feelings of guilt. First, we think we are supposed to be perfect: "I failed; therefore, I'm a bad person." Not at all! We all fail; you are a normal person. Deal with your failure and start over. Our errors in thinking have some of the same roots as those that cause fear and insecurity. We think we should be powerful enough to make the world right and to offset all the wrong choices made by others, including the drinker. But we have already seen what nonsense that idea is.

We also think that somehow we should be able to predict the future. How often we've said, "I should have known what was going to happen so I could have done something differently." However, not knowing all the results of our actions in advance is just something we have to accept.

Sometimes we also have the mistaken idea that we are obligated to undertake whatever anyone asks us to do. When someone decides you are the "perfect person" to take on a volunteer project that's really more than you can handle, do you feel guilty when you say no? Or do you say yes when you shouldn't? It is quite natural to want to be all things to all people, but we can't.

There are times when we say no angrily—especially to children—as a cover-up for this kind of guilt. But then we feel guilty for getting angry. So often we seem to be caught in a vicious cycle. It is important, though, to set priorities, and sometimes that means saying no to good things, not just bad things. In such cases, it's better for everyone when we turn down a request politely, without displaying inappropriate anger.

Approval seeking is another source of inappropriate guilt. In our struggle for approval we try to please everyone. We have a craving for praise and feel crushed if we are criticized. We allow ourselves to be overvulnerable to the opinions of others, believing that if a certain person disapproves of us he or she must be right.

Nonsense. People's opinions are naturally going to differ. You would be leading a very bland life if you never displeased anybody. When you receive criticism, stop and evaluate whether or not it is valid. And even if it is, concentrate on all the other things you did right that day.

Approval seeking may at times put a cruel twist on your relationship with your alcoholic loved one. It may well be that he registers strong approval for your rescuing behavior but then is bitterly critical when you refuse to take on his responsibilities. At such times you may end up feeling guilty for doing what is right. When that happens, just remember "it's the disease talking" and refuse to cater to or reinforce the alcoholic's behavior.

At times feelings of guilt come from lack of acceptance of our own negative feelings. Resentment of bad treatment builds up, and we may experience moments of wishing the alcoholic were dead and out of our life completely. But then we're flooded with remorse and berate ourselves. After all, we're convinced that only a bad person would harbor thoughts like that!

That's the time to accept your feelings and reaffirm that you are not a bad person. Then you won't need to get into rescuing and caretaking just to prove you are a loving person. Just remember when you are overwhelmed with that kind of guilt that love isn't warm, fuzzy feelings. Rather, it's concern for the highest good of the one you love.

Depression

Freud and other early psychoanalysts believed that depression is anger turned inward—that if you keep your anger inside long enough, you'll turn it against yourself. Some modern psychologists think lack of self-esteem is the major cause of depression. It seems to me that both opinions may be partly right—our guilt about our anger may reduce self-esteem until we don't like or trust ourselves enough to do anything constructive. At the same time depression can also be a symptom of various physical problems. Consequently the first thing a seriously depressed person should do is undergo a thorough medical checkup. This is discussed more fully in chapter 17.

Burnout—Time to Refuel

To live with alcoholism is to experience heavy spiritual warfare every day. It's no wonder that you become emotionally drained from time to time; the "poisons" take their toll and rob you of power. That is the time to recharge your "spiritual batteries."

Sometimes this means getting away for a while. Moses, Elijah, John the Baptist, even Jesus—all needed protracted times of solitude and communion with the Father. And they returned from their "desert times" with a fresh burst of power to help others. Maybe you can't escape for a long period of time, but possibly you could manage a weekend a few times a year for solitude, prayer, and rest.

Question: How can you know when you are "burned out" enough to need an extended period of rest and change? You will know for sure when you dip to the disorganized emotional level of your alcoholic loved one, when you are unable to remain detached, and when you can no longer keep your identity separate from the drinker's. You will know you need to get away when you are always worried or obsessed about something you can't change, when you are unable to concentrate on work or serious reading matter, when you live from hour to hour with no particular plan, and when you feel helpless and out of control. But please don't let things get that bad before you take time off for rest and change.

It's true that you may not be able to retreat to an exotic hideaway, but how about an off-season motel cabin, a tent in a quiet state park, or the home of a friend or relative? It's important, though, to be alone in fairly quiet surroundings and with few distractions. Above all, don't feel guilty about leaving your family; they'll survive if you make adequate arrangements, and you'll be better able to meet their needs because of your "break."

While you're away, get lots of rest. Take walks for exercise, read your Bible, and pray often. You may want to try fasting. Do things when you feel like it, and take advantage of the fact that you don't need to keep to a schedule. Be introspective; record your thoughts and feelings in a journal.

Your "poisons" may come to the surface and make you unhappy for a time, but that's because you are getting rid of them. The benefits come later. You'll gain some perspective, and when you're back home, you'll be able to see changes that need to be made. Remember, you are only a "pipeline" for God's love and power; your rest and relaxation time should open your pipeline so that you are better able to give and receive that love.

By changing your way of thinking, you can help prevent poisonous negative emotions from blocking your way to a better life. It will be necessary to develop a certain amount of detachment from your own thoughts, and that is a tricky process. But you'll do well to ask yourself, "Does it make sense to think the way I always have, or is there a better way?" Then as you spend time in God's Word, you'll receive help in putting it all together. And by practicing tough love, you'll give your alcoholic the best chance to get well, and you will have the peace of mind you need so much. The psalmist understood the rewards of being quiet and alone when he wrote, "The Lord is my shepherd, I shall lack nothing. He makes me lie down in green pastures, he leads me beside quiet waters, he restores my soul" (Ps. 23:1–3).

For Further Reflection

On thankfulness versus self-pity, read Psalm 100; Philippians 4:11–13; 1 Thessalonians 5:16–18; and Hebrews 12:28.

On envy, read Psalm 37 and James 3:13–18.

On self-righteousness, read Proverbs 14:12; 15:31–33; 18:17; Romans 3:21–27; 7:15–8:4; 12:3 and 1 John 1:8–10.

On forgiveness, read Psalms 19:12–14; 32; 51; Matthew 6:12–15; 18:21–35; Mark 11:25; and Luke 7:36–50.

On guilt, read Psalm 130:3–4; Isaiah 43:25; John 3:16–18; Romans 8:1–2; Galatians 1:10; Hebrews 10:22; and 1 John 3:18–24.

Part 5   Through Domestic
Misery to a Peaceful
Home

15 *Defuse Those Arguments*

Consider what a great forest is set on fire by a small spark. The tongue also is a fire, a world of evil among the parts of the body. It corrupts the whole person, sets the whole course of his life on fire, and is itself set on fire by hell. . . . With the tongue we praise our Lord and Father, and with it we curse men, who have been made in God's likeness. Out of the same mouth come praise and cursing. My brothers, this should not be.

JAMES 3:5b–6, 9–10

Arguments have to be one of the worst things that happen when you live with an alcohol abuser. The loud, ugly quarrels that shake many of our homes are destructive to the human spirit. They are not proper confrontations (which are limited, controlled, and should be motivated by love) but attempts at confrontation that get out of control and are motivated by anger and spite. Arguments drive wedges between family members, seldom settle any issue, and ruin the peace of the home. No one "wins" an argument!

If there are children in the home, arguments between their parents hurt them worst of all. Whether they are little ones or teenagers, family quarrels destroy their sense of security. And, tragically, the children often blame themselves for problems that have nothing to do with them.

Does It Take Two to Quarrel?

Who starts the arguments in your home? Is it necessarily the one doing all the yelling? Or is it the one who provokes the other with reproving glances, sarcastic jokes, sulky silences, or neglects responsibilities? And once an argument starts, do you feel compelled to help keep it going?

By all means, avoid starting arguments even though your spouse seems to be begging for a fight. (I'm assuming for this chapter that your alcoholic is your marriage partner; if not, maybe there's still something here that you can use.)

If your husband, for example, is intoxicated, he may be very belligerent and uncivil. Everything that goes wrong is your fault, and nothing you say is right. He criticizes anything and everything about you—your housekeeping or home maintenance, cooking, parenting skills, religion, occupation, looks, and family. Eventually comes a shouting match that continues until bedtime, when you both withdraw into a stony silence.

The main reason an alcoholic wants an argument comes under the heading of "projection"—the psychological process by which a person with a crushing load of guilt and self-hatred tries to unload it on someone else by turning it outward as anger. The alcoholic dumps his or her self-loathing on you because you are close and handy. It has nothing to do with your own worth as a person. I once heard an Al-Anon member say, "If Florence Nightingale had been married to an alcoholic, he would have told her she was a lousy nurse."

Once you understand "projection," it should help you not to carry around so much irrational guilt. Just remember that when he lays a guilt trip on you, it's his own guilt talking. At the same time you should also understand why the drinker cuts down your efforts at self-improvement. If you are a wife, you may be baffled and hurt when you spend an entire week cleaning the house in response to your husband's complaints, and then he rants and raves about a curtain that is not quite straight. Just know that he just needs something to complain about, and he'll find it.

Another reason your alcoholic wants to pick a fight is so you can take on the role of the "heavy." If your alcoholic wife can get you to yell at her, she can experience your anger as a punishment or penance, relieving her of any guilt she feels about drinking.

Frontline Maneuvers

Now we agree that a quarrel is a good thing to avoid. And understanding the alcoholic's motives will help you not take the insults so personally, so that your reaction need not be so strong or obvious. Here are some other "frontline maneuvers" that will help you either avoid arguments or lessen their severity:

1. Be good to yourself on a daily basis. It's harder to pick a fight with a happy person. Whatever is good for you is good for the alcoholic.

2. Pray every day that you'll both have a good day and for strength and wisdom in any tricky situation.

3. Learn your alcoholic's "language of love" (see chapter 12) so that you'll know you are doing loving things for him or her and you'll be less vulnerable to guilt. Build up the alcoholic with praise and a big smile when he or she does something that pleases you, no matter how simple a thing it is.

4. Save confrontations for morning. Things are more likely to get out of hand around suppertime and after, when most of us are physically at a low ebb (and when a drinker has more alcohol in the system).

5. Keep working on detachment and acceptance. It would help to use a copy of *One Day at a Time in Al-Anon*, which you can get at a meeting of your local group. Be patient with yourself. Lifetime attitudes and habits aren't going to be reversed overnight.

6. Remember that it's projection when verbal abuse starts. If you keep in mind that it's really the alcoholic's self-hatred talking, you can't help but feel compassion. Don't let your self-esteem be dragged down; you don't deserve bad treatment just because you're getting it.

7. See the humor in it. This calls for a lot of detachment, but the alcoholic's efforts to provoke you by jumping from one ridiculous insult to another can actually be amusing, if you pay attention to what he's doing instead of what he says.

8. Keep your own voice down. Our tendency is to shout when shouted at. If you stick with a quiet answer, the other person may

have to turn down his or her own volume to hear you. Your tone of voice should be calm and gentle. If someone were to tape your discussion, how would *you* sound?

9. Give a vague answer when you need to give one at all. Say something like, "Oh, is that how you see it?" It's better to say something neutral than to keep up a hostile silence. "A gentle answer turns away wrath, but a harsh word stirs up anger" (Prov. 15:1).

10. Don't set the alcoholic off by saying, "You've been drinking again." She knows it and she knows you know it. Don't be furious about denial; denial is normal, remember?

11. React as little as possible when insulted. If you cry, shout, defend yourself, or make counteraccusations when verbally abused, the alcoholic will experience that as a reward: "It worked!" And you'll be sure to hear the same thing the next time. "A fool shows his annoyance at once, but a prudent man overlooks an insult" (Prov. 12:16).

12. Change the subject. A drunk is almost as distractable as a two-year-old, so use this fact to your advantage. When he gets onto a subject that really bothers you, ask him about something else. For example, "Here's an article on the new Chryslers. Do you like the styling?" Do this as many times as you have to, using different topics. He may not calm down, but he may become distracted and switch to another subject.

13. Music hath charms. In the Bible story David used music to soothe the often irrational King Saul. It is useful both in preventing arguments and in distraction. Any kind of good, wholesome music your alcoholic likes will do, whether you play it on the stereo or sing or play an instrument yourself.

14. Listen and agree when possible. It's okay to "tune out" someone who is being verbally abusive. But if you happen to catch what sounds like a reasonable idea, agree with it. It will take the wind out of his sails if he expects automatic opposition. Make sure you understand by repeating back the good idea, "So you think it makes more sense to get a new furnace than to spend the money on repairs?"

15. Don't preach. Witnessing, hymn singing, and Scripture quot-

ing, when done in excess to an angry person, will do more harm than good. A little goes a long way. As a friend of mine once said, "Let the Holy Spirit do the convicting." If you are asked questions about spiritual matters, ask the Holy Spirit to give you the right reply. Otherwise, easy does it. Your attitude is a better witness than your words most of the time.

Sexual Fulfillment in Marriage

Sexuality in marriage is meant to be a natural, beautiful gift from God (see 1 Cor. 7:1–7). Spouses are not to deprive each other under normal circumstances. I have read one well-meaning author who says a husband or wife has a "duty to refuse" sex to a spouse who has been drinking. I feel this is an unfair burden. For one thing, you don't always know for sure when your spouse has been drinking, or how much. For another, if you want to make love and can get some pleasure from it, why should you be deprived? You have enough people wanting to take various choices out of your hands without taking away that one, too. It's not your obligation to use sex as a system of reward and punishment for your spouse.

On the other hand, you may, understandably, want to avoid sex on an occasion when drunkenness has "turned you off." A person under the influence of liquor may not be clean and may smell like alcohol or may use bad language and be verbally abusive. At such times a man may become unable to maintain an erection or may continue intercourse too long without being able to climax. Neither a husband nor wife is obligated under Scripture, I firmly believe, to submit under such degrading conditions.

"Creative avoidance" is the concept to keep in mind when you want to avoid sex. Find a tactful way to say "not right now," and your spouse will understand that you don't mean "not ever." "Let's wait till morning," or "How about tomorrow night?" will meet with less resistance than a plain no. Long baths and similar delaying tactics, until the spouse goes to sleep, can be useful too. Moment by moment, the choice is yours.

Finances

Money is a frequent topic for arguments in any family. But alcohol abuse poses additional problems as money is wasted on liquor and mismanaged in other ways. Although this is controversial, I think the spouse of an alcoholic is justified in keeping his or her money separate from that of the drinking spouse if that will avoid bankruptcy. In extreme cases, legal separations have been obtained for this reason. These are not normally good things to do. Ideally, a husband and wife should act as a team in setting their financial goals and sticking to them. However when this doesn't work, it becomes one more tragic consequence of drunkenness.

Here are some bare-bones principles from Scripture on finances: Trust in the Lord for all your real needs and he will provide. Keep your needs simple. Be thrifty. Don't get into debt. Ideally the husband is the leader, but either spouse can be the bookkeeper. It is a sin to refuse to provide for one's family. Work hard and practice sound management. A home-based craft or business could be ideal for a mother who wants to be with her children, as in Proverbs 31:10–31.

Above all, don't be secretive about finances. Both partners should be fully aware of all bank accounts, debts, investments, insurance policies, and so on. Study carefully the biblical references listed at the end of this chapter. In addition you may find help from a good Christian book on family finances.

It is important to remember, though, that many arguments can be avoided or reduced in severity when you keep your attitudes in line, and a "soft answer" will help to cool off anger. The apostle Paul gave us some good advice when he wrote, "Do not let any unwholesome talk come out of your mouths, but only what is helpful for building others up according to their needs, that it may benefit those who listen" (Eph. 4:29).

For Further Reflection

On arguments, read Proverbs 10:11, 19; 12:18; 13:3; 17:1, 19; 18:13; 19:11; 20:22; 26:2, 4.

On finances, read Psalm 37; Proverbs 13:11; 15:16–17; 16:16; 21:17; 23:4–8; 30:8–9; 31.10–31; Ecclesiastes 4:6; Matthew 25:14–30; Luke 9:10–17; 12:13–34; 2 Corinthians 9:6–7; Colossians 3:23–24; 1 Thessalonians 4:11–12; 2 Thessalonians 3:10–13; and 1 Timothy 5:8

16 *Abuse: It's Not All Right*

> If an enemy were insulting me, I could endure it;
> if a foe were raising himself against me,
>   I could hide from him.
> But it is you, a man like myself,
>   my companion, my close friend,
> with whom I once enjoyed sweet fellowship.   PSALM 55:12–14

To "abuse" is to use wrongly, treat improperly, or violate. It really is a terrible emotional injury to be turned against by someone you love and trust—someone you thought would love you for a lifetime. As Shakespeare's Marc Antony said, it is "the most unkindest cut of all."

Types of Abuse

There are four main classifications of abuse. *Verbal abuse*, as discussed in the last chapter, includes insults and put-downs designed to hurt another person and destroy self-esteem. Put-downs may also be falsely attributed to a third party, as in "So-and-so said this about you." In this case, the purpose is also to drive a wedge between the victim and the third person.

Emotional abuse covers all other kinds of attempts to hurt mentally and emotionally. These sick mind games can include the following:

- Punishing you with prolonged silences.
- Arrogance—he is always right, and his opinion is the only one that matters.
- The King Tut syndrome—his accomplishments are wonderful; yours are meaningless. He implies that he does you a favor by continuing to put up with you.

- Playing "you're the crazy one." He denies the truth of various things you saw or heard for yourself, even when he knows them to be true. "Your imagination is playing tricks on you again, dear."
- Acting like Prince Charming in public and King Tut in private.
- Ignoring you completely in public, refusing to hear your questions or even leaving without telling you.
- Openly flirting with other people of the opposite sex, open admiration of others' physical attributes, implying that they are more attractive than you.

However, don't think for a minute alcoholics believe all this "garbage." They don't. They're like insecure preschoolers trying to puff up their own egos at someone else's expense. Even though such behavior hurts, don't "reward" it with a strong emotional reaction.

Intimidation is the use of force or threats to get one's own way—the use of fear to motivate another. It often starts with "house abuse"—holes punched through walls and so on. You are being intimidated when the alcoholic physically blocks you from leaving the house, disables your car, or threatens to injure or kill you if you step out of line. The lights may be turned off when you are trying to read or turned on when you are trying to sleep. Blankets may be pulled off the bed while you are in it, or dishes of food swept onto the floor. Intimidation includes any action meant to control you through the use of force, threats, or fear.

Physical abuse usually follows closely on the heels of intimidation. It starts in milder ways—not that any of it can be called "mild"—such as shoving the victim around or poking a finger into her chest to emphasize a point. (I say "her" because as a rule most victims of domestic violence are women. But it is equally damaging when a wife resorts to any form of physical abuse.)

Physical abuse can eventually include slapping, burning, kicking, punching, beating, and sometimes even rape. In extreme cases it ends in death by strangulation, head or internal injuries, shooting, or stabbing. And occasionally, the chronic abuser is killed by an abused spouse who finally "reaches the end of her rope."

Physical abuse is progressive. It usually gets worse if allowed to continue. And of one thing you can be sure: It doesn't get better unless action is taken to break the cycle. However, repentance and apologies are not "action."

Denial of physical abuse runs very, very deep in both the abuser and the one abused. The abuser may be horrified the day after an incident and promise it will never happen again. The victim wants to believe it. She can't bring herself to "punish him by leaving or getting professional help just when he is being so nice." Denial says, "It was just this one time. Things will get better now. I have to give him one more chance." This simply means that things are better for a while until they get worse again.

Causes of Abuse

Most domestic violence is connected with drug or alcohol abuse. Some of it is related to family traditions—many abusers of spouse or children were abused as children themselves or saw violence between their parents. Low self-esteem is a factor.

In writing to the Christians in Ephesus the apostle Paul said, "Husbands ought to love their wives as their own bodies. He who loves his wife loves himself" (Eph. 5:28). But the self-destructive use of alcohol and other drugs shows contempt for one's own body. And this self-hatred is just extended to the spouse's body in physical abuse.

The possibility of spiritual or demonic involvement in abuse should not be automatically ruled out, especially if the abuser's personality, voice, and facial expression are totally different than at other times. I think we Christians have sometimes been too blind to these influences. A friend of mine had firsthand experience with this problem. She found that when her husband was under satanic influence, she could control his behavior through the use of God's name. She could say, "In the name of Jesus Christ the Lord, sit down!" when he was threatening her, and he would do it for a short time. Pleading the blood of Jesus in prayer and quoting Scripture are effective weapons in such spiritual warfare.

If there is any question in your mind as to whether you are dealing with a demon, try doing what I have just suggested. If it makes a difference, you probably are—a person who is merely drunk or mentally ill would have no fearful reaction to the Word of God or your prayers. And if you have reason to suspect the worst, get some help from those in your Christian community who are experienced in dealing with such things. My friend did, much to her relief.

What to Do If You Are Abused

If you are suffering abuse, particularly physical abuse or intimidation, there are two things to do right away that are both important. First, ask for God's help and protection, and then seek out whatever human help is available to you. Asking for God's help is serious business and will make a difference, but it doesn't rule out accepting human help. The wisdom writer gave us good advice, "The prudent see danger and take refuge, but the simple keep going and suffer for it" (Prov. 27:12). "Taking refuge" doesn't mean you are weak or don't trust God. Don't let a bad situation continue just because of pride.

Many cities now have shelters for battered women and their children. You can find their phone numbers on public bulletin boards or in the telephone book. There is no shame in using such services. They exist because people really want to help. You may also have friends, especially in your church family, who would love to open their homes to you if they knew you had a need. Talk to a close friend or to your pastor. You may feel in a desperate moment, "There's no way I could disturb a family in the middle of the night." But some people would count it a privilege to help you. Give them a chance.

It is also appropriate to call the police and to file charges in a case of physical abuse. Unfortunately, many police agencies have in the past taken too casual an attitude toward domestic violence and have often refused to do more than give the abuser a warning. But this attitude is somewhat understandable, because many victims file charges and then drop them the next day. If you take such an action, follow through. Recent studies have shown that legal action can help deter further abuse, and many police departments are becoming more responsive to victims of abuse.

It is true that Jesus said on one occasion, "If someone strikes you on one cheek, turn to him the other also" (Luke 6:29). But he was speaking there about suffering religious persecution as Christians. Spouse abuse is a different situation. It is not a bad thing—some would call it a civic duty—to report a crime against you, and that's what assault is.

Once you have dealt with the immediate emergency, you should take steps to get some pastoral or professional counseling. In this way you can gain perspective and rebuild your self-esteem. This is still important even if the abuse is "merely" verbal and emotional. To endure abuse of any kind is to be battered in mind, soul, and spirit, and "a crushed spirit who can bear?" (Prov. 18:14).

The Submission Question

In writing to the Colossian Christians, Paul said, "Wives, submit to your husbands, as is fitting in the Lord" (Col. 3:18). This concept of submission in marriage is difficult for almost everyone these days. And it is even more so when the husband is frequently drunk, irrational, and/or abusive! Frequently, an abused wife hears submission taught in a very strict way in her church. Sometimes the pastor does indicate there are exceptions—a woman shouldn't rob a bank if her husband tells her to. But he seldom says what to do if the husband is drunk, drugged, out of his mind, or violent. A wife can become confused. "If he tells me to jump off a bridge, am I supposed to do that?" she wonders. It's no rhetorical question. Wives are asked every day to do things that make about as much sense as jumping off a bridge.

The concept of submission is still valid today, but it is widely misunderstood and often wrongly preached. Submission isn't blind obedience, and it isn't being a doormat. It is a creative act that calls for intelligence, diplomacy, tact, and wisdom. If a wife is to submit "as is fitting in the Lord," then obviously that cannot include morally wrong or senseless acts that the Lord would not consider "fitting." Virtually everyone agrees that you shouldn't submit when it means doing something morally wrong. But what about requests that are just stupid or pointless?

Len was embarrassed one night when Marilyn insisted on driving home from a fair because he was drunk. Two weeks later, drunk again and still enraged about the incident, he demanded that she get into the car with him, return to the fairgrounds, and apologize to the parking lot attendants. Never mind that the fair was over, and no one was there anymore. Never mind that three sleeping children would be left alone in the house. Marilyn refused, but secretly wondered if she were disobeying God by not doing what her husband wanted. I think it could hardly have been "fitting in the Lord" for her to go. She would have been submitting to craziness and sickness, not to her husband's true self or his best interests.

At the same time a husband has obligations that go hand in hand with wifely submission. He is to provide sane, loving leadership (see 1 Pet. 3:7; Eph. 5:28–29, and Col. 3:19). Each partner's ability to be faithful to the scriptural ideal depends upon the other's obedience. A wife cannot be totally submissive to a husband who isn't providing godly leadership. Neither can a husband lead lovingly if his wife is selfish and rebellious.

When one spouse is being overcompliant and the other is taking advantage through selfish domination, the result is an unhealthy, out-of-balance relationship. The marriage becomes a sick power trip in which neither partner really respects the other. To submit to such destructiveness is not really a loving act. Rather, it is an implied agreeement with your domineering spouse's low opinion of both of you. I really think it's more loving for the dominated partner— husband or wife—to take a strong stand. In doing this, you are saying, "I respect both of us enough to want a better way of life for us."

At the same time, either a husband or wife can show love by letting the spouse have his or her way when the issue has nothing to do with right, wrong, or alcoholism. If you voluntarily give up "having it your way" with a smile on minor issues, your spouse can't say, "You're against me on everything." It is wise to save your strength and newfound firmness for times when you'll really need them.

At all times your primary purpose should be to do the will of God, not to prove anything to your spouse. Nevertheless, your loving, Christ-like example will speak louder than words. Your example will mean more to your spouse and others than you will ever know.

Drunk Driving—a Good Starting Point

If you are looking for a good place to draw a line in refusing to submit to the disease of alcoholism, here's a great place—don't tolerate drunken driving. It's a form of abuse in itself. Don't ride with any drunk driver, ever, and don't permit your minor children to do so.

If there are alcoholics among your relatives and close friends, the people around you are going to think you're being unreasonable in taking your stand. Yes, it will be a hassle. You may have to decline some invitations that you know will end with this possibility. You may have to find another ride or stay somewhere overnight when you weren't planning to. You may even have to refuse to let little David go to the races with his uncle if the uncle is likely to drink while there. You may even have to say to your wife or husband, "If you leave now with that child, I'll call the police as soon as you're gone."

Not three miles from where I live, a car left the road and turned over in a flooded irrigation ditch. The young couple escaped without injury, but their little son was killed. The father was charged with driving while intoxicated. The mother wasn't charged with anything but she will have to live out her life knowing she could have prevented this accident.

What can you do, or should you do, when you know the alcoholic is driving drunk while alone? Innocent people are on the road, and their lives are endangered along with your loved one's. Surely it is fruitless to argue about it, but some people have resorted to "losing" the car keys. Or, if it is too late for that, you might consider reporting the intoxicated driver to the police—if you are very sure about the intoxication.

Can a Christian Separate?

In extreme cases, the only way for an abused spouse to achieve any kind of peace and safety is to live apart for a time. Often, nothing else will convince the abuser that the abuse must stop. Therefore, the question of marital separation must be discussed in this context.

The true remedies for abuse—increased self-esteem, personal growth, and better communication—all take time. In the beginning, such improvements feel like throwing buckets of water into a forest fire. The fire still rages out of control, and someone could get burned—perhaps fatally.

Separation, for a Bible-believing Christian, is quite different from divorce. Secular society assumes that any separation is going to be permanent, and that divorce is merely the legal technicality that makes it final. But the serious Christian reads in the Bible that "a wife must not separate from her husband. But if she does, she must remain unmarried or else be reconciled to her husband. And a husband must not divorce his wife" (1 Cor. 7:10b–11). And Jesus himself said, "Therefore what God has joined together, let man not separate" (Matt. 19:6b).

Consider the words "but if she does" in 1 Corinthians 7. Does the Bible ever speak that way about sin or completely forbidden conduct? The following words tell the right way to separate, implying that separation, while not normally a good idea, may sometimes be necessary. Can you imagine a commandment that says, "Thou shalt not steal—but if you do, here's the right way to do it"?

Christian separation, as I see it, is meant to be temporary—it's like what doctors do when they rebreak and set a broken leg that is healing wrong. It's painful, but in some cases it needs to be done if the patient is ever to walk properly again.

I am not convinced that there is ever a good reason for a Christian to seek a divorce. (Some Christian teachers allow it if the cause is habitual adultery.) I believe that if a Christian leaves a spouse because of drunkenness or abuse, it should be with the intention to remain sexually faithful and with the hope of reconciliation through sobriety. It is reasonable to insist on a good treatment program, and perhaps marriage counseling, as a condition of getting back together.

If your spouse should leave you, the apostle Paul makes it clear that it's all right to let him or her go without a struggle (1 Cor. 7:12–16). (Many Christians believe that this passage conveys the right to remarry in such a case.)

If you don't want a divorce, say so, but don't put up an elaborate resistance. It may be your pride that is hurt more than anything else. When an alcoholic rejects you, it's usually because you are too much of a threat to the disease. It doesn't have anything to do with your attractiveness or desirability as a partner. Just keep working on your own personal growth; otherwise, you could fall into another, similar relationship in spite of your best intentions.

Next, comes the question, How bad must things be before you consider separation? Only you can decide that. No one knows better than you how deeply you have been affected by abuse, or how much you can take and still function well. But spend much time in prayer before making such a decision. And, ignore the unasked-for advice you will get. The people who say "throw the bum out" are not going to be around when you are broke, lonely, and in need of help. The people who are "shocked that you could think of leaving" haven't lived with abuse. (Many Christians, even pastors, have been sheltered from such problems and are pretty naive about abuse.) Watch your ultimatums, though, and don't threaten to leave unless you are planning to follow through.

If you do leave, make sure your spouse knows that you are planning to be faithful—that you have left the house but not the marriage. Be clear about what your conditions are for a reconciliation. A lawyer may be a help in working out financial and child custody arrangements—a Christian lawyer may be more likely to understand your goals.

Be sure to maintain your detachment during the separation. Don't be constantly checking up on your spouse's condition. If your spouse starts dating, you'll have to be prepared to deal with that. Get some counseling, but don't allow anyone to make your decisions for you. Enjoy your freedom and the relative peace and quiet, and if your life seems too empty now, fill the spaces with a new hobby or career skill. If possible, live on your own, not with relatives—you need to be an adult and stand on your own feet. Beware of friendships with someone of the opposite sex: don't lead yourself into temptation.

The bottom line is simply this—you don't have to endure abuse forever, and you aren't being particularly spiritual or loving if you do. Breaking the cycle of abuse may turn out to be the most loving thing you ever do. Ask God to show you the best way for you to break that cycle. It won't be easy, but it is possible and it must be done.

The psalmist spoke to our need when he wrote,

> I cry to you, O Lord;
>   I say, "You are my refuge,
>   my portion in the land of the living.
> Listen to my cry,
>   for I am in desperate need;
> rescue me from those who pursue me,
>   for they are too strong for me.
> Set me free from my prison,
>   that I may praise your name (Ps. 142:5–7).

For Further Reflection

On calling upon God for help, read Psalms 18; 20; 22; 55; 56; 142; 143; and others.

On marriage and divorce, read Proverbs 14:1; Matthew 5:27–32; 19:3–12; Romans 7:1–4; 1 Corinthians 7:10–40; Ephesians 5:22–33; and 1 Peter 3:1–7.

On decision making, read Proverbs 2:1–15; 16; 19:21; 21:30–31.

Part 6 Through Martyrdom
to a Healthy Self-love

17 *Self-esteem Is Not Selfishness*

"Love the Lord your God with all your heart and with all your soul and with all your mind." This is the first and greatest commandment. And the second is like it: "Love your neighbor as yourself." All the Law and the Prophets hang on these two commandments.   MATTHEW 22:37–40

Did you ever stop to think about what this Scripture actually says? Sometimes we overinterpret it and think it says, "Love your neighbor *instead of* yourself." But no—it says to love God first and then your neighbor *as* yourself. Jesus assumes here that we have a natural love for ourselves that we can use as a reference point in loving others. If you don't love yourself, how will you know how to love anyone else? Jesus also says, "In everything, do to others what you would have them do to you" (Matt. 7:12). If you had no ideas about how others should treat you with decency and respect, you wouldn't know how to treat them. So a certain amount of self-love is not only okay, it's a necessity in forming positive relationships with others.

We are all born with the capacity for self-love and only gradually learn how to love others. A baby cries when hungry, uncomfortable, or lonely—never knowing or caring that Mommy is tired or has other things to do. If the baby receives lots of good, loving care, eventually a spark of love is born in him or her and begins to turn outward.

But what happens if no one expresses an adequate amount of love and care for the baby? In such cases, children learn not to trust or depend on anyone else very much. They also think they aren't worth much, if no one hugs or kisses them or says loving things to them. They might learn to meet the needs of others, but they'll be motivated by a need for scraps of approval or the desire to avoid punishment and mistreatment—not by love for its own sake.

The child that is cuddled and cared for has an adequate amount of self-esteem. He or she isn't afraid to "run out of love" because there seems to be a steady supply of it around. This child is secure. The child that doesn't receive love and care has little self-esteem, does not feel lovable, and is afraid to trust anyone too much. This little one is insecure. These are extremes, of course, and many of us fall somewhere between the two.

As we read our Bible, especially Psalms and the Gospels, we get an idea of how important we are to God. It can be hard to understand, if no human being has ever modeled that love to you generously and unconditionally. But Jesus loved you enough to die for you. So when you respect your own worth as a person, you are just agreeing with him.

Question: How is self-esteem lost or damaged? We have seen how early childhood experiences are crucial, as the treatment we receive from others continues to be important in adulthood. Unfortunately, in our Western society, we tend to base self-esteem too much on the work we do. Work is good, of course, but our value to God is the same whether we have a high-paying job, a low-paying job, or a nonpaying job such as that of a mother at home. And it is sad, but many people let their self-esteem be destroyed if they are fired or laid off or when they retire or become disabled.

It is significant that marriage to an alcoholic goes hand in hand with low self-esteem. If our opinion of ourselves is low, we are more likely to choose as a partner someone like an alcoholic—a person wrapped up in himself who will probably not treat us very well. Besides, we aren't sure we deserve good treatment anyway.

Our own negative thought patterns, long established, work against self-esteem. We tell ourselves things like these:

I always fail.
The good things I do don't count; anyone could do them.
Whatever goes wrong, it's my fault.
Nobody loves me; but then, why should they?
Other people are smarter or better than I am.
If someone puts me down, he or she must be right.
No matter what I try to do, it won't work.

We need to counter negative thoughts with positive ones:

God loves me, so there must be something there to love.

Some people like and respect me.

Some of the things I do turn out well.

I have certain gifts and talents.

If I make a mistake sometimes, I'm only human and I'll learn from it.

I'm not always to blame, and others don't always know more than I do.

I am smart and talented and strong enough to succeed with God's help.

Write down your favorite positive thoughts on index cards and keep them where you'll see them often. Include Bible verses such as "I can do everything through him who gives me strength" (Phil. 4:13).

Don't Do Jesus' Job for Him

Negative thinking and irrational guilt lead to false martyrdom. A real Christian martyr is someone who suffers religious persecution and stands up to it well. That isn't what a false martyr does. A false martyr thinks, "It's my job—or it seems to be my fate—to suffer for everyone else and be unhappy so they can be happy." A false martyr bases his or her whole identity on suffering and would hardly know what to do without it. The false martyr is attempting to atone for sin—his own or others'—through suffering. This shows a lack of acceptance for what Jesus did for us on the cross, "For Christ died for sins once for all" (1 Pet. 3:18), and there is nothing you or I can do to "help out" the Lord in this way.

False martyrdom has little to do with love, for it makes the "martyr" angry and bitter eventually when the loved ones for whom he or she has "given up everything" fail to appreciate the sacrifice. If poor self-esteem has led you into this trap, *you can and should give it up*. It only leads to actions that prolong alcoholism and keeps family relationships unhealthy. Don't try to be someone's "savior." There's only one qualified for the job, and it isn't you.

Overcome Depression

Depression is another possible result of a lack of self-esteem, although depression can have other causes, including physical illness or a disturbance in body chemistry.

Low self-esteem and negative thinking lead to depression when we learn to feel helpless and when we no longer believe we have the power to do anything right or change anything for the better. If "nothing I do makes any difference," then sooner or later I'm going to give up trying to do anything. I'll mope around in my bathrobe, emotionally paralyzed. The things I should be doing will seem impossibly difficult.

Fortunately for me personally, when I have a spell like this, it usually lasts only an hour or two. For some, it can go on for days, weeks, or months. Unfortunately, the only way to get out of it is to "pull yourself up by your own socks." There are things you can do to help yourself at home when depression strikes. It is important at such times to *do something constructive*, no matter what, no matter how small. If a job seems too large to tackle, break it down into bite-size steps and just take one bite. If your paperwork is out of control, for instance, just tell yourself you'll sit down at the desk for five minutes, open one envelope, and read what's inside. (You may end up doing more, of course, but after you've fulfilled your "agreement" you can quit anytime you like.)

When "one day at a time" is too much, just take one hour or a few minutes at a time. I'm not a morning person at all. Sometimes I don't think I can stand up and go take a shower in the morning. So I tell myself, "I'll just get out some clean clothes and take them to the bathroom, that's all." Of course, once I get moving I don't mind taking a shower. The key is to think in terms of, "I can't do everything, but I can do something. Here is what I *can* do."

As Erma Bombeck once said: Know thyself. Then trick thyself.

It also helps lift depression when you get out of your rut and do something different. If a trip is too much, then go for a walk or take a different route to work or the store. If these things are too much, then at least vary things by sitting in a different chair. Anything to give yourself, literally, a different perspective.

Learn to Love Yourself

If your self-esteem isn't what it should be, you can work at improving it. Here are some specific things you can do to build up your self-esteem.

1. Praise yourself. Everyone needs to be told what they are doing right. Give yourself a verbal pat on the back when you deserve it: "You sure got a lot of work done today, Sue. Great job!" "You look nice in that new outfit, Fran." You may feel silly doing this; do it anyway.

2. React positively to criticism. Don't let criticism trigger your own negative thoughts. When someone criticizes you, make certain you fully understand what your critic is saying. Then decide whether the criticism is valid. If it is, discuss how you can change or improve your performance, without putting yourself down as a person. If it isn't, you can say, "I don't agree with what you are saying. Would you like to know why I did what I did?"

3. Forgive yourself. A good parent forgives you, and so does God when you confess your wrongs. If you have confessed your wrongs and made amends for them but are still torturing yourself over something that happened long ago, that's condemnation, and it's from Satan! Let it go and forgive yourself aloud. Put your past failures in perspective—you are human; life goes on; you must go on from where you are now.

4. Give yourself little gifts. Do you ever buy or make something nice for yourself "just because"? A new item of clothing, an ounce of cologne, an interesting book, or your own favorite dish for supper can give you a real lift. I'll bet you do nice things for the other people you love. Why not do them for yourself, too?

5. Take some time off. Do you feel worthwhile only when you're working? You wouldn't wish a life of constant drudgery on anyone else. An occasional hour, or even a whole day, to do exactly what you want—or nothing—is good medicine.

6. Look your best. When you look better, you feel better. It doesn't matter where you are going or who's going to see you. An attractive haircut is important. So is cleanliness, and so are clothes that flatter you and make you feel good.

7. Be around positive, supportive people. Have you ever noticed that certain people tend to build you up emotionally and spiritually when you are around them? Try to spend more time with them, and less time with anyone who makes you feel worse about yourself. Don't let your alcoholic cut you off from positive people in an effort to isolate you.

8. Build up others. Notice what it is your positive people do for you, and do it for others. Talk positively—listen to their problems neutrally, without promoting self-pity or giving unwanted advice. Admire and appreciate their good points—people are starving for an honest compliment! Doing this will make you feel better, too.

9. Exercise. Aerobic exercise releases chemicals in your brain that actually improve your mood. Walking is especially good because you can do it almost anywhere, and because a change of scene is also beneficial.

10. Be creative. Because you are made in the image of God, you have a creative force within you, and you can't be completely fulfilled unless you express it somehow. Art, music, dance, crafts, photography, writing, baking, and gardening are only a few of the possible outlets for your creativity. Don't worry about whether you're "good enough." If it makes you happy, that's good enough.

11. Get closer to God. By depending on God in your growth, you'll feel his love flowing through you. And you'll just have to accept his opinion that you are a worthwhile and lovable person.

In short, you love yourself by being a friend to yourself. This is far different from being selfish. We are being selfish when we put our own wants and needs ahead of others' and even ahead of God—when we say, "I'm going to do what I want and I don't care how my behavior affects anyone else!" To be selfish is to withhold love. But a healthy degree of self-love actually increases our love for others, as it increases our understanding of them and our capacity for real giving.

You may have been taught a song long ago in Sunday school entitled "Jesus and Others and You Spells Joy." Maybe the teacher wrote it on the blackboard like this:

Jesus	J
Others	O
You	Y

But that diagram makes it look as if you find joy by invariably putting yourself last, by ignoring your own needs. I think false martyrdom wears out joy in a hurry. A better way to diagram it is like this:

Jesus	
	JOY
Others and You	

This way, you aren't below the others—you're one of them. You're equal. You can love your neighbor and be one of your own neighbors. You can consider your own needs as you would consider anyone else's, without putting yourself above others.

Self-love shouldn't be arrogant, proud, self-important, or narcissistic. Self-love isn't selfish, always needing to have its own way. It's just the recognition that "I am a worthy person, created in the image of God—I have potential to do good things." Jesus died for you. If you're worth dying for, you're worth taking care of. Take care of yourself so that you'll be better able to care for others. Jesus worded it this way, "Consider the ravens: They do not sow or reap, they have no storeroom or barn; yet God feeds them. And how much more valuable you are than birds!" (Luke 12:24).

For Further Reflection

On seeing yourself as God sees you, read Genesis 1:27; Psalm 8:3–9, 139:13–16; Proverbs 19:8; Matthew 10:29–31; Romans 8:37–39; Ephesians 3:14–21; 1 John 3:1–3; and Revelation 1:5–6.

18 *Taking Charge of Yourself*

I will exalt you, O Lord, for you lifted me out of the depths and did not let
    my enemies gloat over me.
O Lord my God, I called to you for help and you healed me.

PSALM 30:1–2

Taking care of yourself doesn't mean being selfish or always putting
yourself first. It means helping yourself grow and change in a responsible, disciplined way. It means becoming the best you can be and
fulfilling the wonderful plan God has for your life. When you overcome the effects on your life of someone else's drinking and/or drug
abuse, you are free to become your best possible self.

Are You Addicted to Crisis?

One reason it's difficult to get the focus of your attention off the
drinker's life and onto your own is "crisis addiction," or what Toby
Rice Drews, in her excellent series *Getting Them Sober*, calls "excited
misery."

Life in the family troubled by *chemical dependency* (this term seems
to be emerging in scientific circles as the most popular one for alcoholism and drug addiction) often seems to drift from one crisis to the
next. (A crisis, for our purposes, is any situation so urgent, traumatic, or upsetting that we feel we must give it our full attention for a
time.) A shouting match, an accident, the loss of a job, an incident of
abuse—these are just a few of the crises that frequently disrupt the
alcohol-troubled family. When a crisis occurs, normal activities
screech to a halt as we get all emotionally worked up about the

predicament at hand. Even when we still have time to attend to everyday chores, we are so totally involved with the crisis that many things go undone.

Quite naturally, we don't like disruptive things to happen. But I think it is possible to become addicted to that high level of excitement. After a period of years, it can get to seem like a normal way of life. We feel there is no point in making plans, as they are only going to be disrupted anyway. So we drift from one distraction to the next. Then when there isn't a crisis at the moment, life seems mundane and boring. We just can't "get into" raking leaves, doing laundry, or helping Joshua learn long division. And when a new emergency comes along, it is a "relief," on one level, to jump into it.

Crisis addiction makes life easier, in a way, because it "lets us off the hook" when we don't take charge of our own lives. After all, "Who can blame me for being disorganized or having little self-discipline when I always have to drop everything because my alcoholic gets into a scrape or picks a fight with me?" This is an understandable mental habit, but one that has to go.

Eileen was addicted to crisis. Even after her separation from her violent alcoholic husband, she was still always wrapped up in some emergency or another. If it didn't involve her husband, it was her son's behavior problems, office politics at work, or a manipulative friend who was "using" her. Each incident threw her into a tizzy for two or three days. During these times she would neglect her appearance and her home, live on coffee and pastries, and spend endless hours on the phone "hashing it out" with friends. Fortunately, after a couple of years of separation she began to calm down.

Of course, many crises are real and genuinely force us to react in some way, but others don't require any action from us at all because they are just predictable steps in the progression of alcoholism. Some emergencies are real turning points that give us opportunities to change our lives for the better. But the important thing when confronted with a crisis is to calm down and reflect carefully on what we should do. Then we need to act rather than merely react.

Ask yourself these question in any crisis:

- Is this truly important?
- Is it my business to be involved in this?
- Is there anything really constructive I can do?
- Am I taking over responsibilities that belong to others?
- How can I regain some peace and detachment right now?

The Mind Is Still the Key

Always remember that you control what goes on in your mind, and your mind controls what goes on in your life. Your emotions don't control you unless you let them. If you want to let go of crisis addiction and lead a real life, you'll need to gain control of your thought life.

Remember that you can improve your attitudes by concentrating on positive things—on what you are doing or will do today. Take pleasure in your work and recreation, because "the cheerful heart has a continual feast" (Prov. 15:15). When destructive or negative thoughts well up, reject them in the name of Jesus, and substitute something better. I'm not telling you to deny an unpleasant truth; just resist the temptation to dwell on bad things and sink into self-pity. Deal with your emotional injuries, and then put them behind you. Allow old wounds to heal—don't let them control you.

Also, drop the practice of using your drinking loved one as an excuse for your own shortcomings. It is no more valid than if the drinker uses you as his excuse.

Going After Your Goals

Would you find it hard to answer if someone asked you what your goals are for today, this week, and this year? Unfortunately, many people caught up in someone else's problems have no immediate answer to that question. They are too accustomed to living from one crisis to another. They might say, "I just want to get through this day."

Well, just "getting through" isn't enough. But if you are in the "getting through" trap, I understand how and why it happened. It's hard to keep making plans when they are always ruined by someone's unpredictable behavior (or by your own overreaction to that behavior). You need patience and flexibility in carrying out your plans, because there will be setbacks. What you don't need is to give up making plans entirely. You need to plan good things, even great and wonderful things, for yourself and those you care about.

It is important, though, to understand that setting goals does not conflict with living one day at a time. Your goals can be pursued "today only"—one little step at a time. If your goal seems big and overwhelming, break it down into tiny, manageable steps, the first small enough to be completed today. For example, if you dream of becoming a lawyer, you could go to the library *today* and compare college catalogs. If your house is chaotic and you want it organized, you could start *today* by giving away all those old magazines you're never going to read.

Incidentally, an organized home is an excellent goal to pursue. You don't want to be perfectionistic or "crazy clean." But neatness is important, because family members can't really relax or feel comfortable with chaos or extreme clutter. The mess becomes a statement of the family's lack of self-esteem and the "mental junk" that clutters minds. Yes, I *am* speaking from experience. If you have trouble getting organized, I recommend a book that helped me. It is *Sidetracked Home Executives*, by Pam Young and Peggy Jones, published by Warner Books. You need not be a full-time homemaker to profit by their experience.

If something happens today that prevents you from taking even one small step toward your goal, take it tomorrow instead. Just keep going. *Don't ever give up.*

Here are some more examples of long-term goals and the immediate steps you could take toward them:

- "I want to read the whole Bible this year." (I'll read three chapters today.)
- "I want to become a better witness for Christ." (Today I'll say hello to my neighbor and get to know her a little better.)

- "I'd like to spend more quality time with my children." (It's going to be hot tomorrow. Maybe we can have a picnic at the beach.)
- "I need a better-paying job." (I'll talk to my supervisor about learning the skills I need to be promoted.)
- "I want to lose twenty pounds." (I don't need this doughnut.)
- "I'd enjoy taking up art as a hobby again." (I'll find a pencil and spend half an hour sketching something today.)

That gives you an idea of what I mean. There's almost nothing you can't do if you start small, but the important thing is to start *now*. Set one or two goals at a time, not eight or ten. (You know what has happened before when you tried to take on your whole life at once.) Keep charts and lists of what you do in moving toward your goal, so you'll be able to see how you've progressed. Use rewards as motivation—decide on some suitable little gift you'd like and what you have to do to earn it. At the same time, progress toward a goal can make you so happy that it serves as its own reward.

In my case I never thought I could write a whole book. But the Lord kept nudging me with the idea. So I finally said, "Okay, maybe I can write a book, and maybe I can't. But I *can* go to the library, find some material on alcoholism, and take a few notes." After I had a thick stack of note cards, one day I decided I could start to organize them into categories and put together a rough table of contents. This all took years, with setbacks both major and minor.

Starting the actual writing was a hurdle, even though I'd been publishing smaller pieces for a long time. But one day I said, "I think I could start with chapter five. I have a fair idea of what I want to say in it." Now thousands of one-day-at-a-time hours later, the book is coming together. Getting it published is part of the goal. But even if no one else ever reads it, it would still be worthwhile for me to have written it, because I have written it to myself as much as to you, and it has helped me with my own recovery and growth.

What About the Children?

If you are raising one or more children, they are some of the best reasons you have to get control of and take charge of your life. If they are the children of an alcoholic, they have a greater than average chance of becoming alcoholics or codependents themselves. Your best chance of helping them is to help yourself. When you break the cycle of sick relationships within the family, when you are emotionally strong enough to nurture the children, make them feel fully loved, and provide a more normal family environment, they will be stronger and more able to make sane choices as adults.

Children's physical needs—for protection, good food, sleep, cleanliness, decent clothing, shelter, supervision, and medical care— must be met no matter what. Chemical dependency in the family often leads to lapses in care of children even when adults know better. Remember, though, there is nothing you have to do that is more urgent or important than meeting the needs of the children in your life.

A child's emotional needs are as important as the physical needs. Children need direct expressions of your love—they don't just "know" they are loved without being told, hugged, and kissed. They also need spiritual training, consistent discipline, and protection from any kind of abuse. They need to be able to discuss alcoholism and other family problems openly and honestly with at least one parent or other close adult. (Al-Anon offers books and materials that can help you start such a discussion.) Children need to have responsibilities at home, but within reason. Unfortunately, some children of alcoholics are pushed into adult roles prematurely, becoming little homemakers, confidants, and "parents" to their parents.

Don't interfere with the child's relationship with an alcoholic parent any more than necessary. If there is physical or sexual abuse, that to me would be reason enough to separate and take the children to live elsewhere. But if there is no abuse, don't stand in the way when the alcoholic wants to provide good discipline or become involved in the children's lives. Also, there is no need to "protect" the alcoholic from the child by acting as peacemaker in their disagreements or by keeping children out of the way when the drinker "doesn't feel well." The goal here is to have as normal a parent-child relationship as possible.

If the "children" in your life are teens or young adults and have already been damaged to a degree by alcoholism in the home, don't think it's too late to make a difference. Your example is still important to them. If they see you make dramatic improvements in your own quality of life, they will want to know why and how. And then you can tell them.

Self-discipline and Integrity

To overcome a bad habit may be another of your goals in taking charge of your life. You cannot really be in charge if you are enslaved by overeating, pills, smoking, or excessive shopping, television watching, or anything else that seems beyond your control. Your habit may seem to be a comfort because it fills a gap created by the real unmet needs in your life. But wouldn't you rather have your real needs fulfilled?

Remember those wise words of Paul to the Christians in Corinth: "So, if you think you are standing firm, be careful that you don't fall! No temptation has seized you except what is common to man. And God is faithful; he will not let you be tempted beyond what you can bear. But when you are tempted, he will also provide a way out so that you can stand up under it" (1 Cor. 10:12–13). God promises you two things in these verses. First, you are not alone or unique in your temptation, and second, you can resist it.

Two other principles may help you resist what is bad for you. One, you can substitute something better—when tempted, keep busy with something constructive, and think positive thoughts. Two, don't provide for or cater to the desires of your sinful nature in advance. That can mean different things, depending on what your temptation is. If it's food, don't bring home the doughnuts and cookies. If it's spending, cut up your credit cards. If it's pornography, don't enter a store where they sell it. If adultery is a possibility, don't make a lunch date with the person in question.

What about drinking? Although I don't believe an occasional alcoholic drink is a sin, I do think anyone who has lived with alcoholism is wise to be extremely cautious, if not totally abstinent. You could put yourself in danger through various kinds of accidents and through lowered inhibitions if you drink. If you had an alcoholic parent or grandparent, you may be genetically vulnerable to addiction. And even if you are not going to do yourself any harm, you should think about the example you set for others who may be more vulnerable than you are. You have a unique opportunity to show your loved ones that a person can seldom or never drink and still be happy and fulfilled.

Is there anything on your conscience—even something small or something that happened long ago—that keeps you from feeling right about yourself today? Read again the section on guilt in chapter 14. Then make amends to anyone you have hurt, if that's what you need to do. Amends are anything you can do to make things right—an apology, the payment of an old debt, and so on. Sometimes "indirect amends" are the best and most useful kind. An improved attitude toward your loved ones or a reconciliation with someone from whom you have been alienated can be the best policy and can do more good than a "confession" that will only hurt someone.

It takes *self-discipline* to live with a sense of purpose; to take the small, everyday steps that lead to reaching your goals. It takes self-discipline to resist doing what is wrong or is wrong for you. And it takes self-discipline to take care of your rightful responsibilities and take charge of your life rather than be blown around by every wind that comes along. Self-discipline is similar in meaning to "self-control"—one of the fruits of the Spirit (see Gal. 5:16–26). Finally, self-discipline means often doing things that you don't particularly feel like doing at the moment but in the long run will lead to a better way of life.

We have covered a lot of seemingly unrelated topics in this chapter. What makes them all hang together is the concept of "integrity." Integrity is your wholeness or completeness; it is your ability to live according to your own beliefs and be the best possible you that you can be. When you have integrity, you have nothing to hide—your conscience is clear. You can act with confidence rather than react with fear, insecurity, and people-pleasing.

A person with integrity does what is right because it is right, not because of the way other people will or won't react. A person with integrity has values, goals, and faith that are more important than what anyone else thinks. "What you see is what you get" with such a person—all communications are straightforward and honest.

When you have grown into integrity, it won't bother you as much that you can't make your alcoholic happy. You will realize that no one can make another person happy. Each person is responsible for his or her own happiness. You will concern yourself with your own clearly defined responsibilities. You know where the boundaries are between yourself and others. You don't have high walls, but you do have borders. You aren't addicted to crises, because the pursuit of your goals makes your everyday life full and exciting. In short, you are in charge of yourself, and you can be a strong example to the next generation. And with the psalmist you can say to the Lord, "I know that you are pleased with me, for my enemy does not triumph over me. In my integrity you uphold me and set me in your presence forever" (Ps. 41:11–12).

For Further Reflection

On the mind and attitudes, read Romans 8:5–8; 12:2; Ephesians 4:17–24; Philippians 4:4–9; and 1 Peter 1:13–16; 4:7.

On goals, read 2 Corinthians 5:9–10 and Philippians 2:3–4; 3:12–14.

On temptation, read Matthew 5:27–30; 26:41; 6:13; Luke 4:1–13; Romans 6:11–14; 7:14–8:17; Galatians 6:1; and James 1:13–15.

On making amends, read Proverbs 14:9 and Matthew 5:23–26.

On integrity, read 1 Chronicles 29:17; Nehemiah 7:2; and Psalm 25:20–21.

On children, read Psalms 78:1–7; 127:3–5; Proverbs 14:26; 19:18; 22:6, 15; 29:15, 17; Matthew 7:9–12; 18:1–6; 19:13–14; Ephesians 6:1–4; and Colossians 3:20–21.

Part 7 Toward Healthy
Relationships

19 *Expanding Your Horizons*

He who walks with the wise grows wise, but a companion of fools suffers harm.
                                                              PROVERBS 13:20

Until now, we have concentrated on your relationship with your alcoholic loved one and your relationship with yourself. Now let's look at how you relate to the rest of the world.

Overcome Isolation

It is possible, you know, to be around people all day long and never really "connect" with anyone. You can know that you are getting to be too isolated emotionally if

- There is no one with whom you can discuss your problems.
- Your social life is confined to other chemical dependents and their families.
- You can't have "normal" friends, because it's too embarrassing for them to see how you live.
- Old friends have dropped you because they can't take the alcoholic's bizarre behavior.
- You have dropped old friends or involvement in a church or organization you enjoyed because your alcoholic objected to them and gave you a hard time about it.
- You have been talked into moving to some remote place where you don't know anyone.
- You couldn't possibly get into a self-help group or counseling,

because of your drinker's objections or because such things can't even be discussed.

• You feel "no one understands."

As we have said before, the alcoholic wants you isolated so that he or she—and the disease—will come to have total control over you. In the name of tough love, you must learn to recognize this manipulation and refuse to knuckle under to it.

Overcome your fears and taboos. Go to church or your club. See your "normal" friends—alone during the day, if necessary. Discourage any talk about moving away or to the mountains. Get help when you feel you need it. If the drinker keeps you home by being "unable to take care of the children" when you are going out, make other arrangements for them. Above all, don't believe the nonsense that it will "help him or her get sober" when you devote yourself exclusively to the drinker.

Confide with Care

Confide your troubles to God first. After that, most of us have the need for at least one close friend—a person close enough to hear all our troubles and know everything about us. A good confidant helps you overcome self-pity, feel less alone, and relieve the tension that comes from keeping everything inside. In all probability we're talking about one such friend, or a very few at the most. Don't make a bid for sympathy by confiding in practically everyone you know.

What kind of person is the ideal confidant? He or she

• Is a mature Christian with a good spiritual perspective.
• Has some understanding of chemical dependency.
• Is a good listener who won't interrupt you, misinterpret what you say, or quickly give unasked-for advice.
• Is not related to you or the alcoholic. Relatives seldom have the necessary detachment; they take sides.
• Can keep a confidence. (Watch out for friends who gossip. If they do it to everyone else, they'll do it to you.)

- Doesn't overload you with sympathy but helps you see that you have choices.
- Is in no danger of starting to "rescue" you—take over your decisions or do things for you that you should do for yourself.

Remember the wise words of the wisdom writer, "A righteous man is cautious in friendship" (Prov. 12:26).

Relatively Speaking

Even without chemical dependency, extended families involve complicated relationships. Relatives tend to become too emotionally involved with one another's problems. There is a tendency to feel they must come up with "answers" for you. It's wonderful to have them around when you need practical help, but do all you can to discourage them from becoming overinvolved or rescuing either you or the drinker.

If there are other alcoholics, drug abusers, and codependents in the family, these problems are greatly magnified. Unhealthy, overinvolved family relationships will likely be so common that family members don't understand what a normal relationship is. Then, when you get into a recovery program and begin to regain control over your own life and responsibilities, they won't understand you at all.

If family members are always getting you down or spoiling the good effects of your recovery, you may need to stay away from them for a time. If that makes them angry, you'll have to accept their anger as normal. Just say to yourself, "Of course, they don't understand. They're just like I used to be." Don't push the truth too hard; they will see it when the time is right, just as you did.

Keep in mind, too, that it is always possible that some relative or close friend will take over your role in "rescuing" your drinker after you give it up. He or she may lend him money, drive her home, bail him out, lie for her, take over his work for him. In all probability this will make you feel angry and frustrated now that you know how bad this is for an alcoholic. In addition it may trigger your irrational guilt, too, and cause you to say, "That's *my* job." But that makes no sense at all; that's why we call it irrational.

What is even more upsetting to you is that you feel you are being considered a bad person for giving up your rescuing role. But, let's face it, there is nothing you can do about this situation without making yourself look even worse to the other "rescuer." Just wait it out, and hope the do-gooder wakes up to what is happening. At least your time is now free for more useful activities.

You Can't Rescue the World

In all probability you are a very nurturing and loving person, and that's a wonderful attribute. The world needs more like you. But it can be overdone.

It is possible you have what I call the mother-of-the-world syndrome. Are your friends always the ones who need you rather than the ones you need? Do you jump into other people's arguments in the peacemaker role? Do you sometimes get into trouble by giving unwanted advice? Do you do things for others that they could and should be doing for themselves? Watch out for excesses in your nurturing, because they can spill over into unhealthy rescuing.

If you are doing over 50 percent of the "work" in a relationship over a long period of time, you are probably acting out the role of rescuer. What do you get out of it? And while it is true this role makes you feel indispensable and saintly, it is liable to destroy the relationship sooner or later because of the resentment that can so easily surface. You may feel rejected if your advice isn't followed. And the other person may become resentful because of the feeling you are interfering.

Every person needs to examine his or her "rescuing" motives. Are you bent on being a "rescue" person because of your great love for humanity? Or do you really like having a certain amount of power and control over another person? If you're thinking the other person "can't make it without me," that's your ego talking.

Many codependents end up in the "helping professions": nursing, social work, and counseling. Even here, you can avoid rescuing.

Though the professional-client relationship is inherently unequal, there are certain proper boundaries and limitations to it. You can observe those. Also, you should be encouraging your patients and clients to become less dependent, not more.

It is also possible that your alcoholic's drinking buddies may appeal to you as an outlet for your "mothering" energies. This is a unique sort of friendship. Sometimes a cozy group of loyal drinking friends exists together in a fantasy world of their own creation. They believe one another's denial as if it were the gospel and see the world as conspiring against them.

Though such people can be both pathetic and appealing, avoid the temptation to "save" them. If you let them, they will consume all your time. Instead, work on your own life and problems. Spend time with people who are good for you. And if you are sometimes thrown together with the drinking buddies' codependent family members, share with them what you are learning, but be gentle if they aren't ready for it.

Getting Help

It is important to understand that alcoholism is too much for a person to deal with alone. Reading a book like this may not be enough. Human beings are meant to work together in partnership and in dependence on God. In this way, we come up with better answers and learn more about love and how it works. There are several different kinds of outside help available to you. Be selective, and utilize those particular aids that meet your needs at a given moment. In doing so, you'll come across secular influences and ideas that may conflict with your beliefs. That's okay. Just run everything through your mental and spiritual "filters," and take only what you can use effectively.

Al-Anon Family Groups, an offshoot of Alcoholics Anonymous, is a self-help organization for family members and close friends who need help in dealing with someone else's drinking. At first some people go to meetings to learn "how to make him stop drinking." But that isn't what the group is about. The emphasis is on helping yourself by changing your response to the drinking. Its philosophy is similar to what you've already been reading in this book. If you go, the members won't let you focus on complaining about the drinker. Instead they will help you examine yourself to see how you can improve your reactions.

Some well-meaning Christians object to Al-Anon because it isn't specifically Christian. I have never felt there is anything in it that is incompatible with my faith. Al-Anon encourages you to depend on a Higher Power, so all you have to do is define your Higher Power as Jesus Christ. It is true that some people define their Higher Power differently. But AA and Al-Anon need to have this kind of openness if they are to help a variety of people with many different beliefs and backgrounds. However, many members acquire a hunger for deeper spiritual truths through this process and move on to a deeper understanding of Christian faith.

You may ask, Why do I need Al-Anon when I have my church? Well, it could be that many of your church leaders know little about chemical dependency. That is often the case. So why not let church and Al-Anon work together in your life to teach you how to apply the wisdom of God's Word to this particular situation?

You can find Al-Anon meetings by calling the number listed in most big-city telephone books, or through your local police agency, church office, or Chamber of Commerce. If one group doesn't suit you, try another.

You can also seek help through individual counseling. Most likely you can find a therapist or counselor through your church, your medical doctor, or a community health center. In selecting a counselor, it is important that he or she be knowledgeable about alcoholism. And, of course, it is a plus if he or she is a Christian. Such relationships are highly individual, so if you don't mesh with one counselor, ask to be referred to another.

Be prepared for therapy to be hard work, as you face unpleasant feelings and decide what changes need to be made in your life. It is likely, too, that therapy will help you find more strength than you thought you had. Be prepared, too, for your alcoholic to feel threatened by your therapy or your participation in Al-Anon or any other self-help group. But if that happens, just keep on doing what's best for you. Don't let your strings be pulled by somebody else.

In addition, if there is need, there are shelters for battered women and children, support groups for those who have suffered abuse, and programs for displaced homemakers who need to return to the job market. And there is legal aid available if you are considering a legal separation or need a court order to keep a violent person away from you.

At the same time don't overlook the help that can be yours through the church. Pastoral counseling can be a big help. Though some pastors have little experience with alcohol or drug abuse, others are quite knowledgeable. When I went through a brief separation years ago, I got good advice from my pastor. I also received practical help in setting up an apartment from church people I had thought would be judgmental and reject me!

Help for the Alcoholic

I would also encourage you to check out the programs for alcoholics that are available in your area—AA, inpatient and outpatient hospital programs, counselors, therapy groups, and so on. Also check out the services that your health insurance will cover. In this way you'll be well prepared when your alcoholic is ready to accept help.

Treatment can save lives. But over the long term much depends on the alcoholic's own motivation. Treatment can't make a person get well who doesn't want to. Sometimes, however, a drinker may enter treatment just to get a spouse or employer off his or her back but then will get the proper motivation to undertake what is necessary for recovery. It is important not to pin all your hopes on any program: if your loved one gets into treatment, be happy, keep praying, and keep working on your own recovery so that you'll be prepared for whatever happens.

Again, the wisdom writer gives us good advice, "Perfume and incense bring joy to the heart, and the pleasantness of one's friend springs from his earnest counsel" (Prov. 27:9).

For Further Reflection

On friendship and help, read Psalm 18; Proverbs 12:26; 16:28; 17:17; 18:24; 20:18; 27:6; Romans 8:26–39; and 1 Corinthians 12:12–28.

20 *The Bottom Line*

God is our refuge and strength, an ever-present help in trouble.

PSALM 46:1

I'd like to close this book by restating its main ideas, chapter by chapter:

1. Drinking is a firmly entrenched social custom, but alcohol addiction is a serious social problem from which we all suffer.
2. Abusers of alcohol (and other harmful drugs) harm themselves physically, financially, mentally, emotionally, and spiritually. Others around them suffer too.
3. It isn't a contradiction to say that drunkenness is a sin *and* alcoholism is a disease. Some people may have a genetic predisposition to alcohol addiction.
4. By the time you have to ask whether someone has a drinking problem, most likely the answer is yes. When someone's drinking disturbs you, it's more important to deal with your problem than to find the "right" term for it.
5. You can't stop someone else from drinking, but you can improve your own life by changing your reactions to the drinking and related behavior.
6. Alcoholics and their affected loved ones (codependents) tend to deny the problem and pretend it doesn't exist, but we must give up denial before we can get anywhere.
7. There is a right way and a wrong way to confront the drinker about the effects of his or her behavior on *you*. It isn't judgmental to point out that there is a problem.

8. Alcoholism breeds fear, but God provides practical ways to overcome your fears.

9. Faith is the answer to fear, but faith in anyone or anything but God is misplaced.

10. Faith that is real will be put to work, but we must do some thinking and praying about which actions are really good works. Love that is tough love is motivated by what is best in the long run for the one you love.

11. Detachment, or letting go of emotional overinvolvement and obsession with the drinker, leads to serenity and peace.

12. We each have responsibility for our own actions, not for others'. We must stop protecting alcoholics from the consequences of their own behavior.

13. To be angry is not wrong in itself. It is better to recognize anger and deal with it constructively, and to accept others realistically, than to swallow our anger and hold grudges.

14. Like anger, spiritual poisons like self-pity, envy, self-righteousness, lack of forgiveness, inappropriate guilt, and depression must be faced and replaced with more positive feelings. It's good to take some time out to refuel when "burned out."

15. Even when the alcoholic dumps his or her self-loathing on you through projection, most domestic arguments can be avoided or minimized through wise management on your part.

16. Verbal and emotional abuse, intimidation, and physical abuse are serious problems that call for firm action. It is not an act of love to submit to mutual destruction. There is a right way for a married Christian to separate if necessary.

17. To love yourself is to recognize the high value God puts on you as a person. Self-esteem is not selfishness, and you can rebuild yours if it has been damaged.

18. Rather than "go with the flow" of alcohol-related crises, we must take charge of our lives by setting goals and working toward them. Integrity is being true to yourself and your own beliefs.

19. If alcoholism has isolated you emotionally, you can reach out